DRAGON RACER

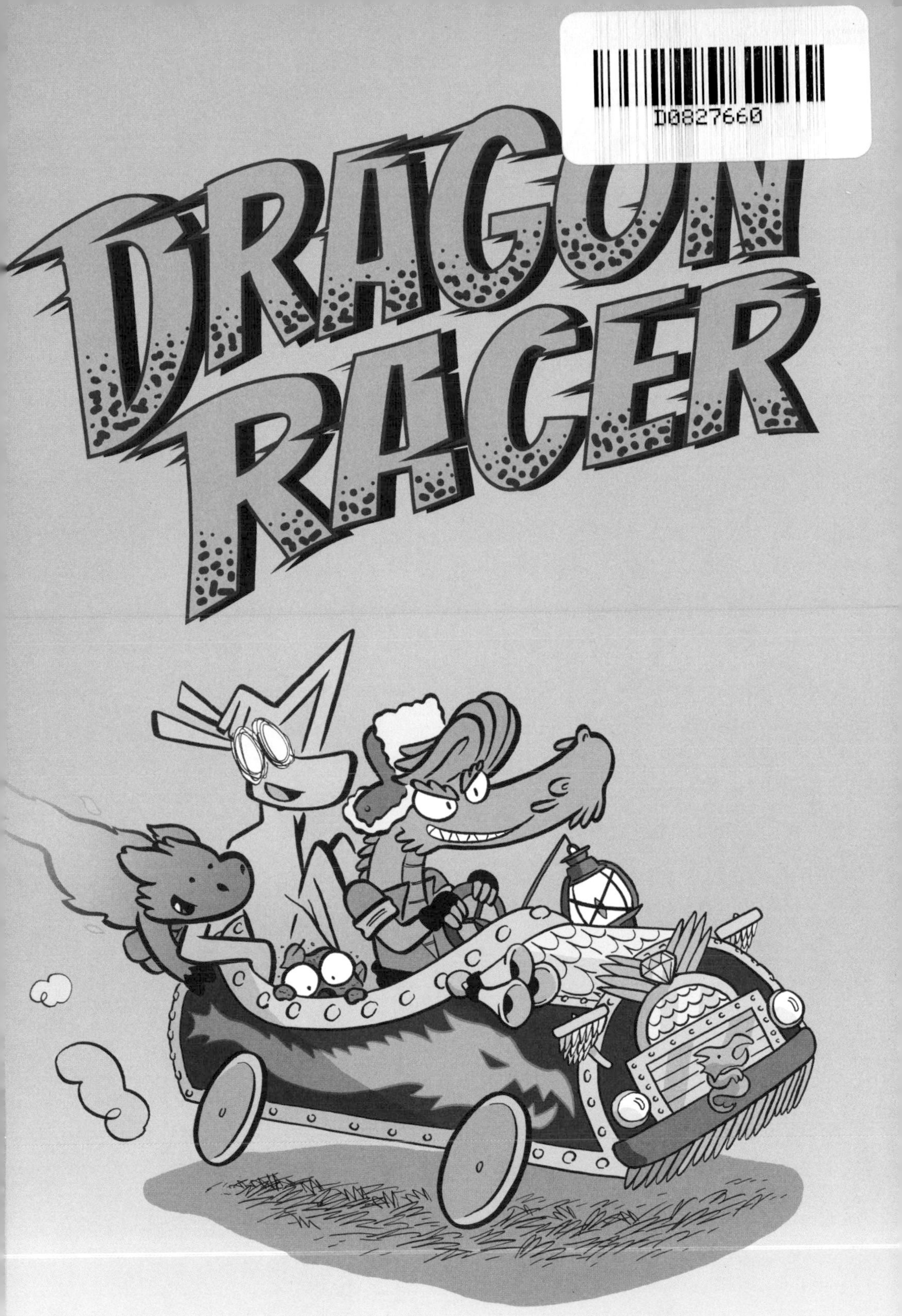

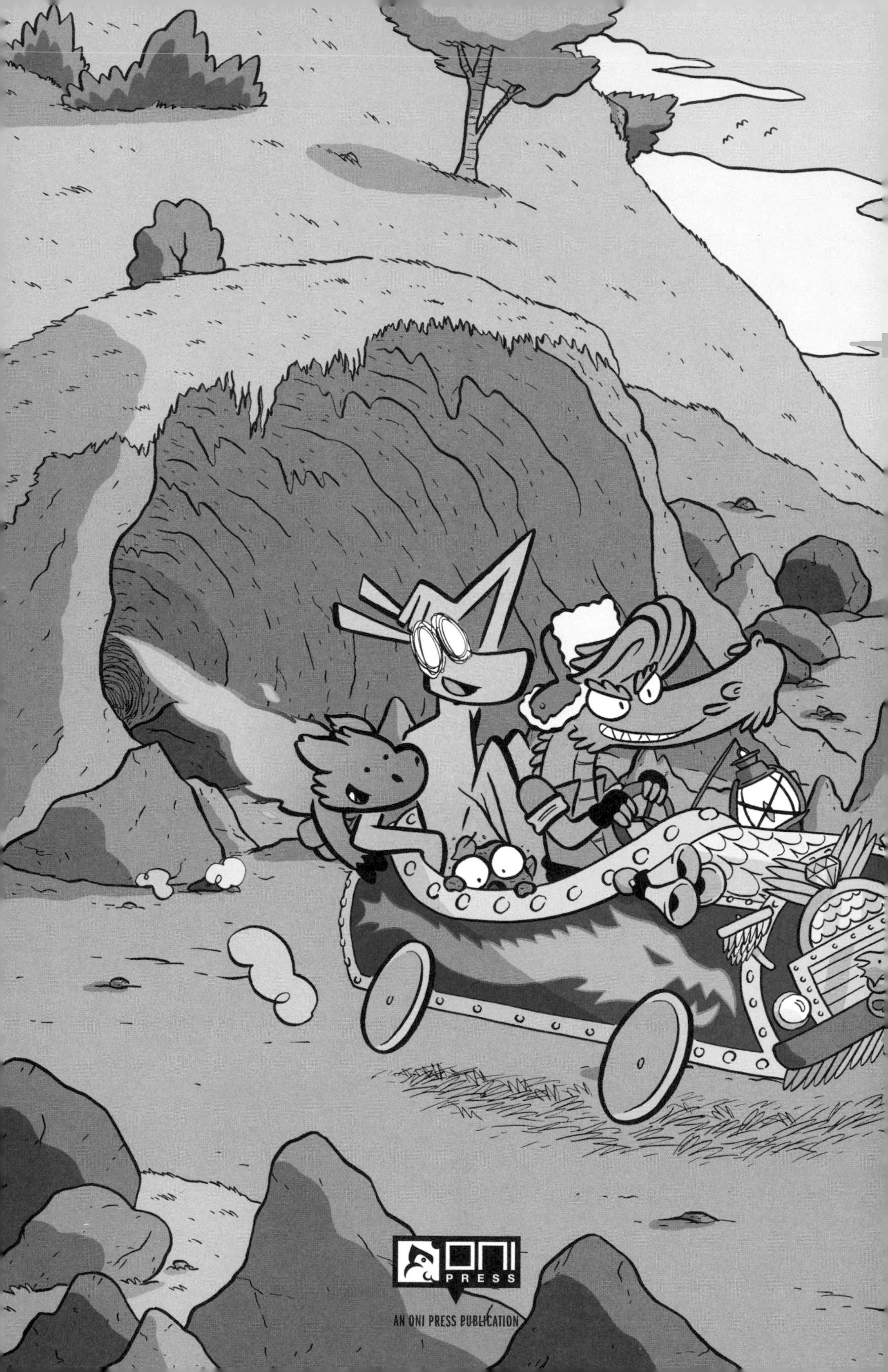
AN ONI PRESS PUBLICATION

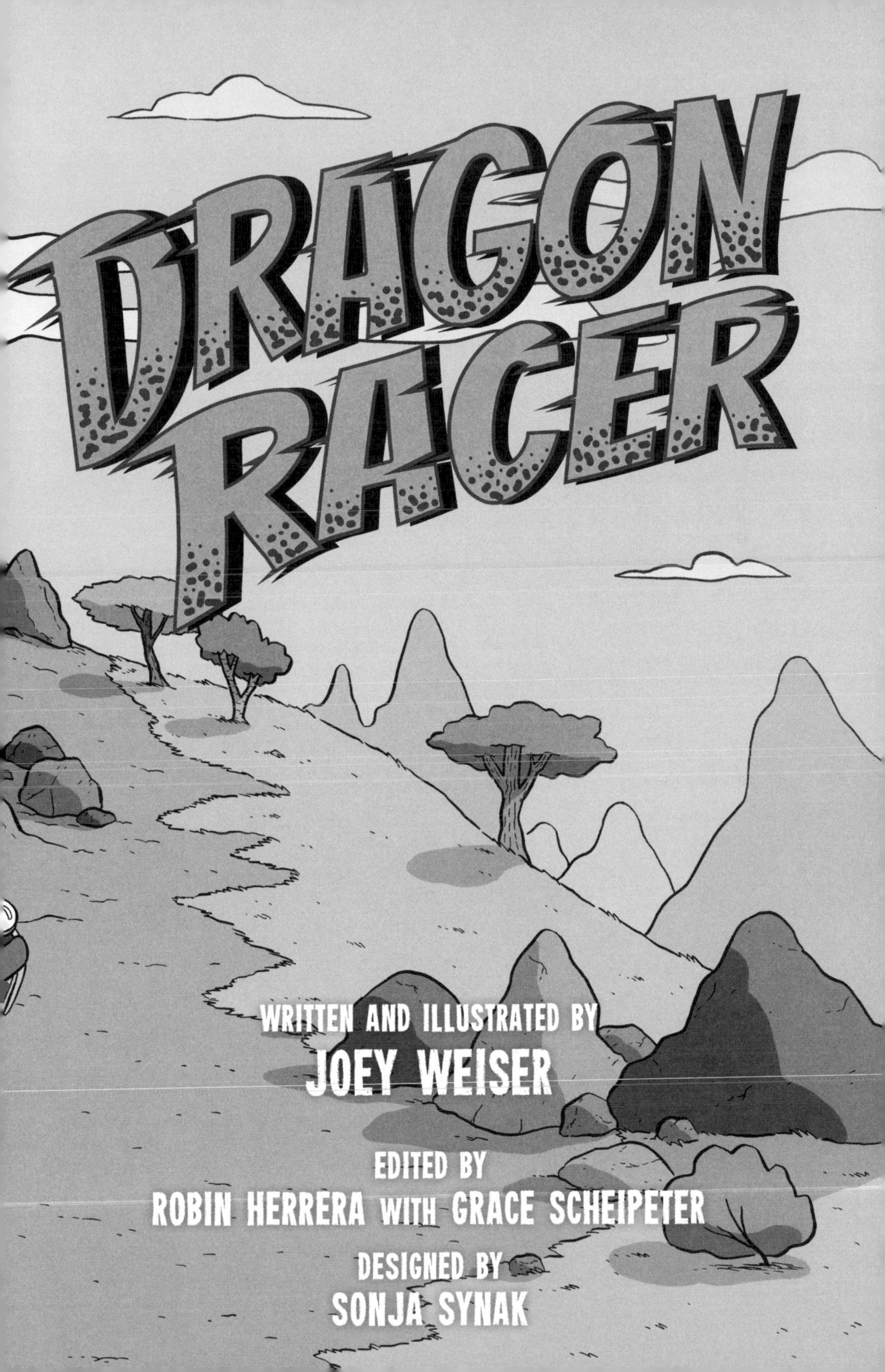

DRAGON RACER

WRITTEN AND ILLUSTRATED BY
JOEY WEISER

EDITED BY
ROBIN HERRERA WITH GRACE SCHEIPETER

DESIGNED BY
SONJA SYNAK

Published by Oni-Lion Forge Publishing Group, LLC

James Lucas Jones, president & publisher • **Sarah Gaydos,** editor in chief
Charlie Chu, e.v.p. of creative & business development • **Brad Rooks,**
director of operations • **Amber O'Neill,** special projects manager • **Margot Wood,** director of marketing & sales • **Devin Funches,** sales & marketing
manager • **Katie Sainz,** marketing manager • **Tara Lehmann,** publicist
Troy Look, director of design & production • **Kate Z. Stone,** senior graphic
designer • **Sonja Synak,** graphic designer • **Hilary Thompson,** graphic
designer • **Sarah Rockwell,** graphic designer • **Angie Knowles,** digital
prepress lead • **Vincent Kukua,** digital prepress technician • **Jasmine
Amiri,** senior editor • **Shawna Gore,** senior editor • **Amanda Meadows,**
senior editor • **Robert Meyers,** senior editor, licensing • **Desiree
Rodriguez,** editor • **Grace Scheipeter,** editor • **Zack Soto,** editor • **Chris
Cerasi,** editorial coordinator • **Steve Ellis,** vice president of games
Ben Eisner, game developer • **Michelle Nguyen,** executive assistant • **Jung
Lee,** logistics coordinator

Joe Nozemack, publisher emeritus

onipress.com 🄵 🄳 🄸 lionforge.com

tragic-planet.com
@joeyweiser

First Edition: June 2021

ISBN 978-1-62010-932-8
eISBN 978-1-62010-945-8

Printed in Canada

Library of Congress Control Number: 2020947309

10 9 8 7 6 5 4 3 2 1

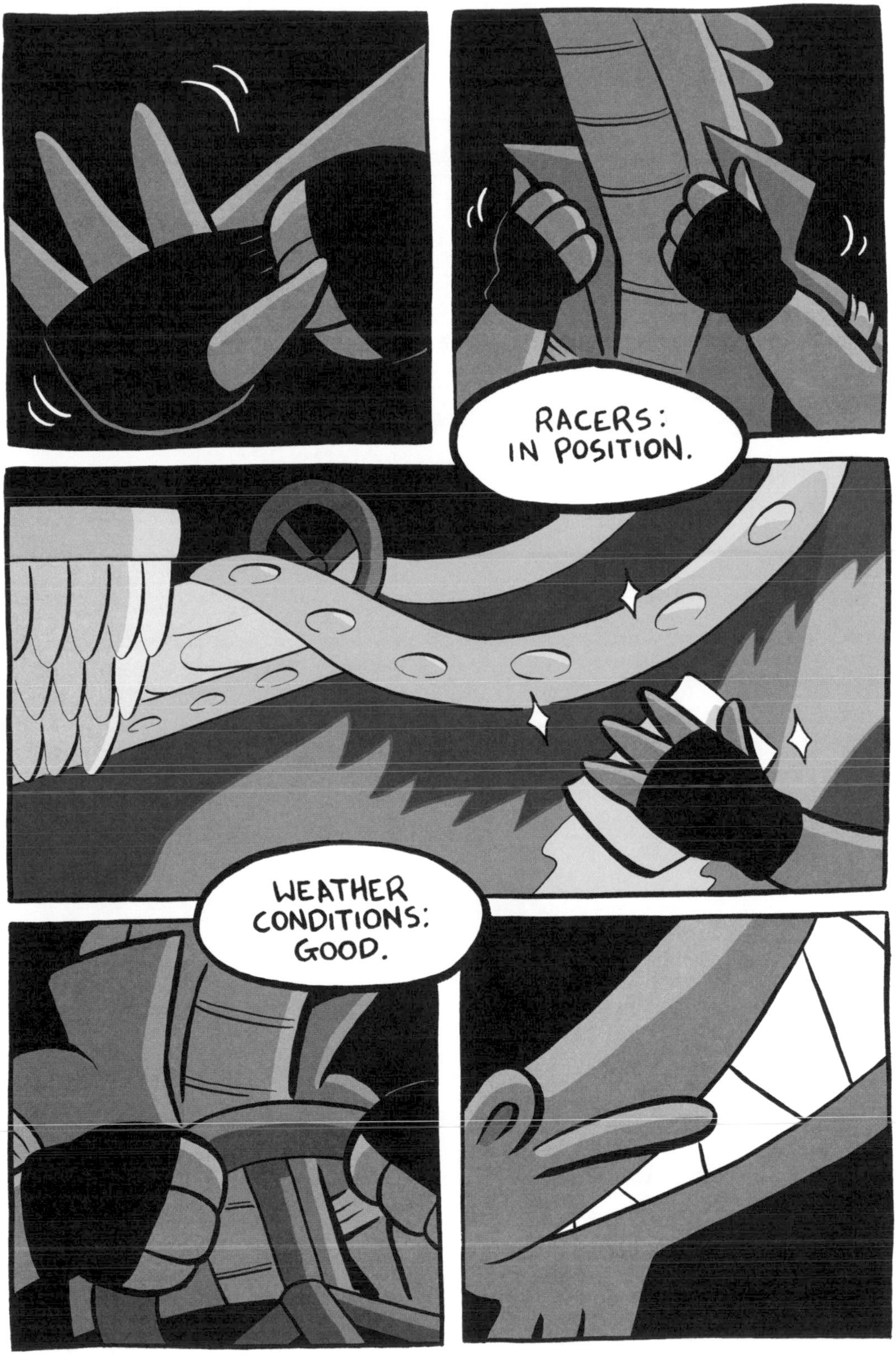
RACERS: IN POSITION.
WEATHER CONDITIONS: GOOD.

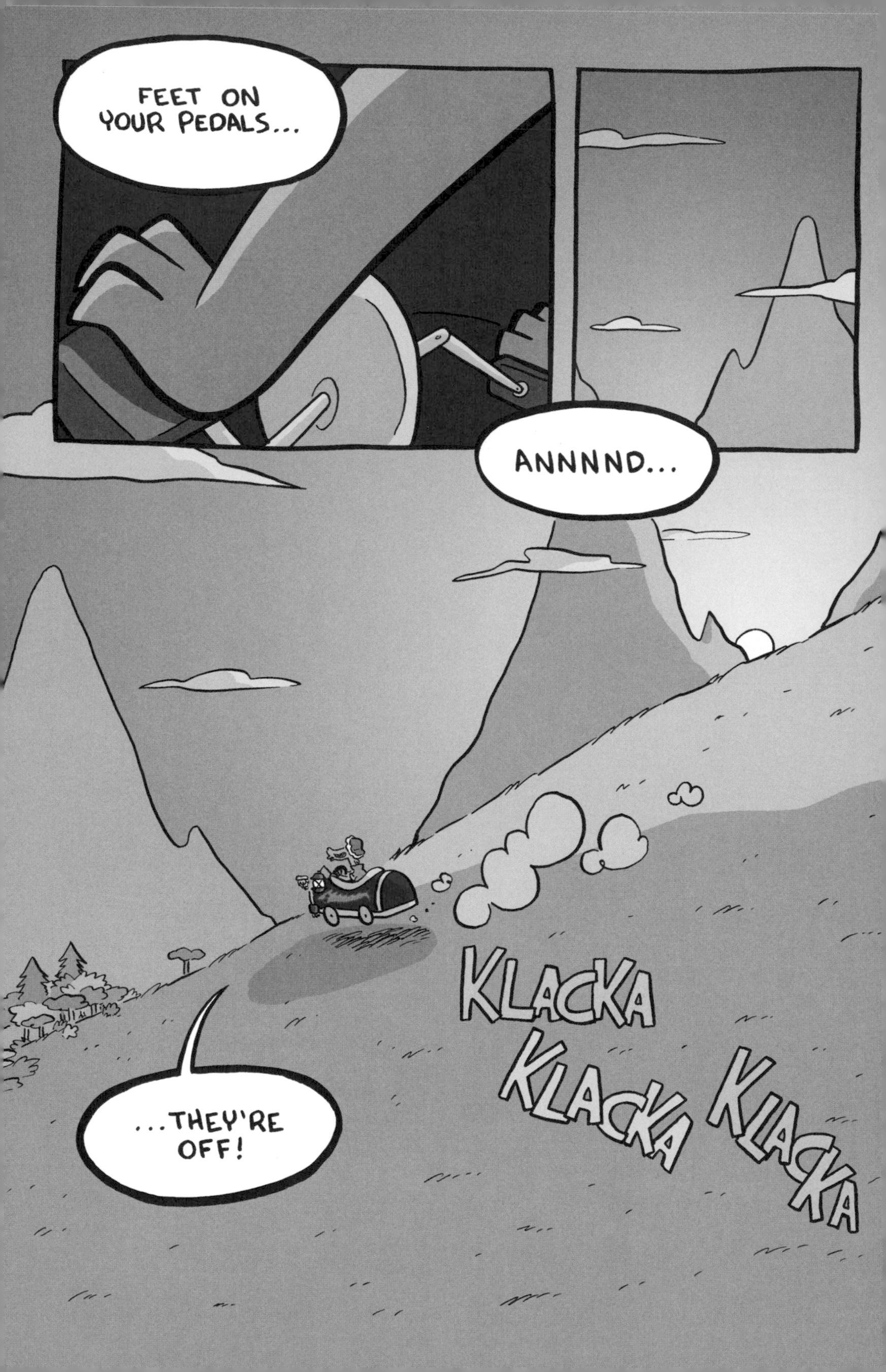

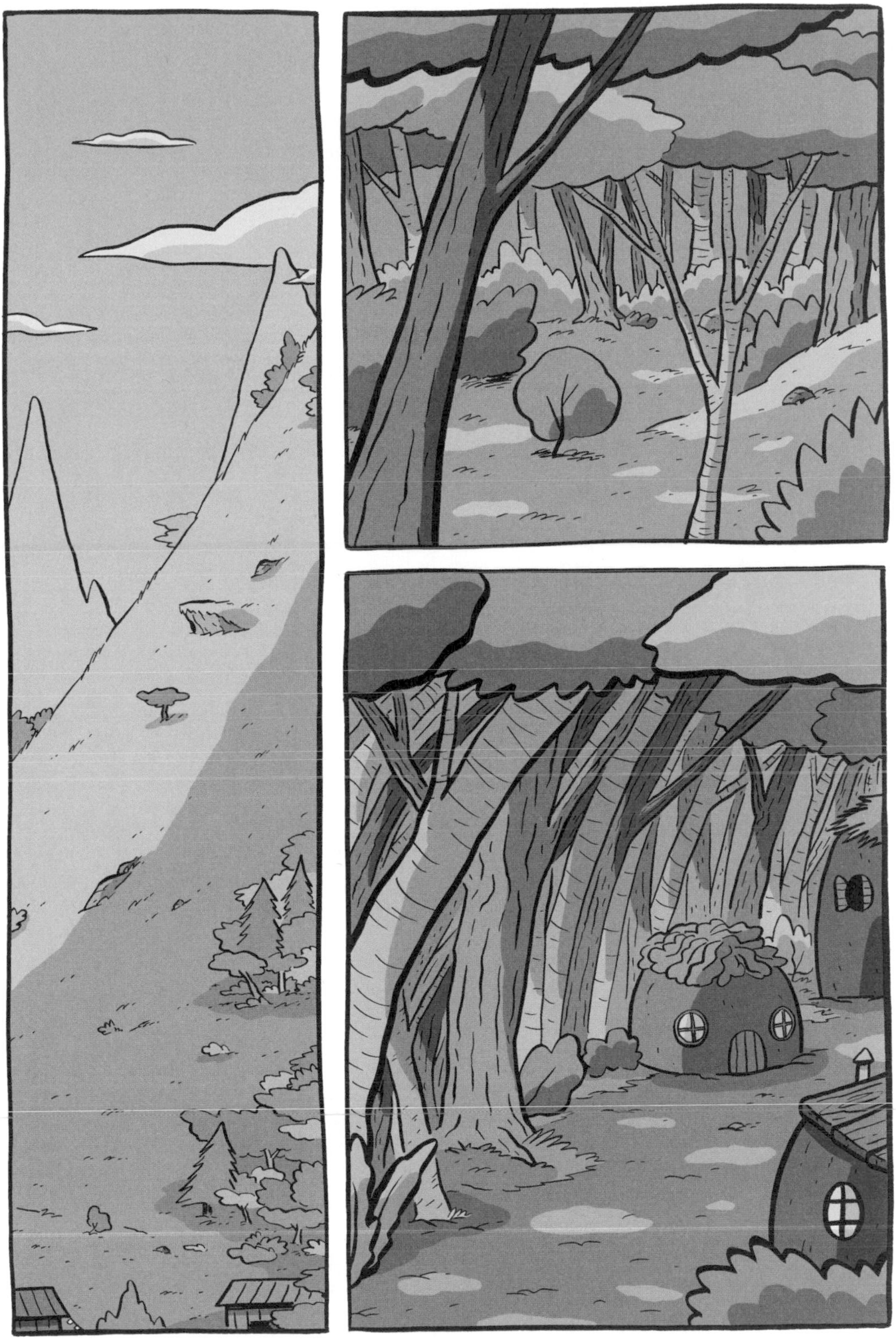

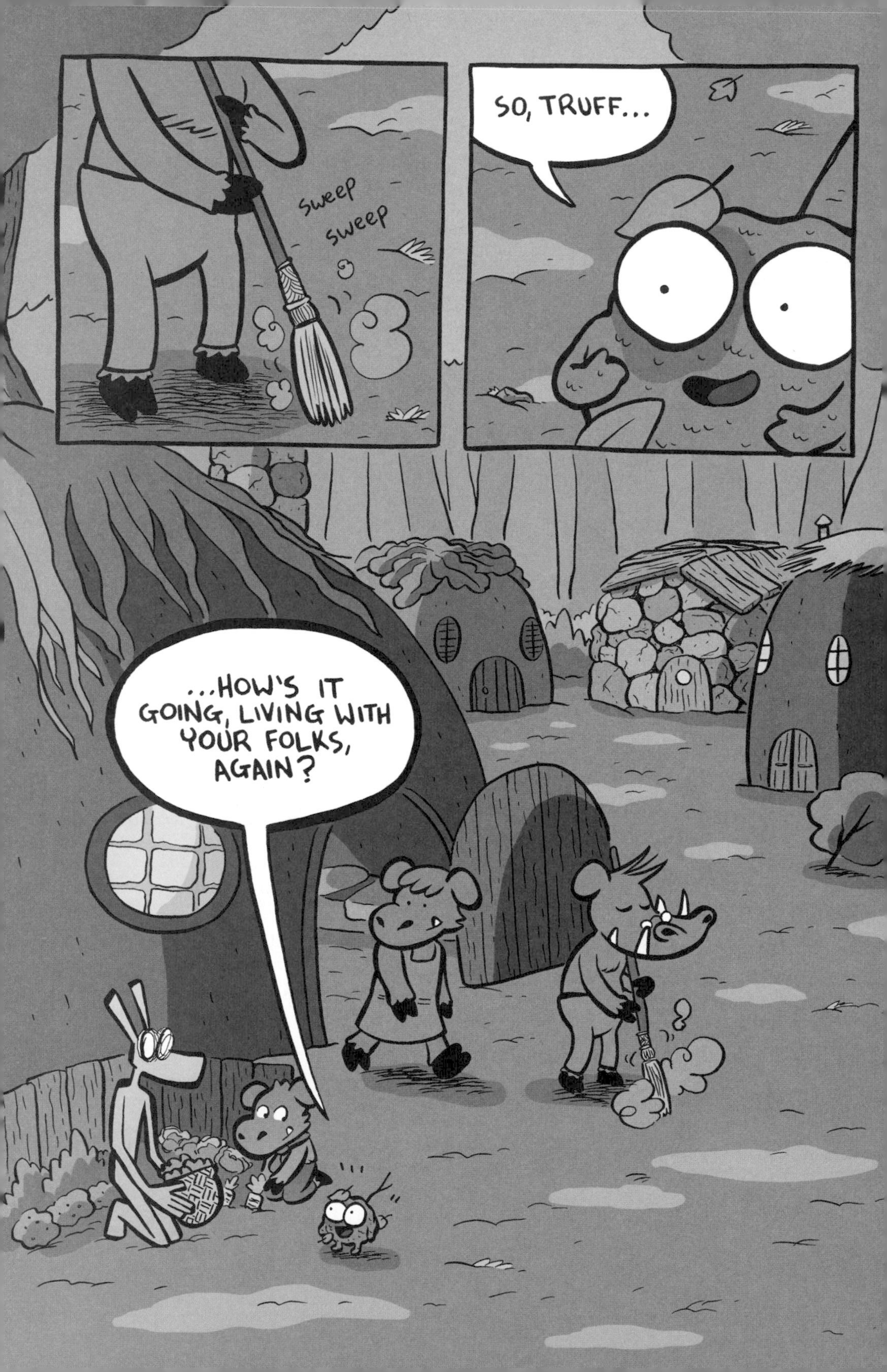

Sweep
sweep
SO, TRUFF...
...HOW'S IT GOING, LIVING WITH YOUR FOLKS, AGAIN?

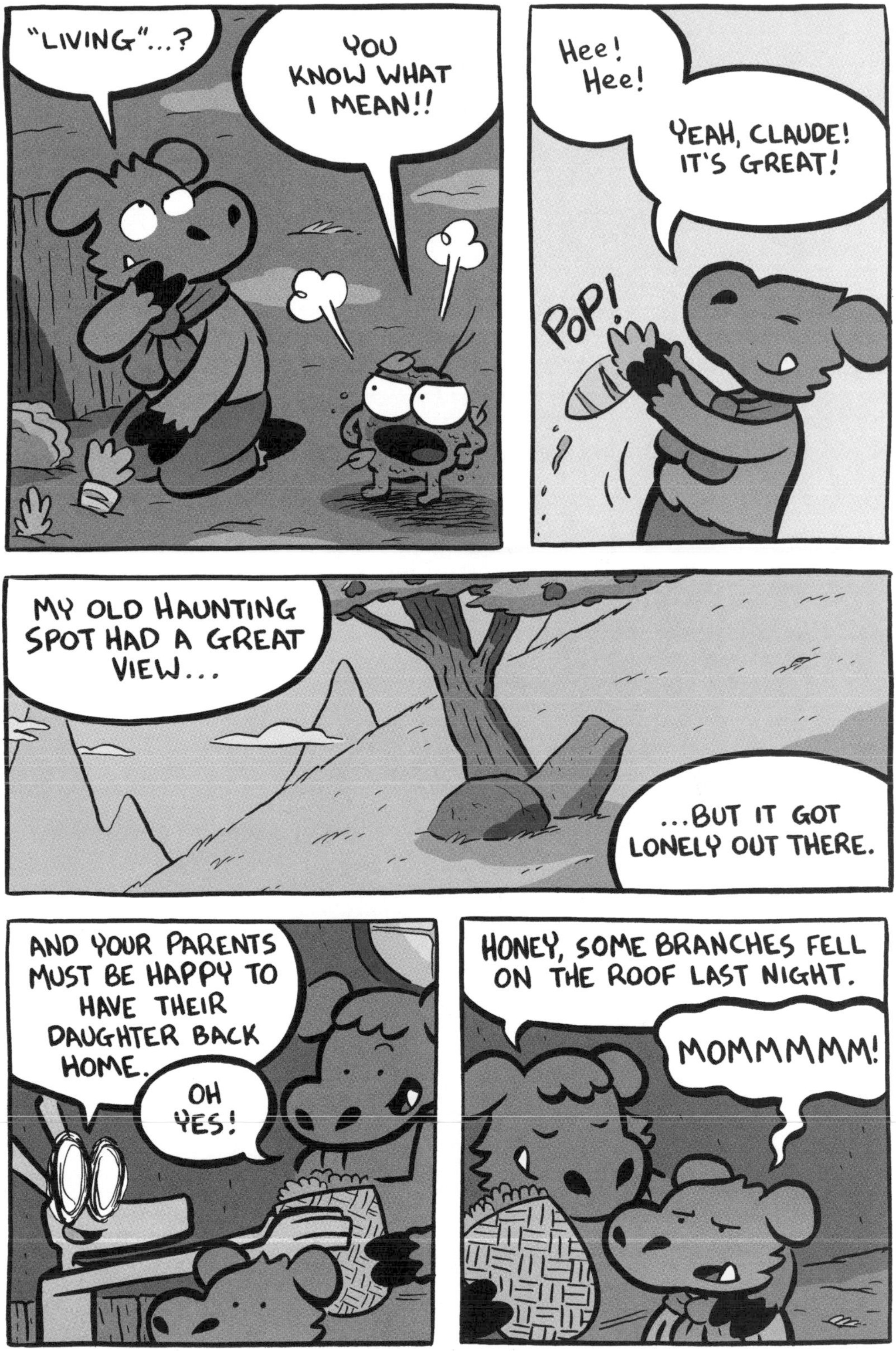
"LIVING"...?
YOU KNOW WHAT I MEAN!!
Hee! Hee!
YEAH, CLAUDE! IT'S GREAT!
POP!
MY OLD HAUNTING SPOT HAD A GREAT VIEW...
...BUT IT GOT LONELY OUT THERE.
AND YOUR PARENTS MUST BE HAPPY TO HAVE THEIR DAUGHTER BACK HOME.
OH YES!
HONEY, SOME BRANCHES FELL ON THE ROOF LAST NIGHT.
MOMMMMM!

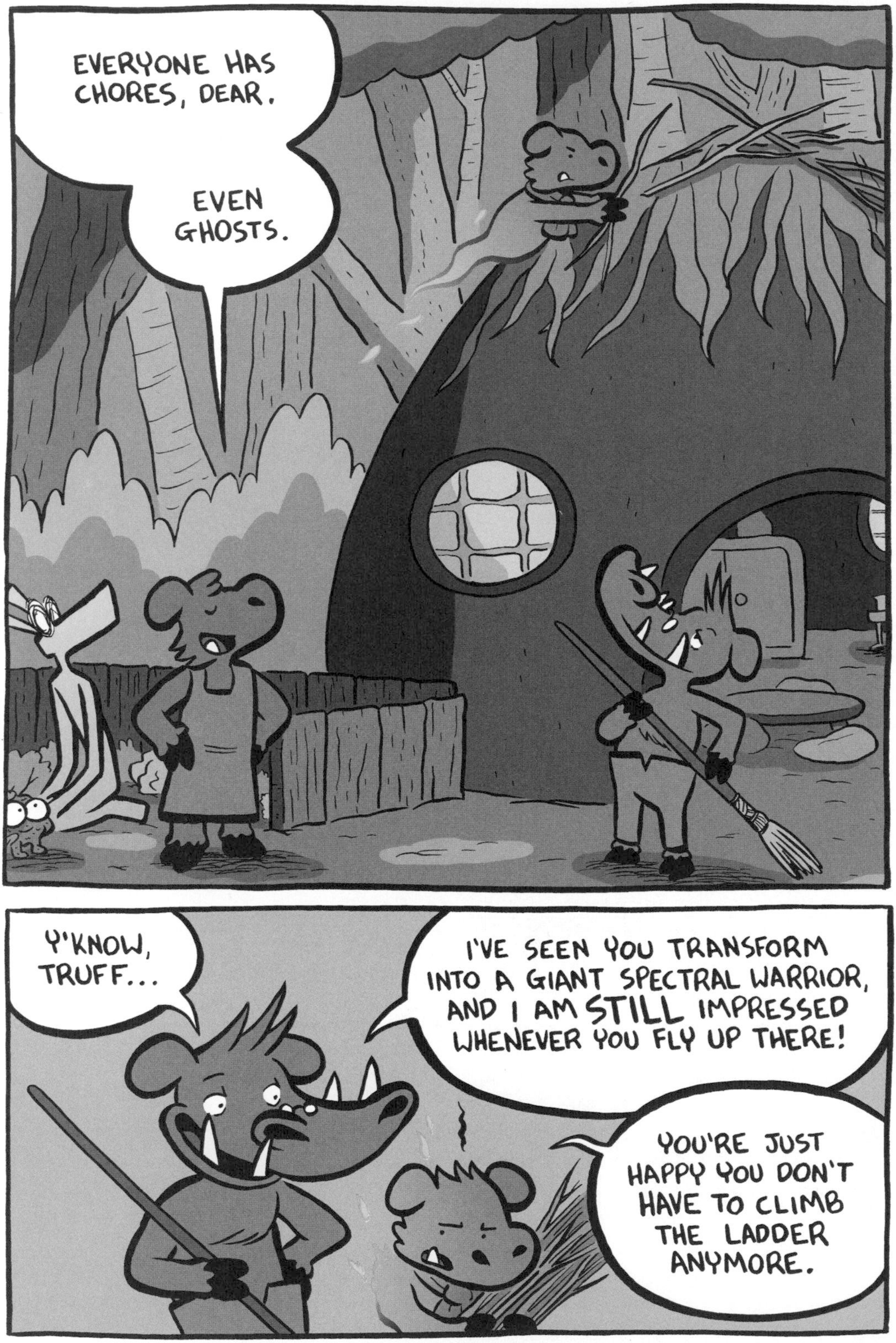
EVERYONE HAS CHORES, DEAR.
EVEN GHOSTS.
Y'KNOW, TRUFF...
I'VE SEEN YOU TRANSFORM INTO A GIANT SPECTRAL WARRIOR, AND I AM STILL IMPRESSED WHENEVER YOU FLY UP THERE!
YOU'RE JUST HAPPY YOU DON'T HAVE TO CLIMB THE LADDER ANYMORE.

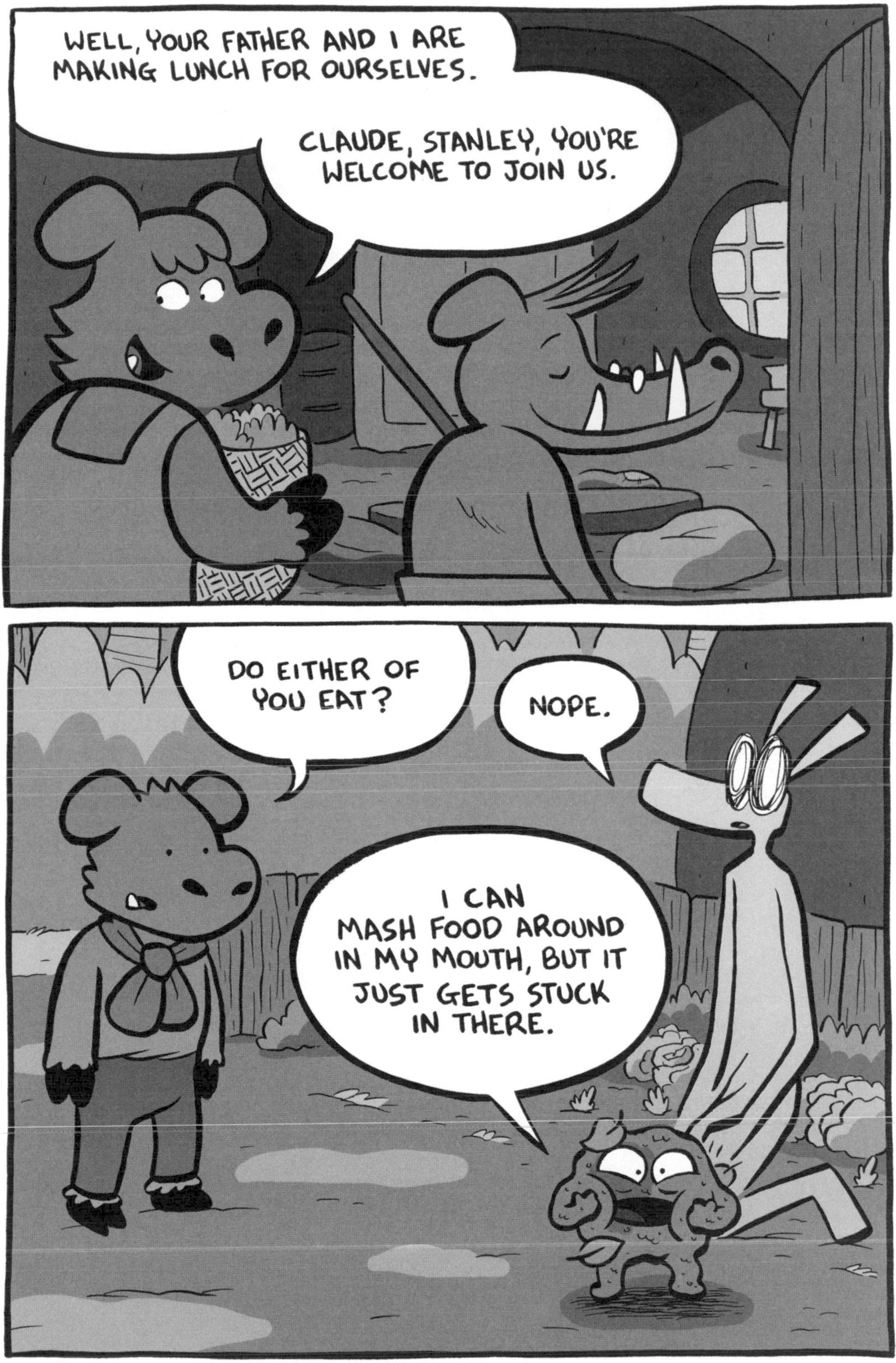
WELL, YOUR FATHER AND I ARE MAKING LUNCH FOR OURSELVES.
CLAUDE, STANLEY, YOU'RE WELCOME TO JOIN US.
DO EITHER OF YOU EAT?
NOPE.
I CAN MASH FOOD AROUND IN MY MOUTH, BUT IT JUST GETS STUCK IN THERE.

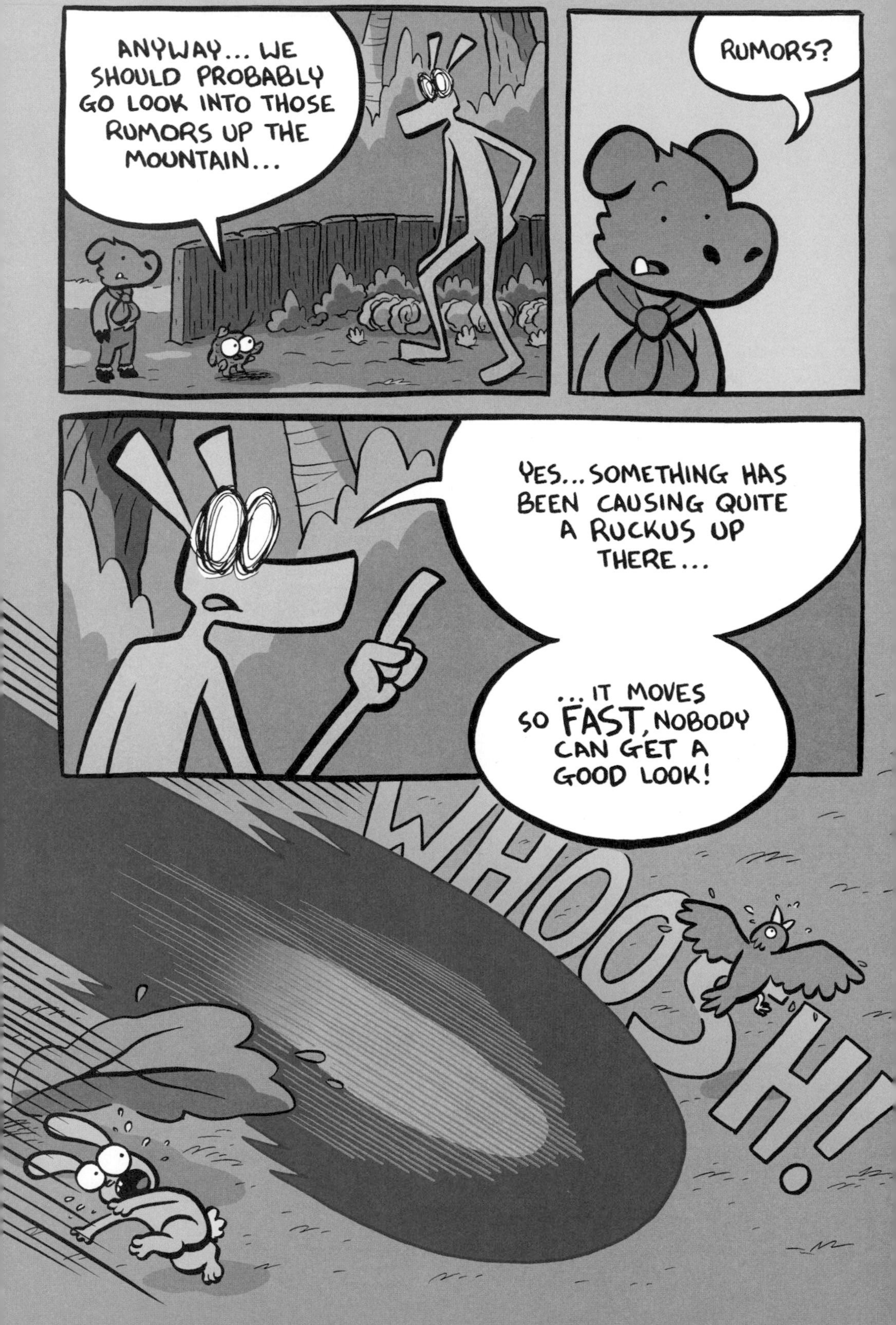
ANYWAY... WE SHOULD PROBABLY GO LOOK INTO THOSE RUMORS UP THE MOUNTAIN...
RUMORS?
YES...SOMETHING HAS BEEN CAUSING QUITE A RUCKUS UP THERE...
...IT MOVES SO FAST, NOBODY CAN GET A GOOD LOOK!
WHOOSH!!

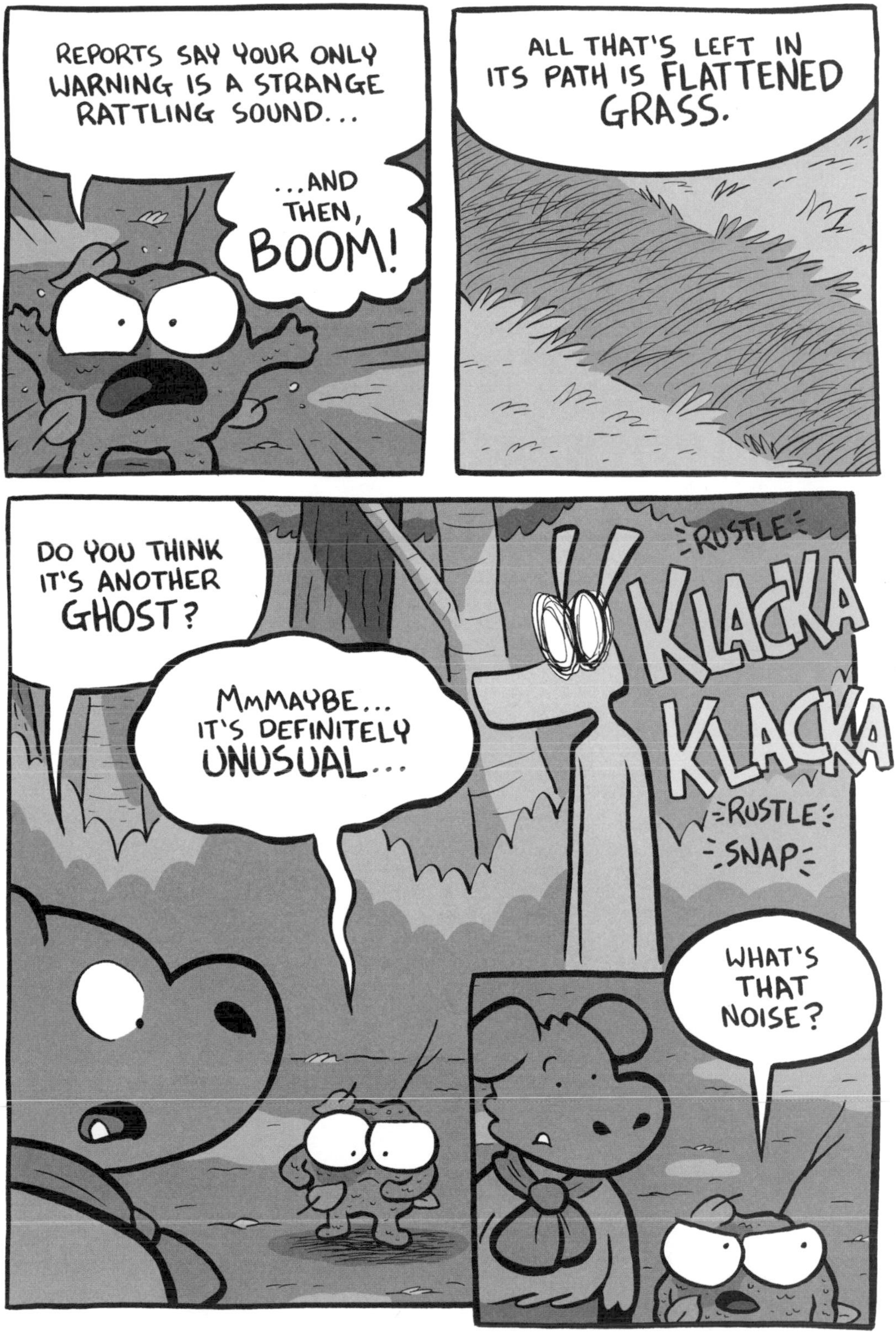
REPORTS SAY YOUR ONLY WARNING IS A STRANGE RATTLING SOUND...
...AND THEN, BOOM!
ALL THAT'S LEFT IN ITS PATH IS FLATTENED GRASS.
DO YOU THINK IT'S ANOTHER GHOST?
MMMAYBE... IT'S DEFINITELY UNUSUAL...
RUSTLE
KLACKA
KLACKA
RUSTLE
SNAP
WHAT'S THAT NOISE?

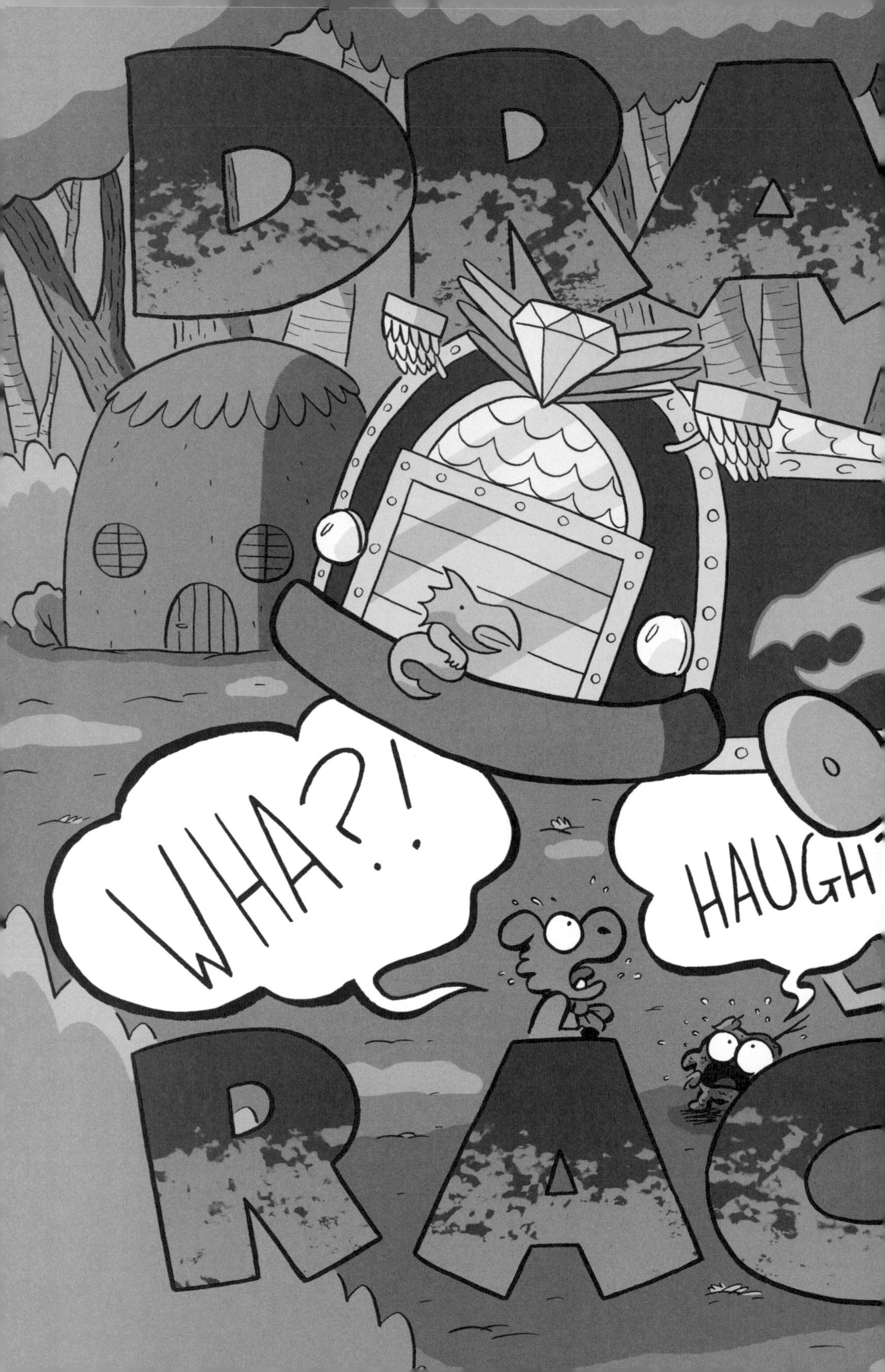
DRA
WHA?!
HAUGH
RAC

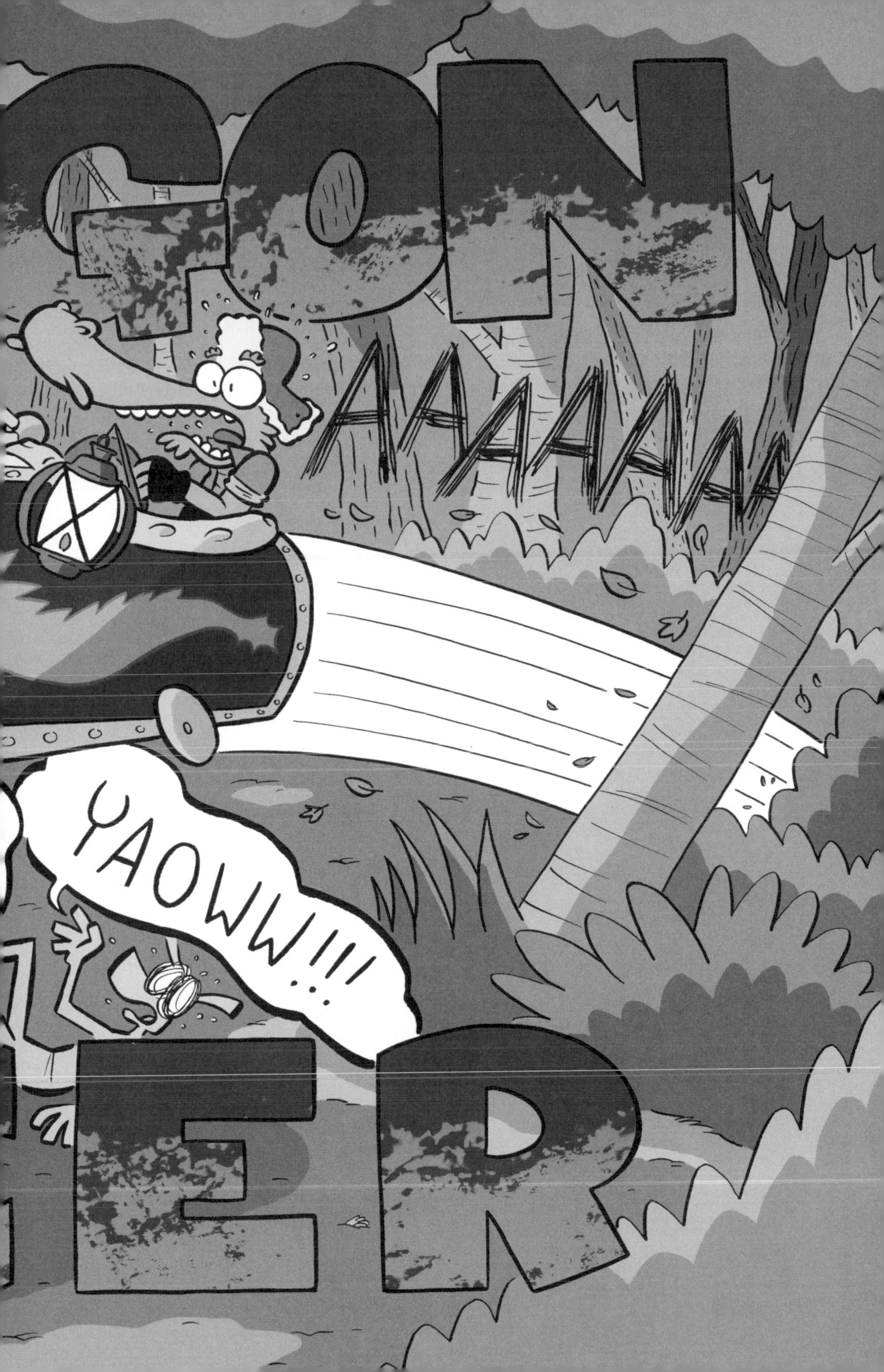
CON
AAAAAAAA
YAOWW!!!...
ER

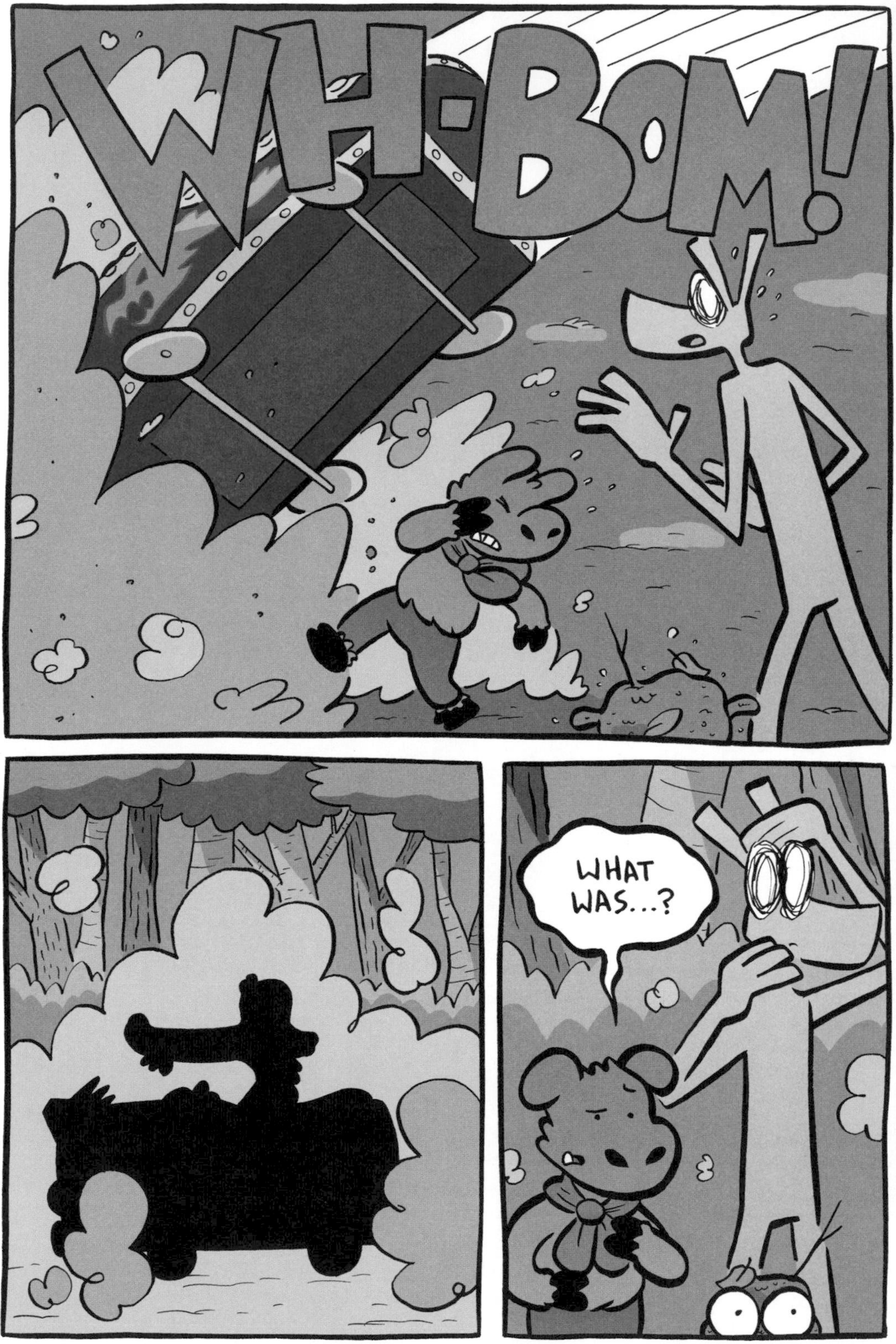
WH-BOM!
WHAT WAS...?

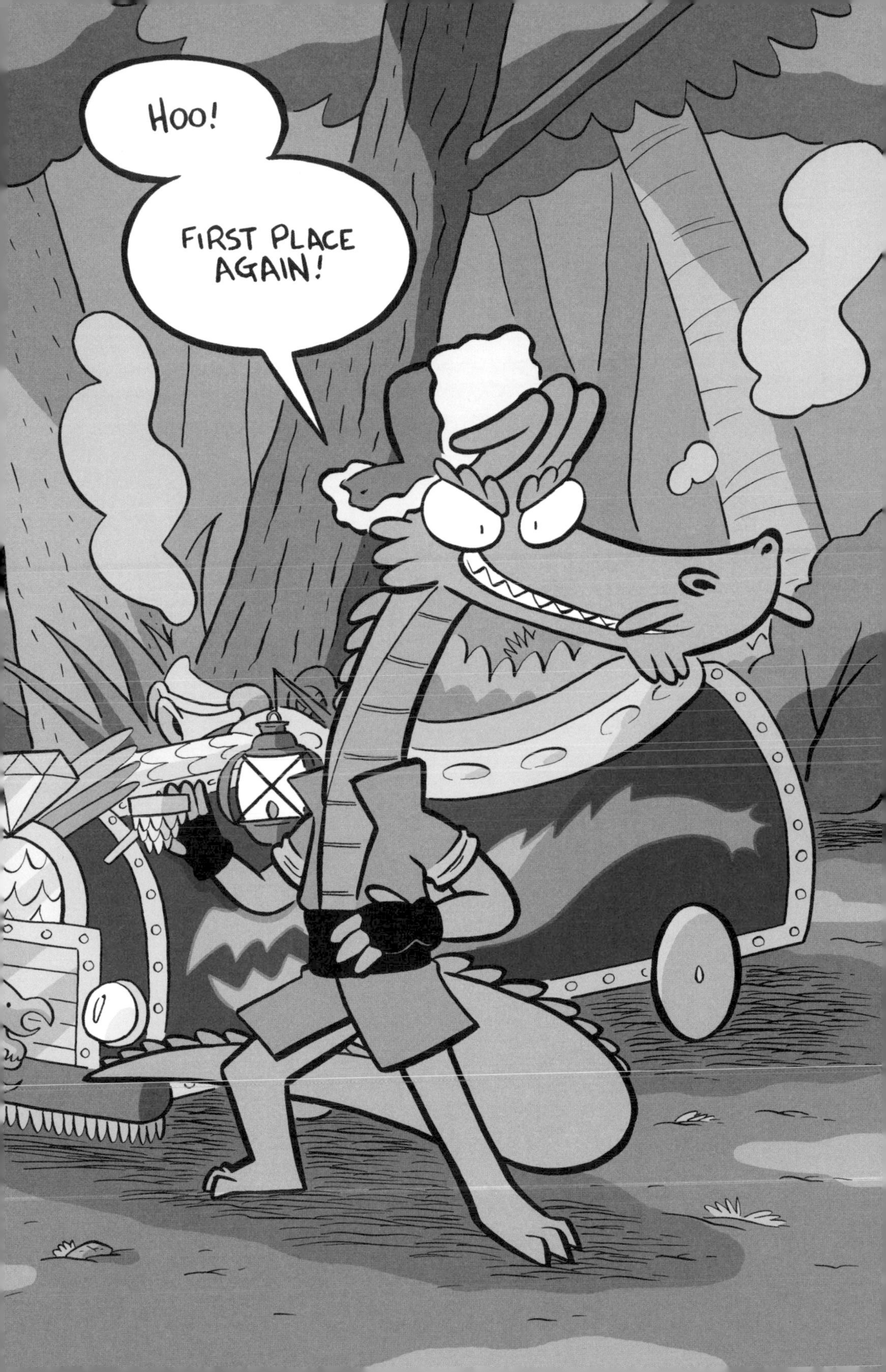
HOO!
FIRST PLACE AGAIN!

"FIRST"...?

HA HA HA HA

JUST A PRACTICE RUN...

...BUT IF IT HAD BEEN A **REAL RACE**, I'D SURELY WIN!

OKAY, BOZO. WHO ARE YOU?

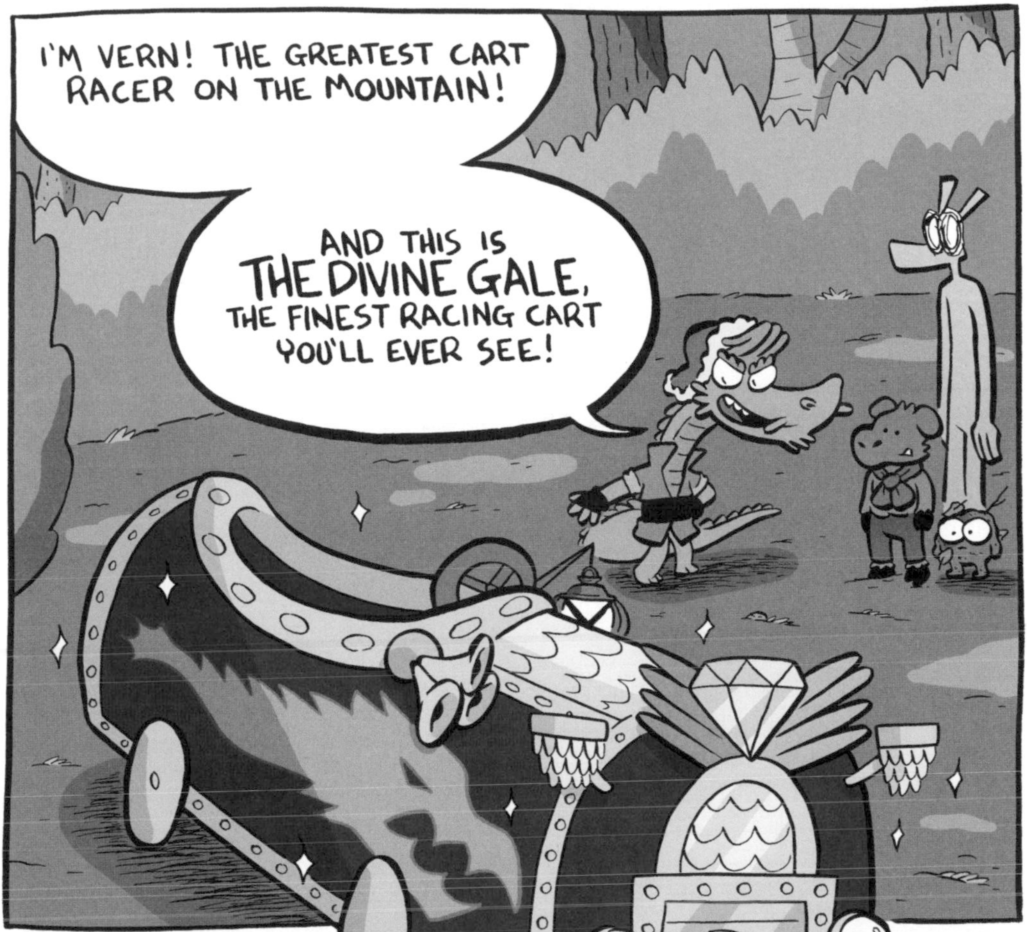
I'M VERN! THE GREATEST CART RACER ON THE MOUNTAIN!
AND THIS IS THE DIVINE GALE, THE FINEST RACING CART YOU'LL EVER SEE!

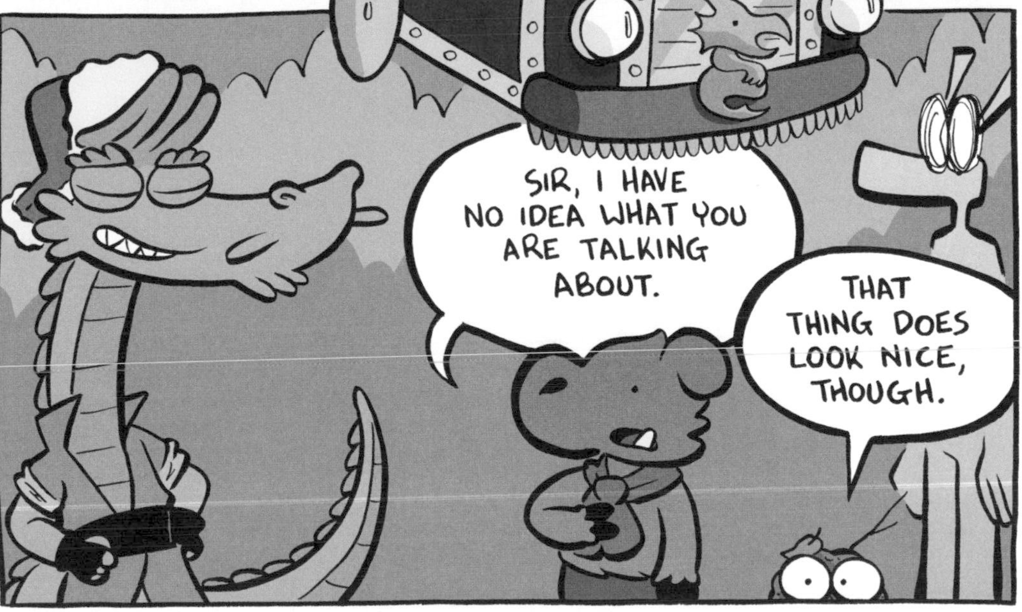
SIR, I HAVE NO IDEA WHAT YOU ARE TALKING ABOUT.
THAT THING DOES LOOK NICE, THOUGH.

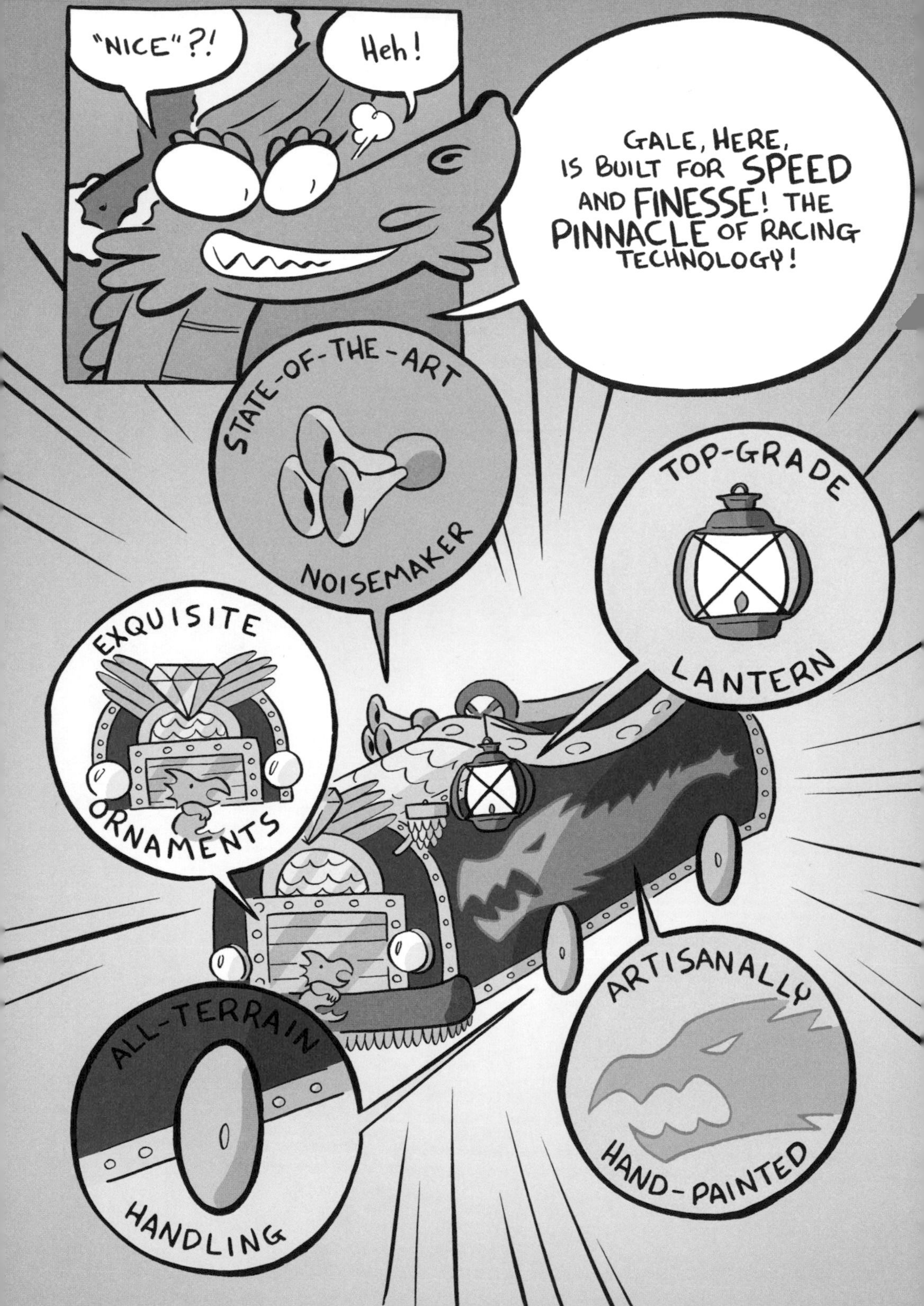
"NICE"?!
Heh!
GALE, HERE, IS BUILT FOR SPEED AND FINESSE! THE PINNACLE OF RACING TECHNOLOGY!
STATE-OF-THE-ART NOISEMAKER
TOP-GRADE LANTERN
EXQUISITE ORNAMENTS
ALL-TERRAIN HANDLING
ARTISANALLY HAND-PAINTED

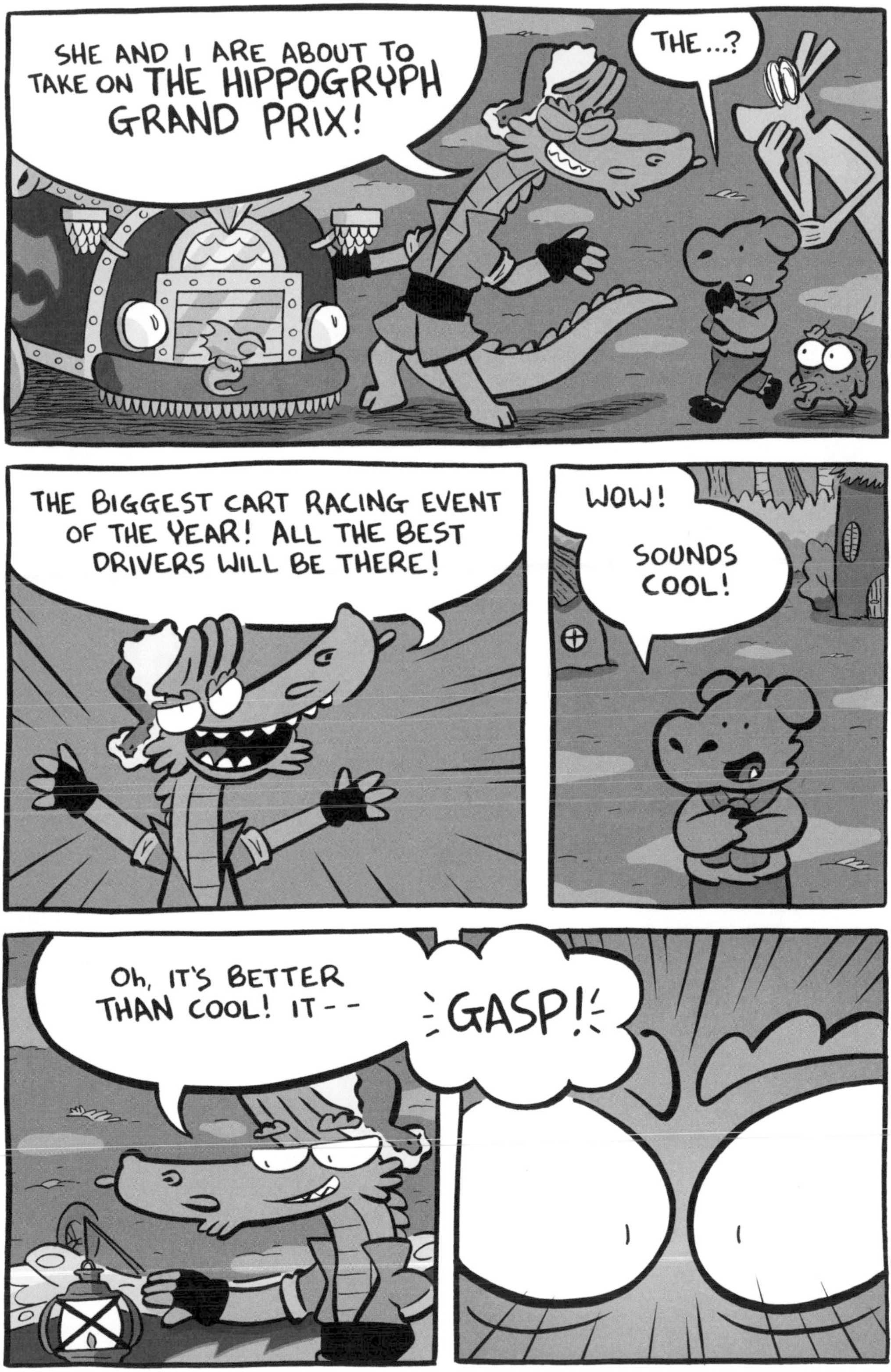
SHE AND I ARE ABOUT TO TAKE ON THE HIPPOGRYPH GRAND PRIX!
THE...?
THE BIGGEST CART RACING EVENT OF THE YEAR! ALL THE BEST DRIVERS WILL BE THERE!
WOW!
SOUNDS COOL!
Oh, IT'S BETTER THAN COOL! IT--
GASP!

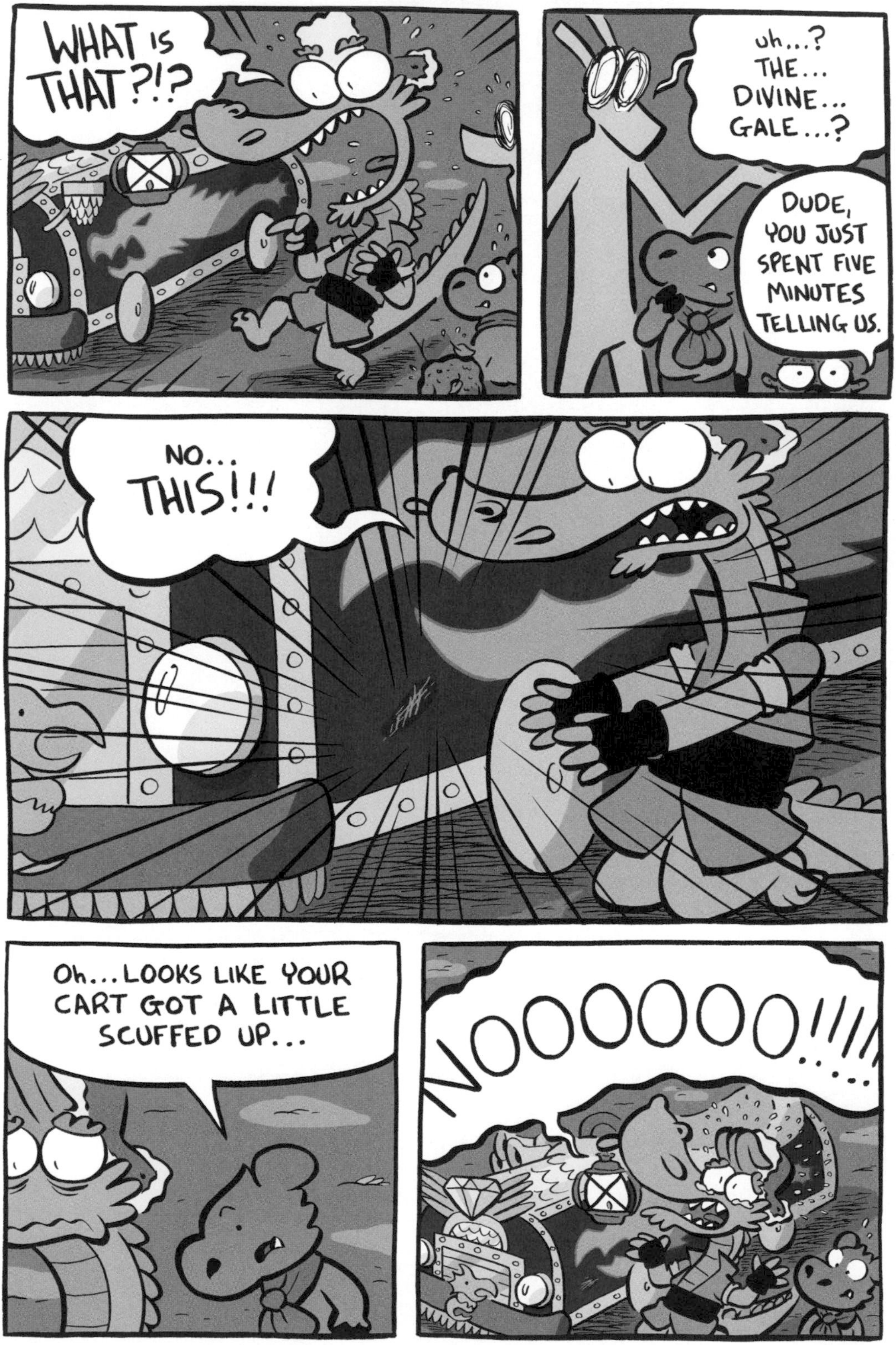
WHAT IS THAT?!?
uh...? THE... DIVINE... GALE...?
DUDE, YOU JUST SPENT FIVE MINUTES TELLING US.
NO... THIS!!!
Oh... LOOKS LIKE YOUR CART GOT A LITTLE SCUFFED UP...
NOOOOOO!!!!......

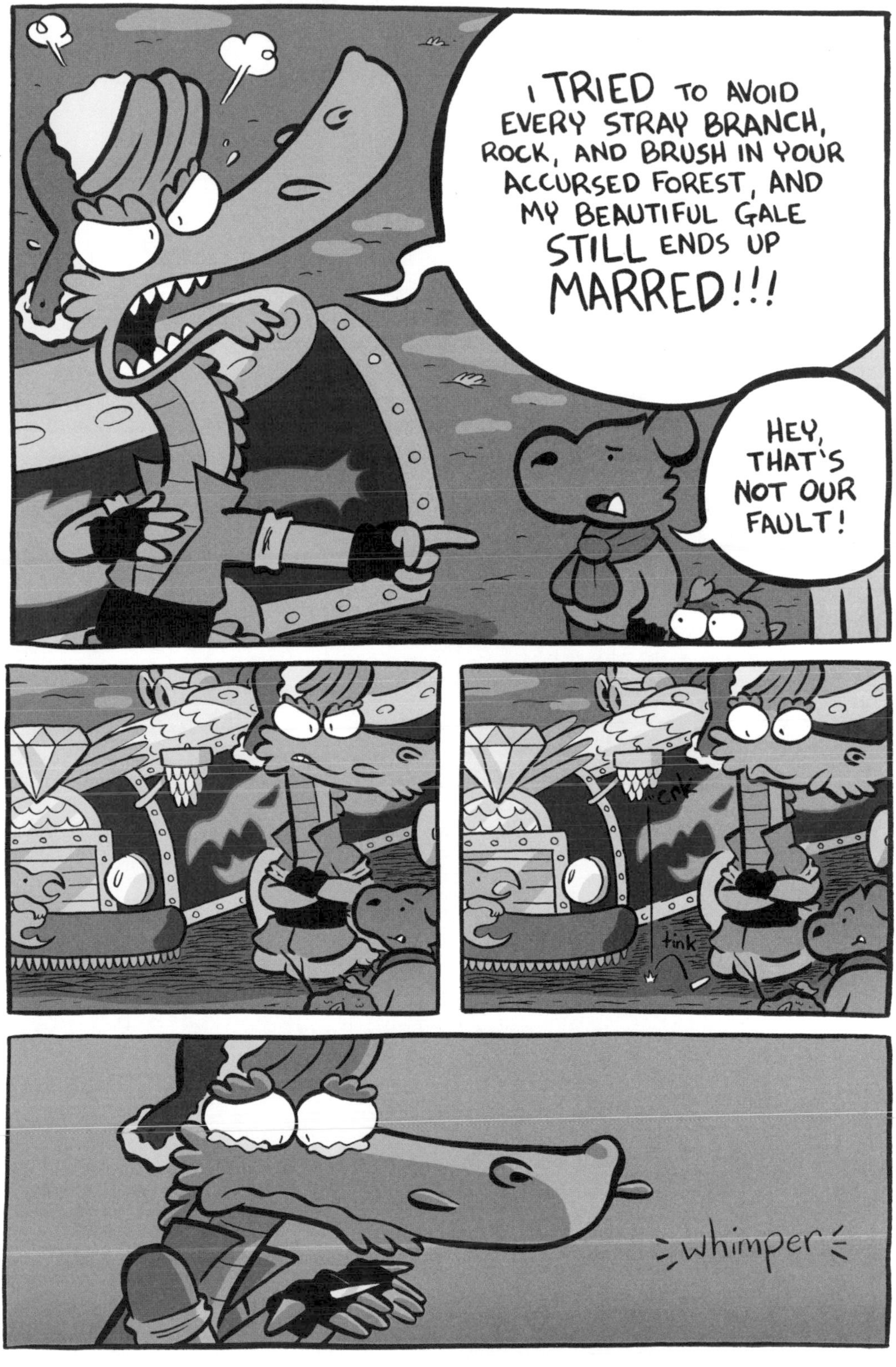
I TRIED TO AVOID EVERY STRAY BRANCH, ROCK, AND BRUSH IN YOUR ACCURSED FOREST, AND MY BEAUTIFUL GALE STILL ENDS UP MARRED!!!
HEY, THAT'S NOT OUR FAULT!
crk
tink
whimper

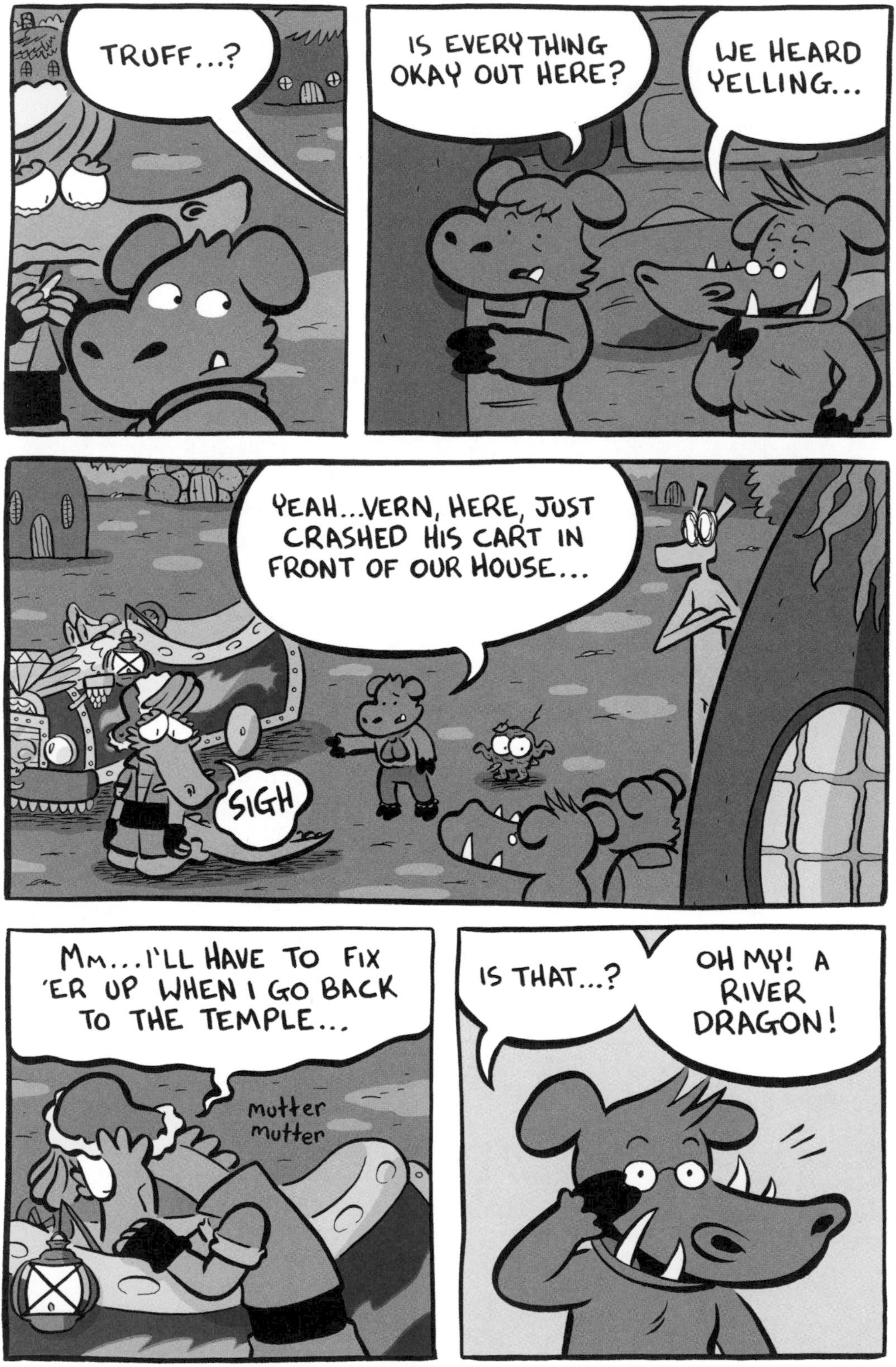
TRUFF...?
IS EVERYTHING OKAY OUT HERE?
WE HEARD YELLING...
YEAH...VERN, HERE, JUST CRASHED HIS CART IN FRONT OF OUR HOUSE...
SIGH
MM...I'LL HAVE TO FIX 'ER UP WHEN I GO BACK TO THE TEMPLE...
mutter mutter
IS THAT...?
OH MY! A RIVER DRAGON!

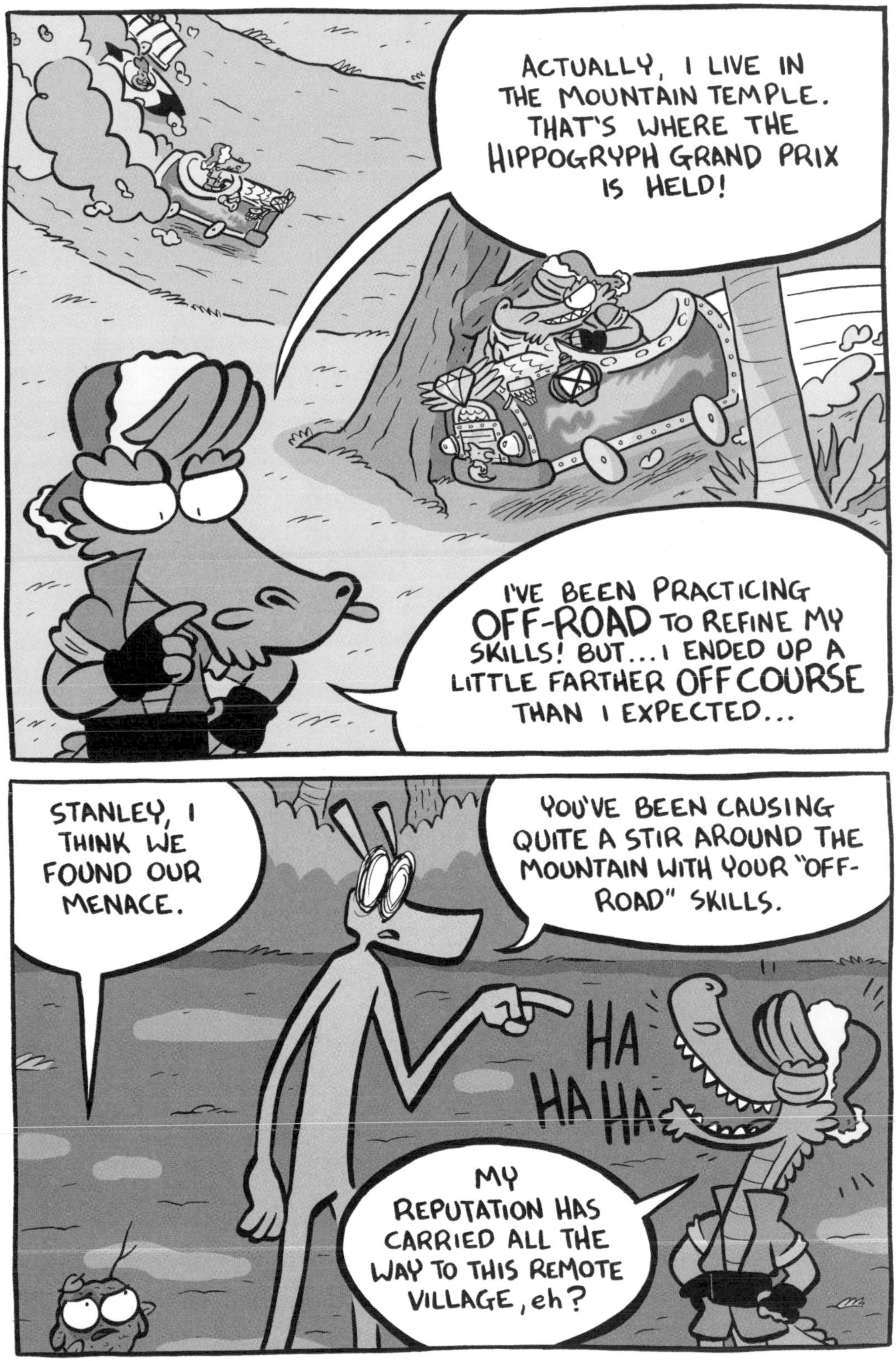
ACTUALLY, I LIVE IN THE MOUNTAIN TEMPLE. THAT'S WHERE THE HIPPOGRYPH GRAND PRIX IS HELD!
I'VE BEEN PRACTICING OFF-ROAD TO REFINE MY SKILLS! BUT... I ENDED UP A LITTLE FARTHER OFF COURSE THAN I EXPECTED...
STANLEY, I THINK WE FOUND OUR MENACE.
YOU'VE BEEN CAUSING QUITE A STIR AROUND THE MOUNTAIN WITH YOUR "OFF-ROAD" SKILLS.
HA HA HA HA
MY REPUTATION HAS CARRIED ALL THE WAY TO THIS REMOTE VILLAGE, eh?

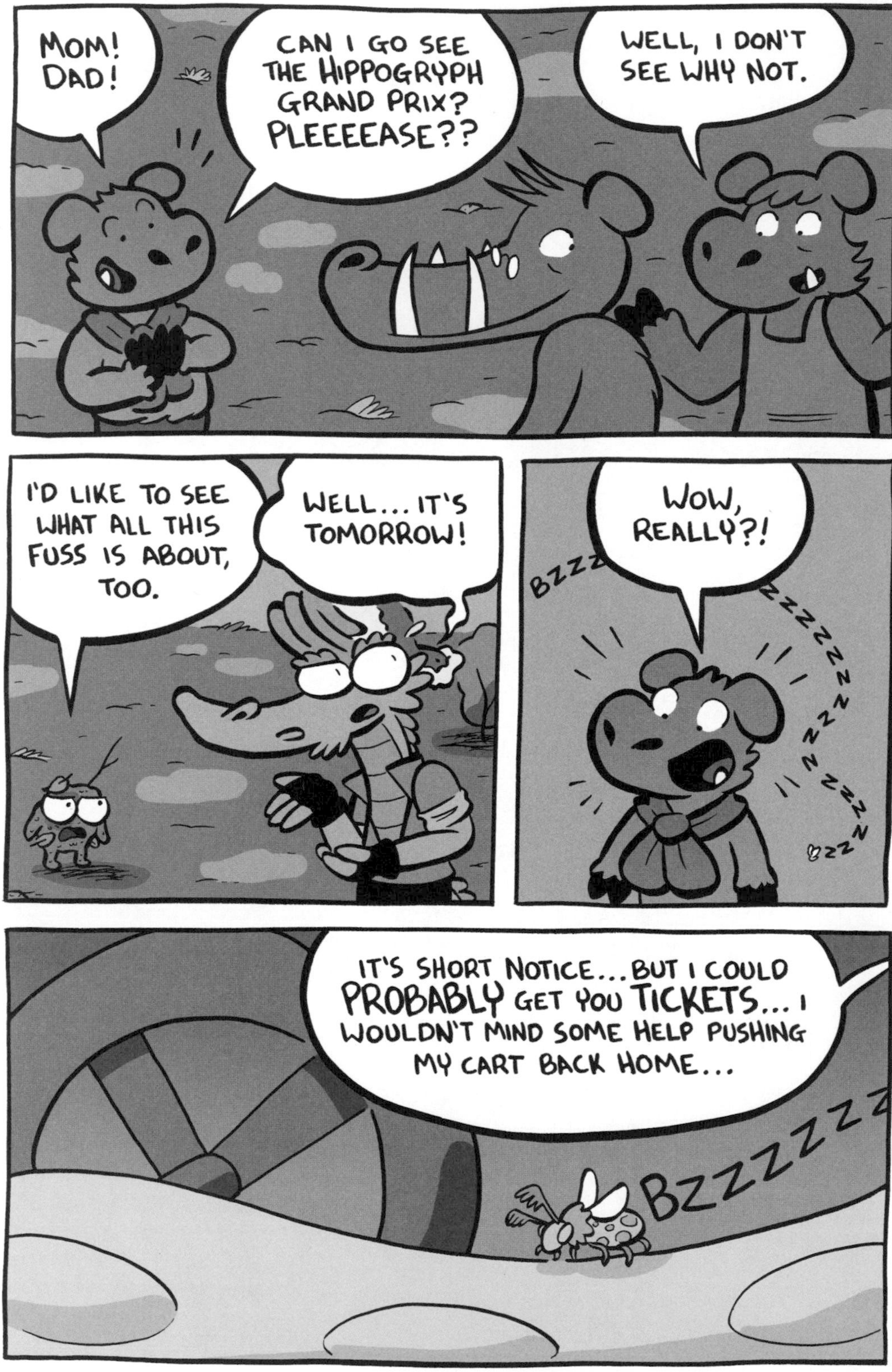
MOM! DAD!
CAN I GO SEE THE HIPPOGRYPH GRAND PRIX? PLEEEEASE??
WELL, I DON'T SEE WHY NOT.
I'D LIKE TO SEE WHAT ALL THIS FUSS IS ABOUT, TOO.
WELL... IT'S TOMORROW!
WOW, REALLY?!
BZZZ
ZZZZZZZZZZZZZZ
IT'S SHORT NOTICE... BUT I COULD PROBABLY GET YOU TICKETS... I WOULDN'T MIND SOME HELP PUSHING MY CART BACK HOME...
BZZZZZZZ

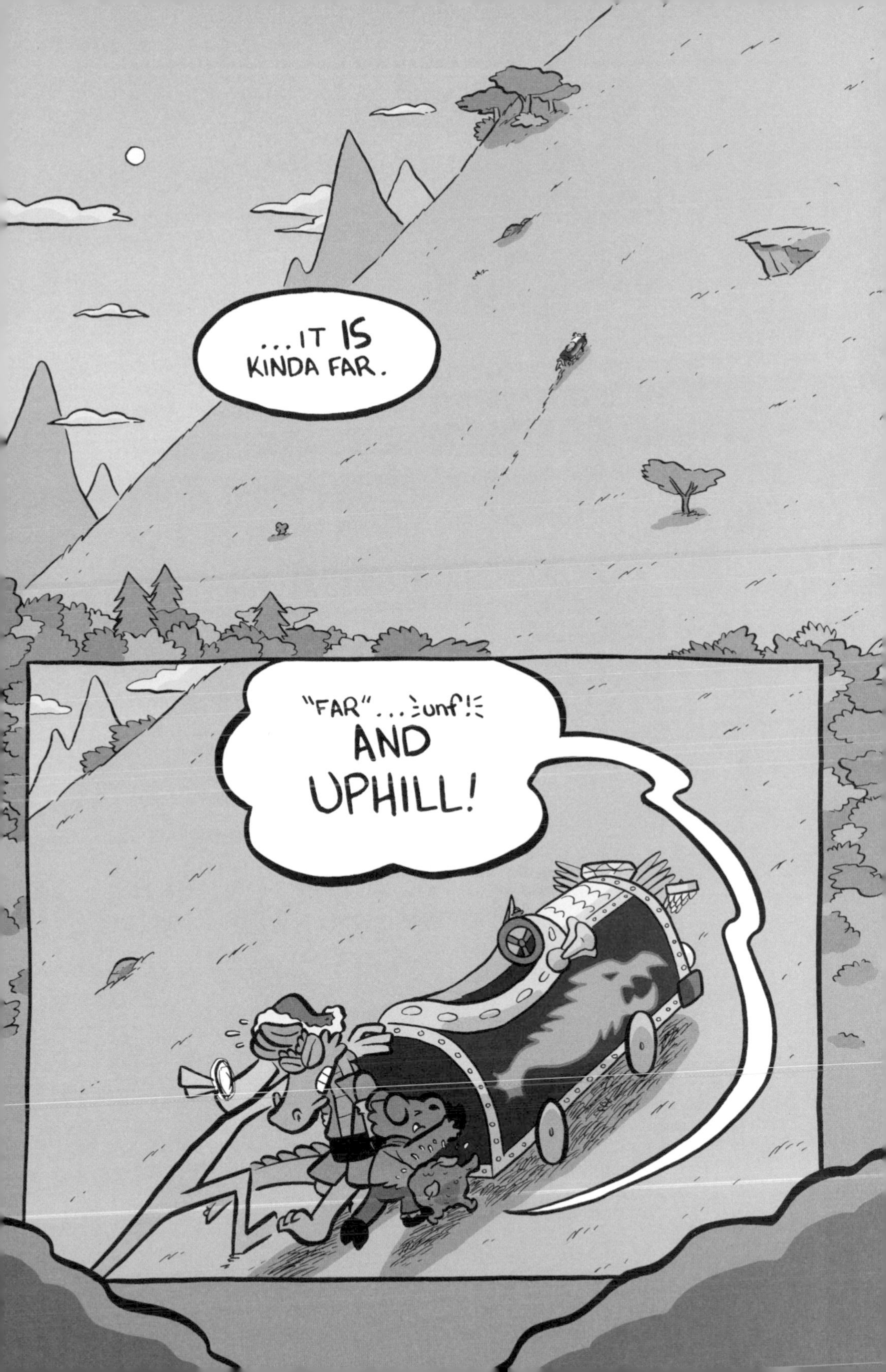
...IT IS KINDA FAR.
"FAR"... unf!
AND UPHILL!

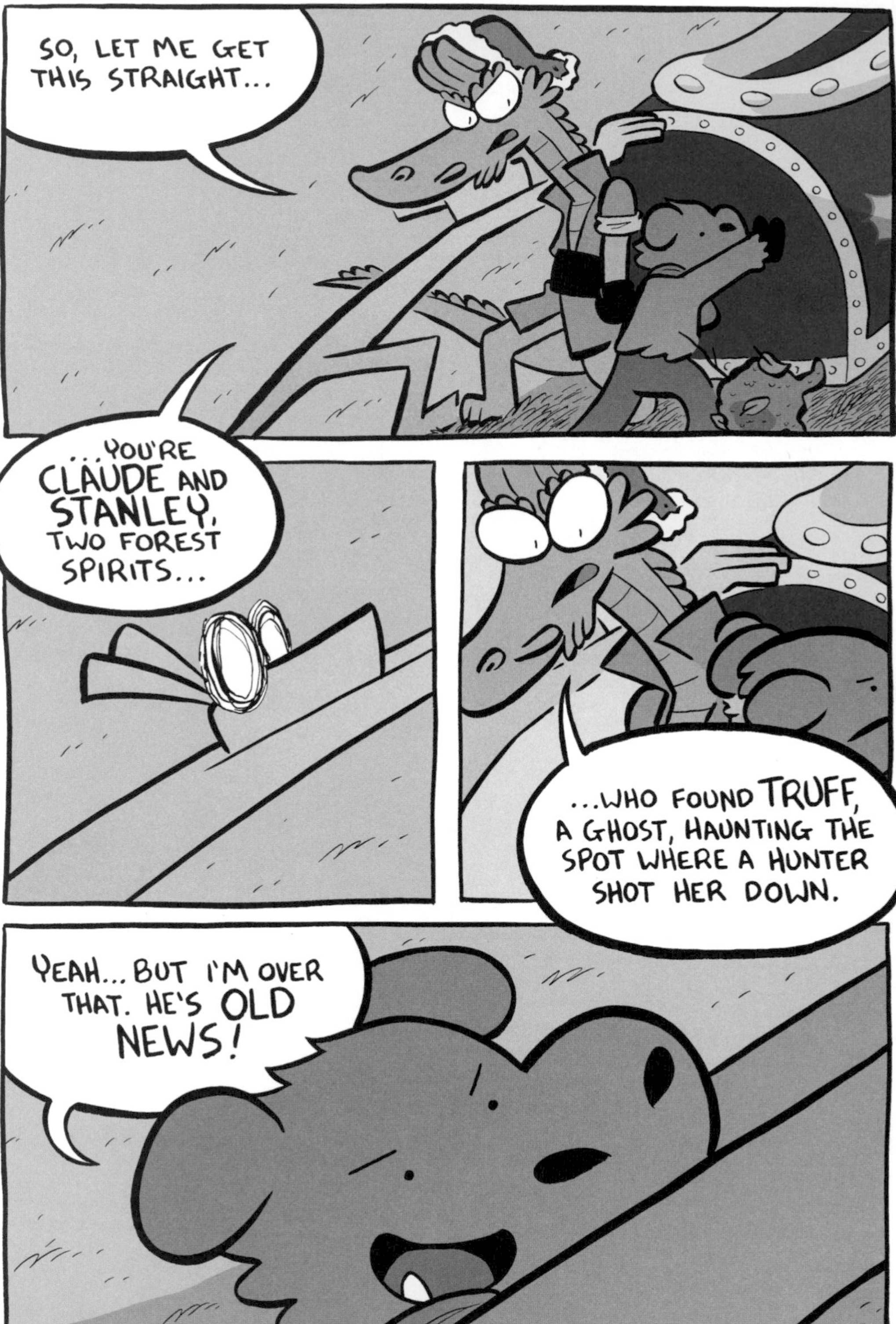
SO, LET ME GET THIS STRAIGHT...
...YOU'RE CLAUDE AND STANLEY, TWO FOREST SPIRITS...
...WHO FOUND TRUFF, A GHOST, HAUNTING THE SPOT WHERE A HUNTER SHOT HER DOWN.
YEAH... BUT I'M OVER THAT. HE'S OLD NEWS!

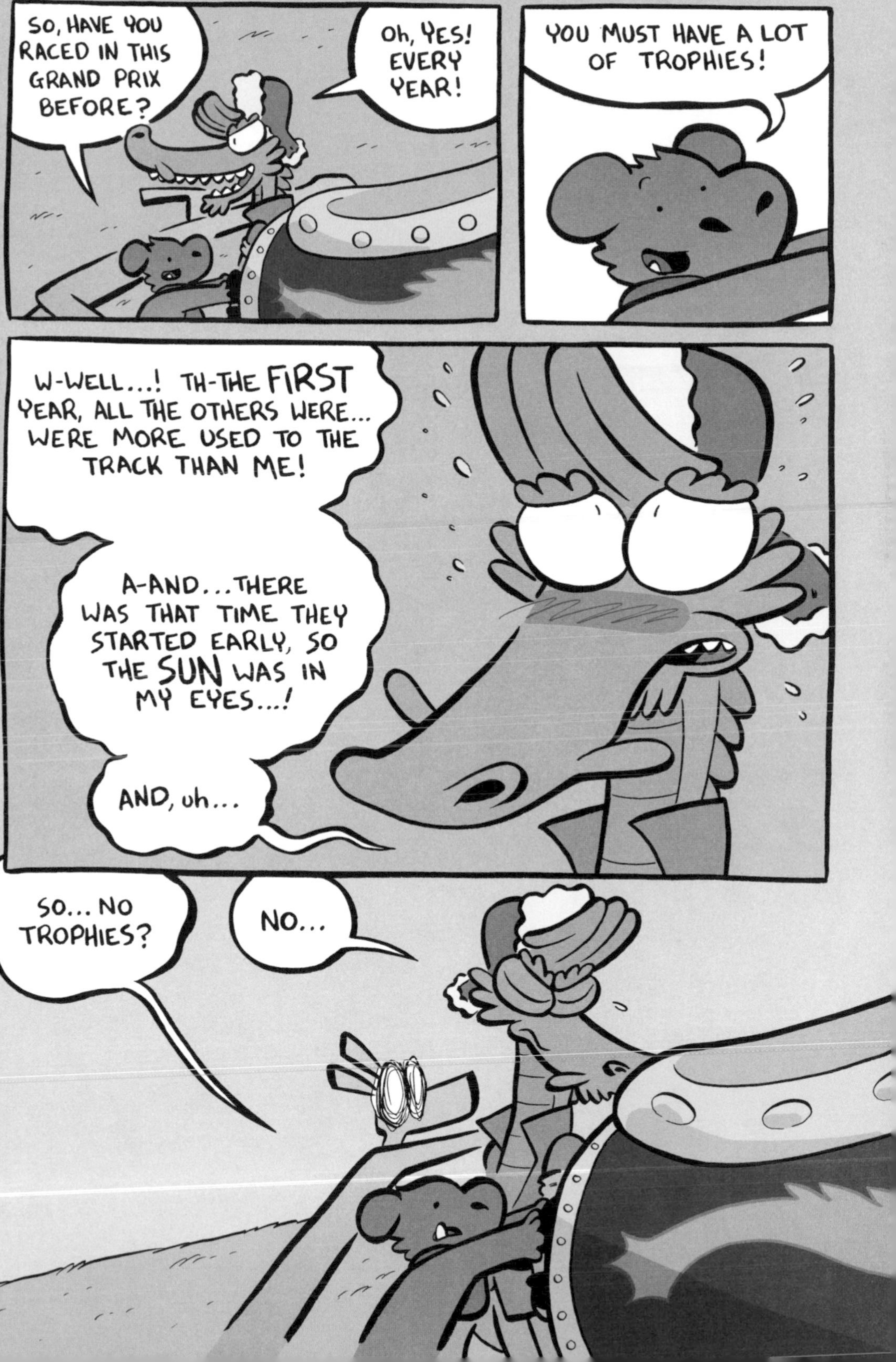
SO, HAVE YOU RACED IN THIS GRAND PRIX BEFORE?
Oh, YES! EVERY YEAR!
YOU MUST HAVE A LOT OF TROPHIES!
W-WELL...! TH-THE FIRST YEAR, ALL THE OTHERS WERE... WERE MORE USED TO THE TRACK THAN ME!
A-AND...THERE WAS THAT TIME THEY STARTED EARLY, SO THE SUN WAS IN MY EYES...!
AND, uh...
SO... NO TROPHIES?
NO...

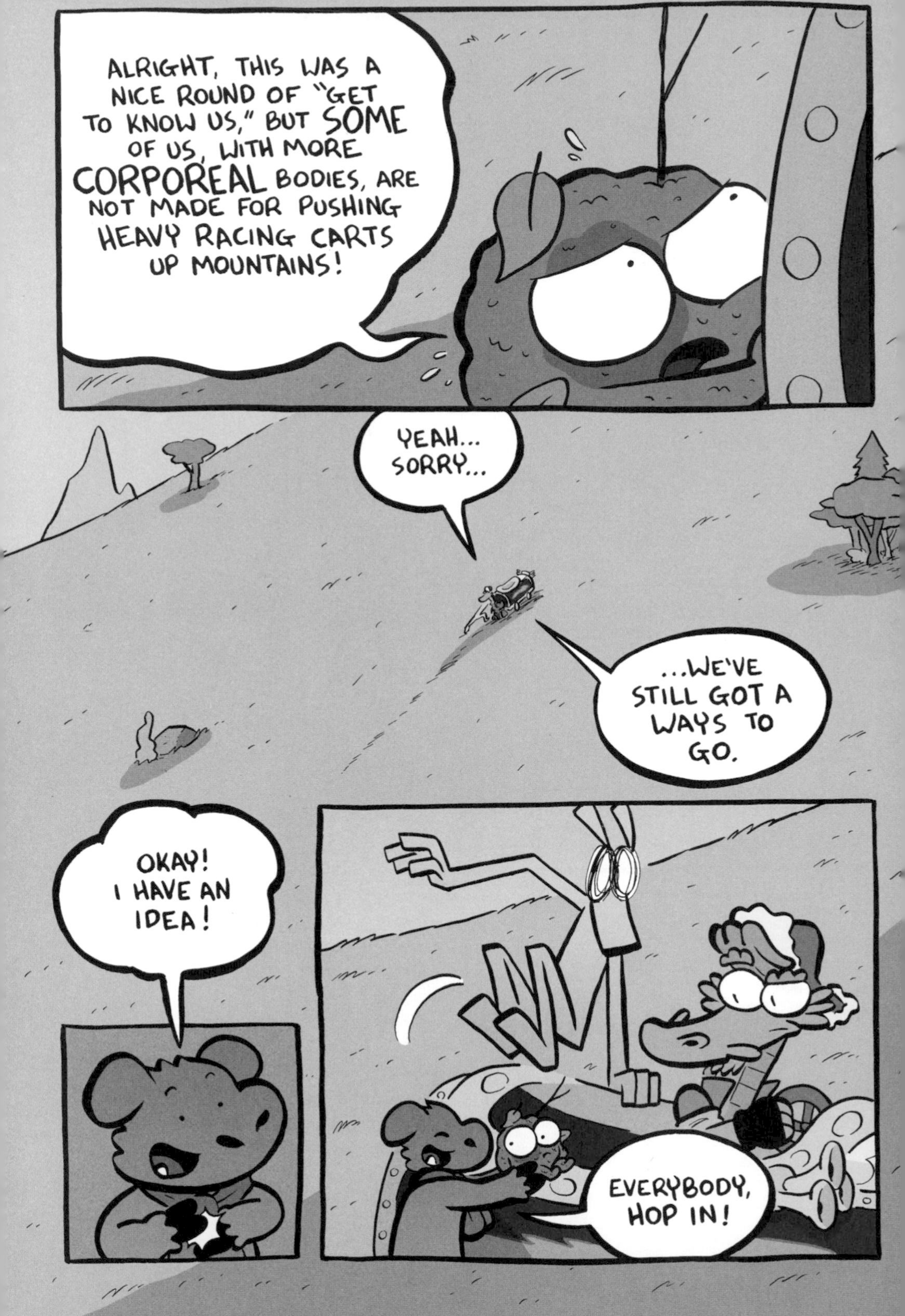
ALRIGHT, THIS WAS A NICE ROUND OF "GET TO KNOW US," BUT SOME OF US, WITH MORE CORPOREAL BODIES, ARE NOT MADE FOR PUSHING HEAVY RACING CARTS UP MOUNTAINS!
YEAH... SORRY...
...WE'VE STILL GOT A WAYS TO GO.
OKAY! I HAVE AN IDEA!
EVERYBODY, HOP IN!

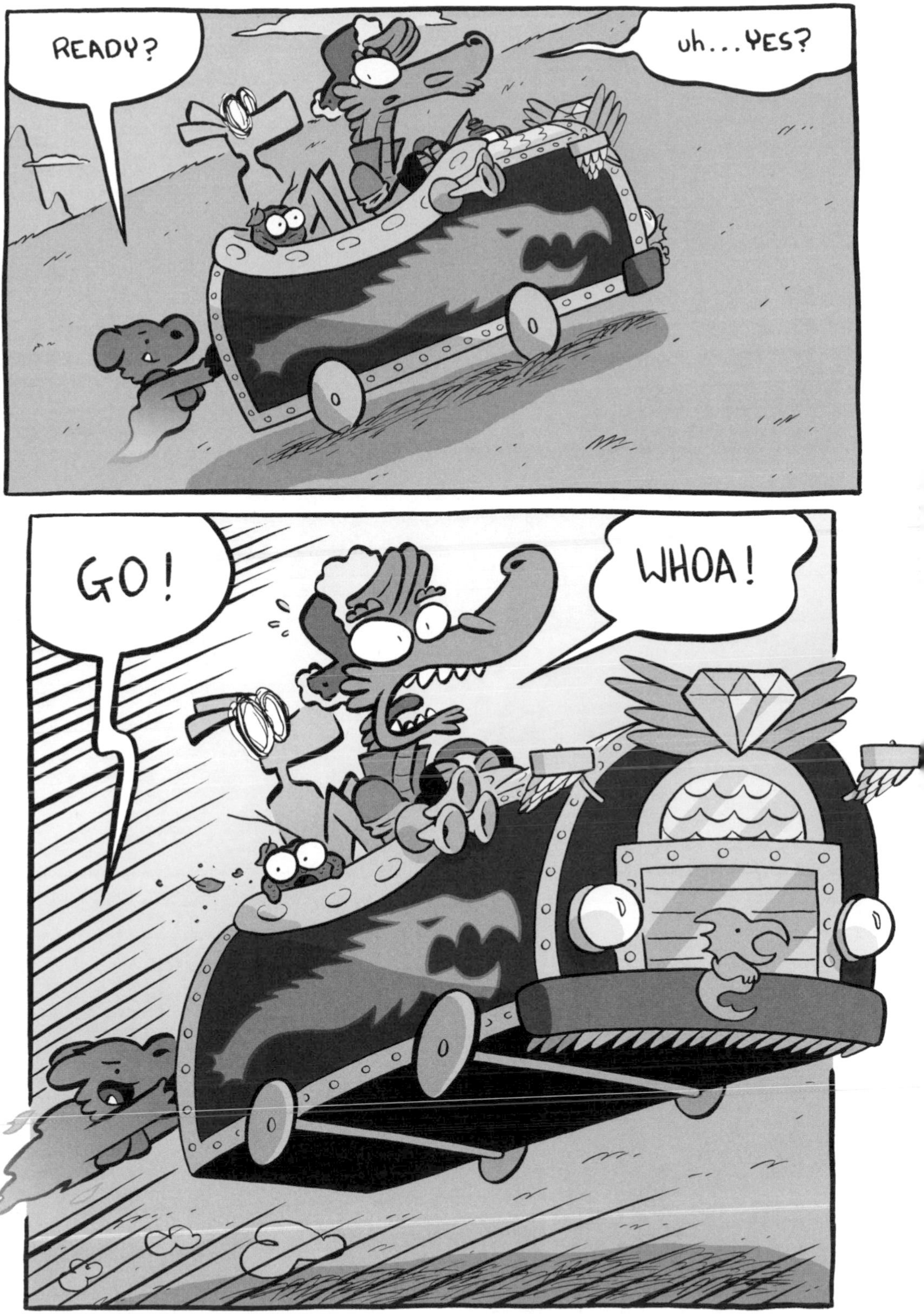
READY?
uh... YES?
GO!
WHOA!

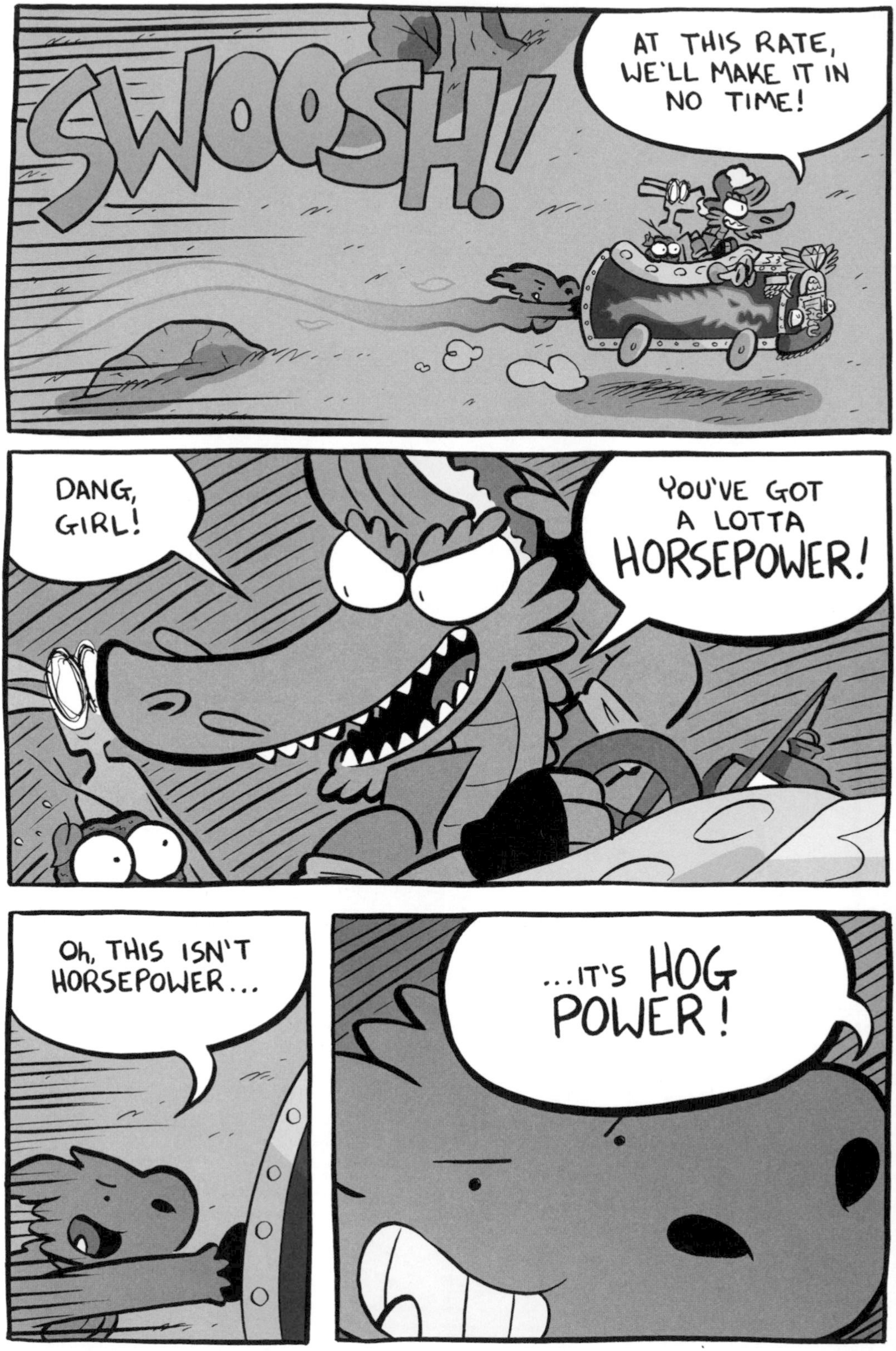
SWOOSH!
AT THIS RATE, WE'LL MAKE IT IN NO TIME!
DANG, GIRL!
YOU'VE GOT A LOTTA HORSEPOWER!
Oh, THIS ISN'T HORSEPOWER...
...IT'S HOG POWER!

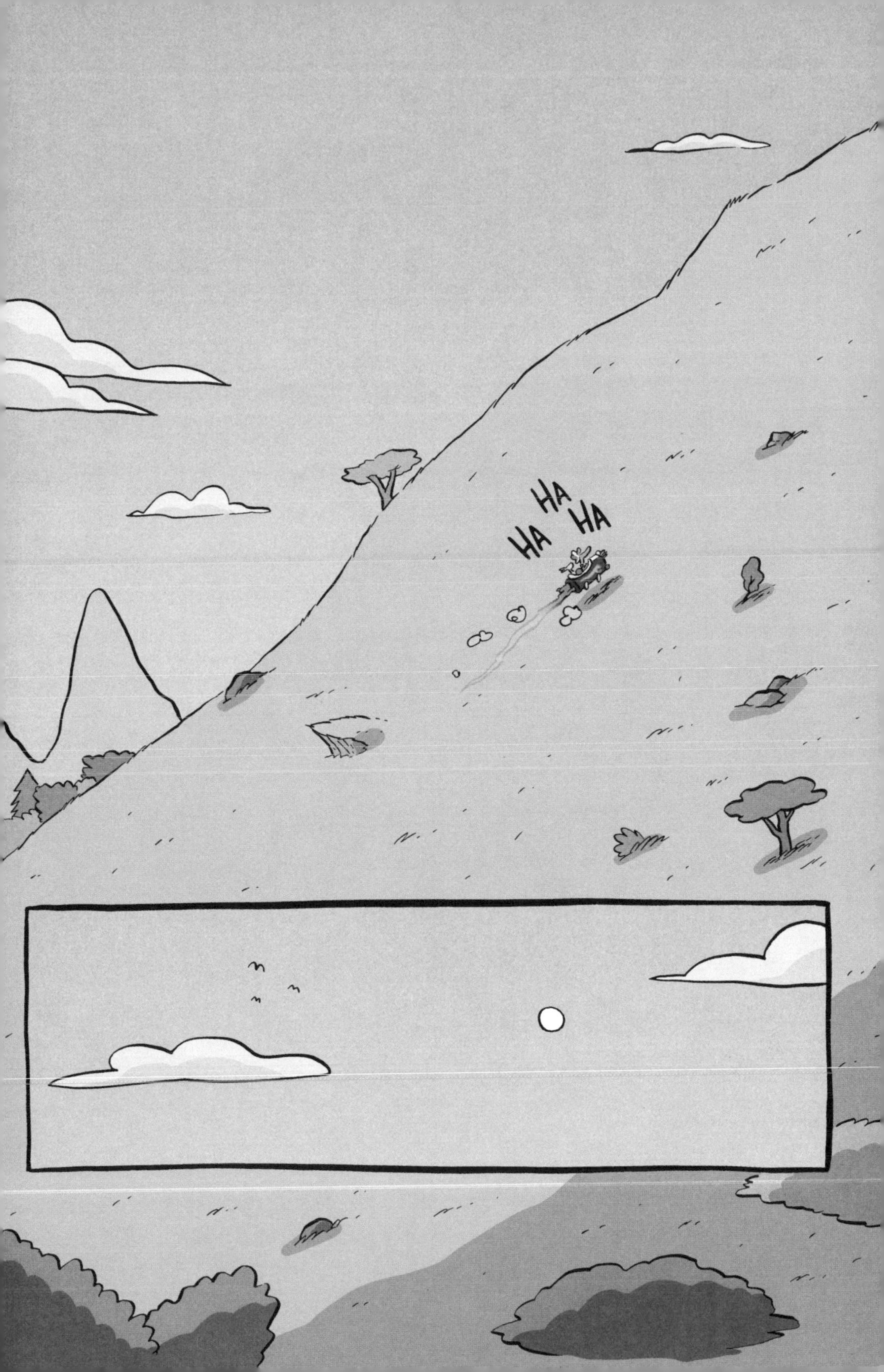
HA HA HA

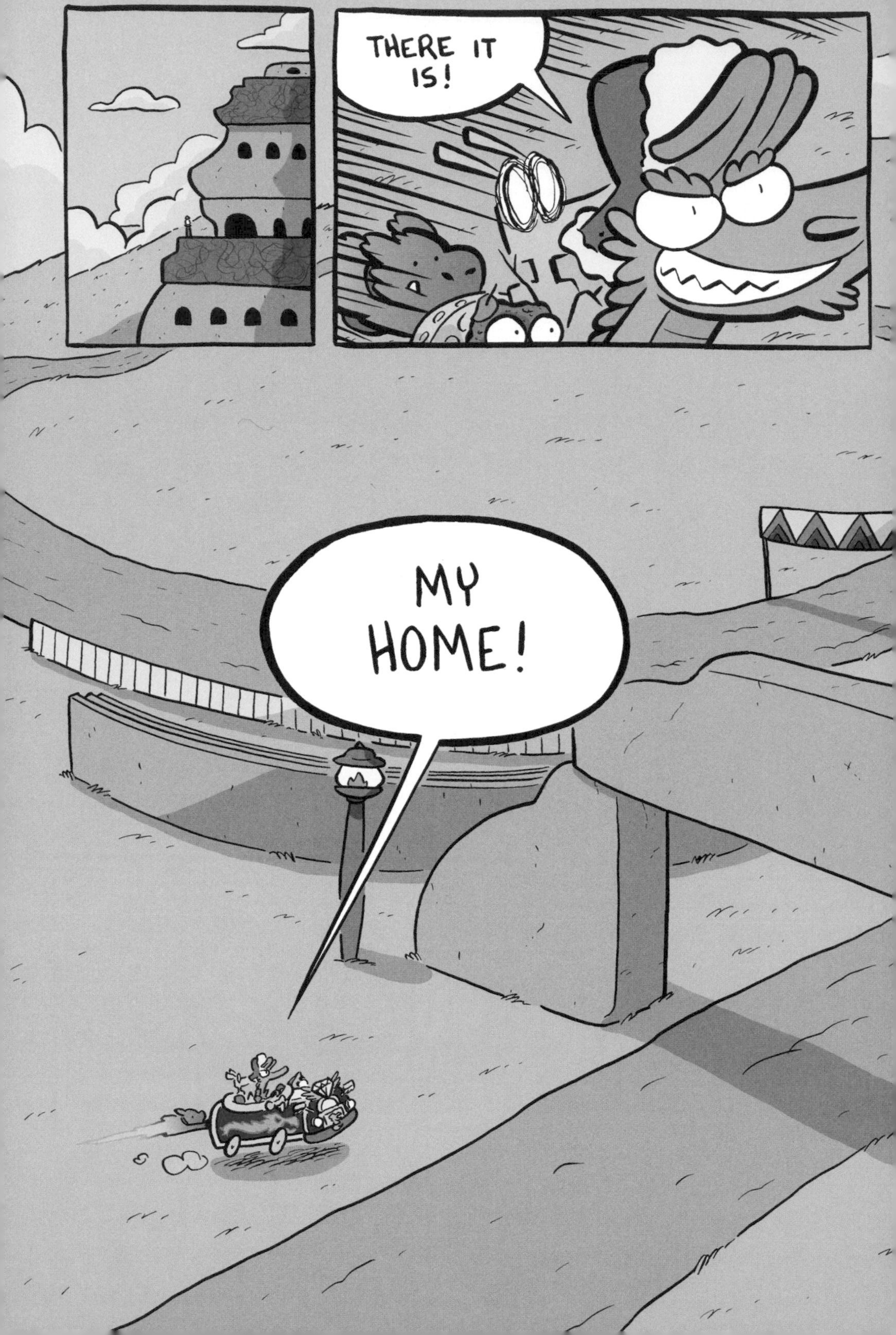
THERE IT IS!
MY HOME!

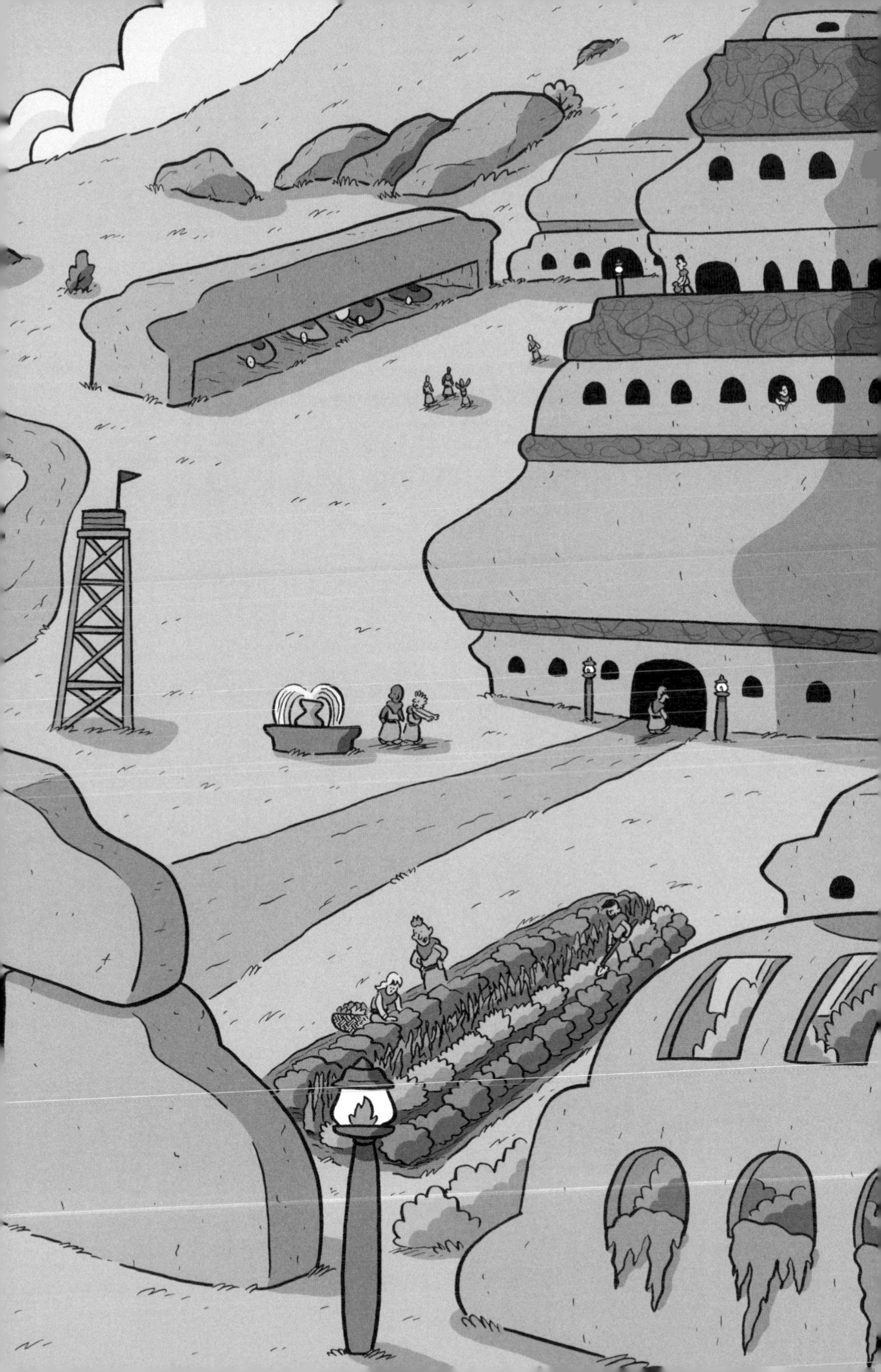

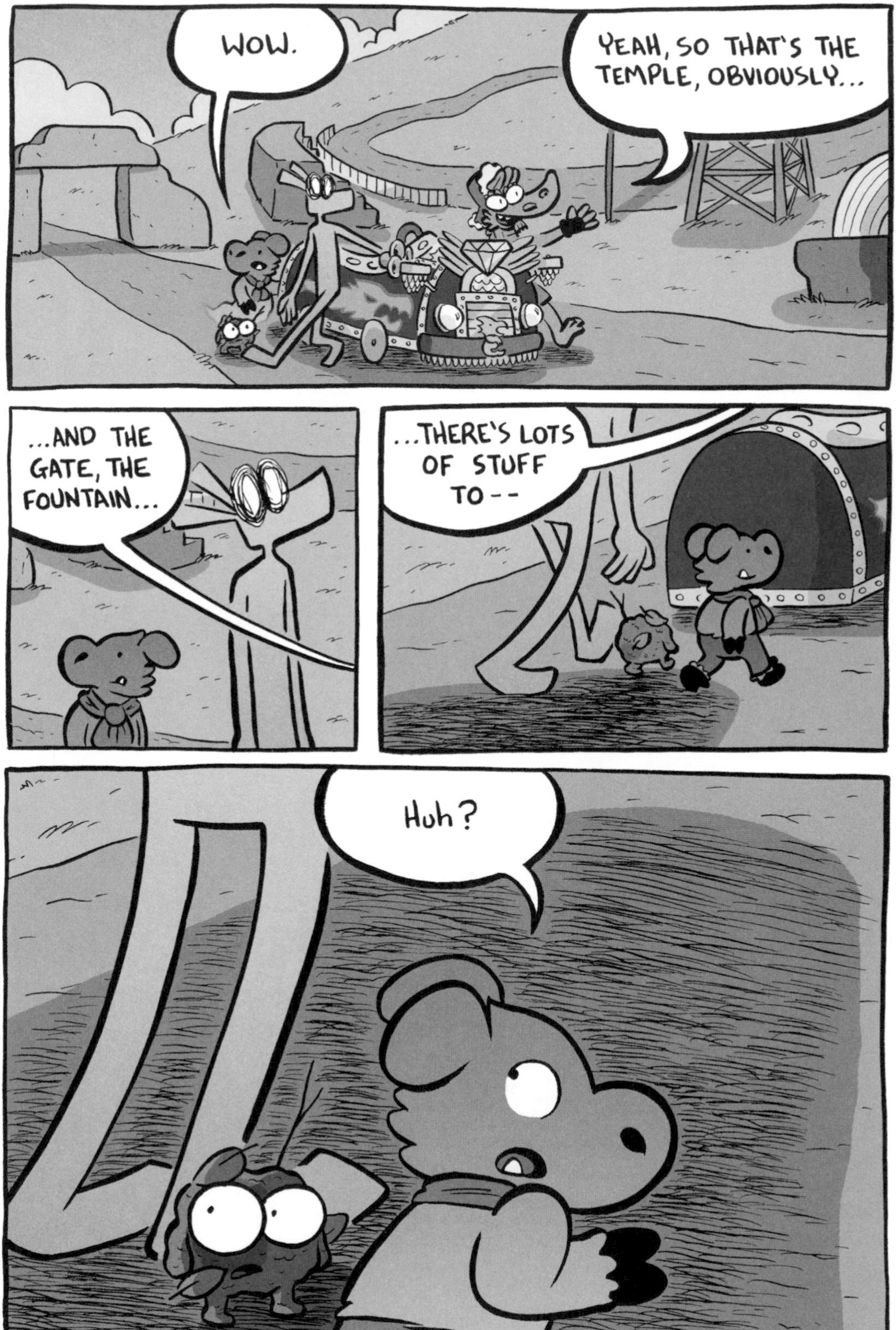
WOW.
YEAH, SO THAT'S THE TEMPLE, OBVIOUSLY...
...AND THE GATE, THE FOUNTAIN...
...THERE'S LOTS OF STUFF TO--
Huh?

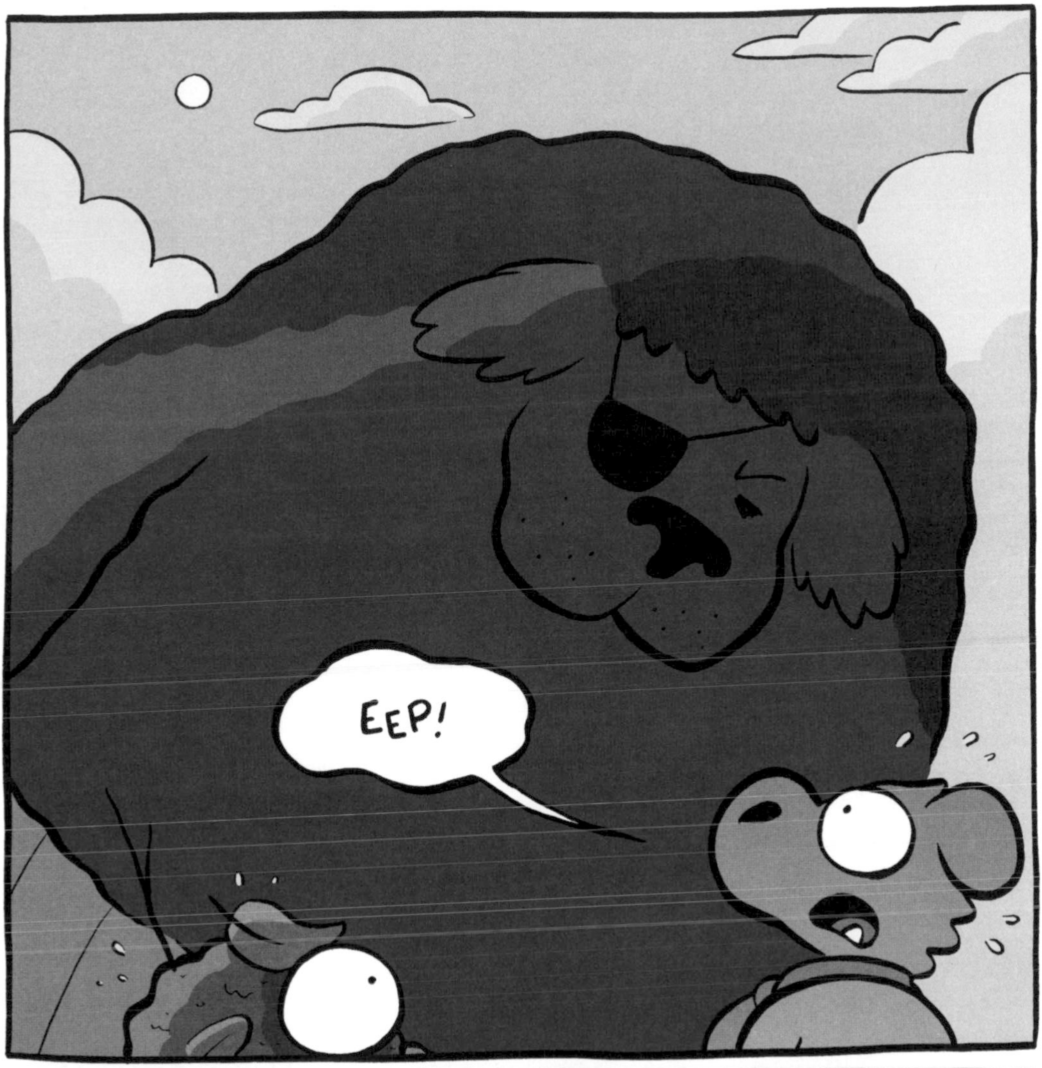
EEP!

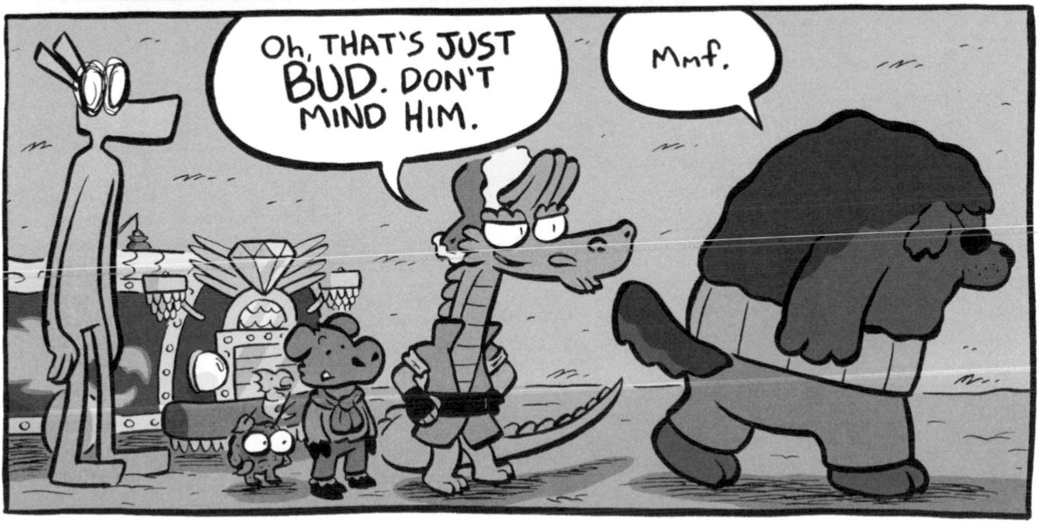
Oh, THAT'S JUST BUD. DON'T MIND HIM.
Mmf.

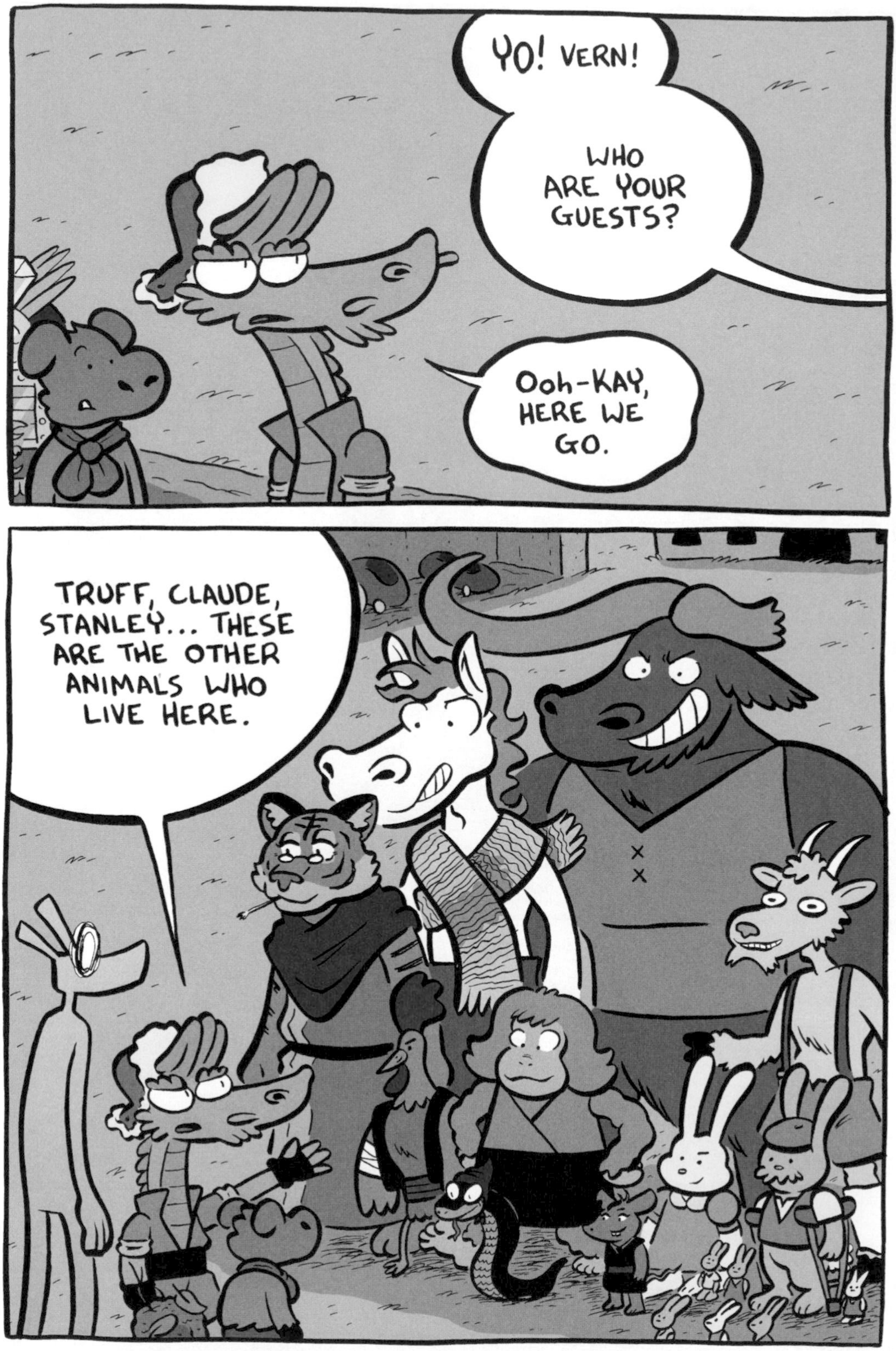
YO! VERN!
WHO ARE YOUR GUESTS?
Ooh-KAY, HERE WE GO.
TRUFF, CLAUDE, STANLEY... THESE ARE THE OTHER ANIMALS WHO LIVE HERE.

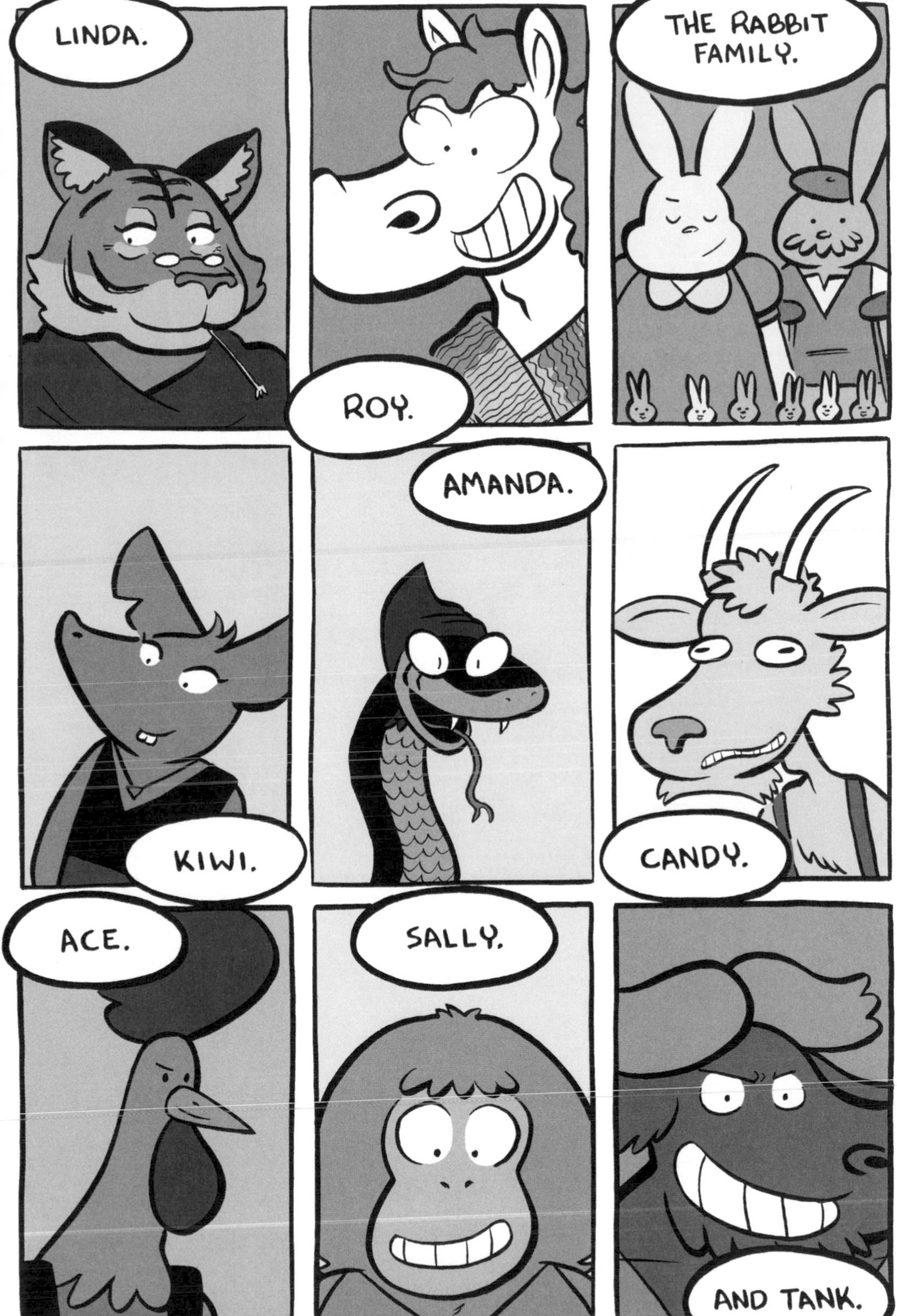
LINDA.
ROY.
THE RABBIT FAMILY.
AMANDA.
KIWI.
CANDY.
ACE.
SALLY.
AND TANK.

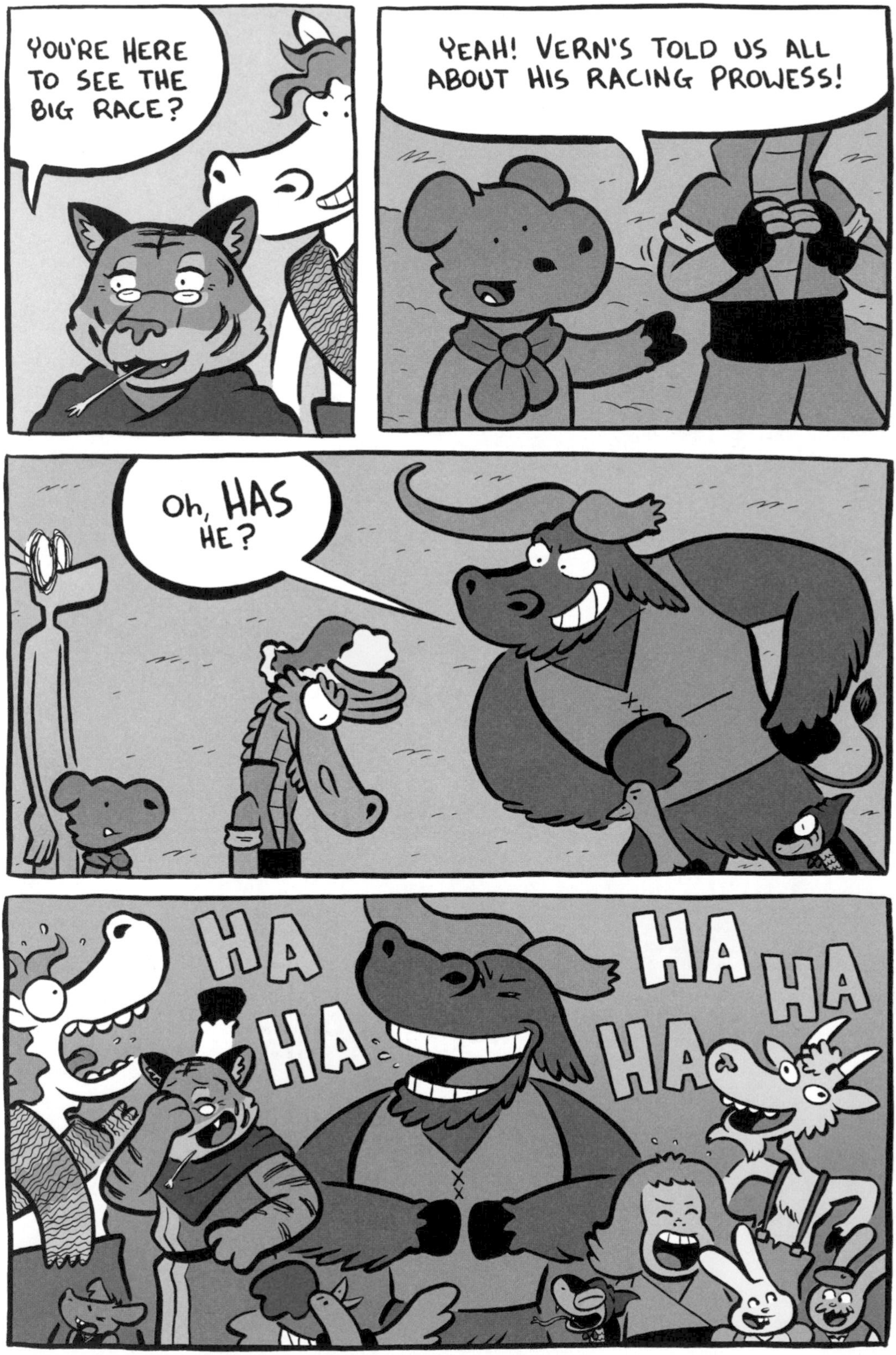
YOU'RE HERE TO SEE THE BIG RACE?
YEAH! VERN'S TOLD US ALL ABOUT HIS RACING PROWESS!
Oh, HAS HE?
HA HA HA HA HA HA

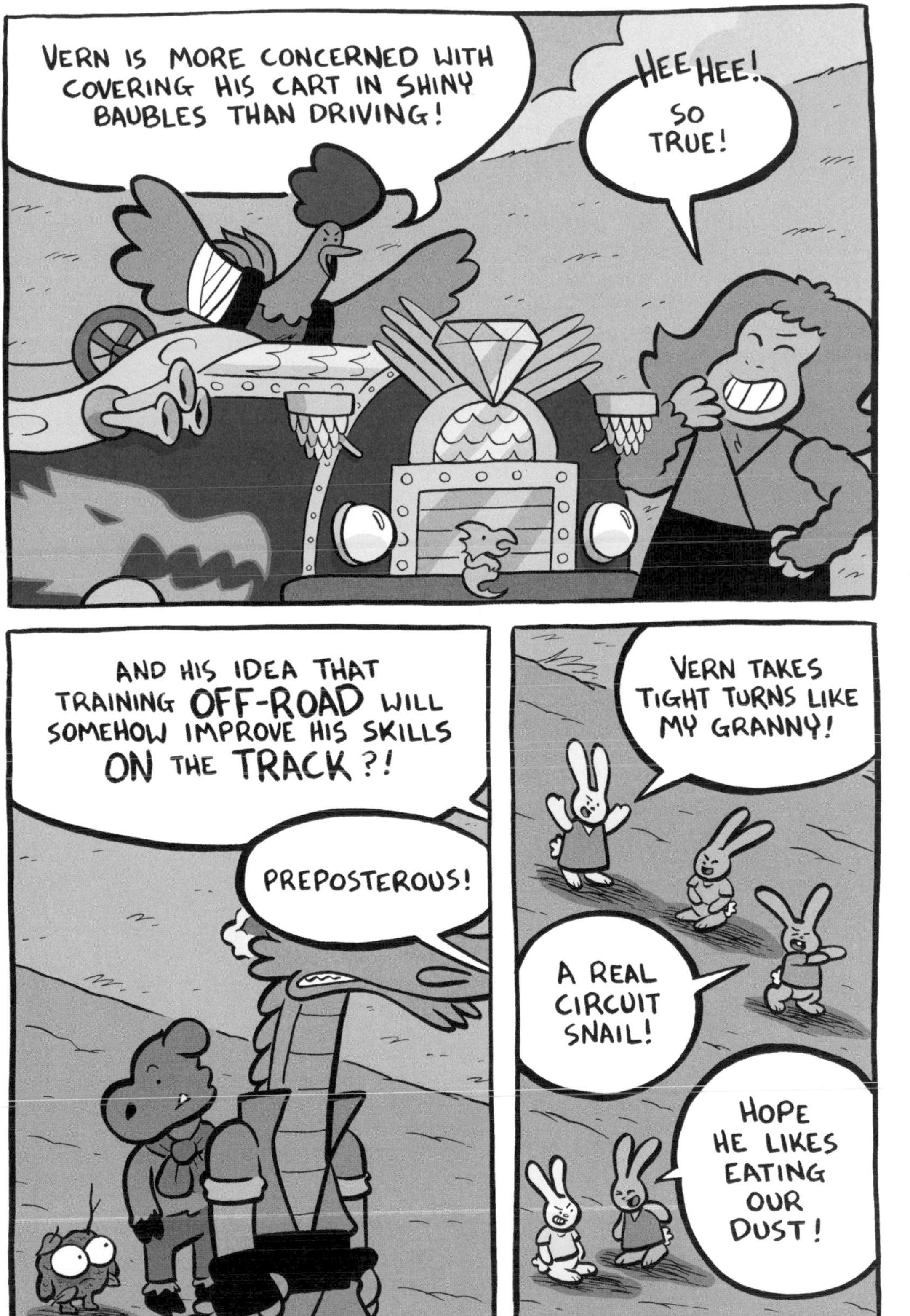
VERN IS MORE CONCERNED WITH COVERING HIS CART IN SHINY BAUBLES THAN DRIVING!
HEE HEE!
SO TRUE!
AND HIS IDEA THAT TRAINING OFF-ROAD WILL SOMEHOW IMPROVE HIS SKILLS ON THE TRACK?!
PREPOSTEROUS!
VERN TAKES TIGHT TURNS LIKE MY GRANNY!
A REAL CIRCUIT SNAIL!
HOPE HE LIKES EATING OUR DUST!

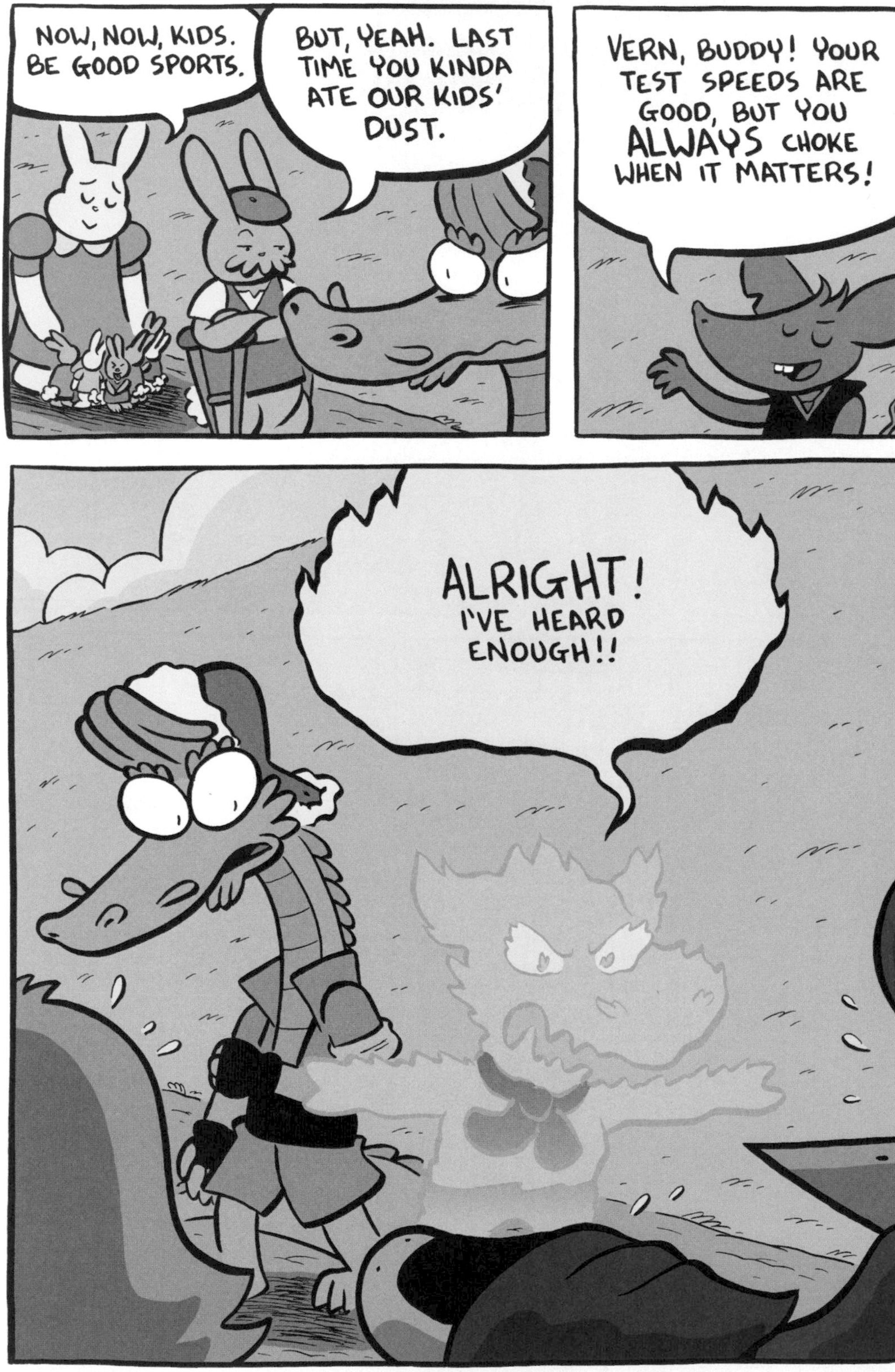
NOW, NOW, KIDS. BE GOOD SPORTS.
BUT, YEAH. LAST TIME YOU KINDA ATE OUR KIDS' DUST.
VERN, BUDDY! YOUR TEST SPEEDS ARE GOOD, BUT YOU ALWAYS CHOKE WHEN IT MATTERS!
ALRIGHT! I'VE HEARD ENOUGH!!

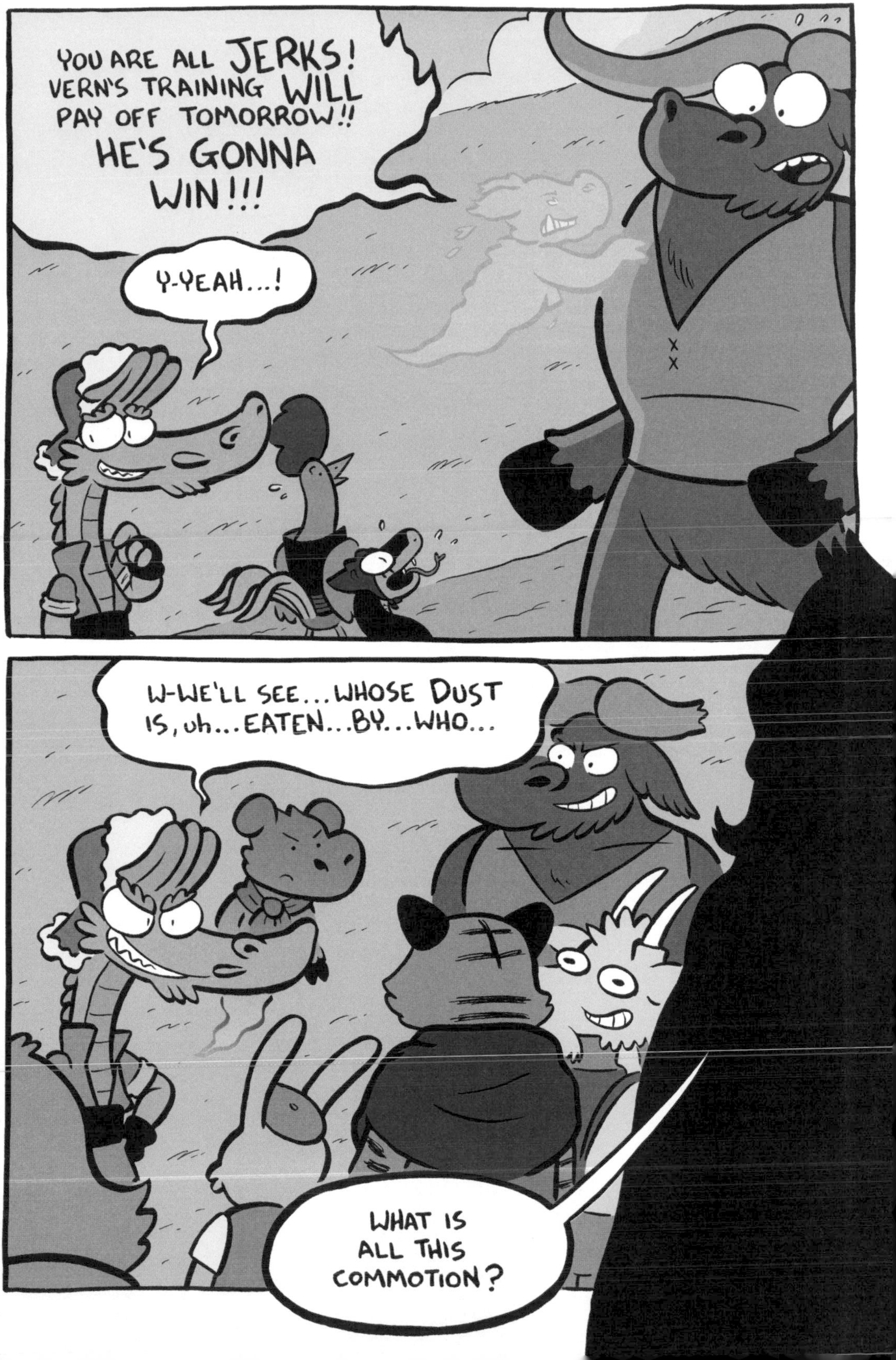
YOU ARE ALL JERKS! VERN'S TRAINING WILL PAY OFF TOMORROW!! HE'S GONNA WIN!!!
Y-YEAH...!
W-WE'LL SEE... WHOSE DUST IS, uh... EATEN... BY... WHO...
WHAT IS ALL THIS COMMOTION?

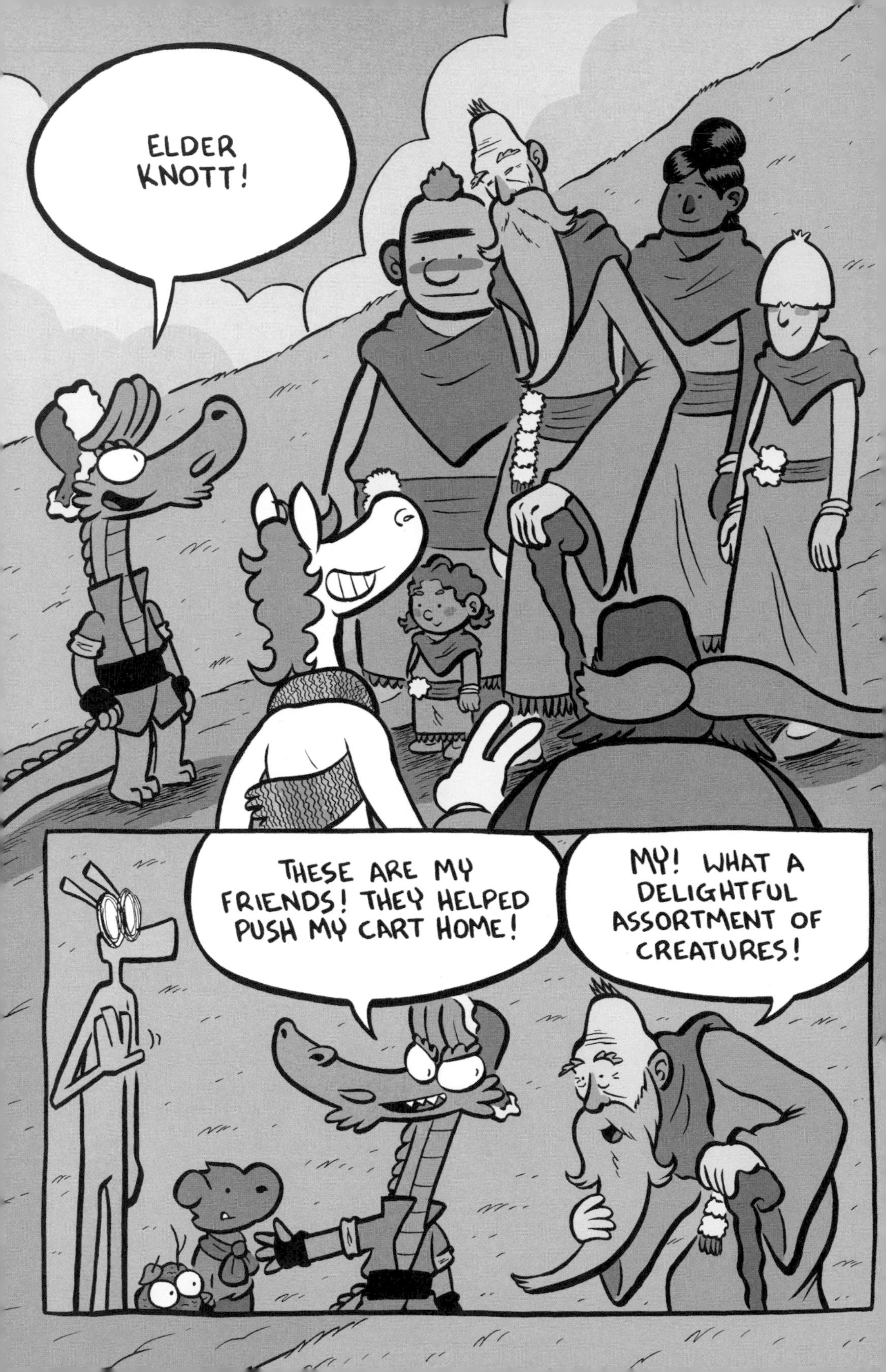
ELDER KNOTT!
THESE ARE MY FRIENDS! THEY HELPED PUSH MY CART HOME!
MY! WHAT A DELIGHTFUL ASSORTMENT OF CREATURES!

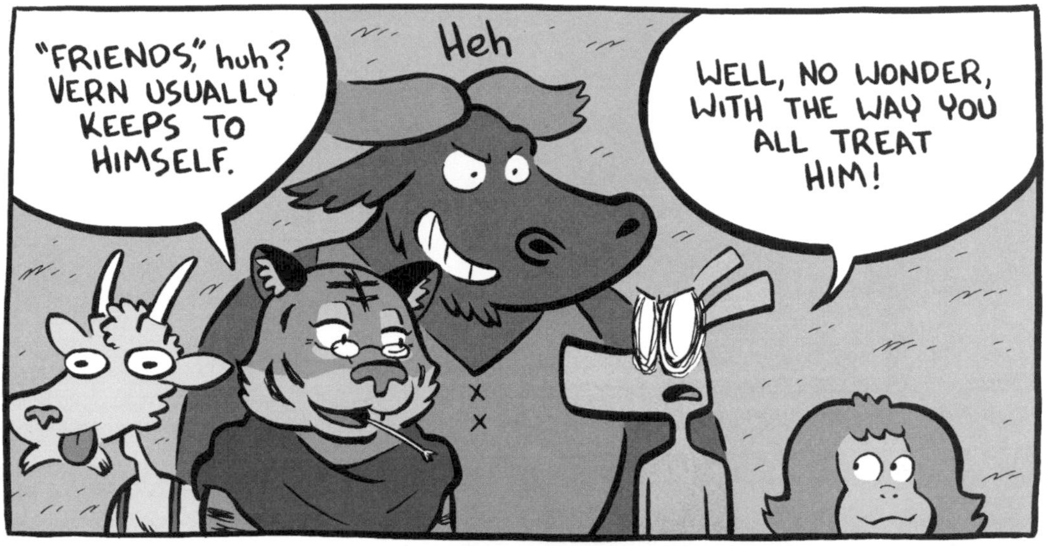
"FRIENDS," huh? VERN USUALLY KEEPS TO HIMSELF.
Heh
WELL, NO WONDER, WITH THE WAY YOU ALL TREAT HIM!

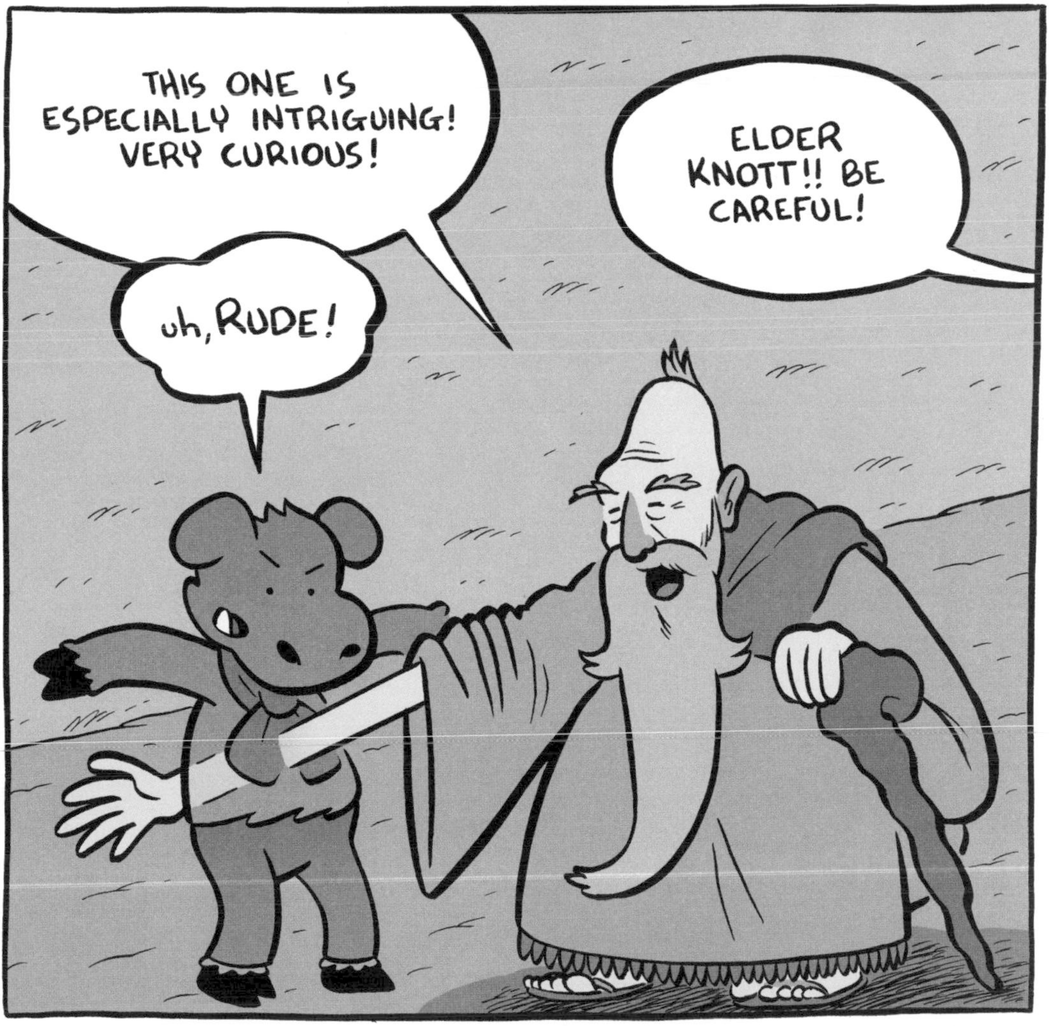
THIS ONE IS ESPECIALLY INTRIGUING! VERY CURIOUS!
uh, RUDE!
ELDER KNOTT!! BE CAREFUL!

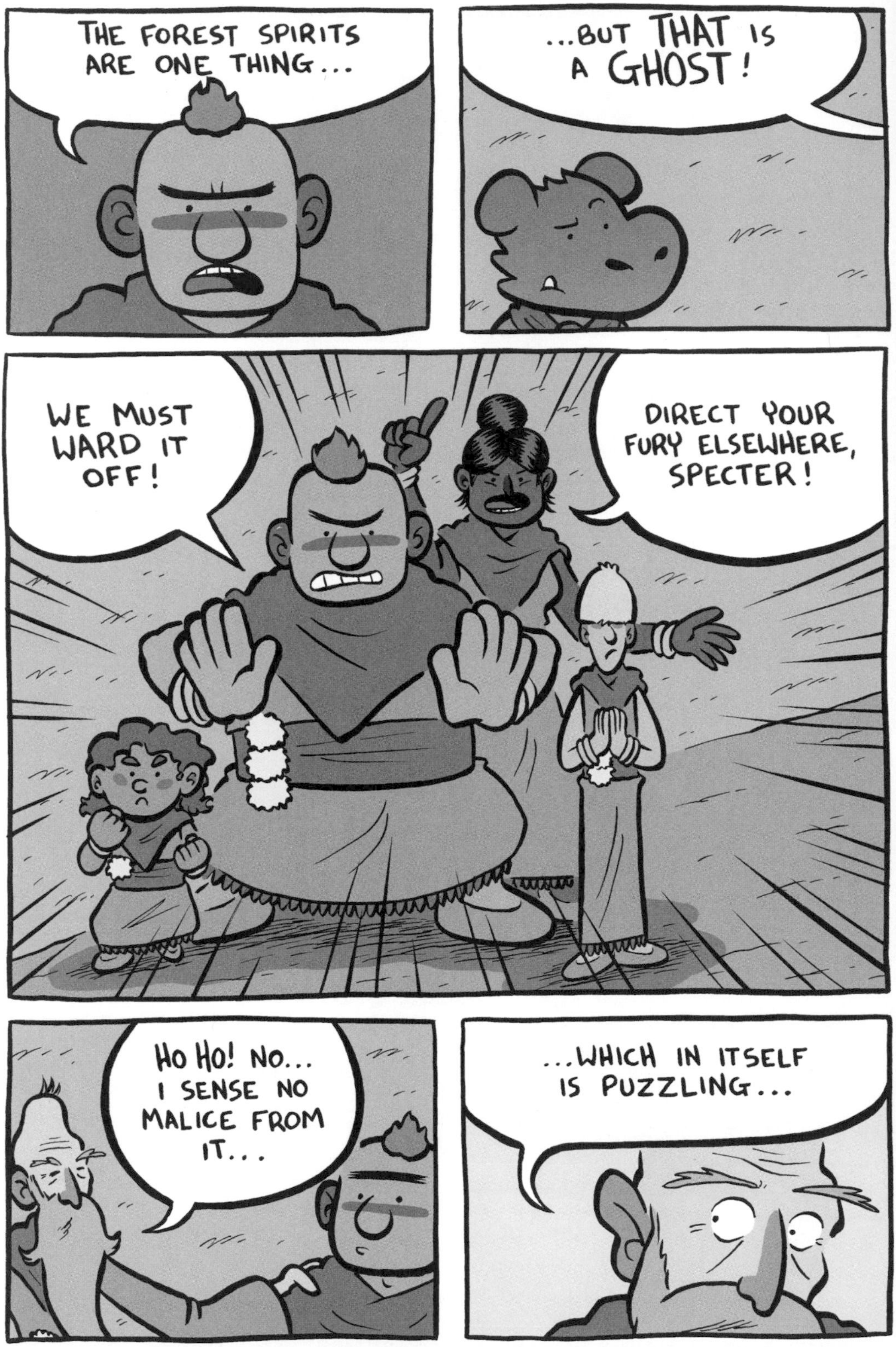
THE FOREST SPIRITS ARE ONE THING...
...BUT THAT IS A GHOST!
WE MUST WARD IT OFF!
DIRECT YOUR FURY ELSEWHERE, SPECTER!
HO HO! NO... I SENSE NO MALICE FROM IT...
...WHICH IN ITSELF IS PUZZLING...

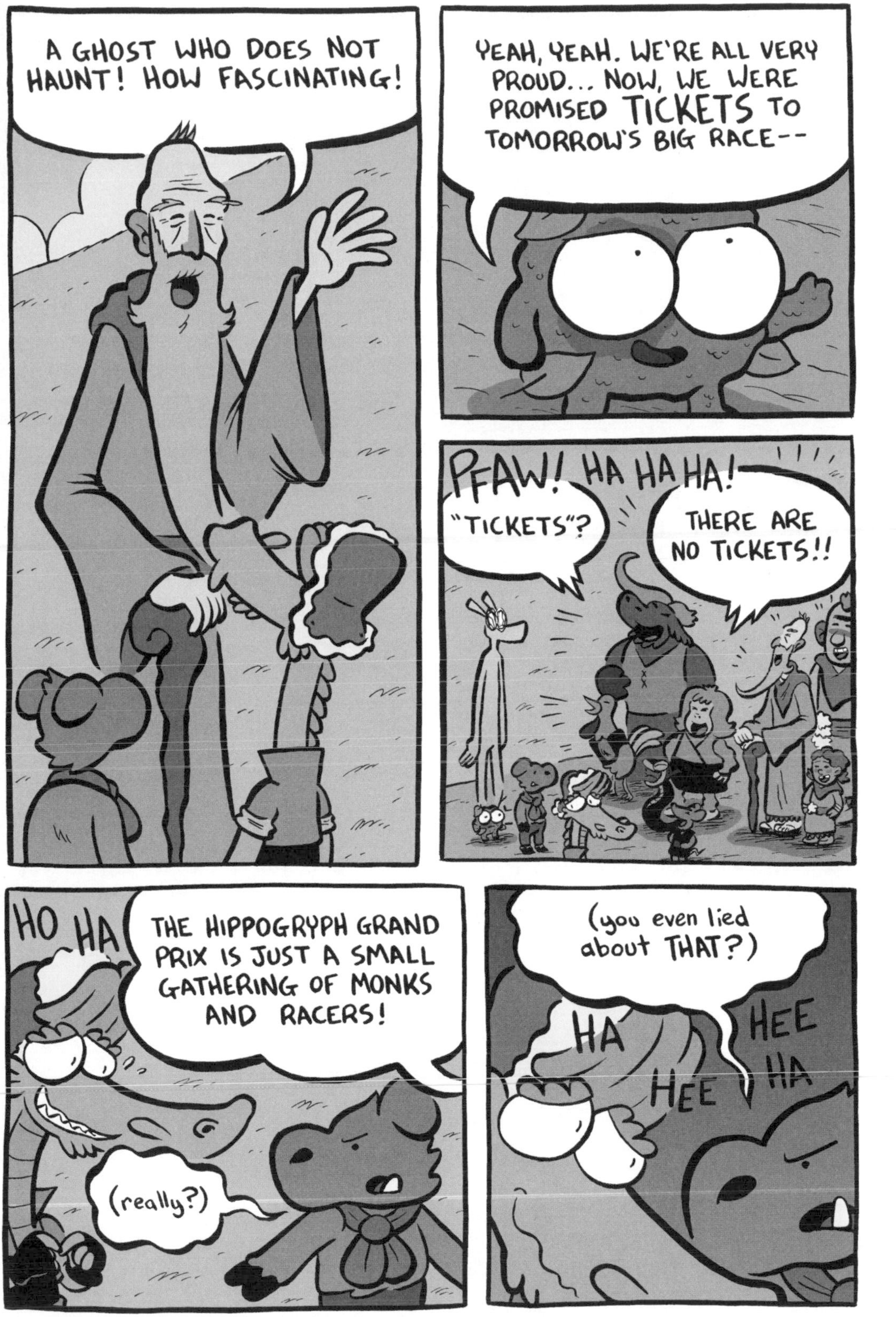

A GHOST WHO DOES NOT HAUNT! HOW FASCINATING!
YEAH, YEAH. WE'RE ALL VERY PROUD... NOW, WE WERE PROMISED TICKETS TO TOMORROW'S BIG RACE--
PFAW! HA HA HA!
"TICKETS"?
THERE ARE NO TICKETS!!
HO HA
THE HIPPOGRYPH GRAND PRIX IS JUST A SMALL GATHERING OF MONKS AND RACERS!
(really?)
(you even lied about THAT?)
HA
HEE HA
HEE

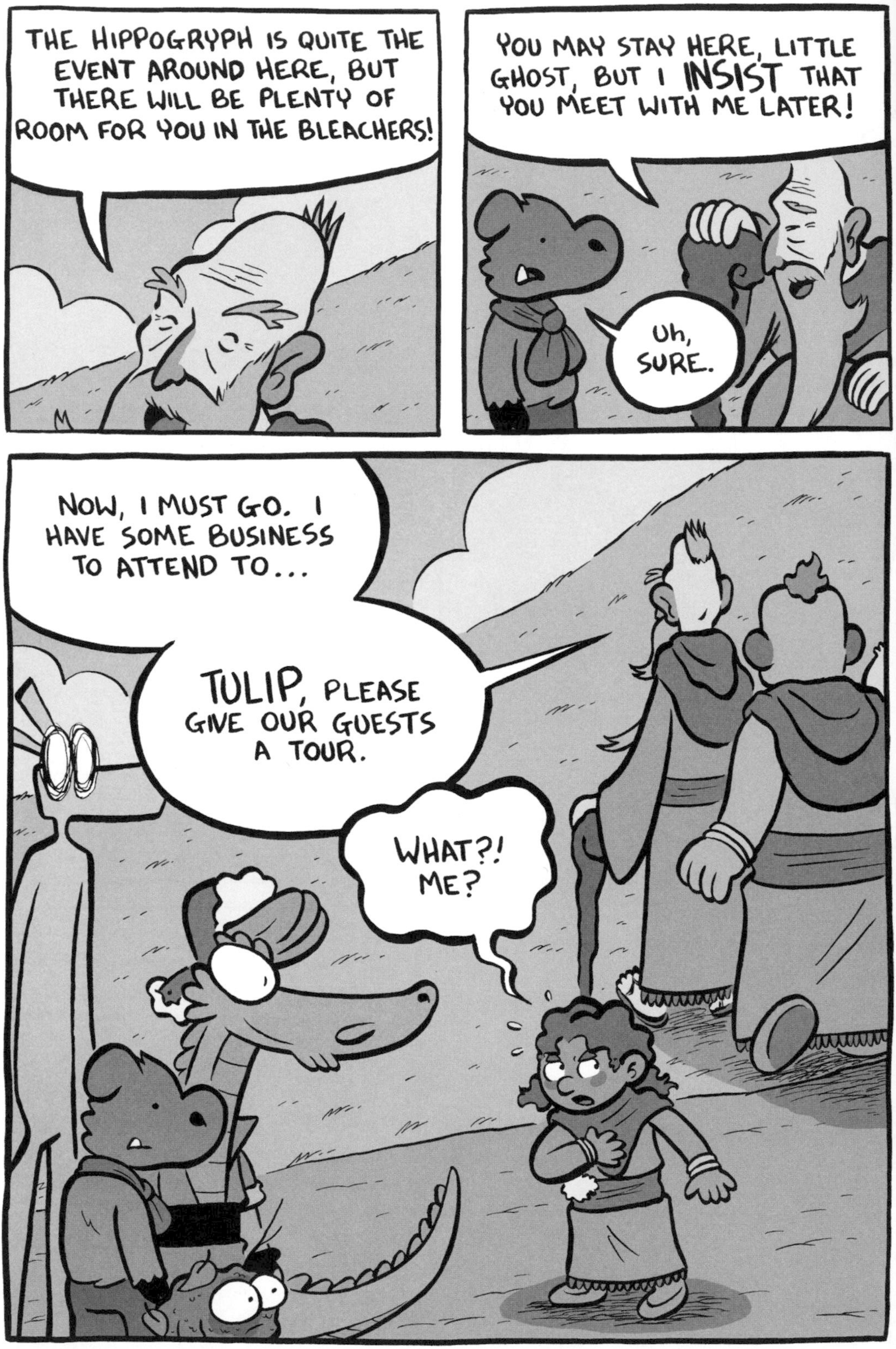
THE HIPPOGRYPH IS QUITE THE EVENT AROUND HERE, BUT THERE WILL BE PLENTY OF ROOM FOR YOU IN THE BLEACHERS!
YOU MAY STAY HERE, LITTLE GHOST, BUT I INSIST THAT YOU MEET WITH ME LATER!
Uh, SURE.
NOW, I MUST GO. I HAVE SOME BUSINESS TO ATTEND TO...
TULIP, PLEASE GIVE OUR GUESTS A TOUR.
WHAT?! ME?

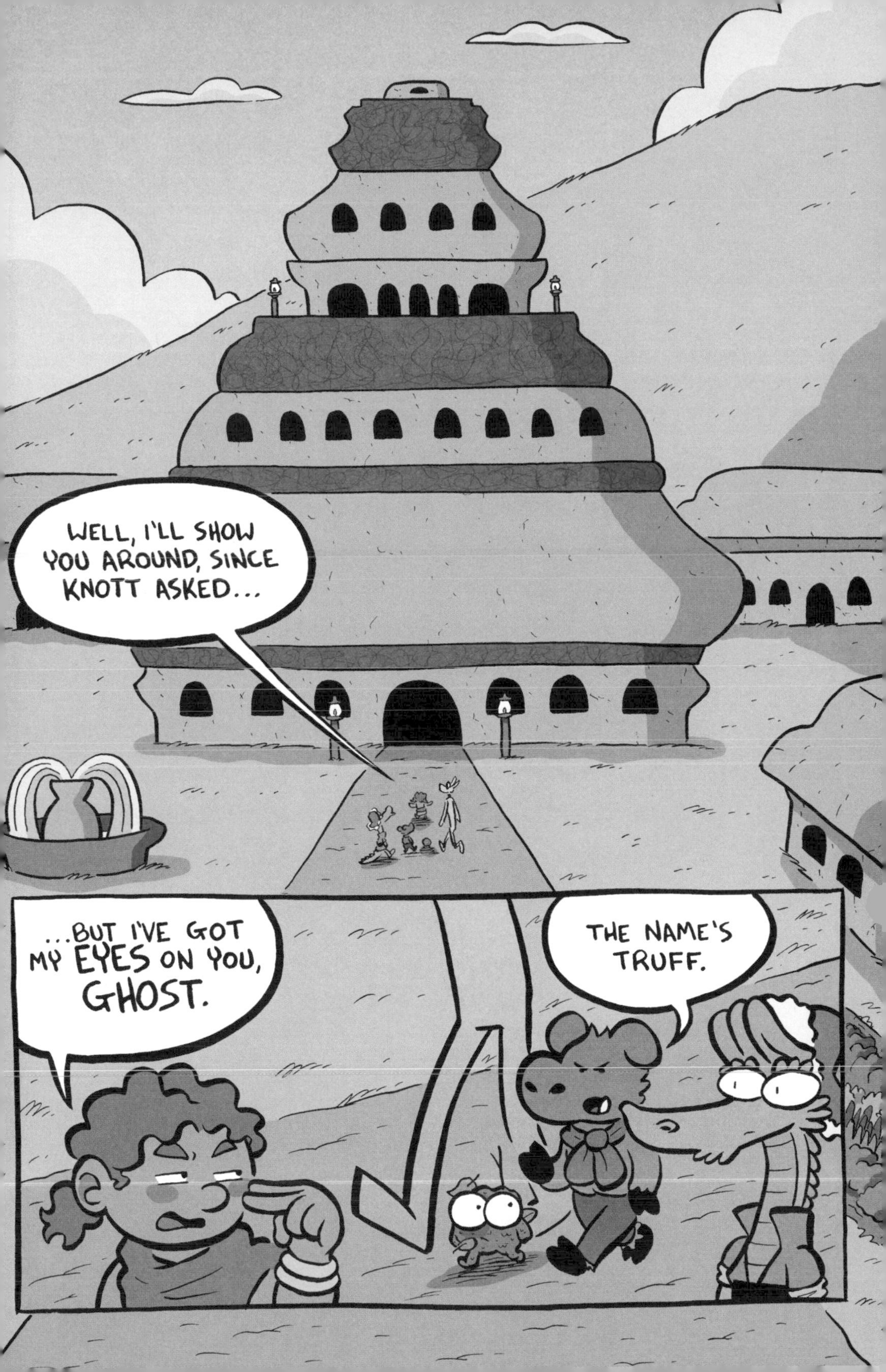
WELL, I'LL SHOW YOU AROUND, SINCE KNOTT ASKED...
...BUT I'VE GOT MY EYES ON YOU, GHOST.
THE NAME'S TRUFF.

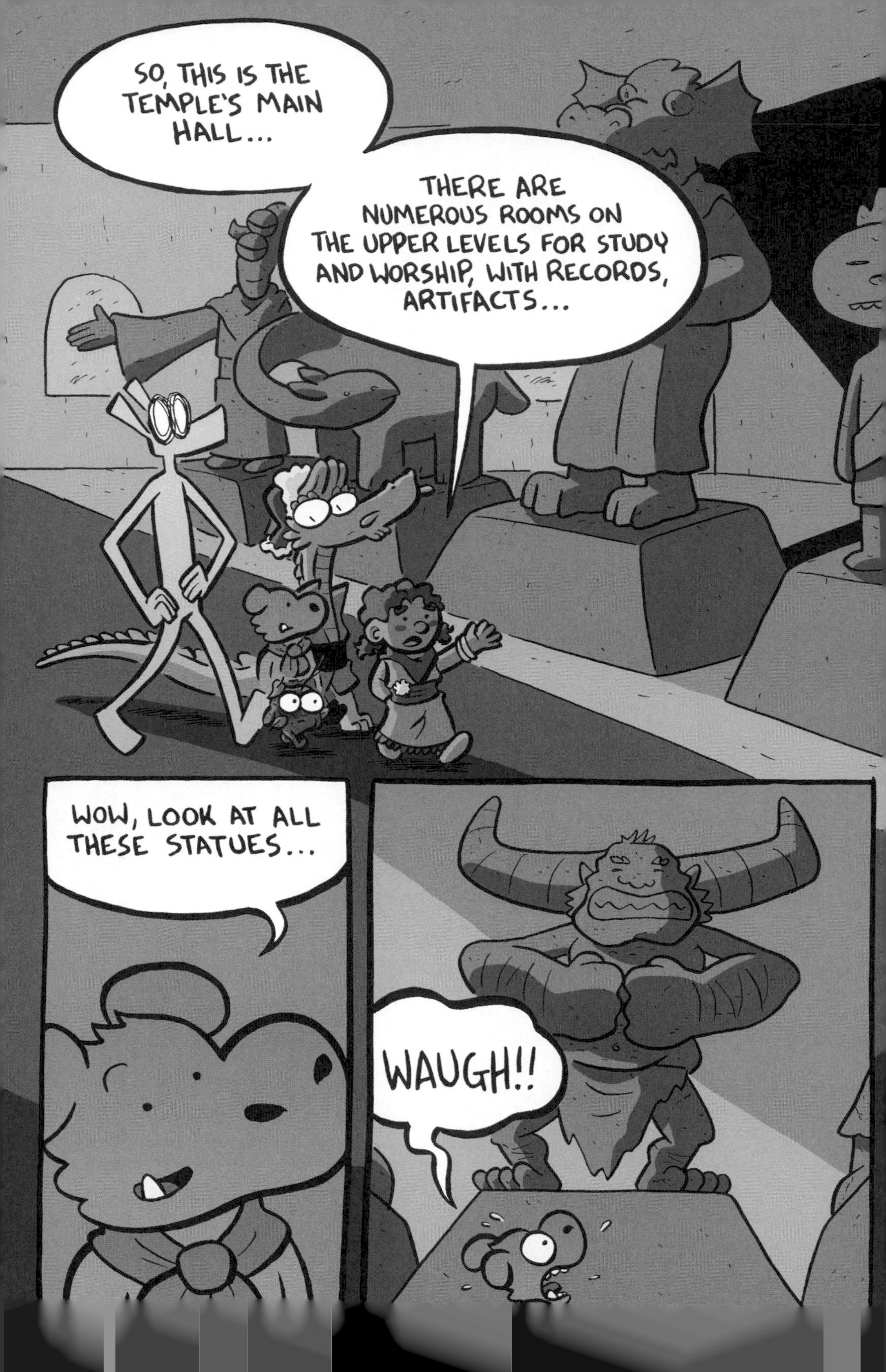
SO, THIS IS THE TEMPLE'S MAIN HALL...
THERE ARE NUMEROUS ROOMS ON THE UPPER LEVELS FOR STUDY AND WORSHIP, WITH RECORDS, ARTIFACTS...
WOW, LOOK AT ALL THESE STATUES...
WAUGH!!

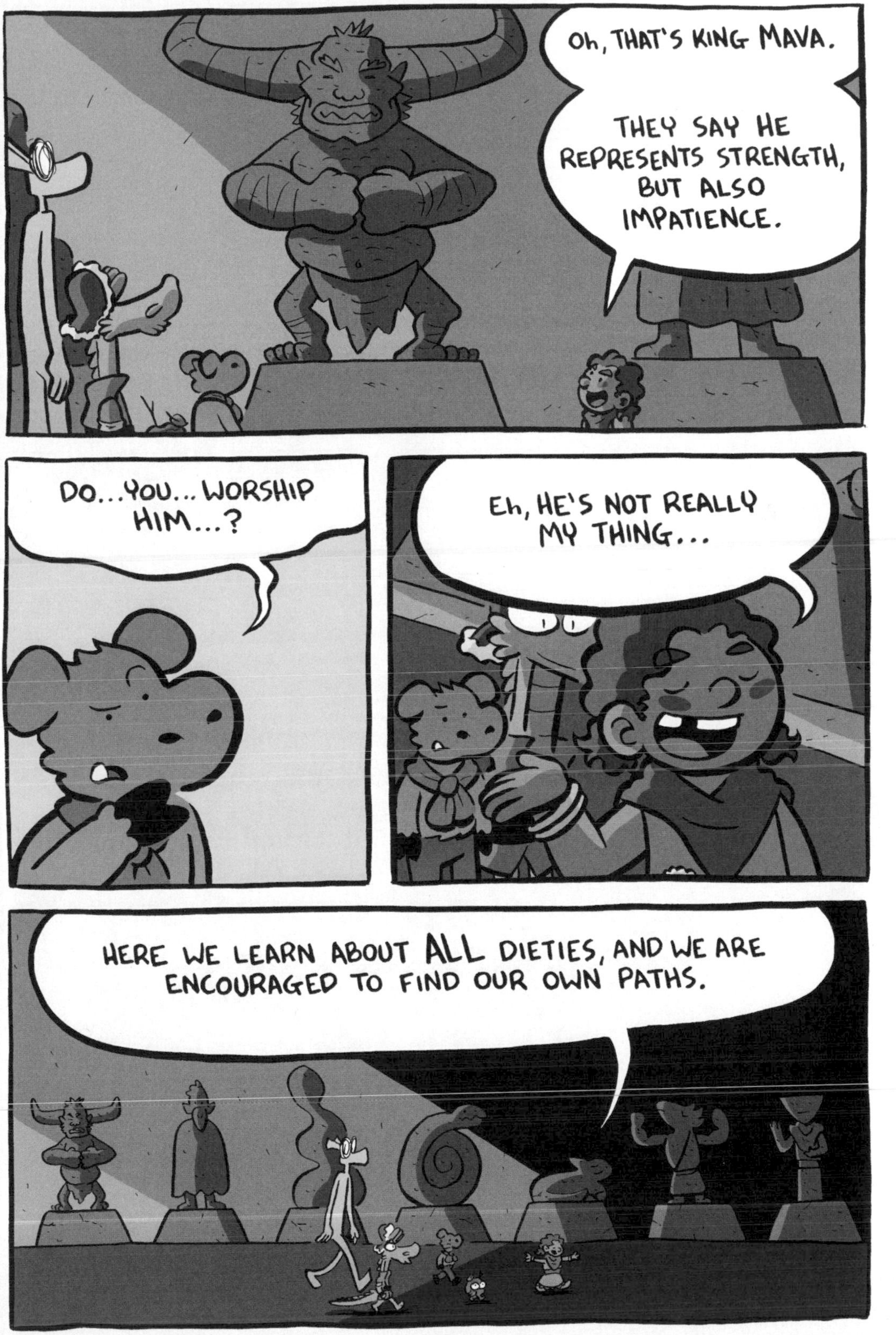
Oh, THAT'S KING MAVA.
THEY SAY HE REPRESENTS STRENGTH, BUT ALSO IMPATIENCE.
DO...YOU...WORSHIP HIM...?
Eh, HE'S NOT REALLY MY THING...
HERE WE LEARN ABOUT ALL DIETIES, AND WE ARE ENCOURAGED TO FIND OUR OWN PATHS.

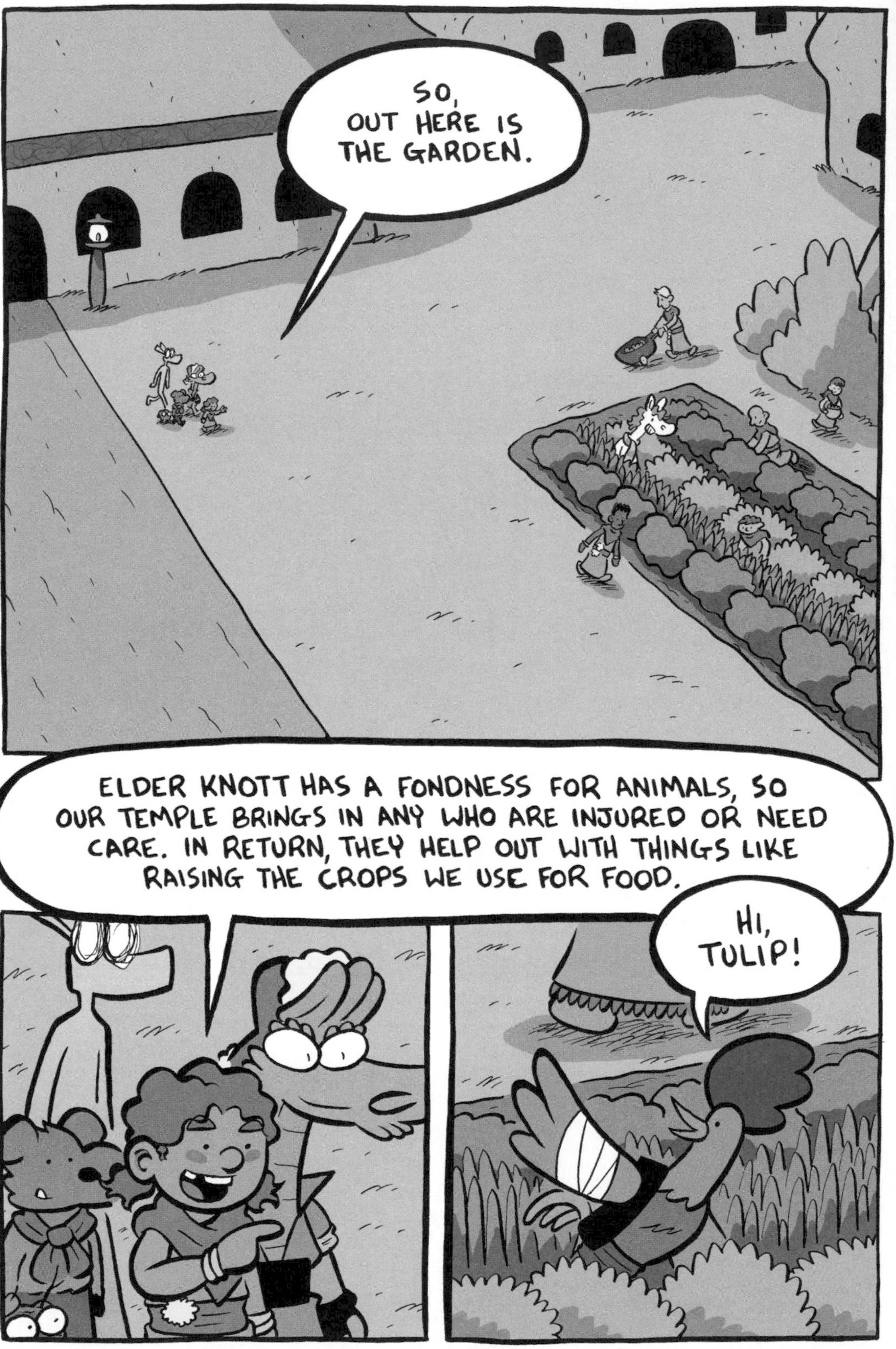
SO, OUT HERE IS THE GARDEN.
ELDER KNOTT HAS A FONDNESS FOR ANIMALS, SO OUR TEMPLE BRINGS IN ANY WHO ARE INJURED OR NEED CARE. IN RETURN, THEY HELP OUT WITH THINGS LIKE RAISING THE CROPS WE USE FOR FOOD.
HI, TULIP!

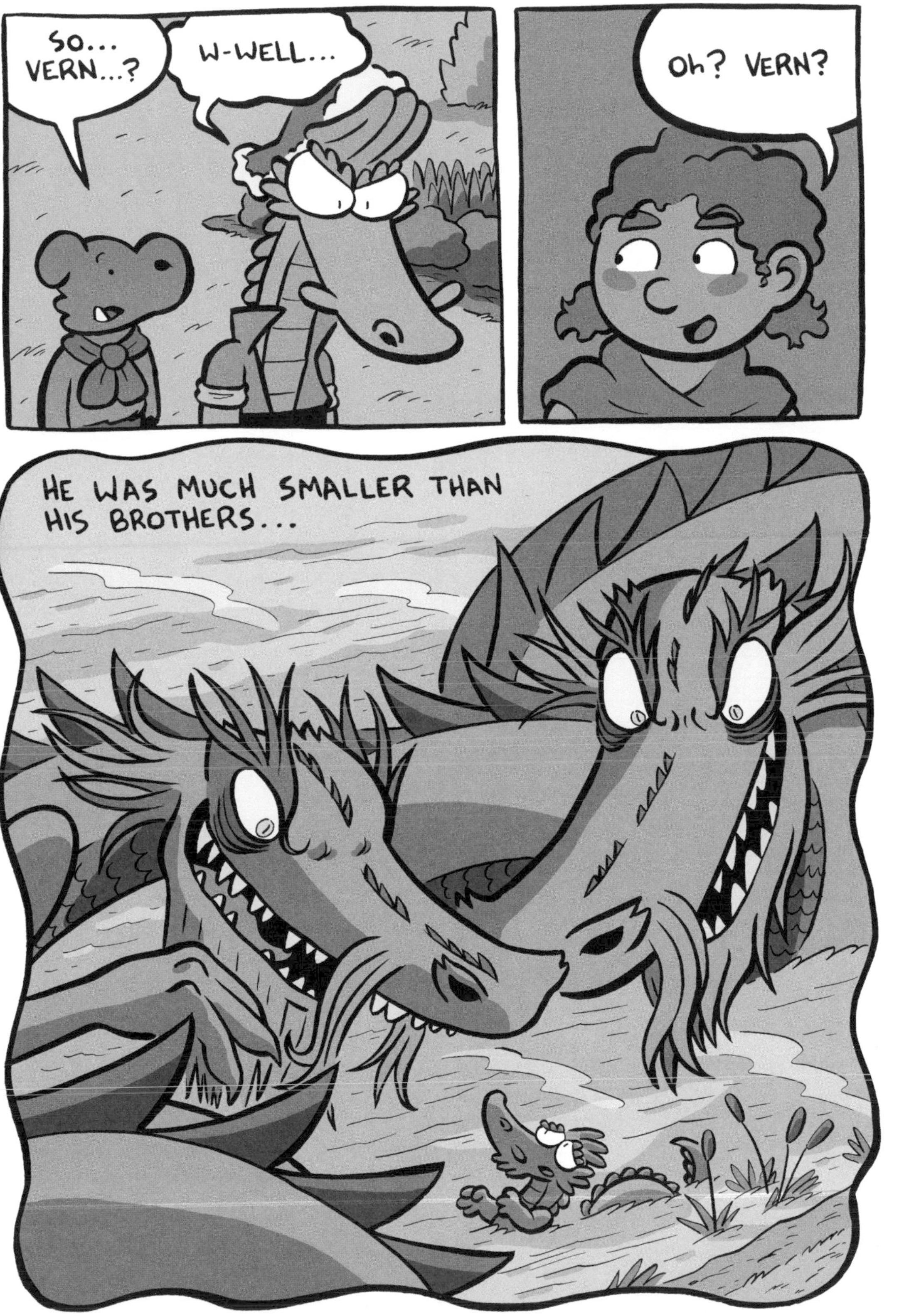
SO... VERN...?
W-WELL...
Oh? VERN?
HE WAS MUCH SMALLER THAN HIS BROTHERS...

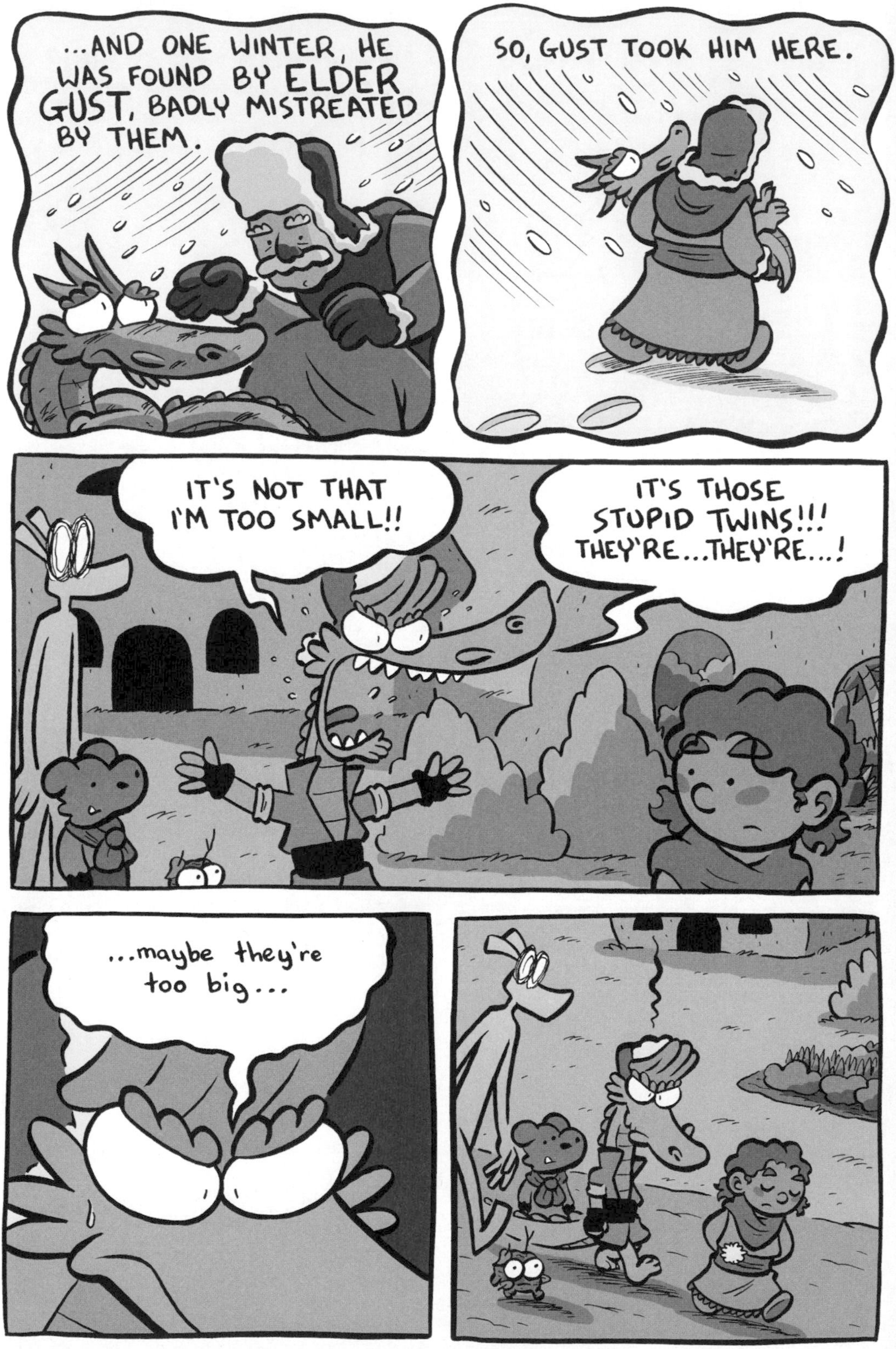
...AND ONE WINTER, HE WAS FOUND BY ELDER GUST, BADLY MISTREATED BY THEM.
SO, GUST TOOK HIM HERE.
IT'S NOT THAT I'M TOO SMALL!!
IT'S THOSE STUPID TWINS!!! THEY'RE...THEY'RE...!
...maybe they're too big...

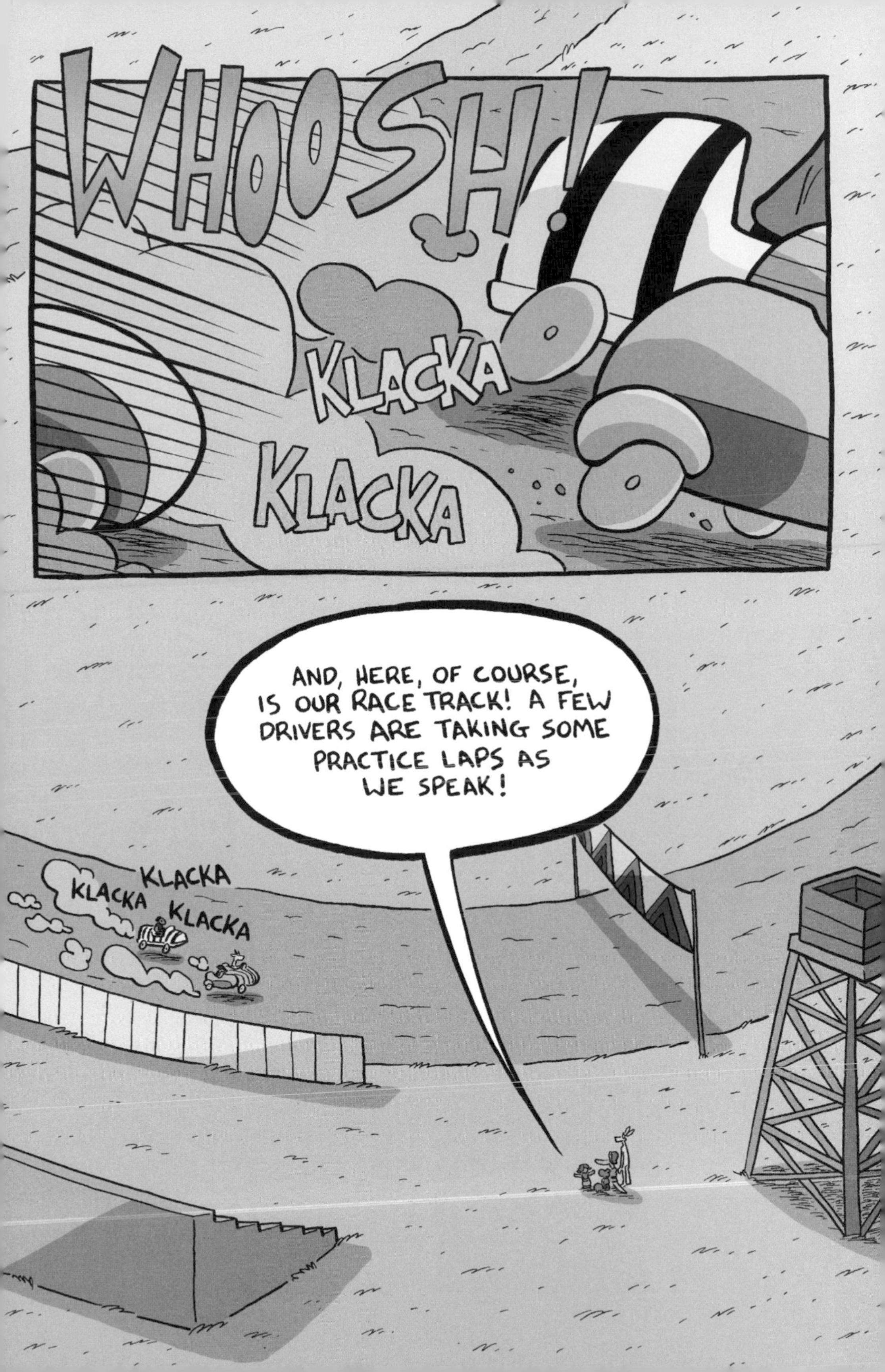
WHOOSH!
KLACKA
KLACKA
AND, HERE, OF COURSE, IS OUR RACE TRACK! A FEW DRIVERS ARE TAKING SOME PRACTICE LAPS AS WE SPEAK!
KLACKA
KLACKA
KLACKA

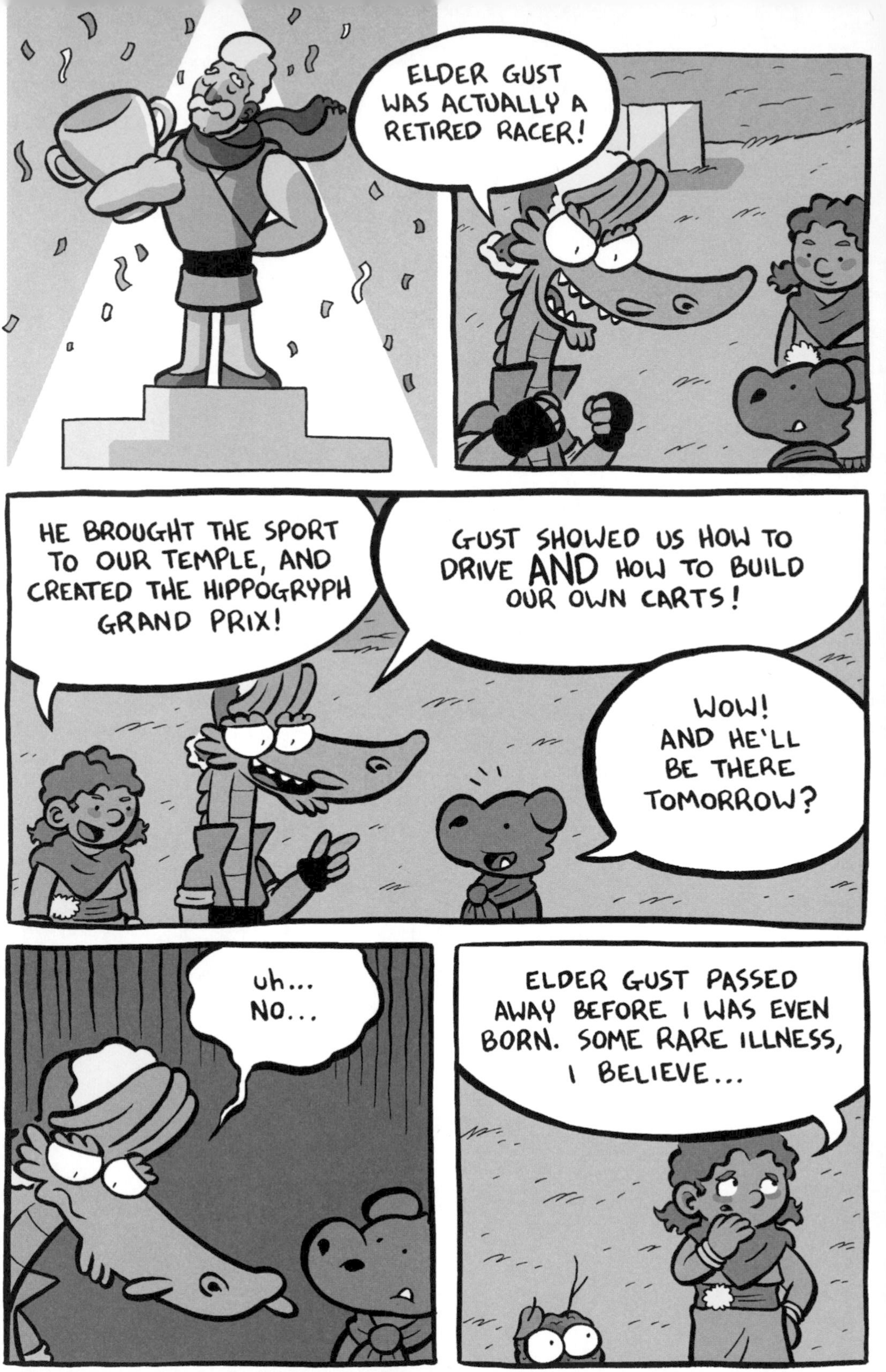
ELDER GUST WAS ACTUALLY A RETIRED RACER!
HE BROUGHT THE SPORT TO OUR TEMPLE, AND CREATED THE HIPPOGRYPH GRAND PRIX!
GUST SHOWED US HOW TO DRIVE AND HOW TO BUILD OUR OWN CARTS!
WOW! AND HE'LL BE THERE TOMORROW?
uh... NO...
ELDER GUST PASSED AWAY BEFORE I WAS EVEN BORN. SOME RARE ILLNESS, I BELIEVE...

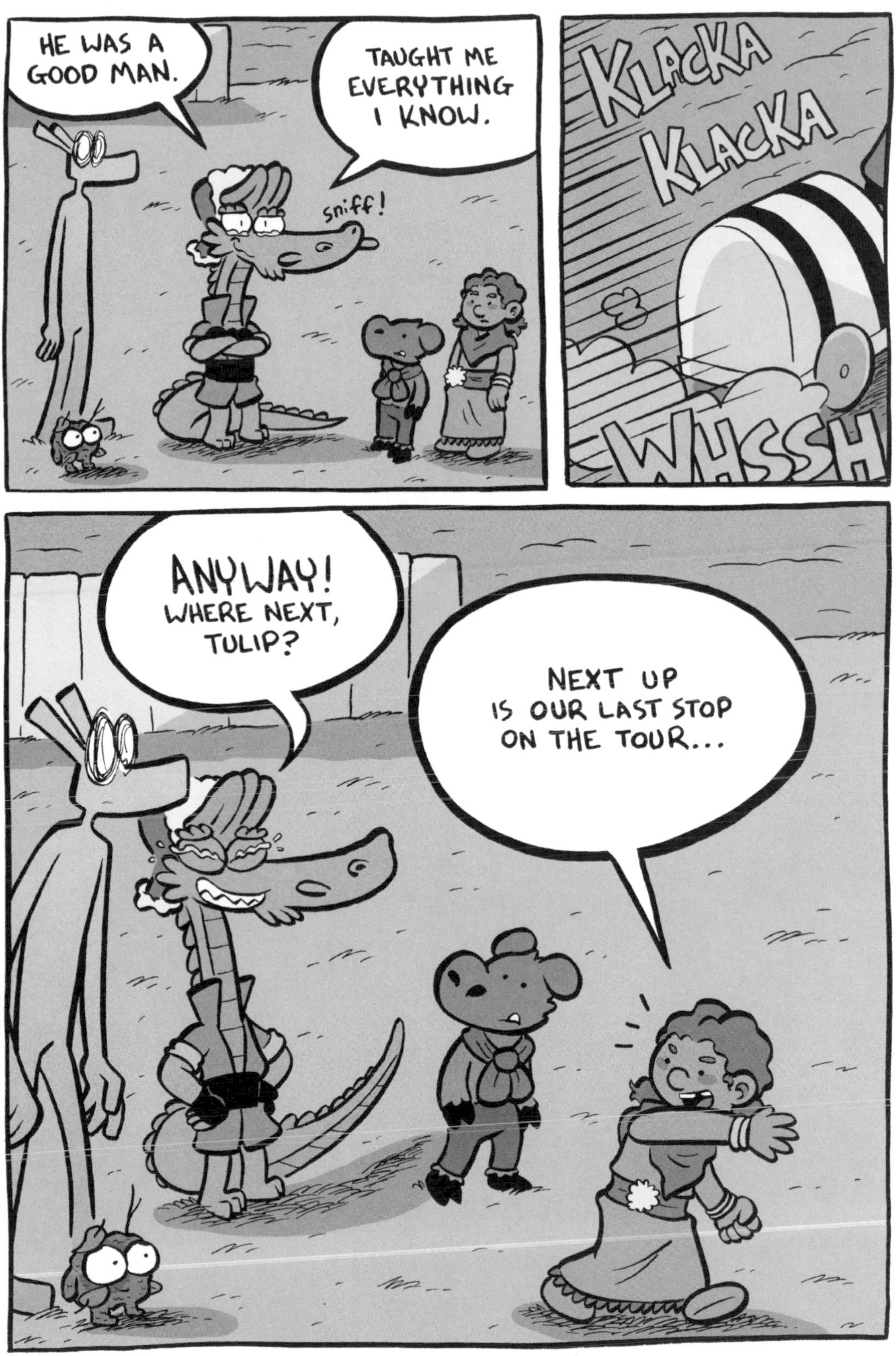
HE WAS A GOOD MAN.
TAUGHT ME EVERYTHING I KNOW.
sniff!
KLACKA KLACKA
WHSSH
ANYWAY! WHERE NEXT, TULIP?
NEXT UP IS OUR LAST STOP ON THE TOUR...

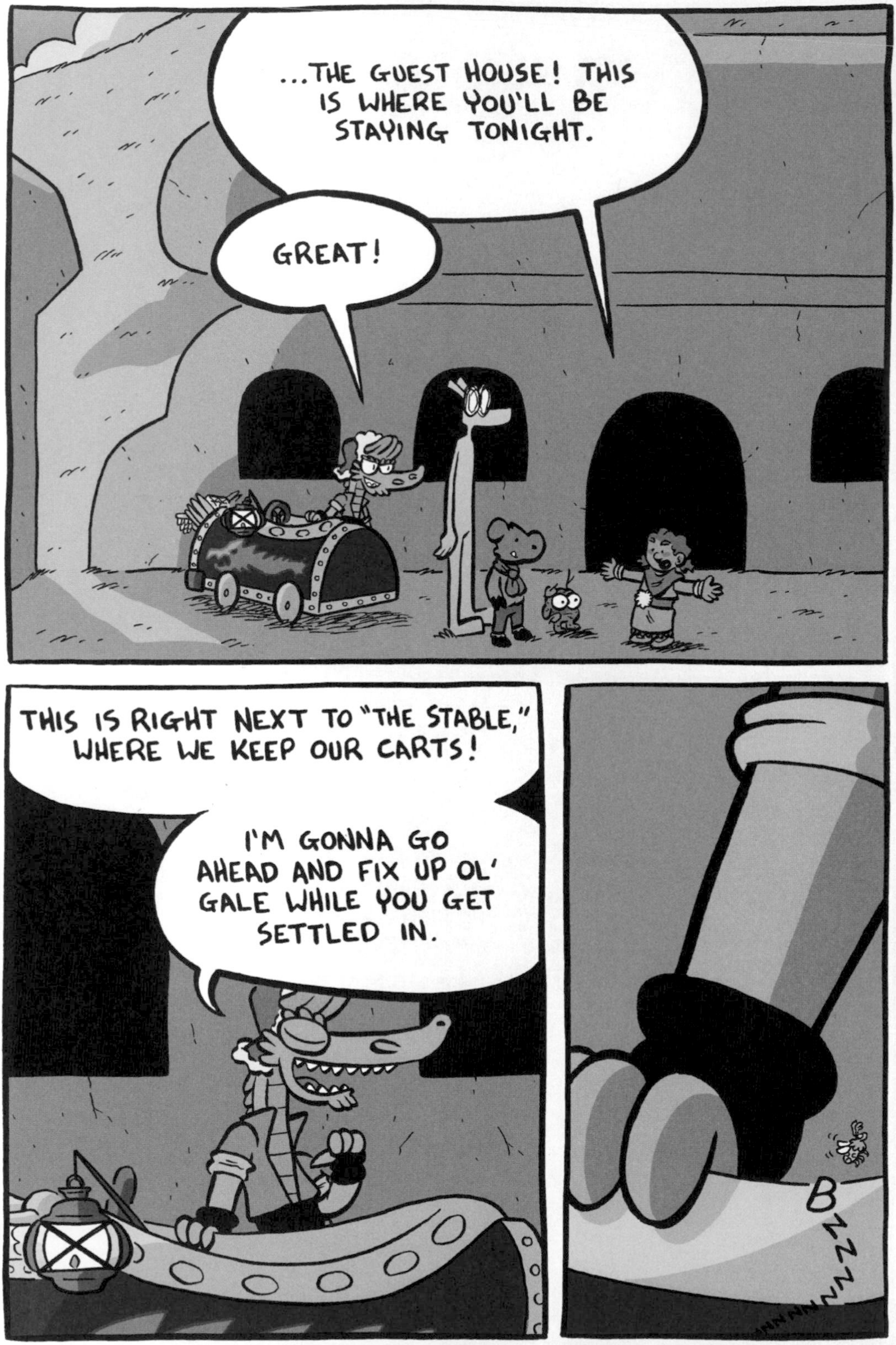
...THE GUEST HOUSE! THIS IS WHERE YOU'LL BE STAYING TONIGHT.
GREAT!
THIS IS RIGHT NEXT TO "THE STABLE," WHERE WE KEEP OUR CARTS!
I'M GONNA GO AHEAD AND FIX UP OL' GALE WHILE YOU GET SETTLED IN.
BZZZ

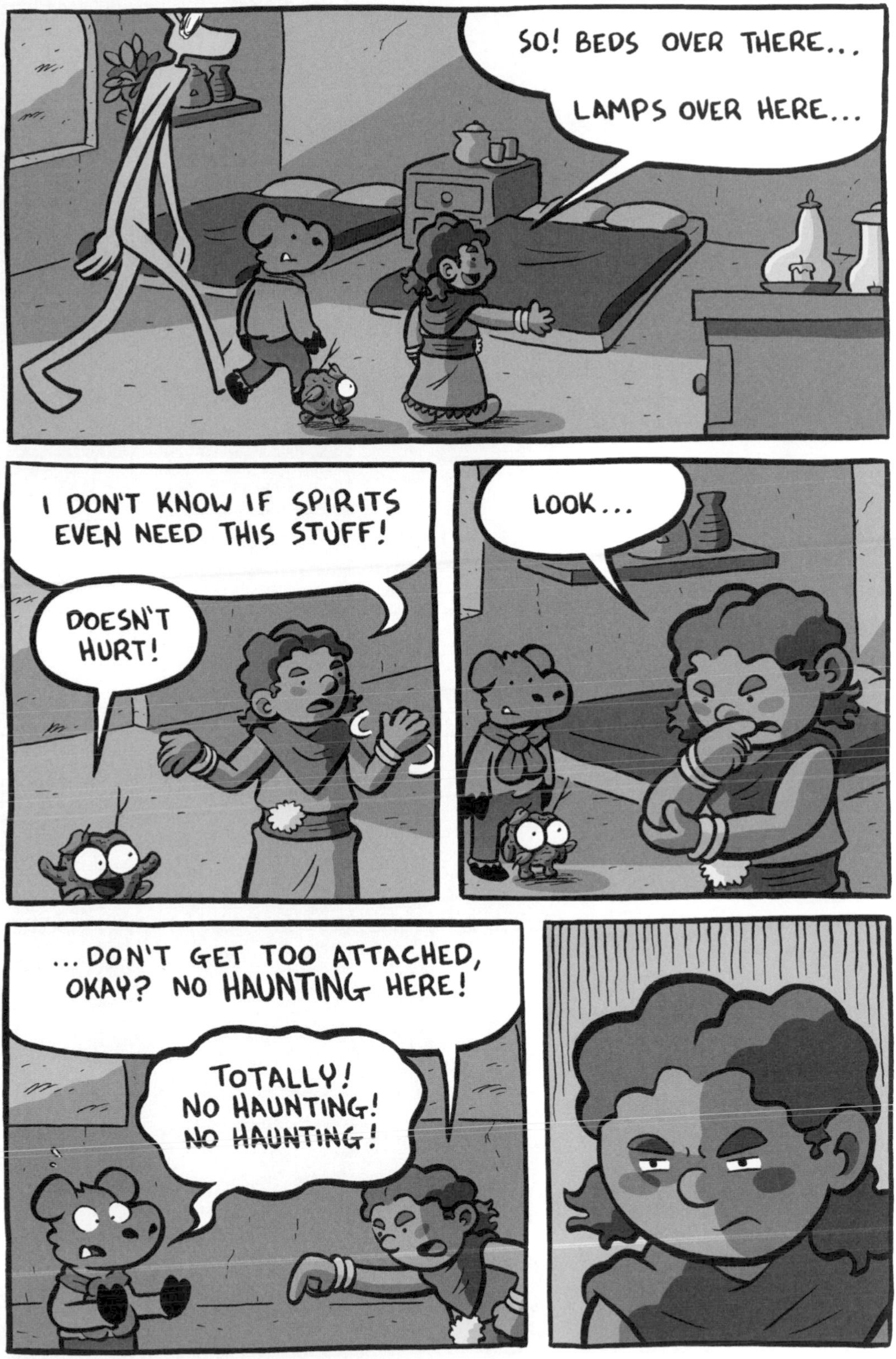
SO! BEDS OVER THERE...
LAMPS OVER HERE...
I DON'T KNOW IF SPIRITS EVEN NEED THIS STUFF!
DOESN'T HURT!
LOOK...
...DON'T GET TOO ATTACHED, OKAY? NO HAUNTING HERE!
TOTALLY! NO HAUNTING! NO HAUNTING!

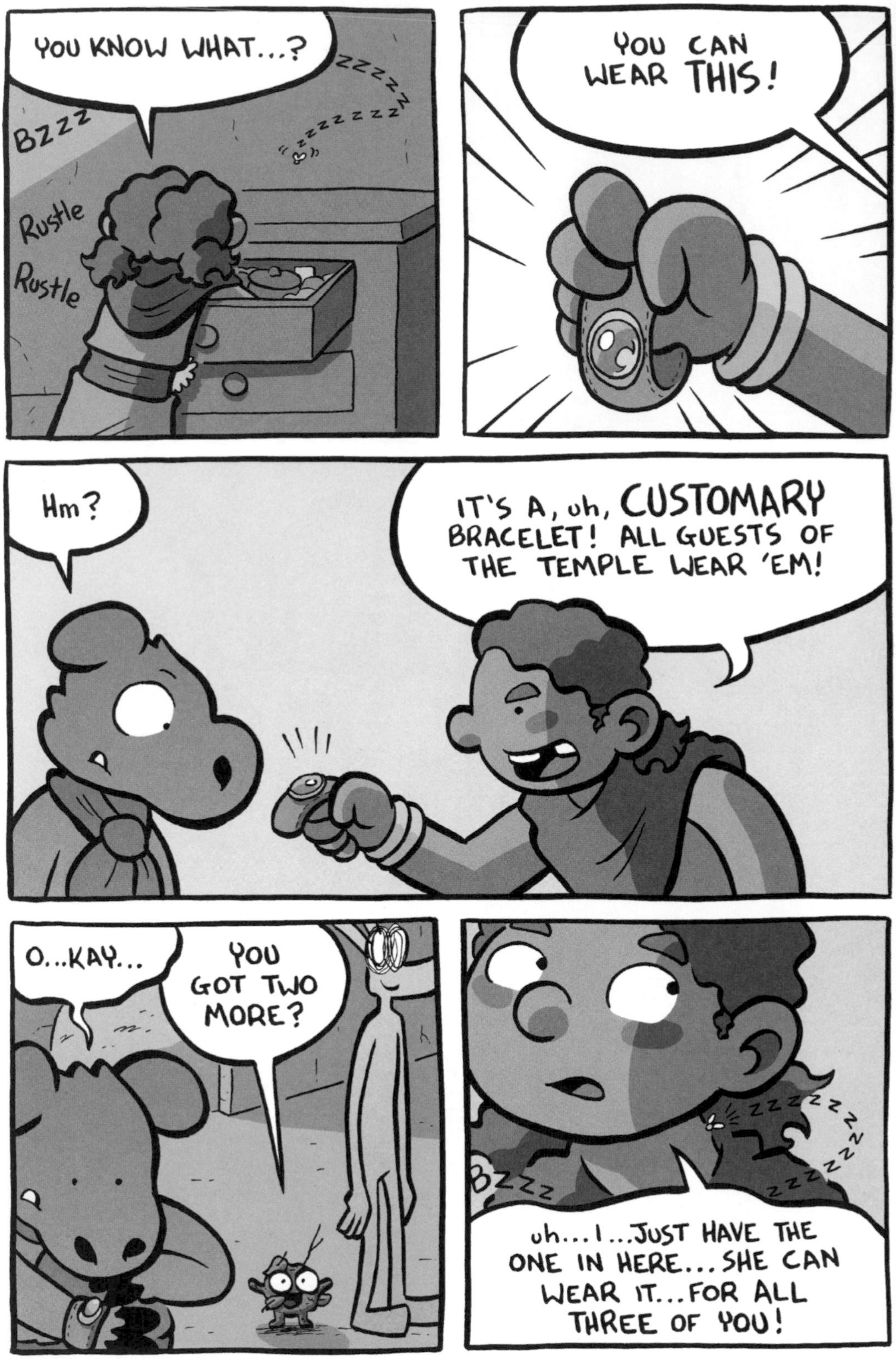
YOU KNOW WHAT...?
BZZZ
ZZZZZ
ZZZZZZZZ
Rustle
Rustle
YOU CAN WEAR THIS!
Hm?
IT'S A, uh, CUSTOMARY BRACELET! ALL GUESTS OF THE TEMPLE WEAR 'EM!
O...KAY...
YOU GOT TWO MORE?
ZZZZZZZ
ZZZZZ
BZZZ
uh...I...JUST HAVE THE ONE IN HERE... SHE CAN WEAR IT...FOR ALL THREE OF YOU!

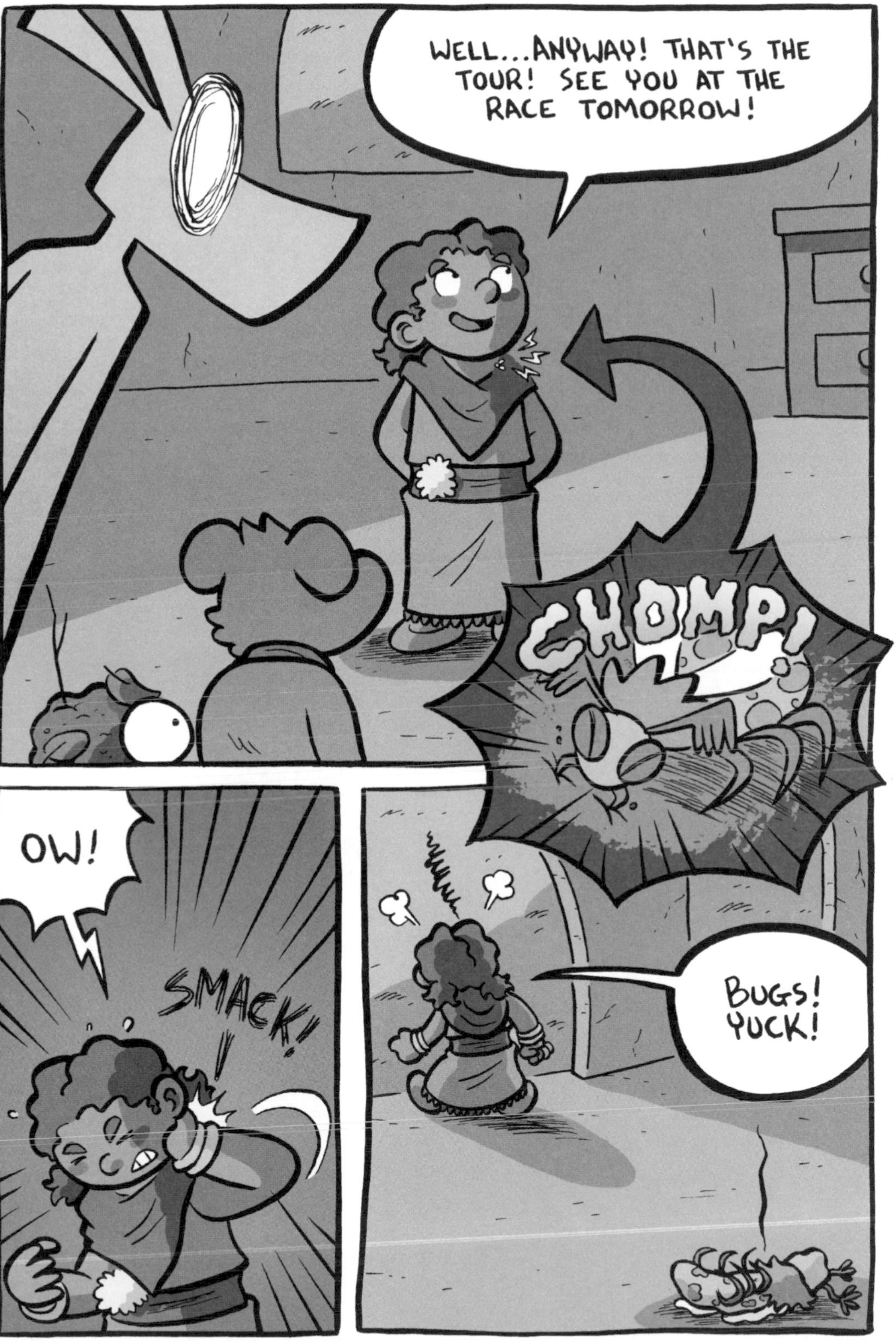
WELL...ANYWAY! THAT'S THE TOUR! SEE YOU AT THE RACE TOMORROW!
CHOMP!
OW!
SMACK!
BUGS! YUCK!

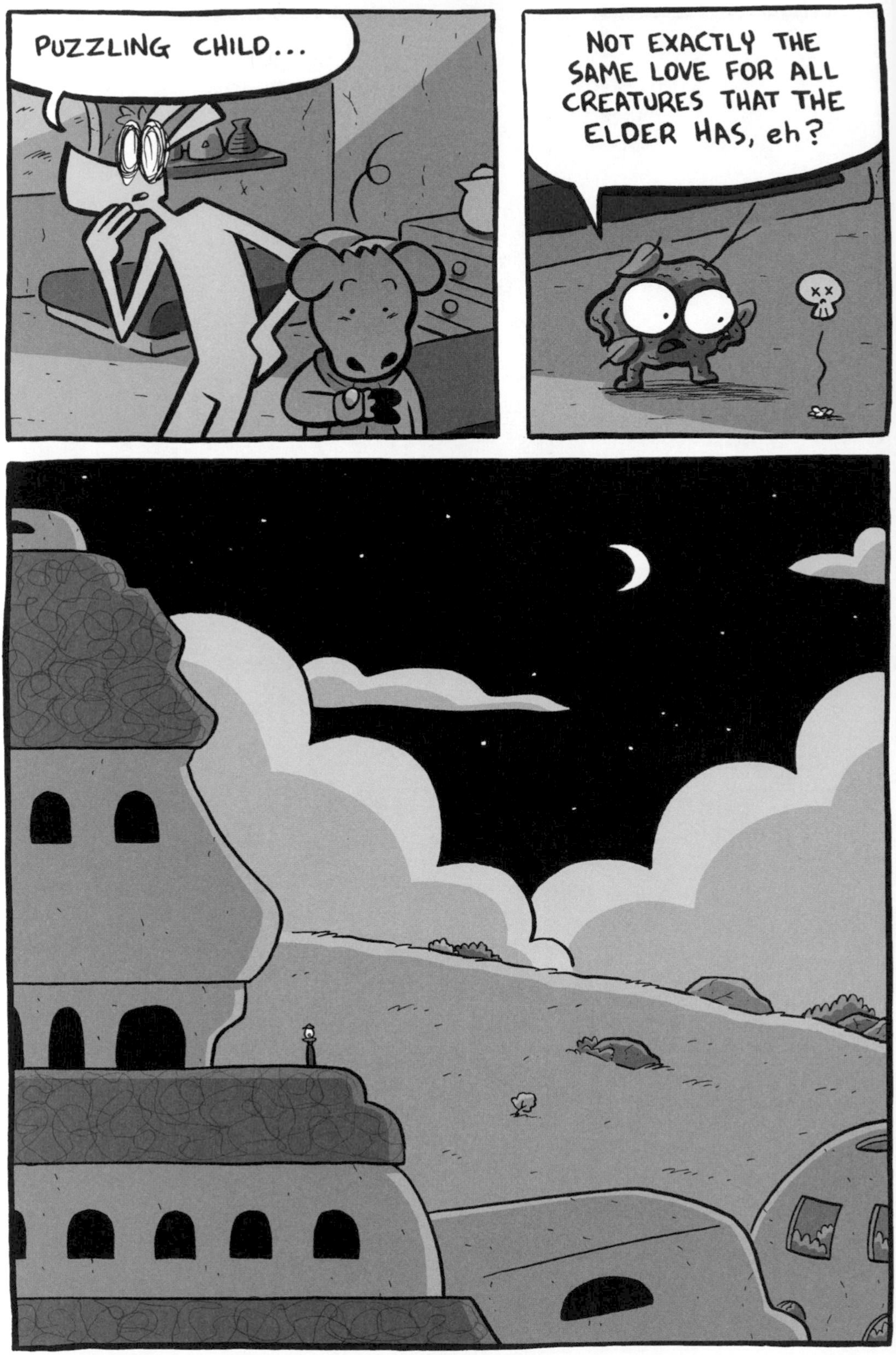
PUZZLING CHILD...
NOT EXACTLY THE SAME LOVE FOR ALL CREATURES THAT THE ELDER HAS, eh?

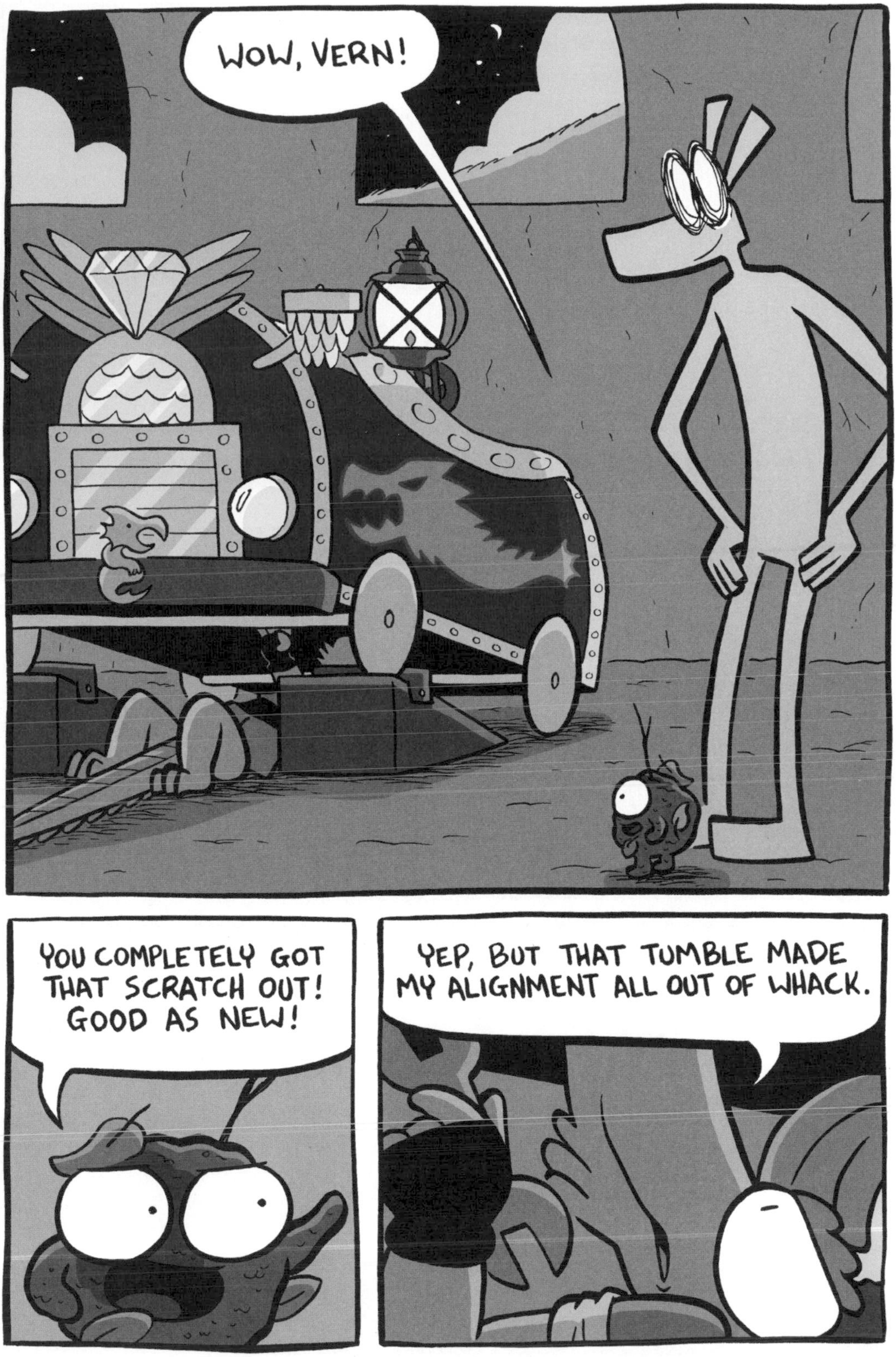
WOW, VERN!
YOU COMPLETELY GOT THAT SCRATCH OUT! GOOD AS NEW!
YEP, BUT THAT TUMBLE MADE MY ALIGNMENT ALL OUT OF WHACK.

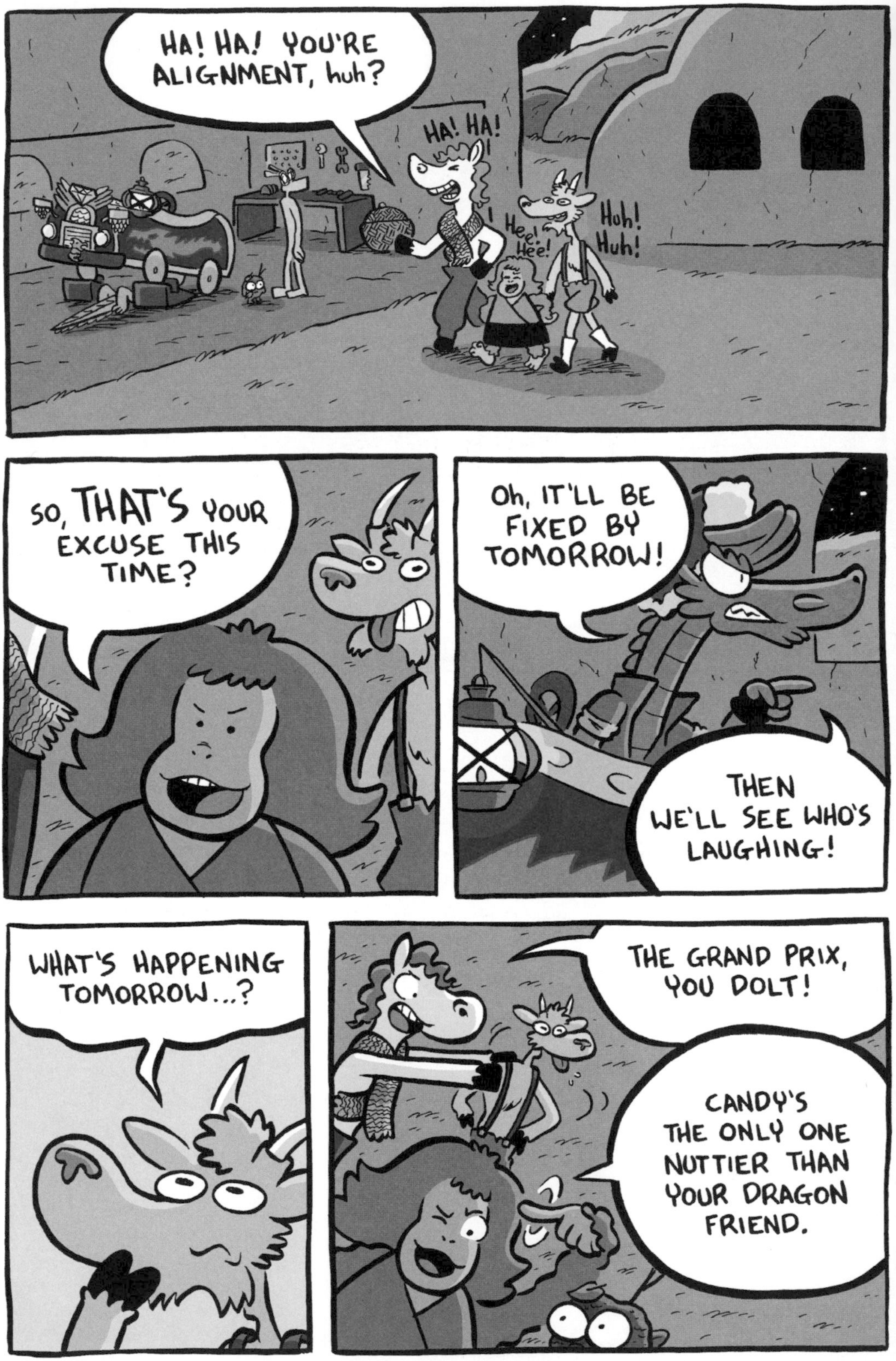
HA! HA! YOU'RE ALIGNMENT, huh?
HA! HA!
Hee! Hee!
Huh! Huh!
SO, THAT'S YOUR EXCUSE THIS TIME?
Oh, IT'LL BE FIXED BY TOMORROW!
THEN WE'LL SEE WHO'S LAUGHING!
WHAT'S HAPPENING TOMORROW...?
THE GRAND PRIX, YOU DOLT!
CANDY'S THE ONLY ONE NUTTIER THAN YOUR DRAGON FRIEND.

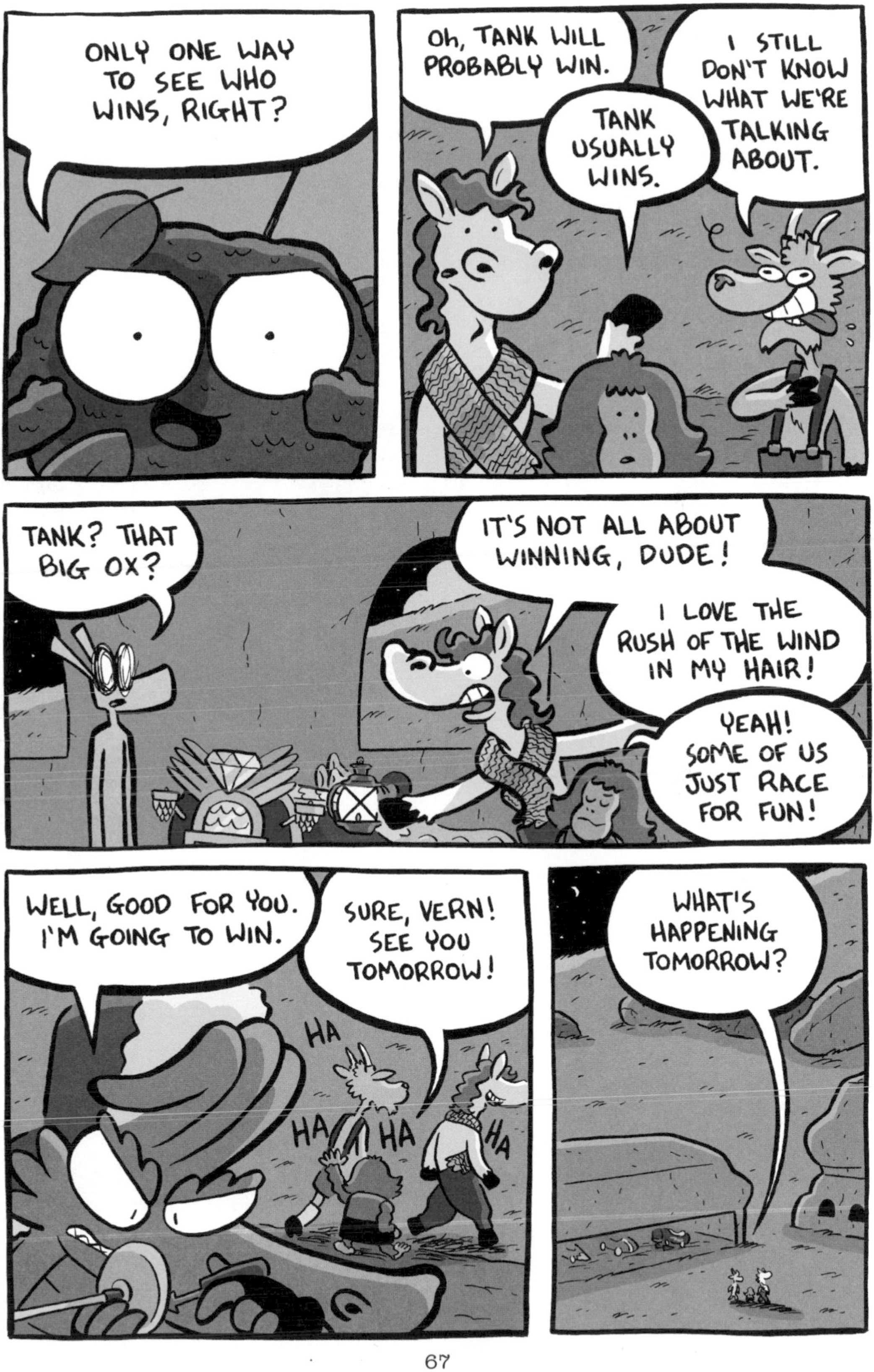
ONLY ONE WAY TO SEE WHO WINS, RIGHT?
Oh, TANK WILL PROBABLY WIN.
TANK USUALLY WINS.
I STILL DON'T KNOW WHAT WE'RE TALKING ABOUT.
TANK? THAT BIG OX?
IT'S NOT ALL ABOUT WINNING, DUDE!
I LOVE THE RUSH OF THE WIND IN MY HAIR!
YEAH! SOME OF US JUST RACE FOR FUN!
WELL, GOOD FOR YOU. I'M GOING TO WIN.
SURE, VERN! SEE YOU TOMORROW!
HA
HA HA HA
WHAT'S HAPPENING TOMORROW?

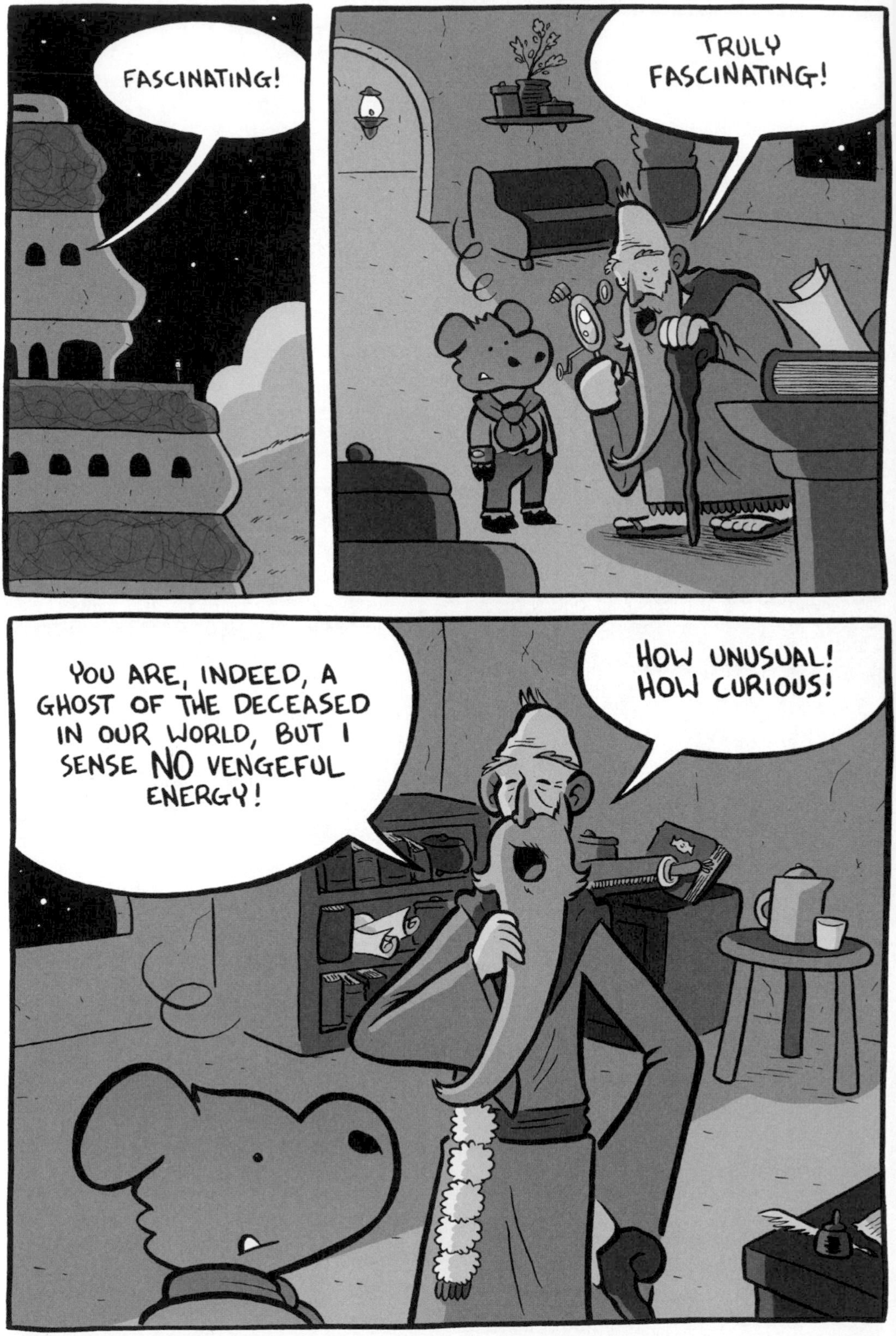
FASCINATING!
TRULY FASCINATING!
YOU ARE, INDEED, A GHOST OF THE DECEASED IN OUR WORLD, BUT I SENSE NO VENGEFUL ENERGY!
HOW UNUSUAL! HOW CURIOUS!

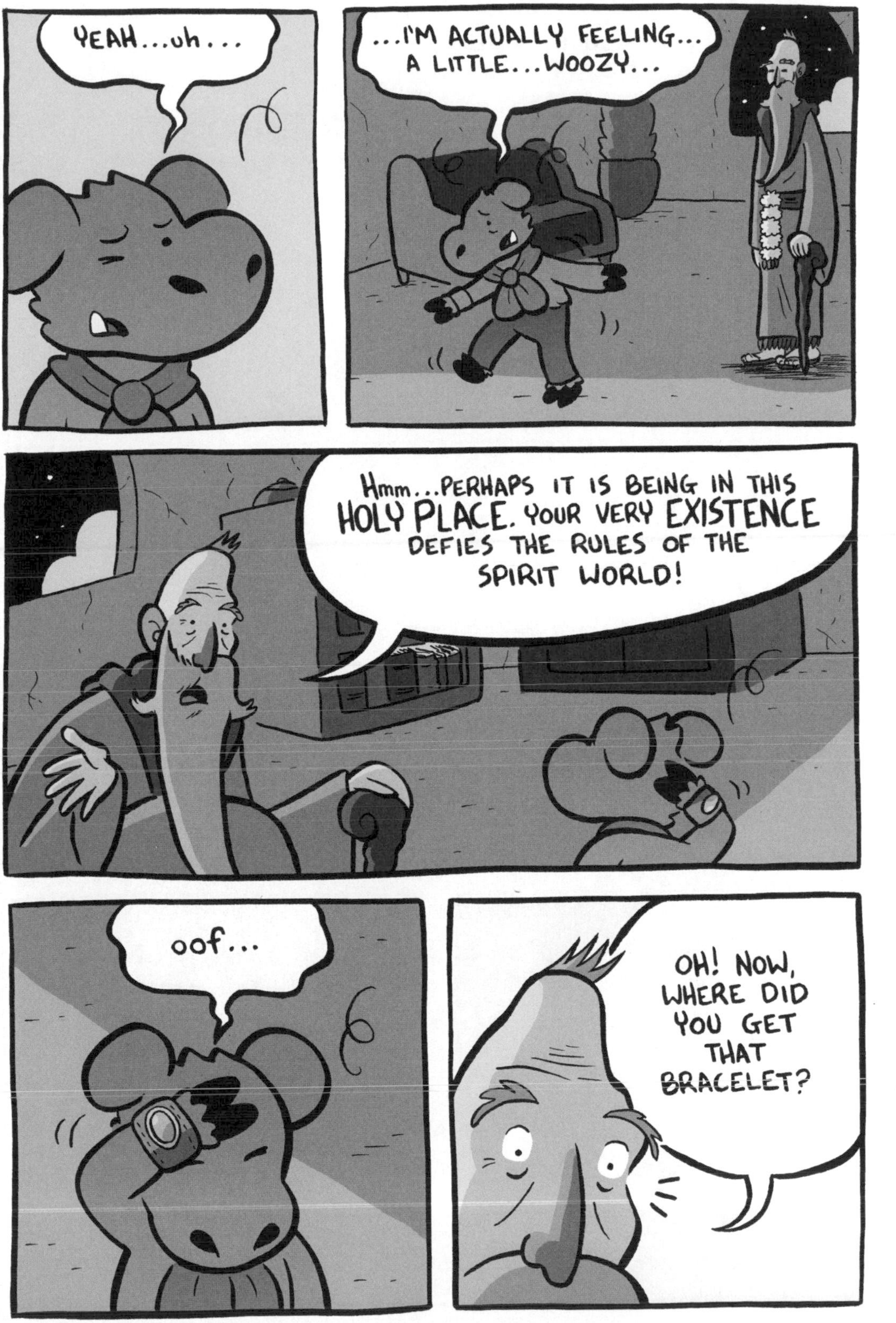
YEAH...uh...
...I'M ACTUALLY FEELING... A LITTLE...WOOZY...
Hmm...PERHAPS IT IS BEING IN THIS HOLY PLACE. YOUR VERY EXISTENCE DEFIES THE RULES OF THE SPIRIT WORLD!
oof...
OH! NOW, WHERE DID YOU GET THAT BRACELET?

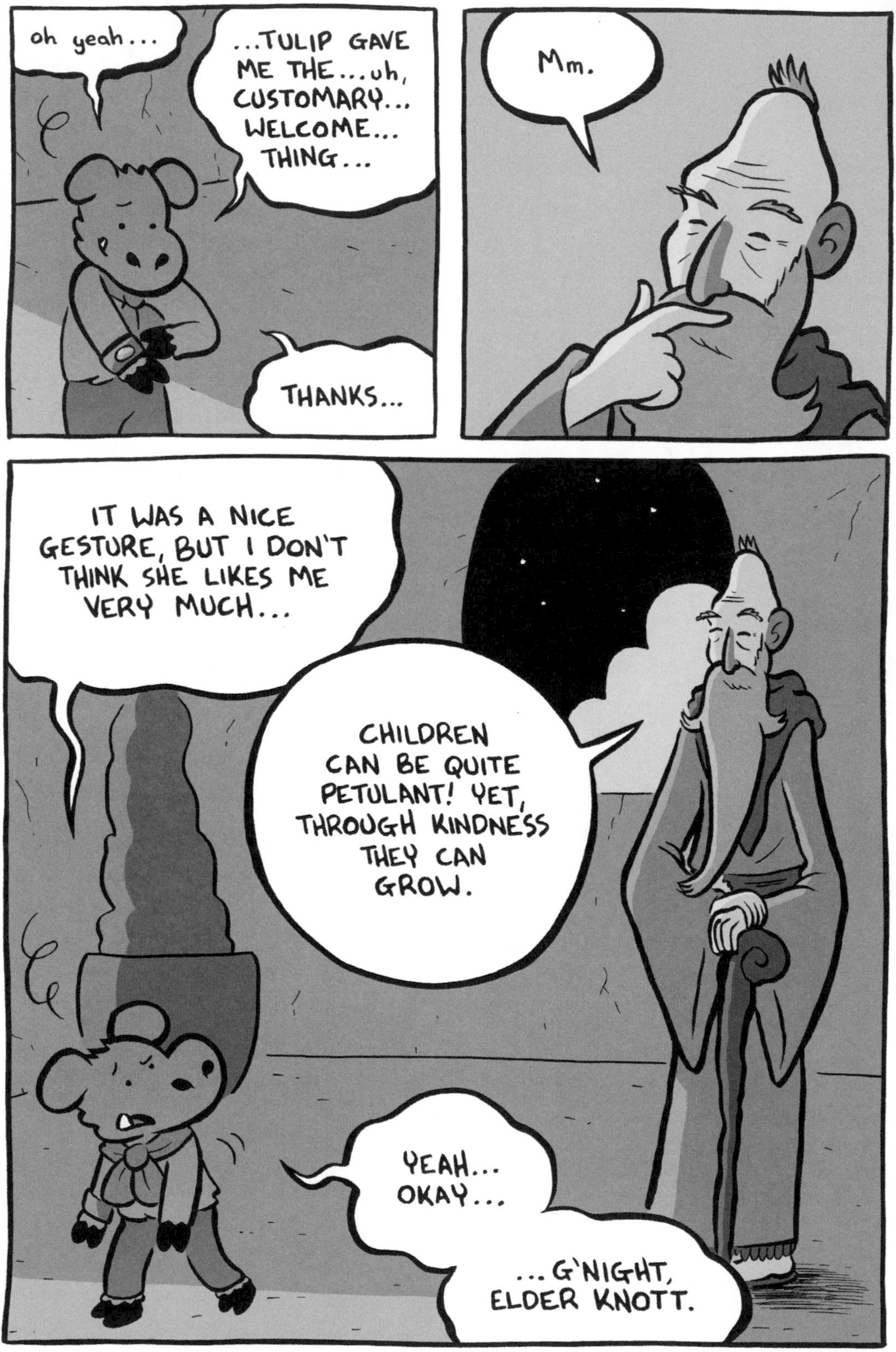
oh yeah...
...TULIP GAVE ME THE...uh, CUSTOMARY... WELCOME... THING...
THANKS...
Mm.
IT WAS A NICE GESTURE, BUT I DON'T THINK SHE LIKES ME VERY MUCH...
CHILDREN CAN BE QUITE PETULANT! YET, THROUGH KINDNESS THEY CAN GROW.
YEAH... OKAY...
...G'NIGHT, ELDER KNOTT.

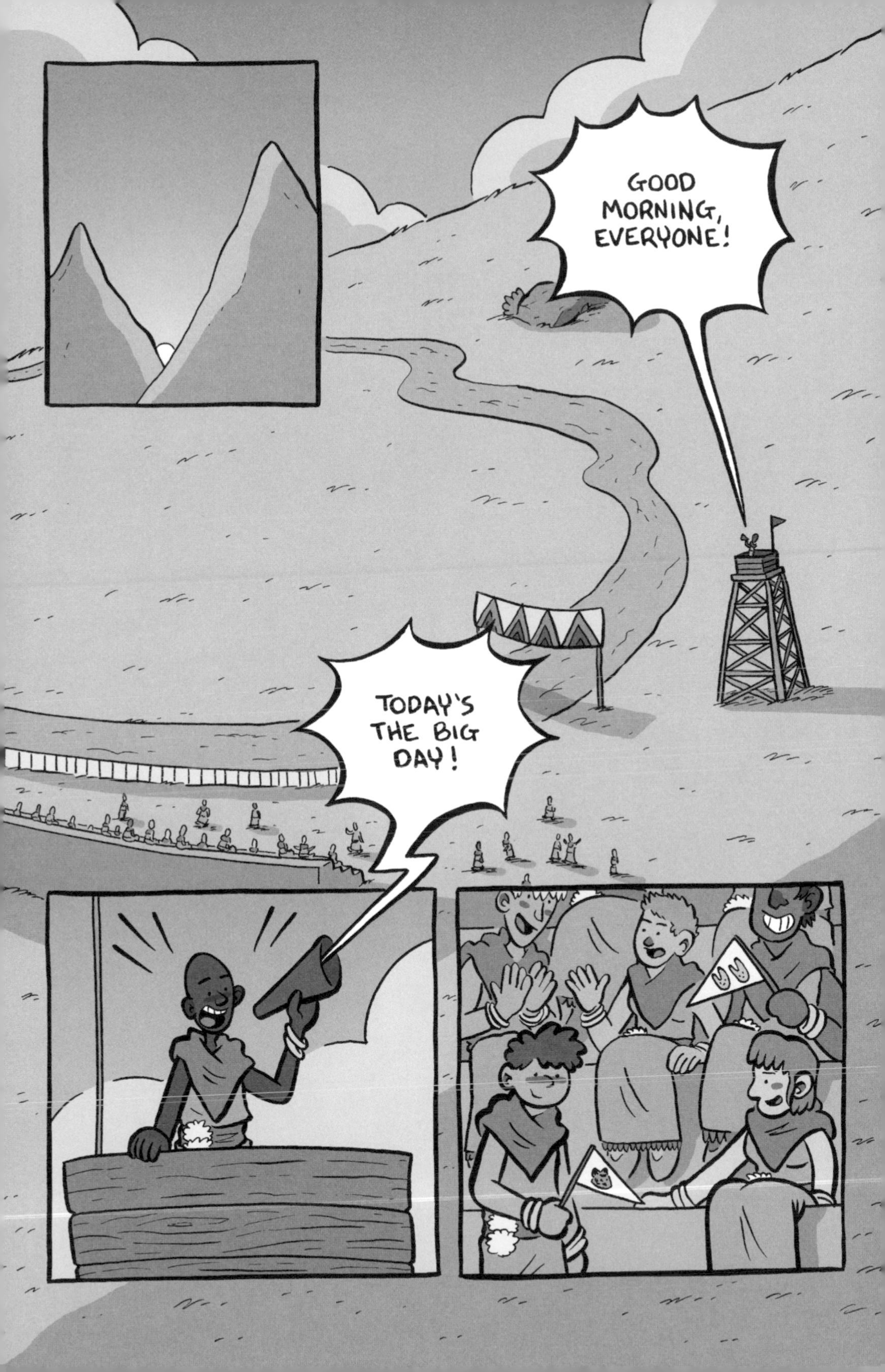
GOOD MORNING, EVERYONE!
TODAY'S THE BIG DAY!

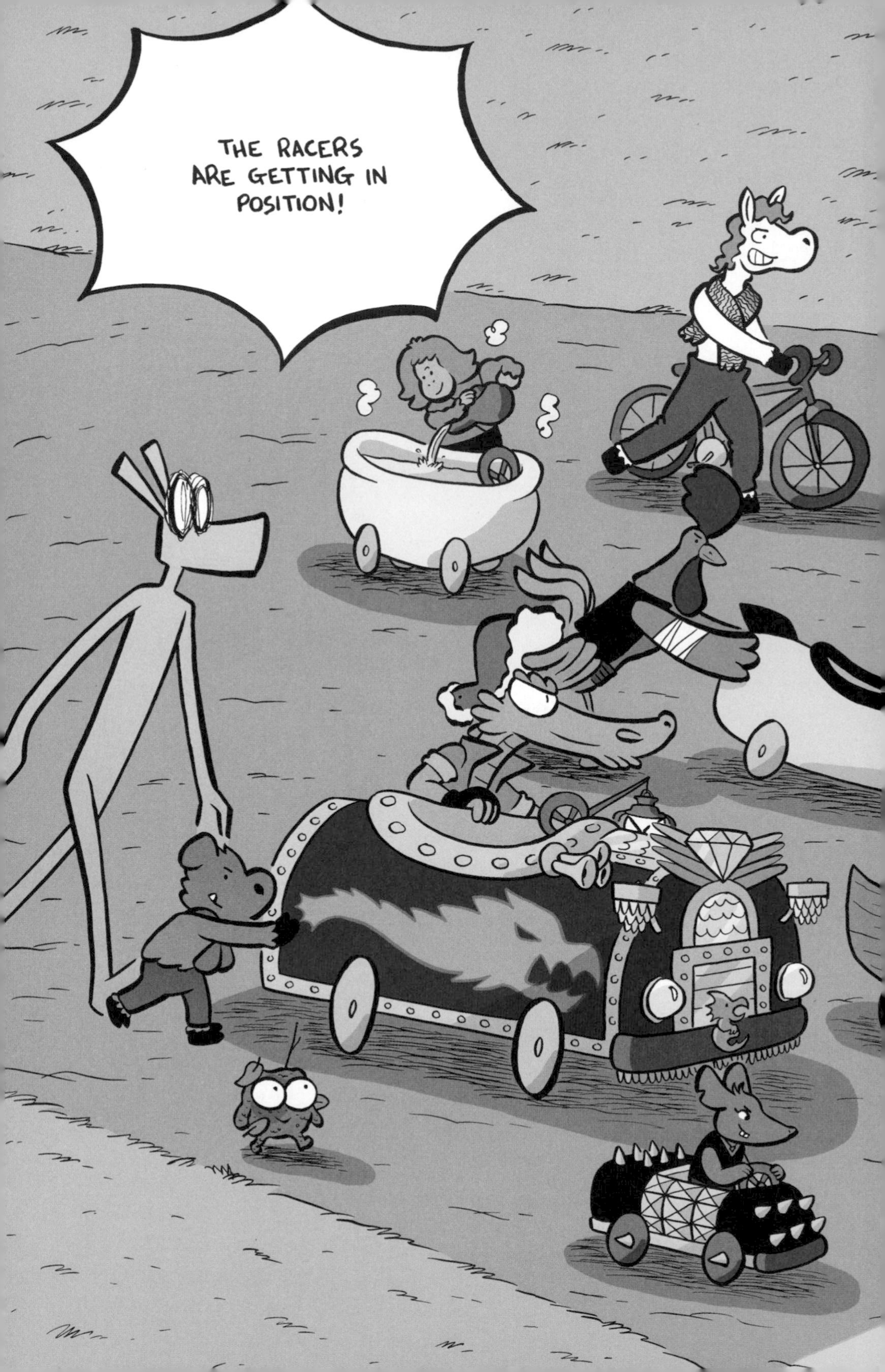
THE RACERS ARE GETTING IN POSITION!

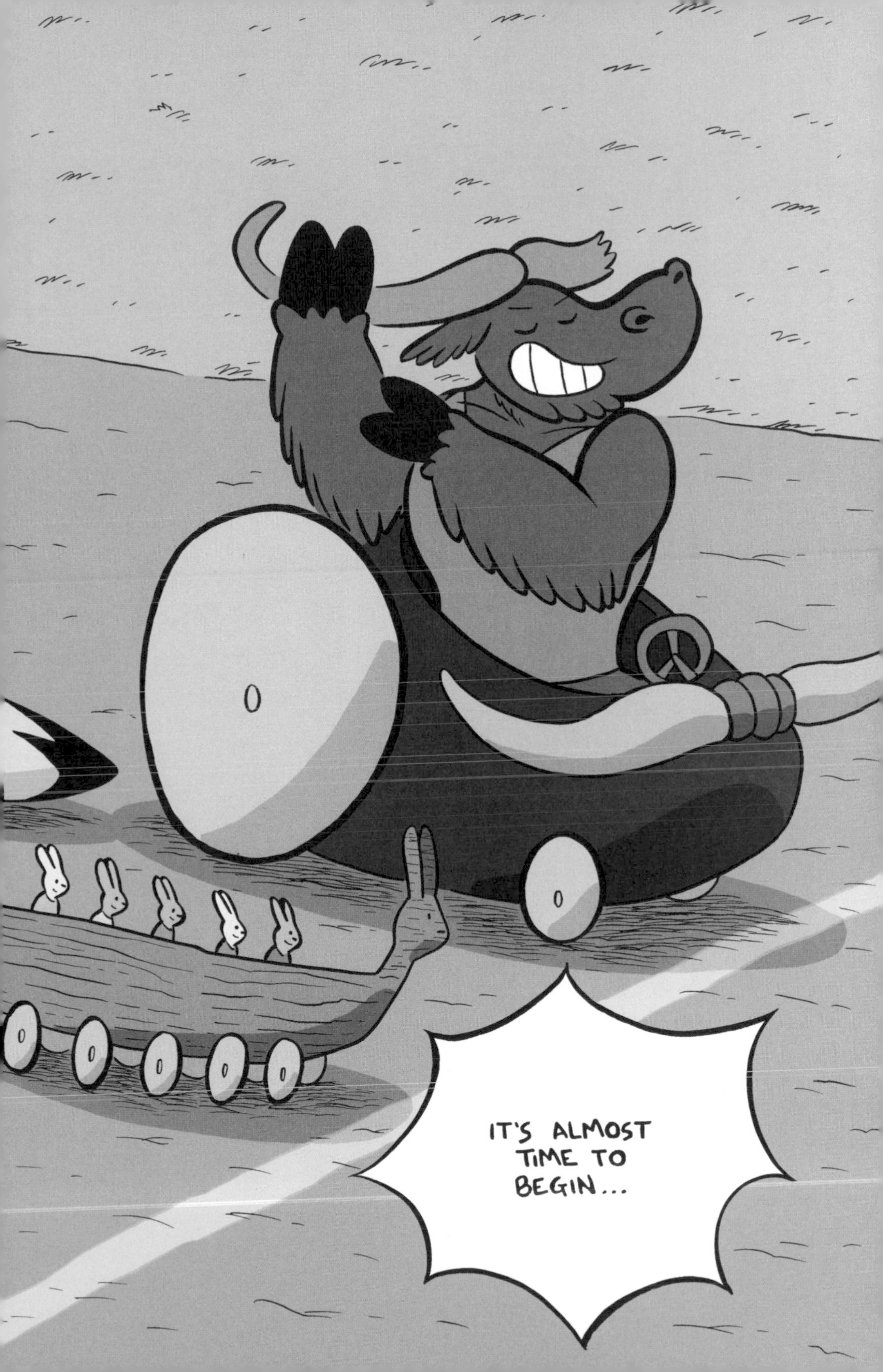
IT'S ALMOST TIME TO BEGIN...

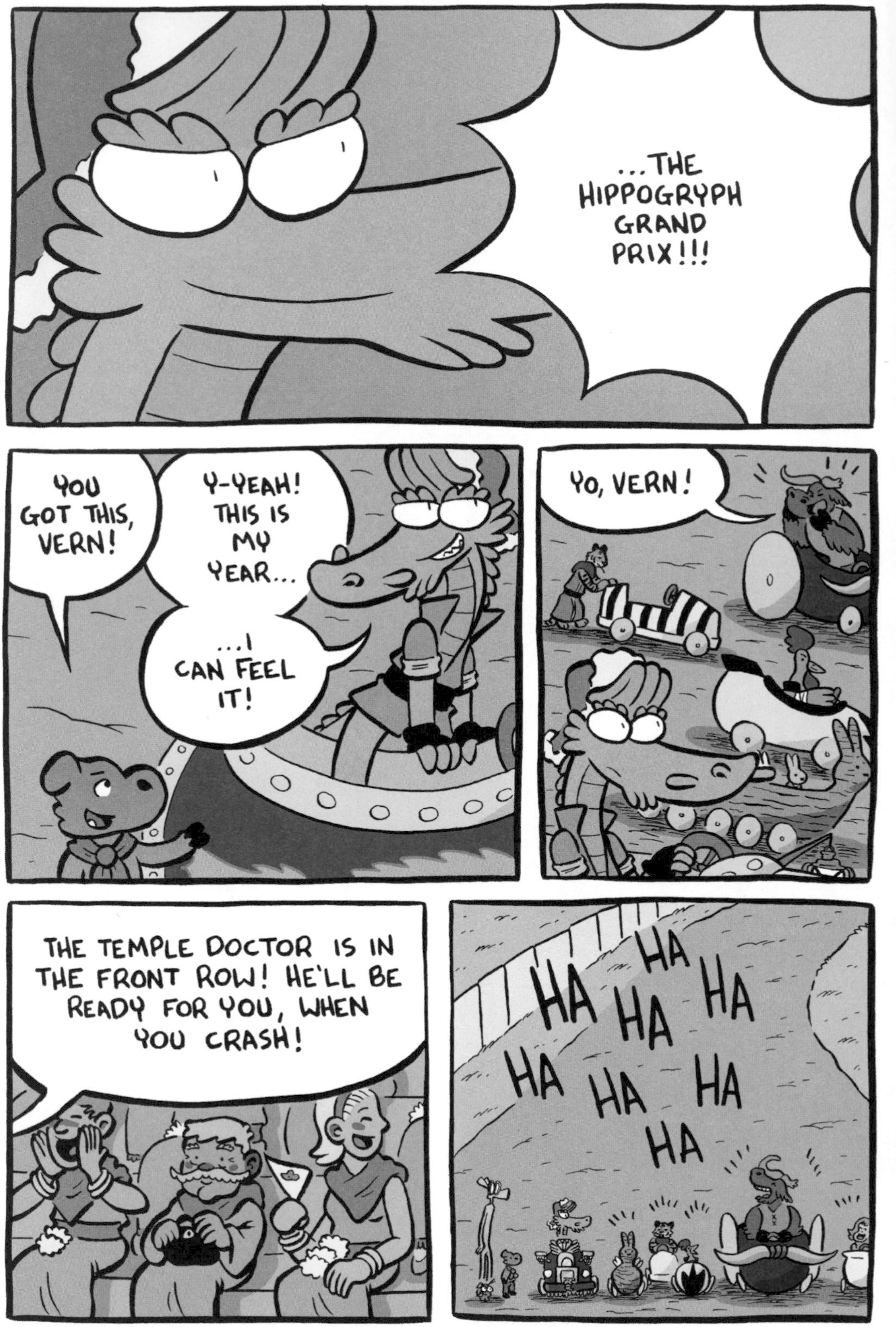
...THE HIPPOGRYPH GRAND PRIX!!!
YOU GOT THIS, VERN!
Y-YEAH! THIS IS MY YEAR...
...I CAN FEEL IT!
YO, VERN!
THE TEMPLE DOCTOR IS IN THE FRONT ROW! HE'LL BE READY FOR YOU, WHEN YOU CRASH!
HA HA HA HA HA HA HA HA HA

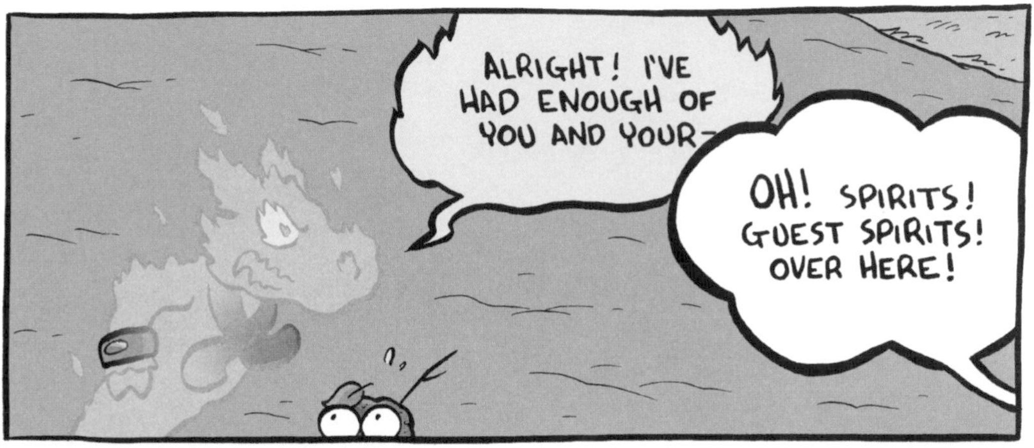
ALRIGHT! I'VE HAD ENOUGH OF YOU AND YOUR-
OH! SPIRITS! GUEST SPIRITS! OVER HERE!

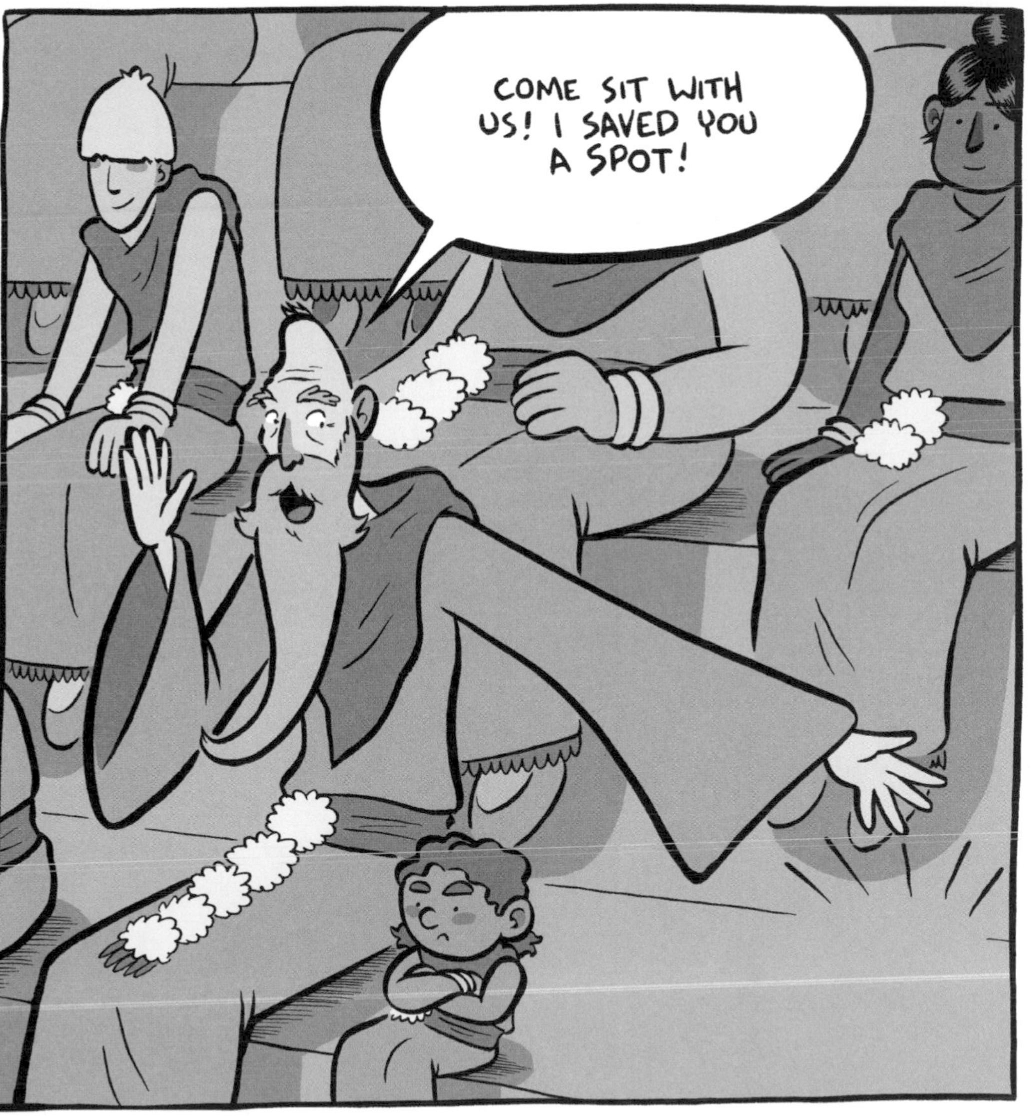
COME SIT WITH US! I SAVED YOU A SPOT!

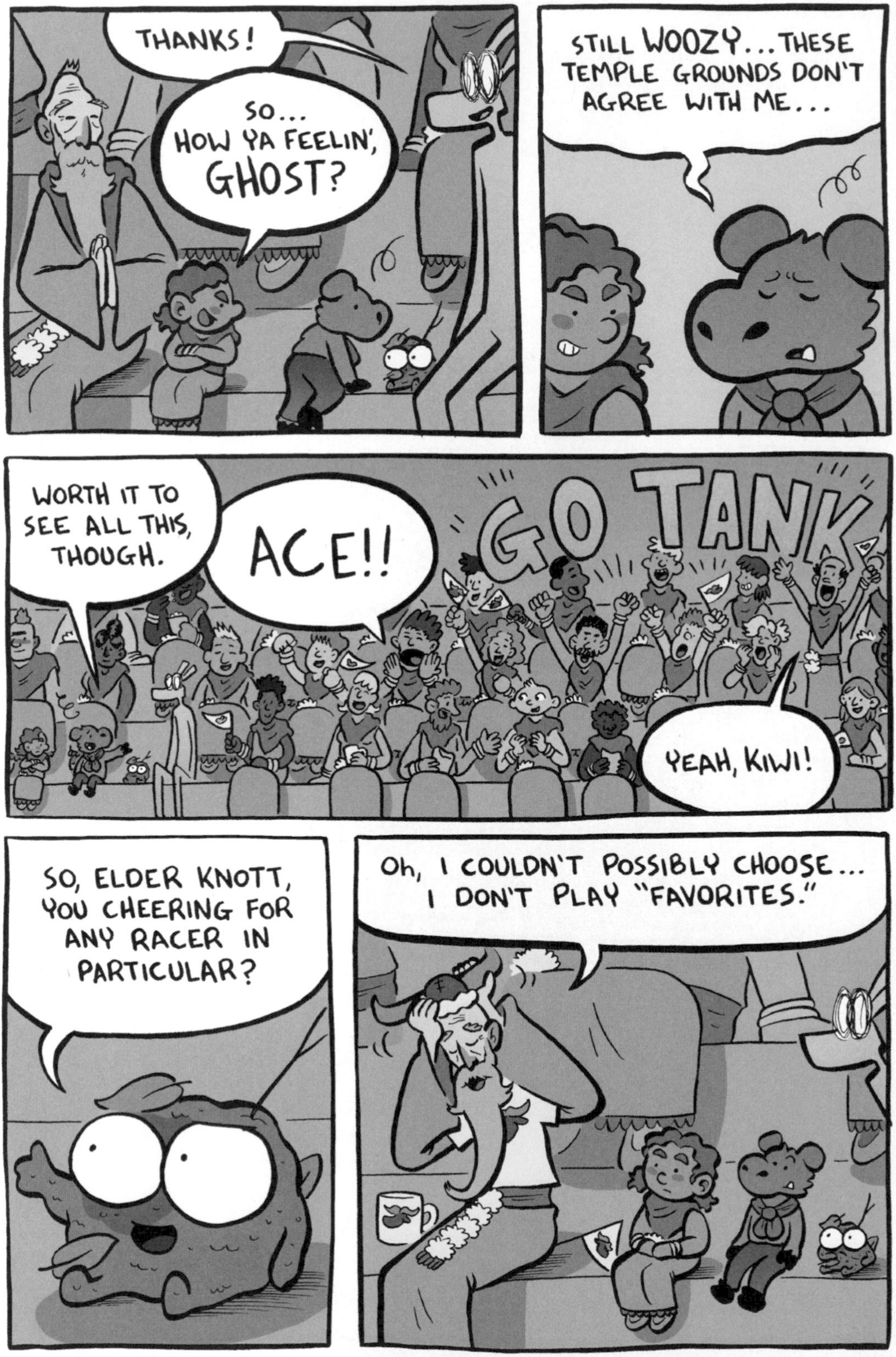
THANKS!
SO... HOW YA FEELIN', GHOST?
STILL WOOZY... THESE TEMPLE GROUNDS DON'T AGREE WITH ME...
WORTH IT TO SEE ALL THIS, THOUGH.
ACE!!
GO TANK
YEAH, KIWI!
SO, ELDER KNOTT, YOU CHEERING FOR ANY RACER IN PARTICULAR?
Oh, I COULDN'T POSSIBLY CHOOSE... I DON'T PLAY "FAVORITES."

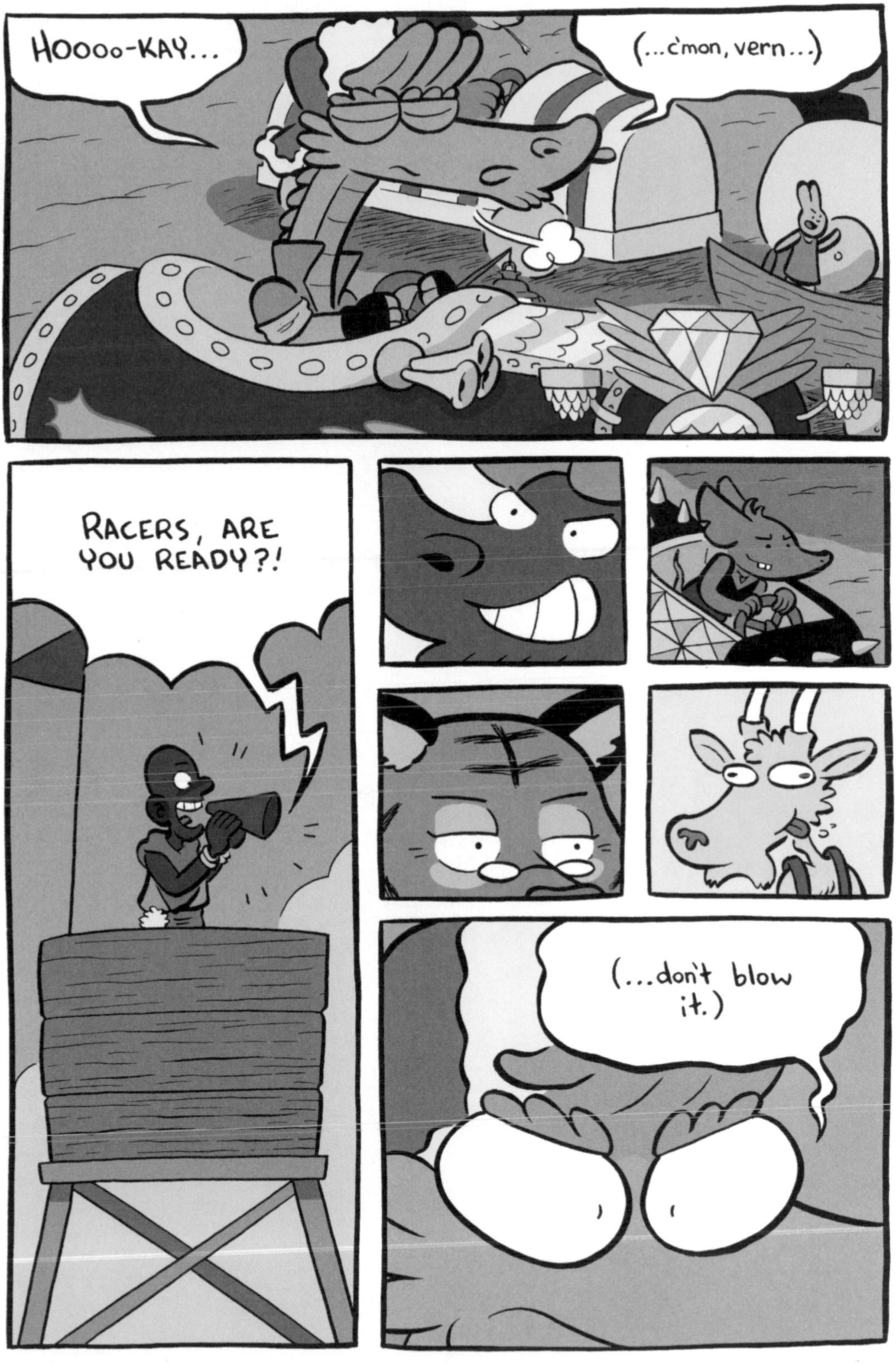
HOOOo-KAY...
(...c'mon, vern...)
RACERS, ARE YOU READY?!
(...don't blow it.)

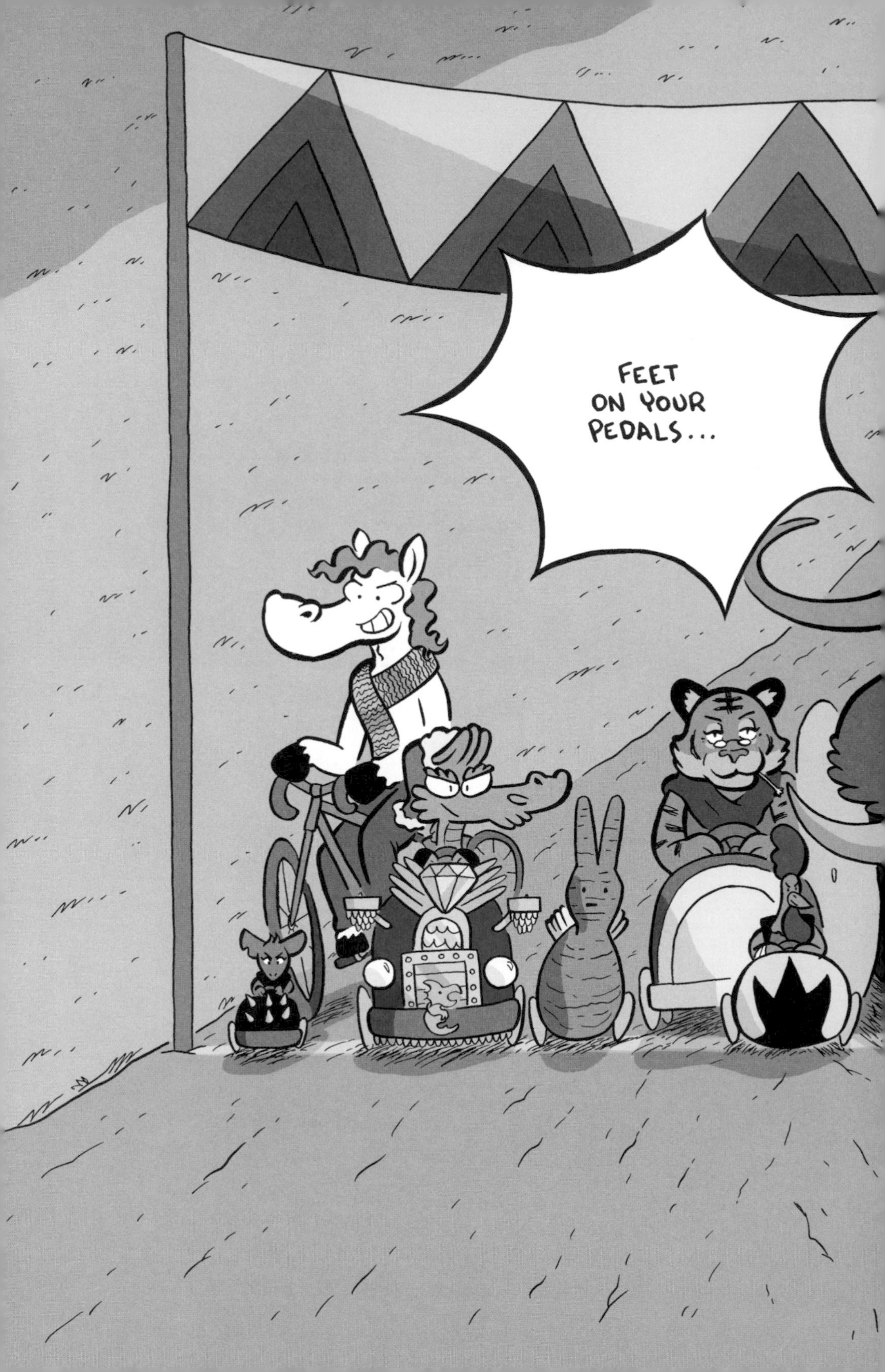
FEET ON YOUR PEDALS...

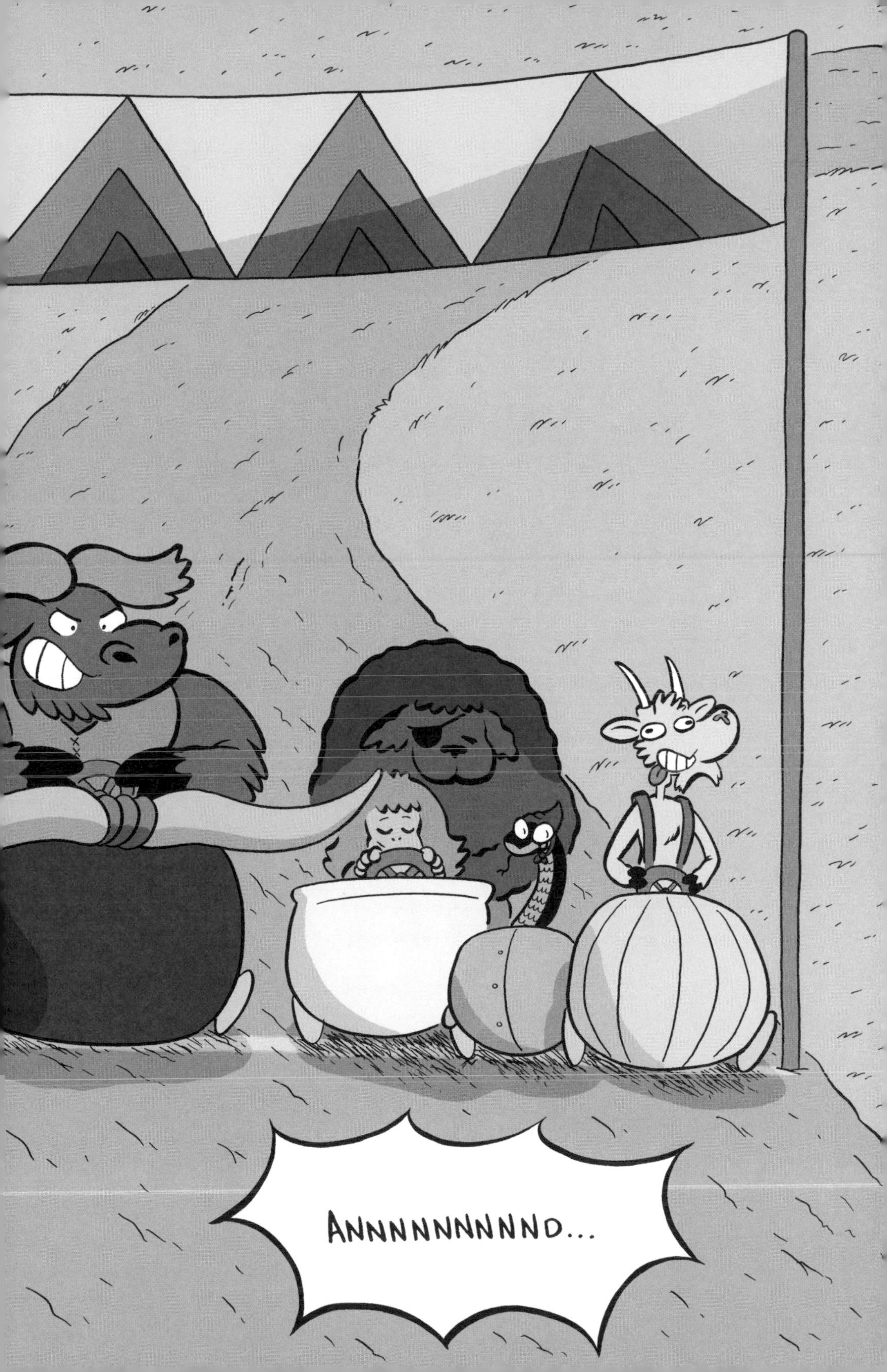
ANNNNNNNNND...

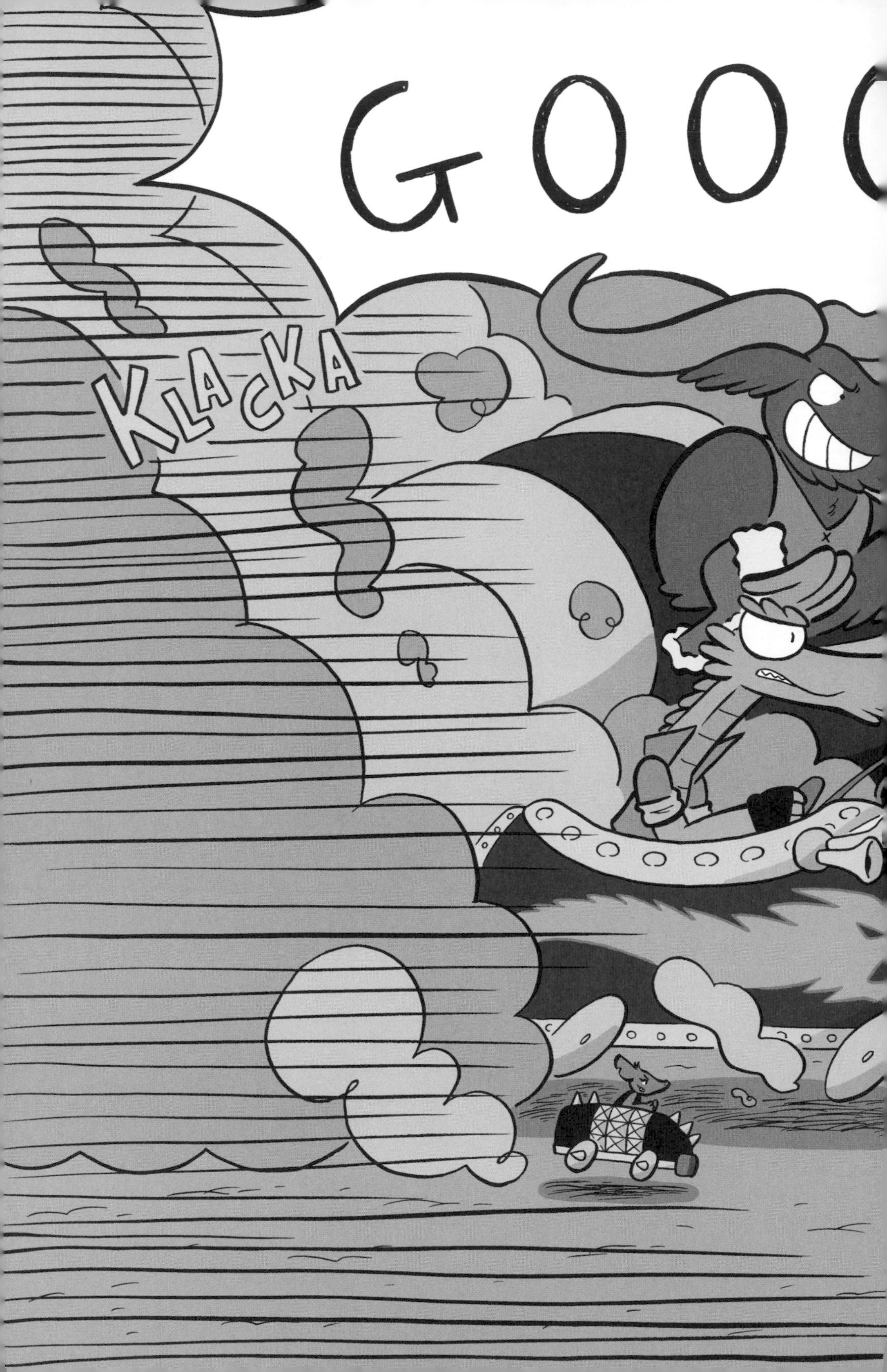
GOOO
KLACKA

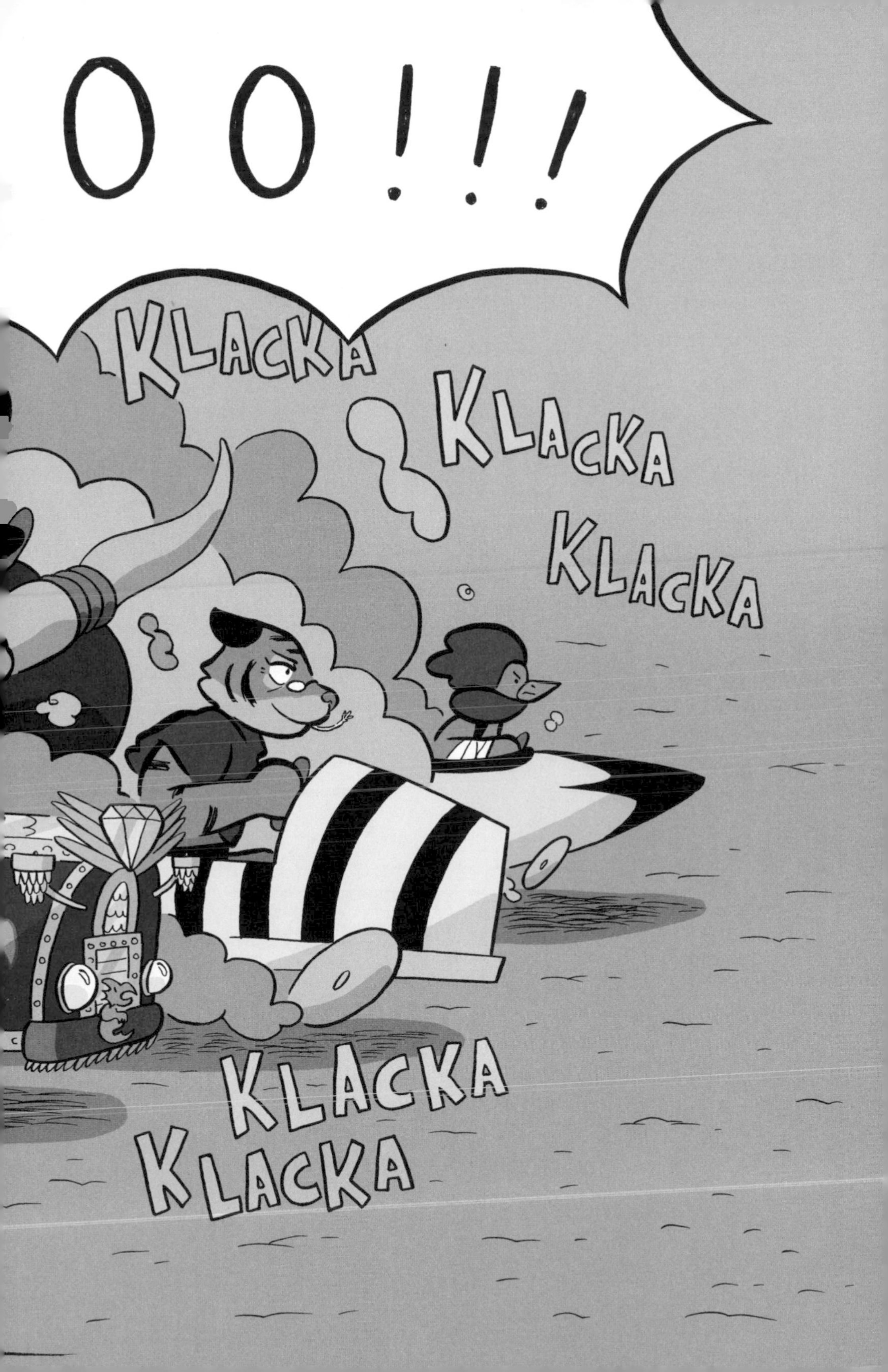
OO!!!
KLACKA
KLACKA
KLACKA
KLACKA
KLACKA

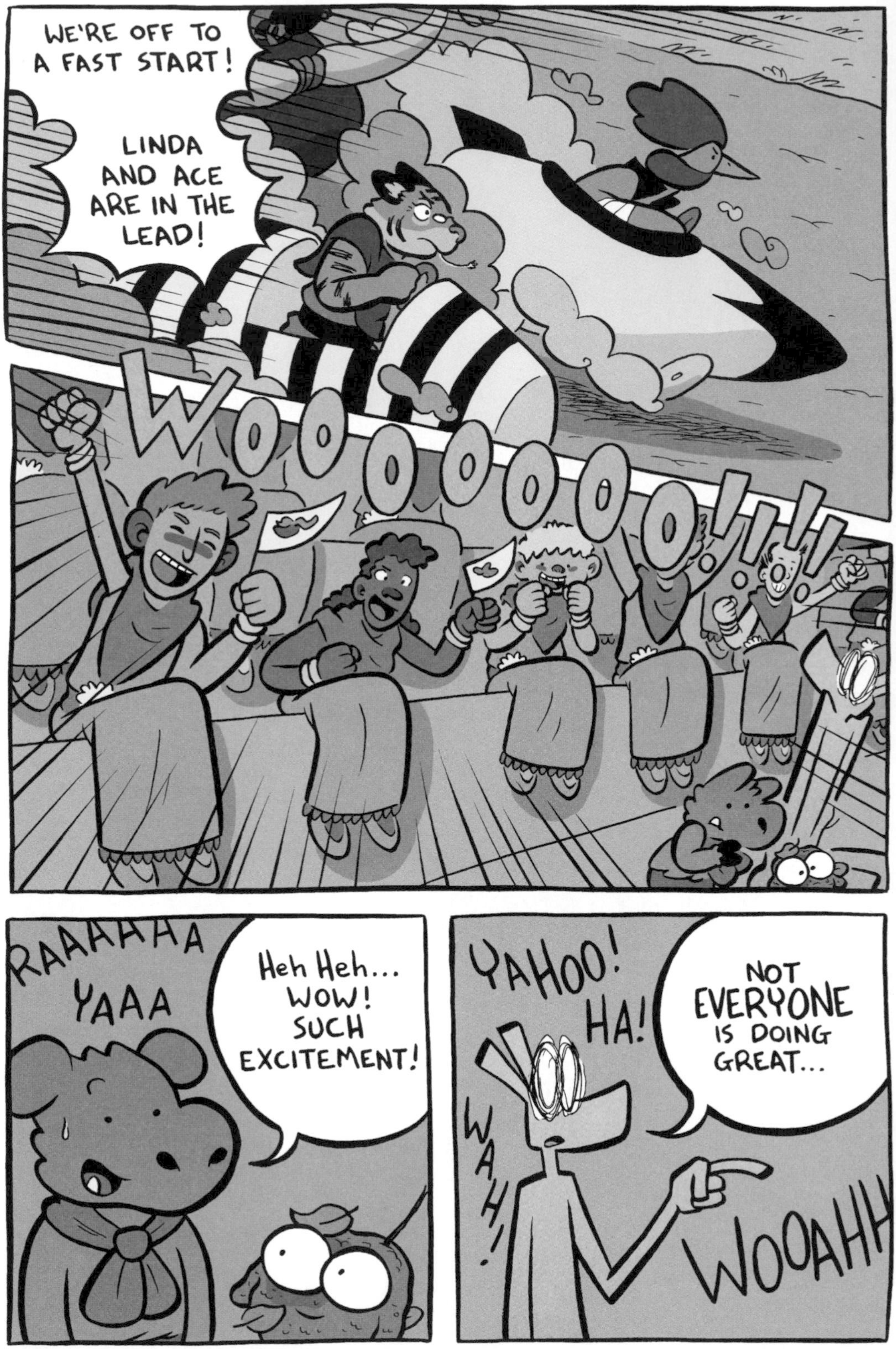
WE'RE OFF TO A FAST START!
LINDA AND ACE ARE IN THE LEAD!
WOOOOOOOOO!!!!!
RAAAAAA YAAA
Heh Heh... WOW! SUCH EXCITEMENT!
YAHOO! HA!
WAH!
NOT EVERYONE IS DOING GREAT...
WOOAHH

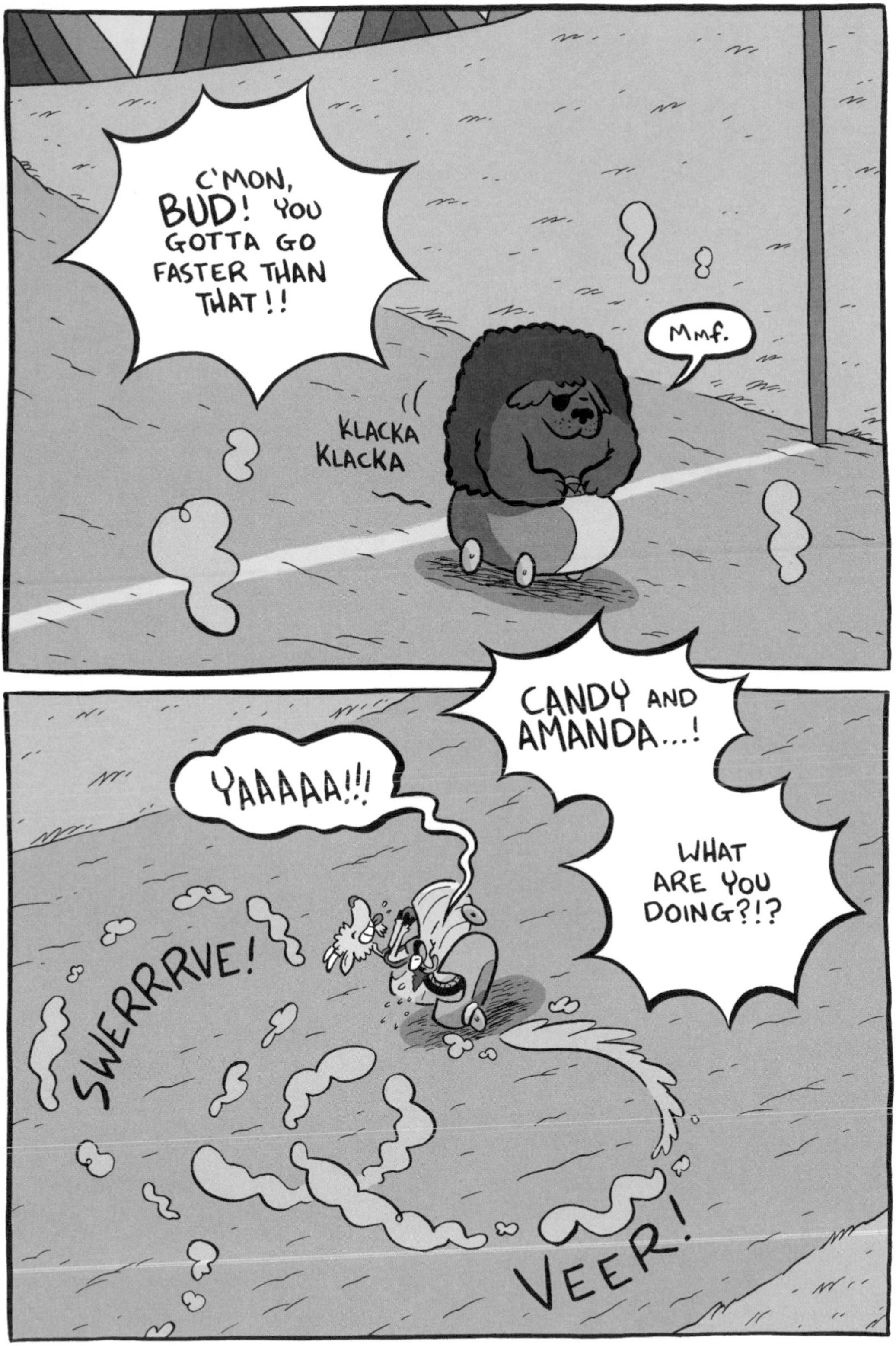
C'MON, BUD! YOU GOTTA GO FASTER THAN THAT!!
Mmf.
KLACKA KLACKA
CANDY AND AMANDA...!
YAAAAA!!!
WHAT ARE YOU DOING?!?
SWERRRVE!
VEER!

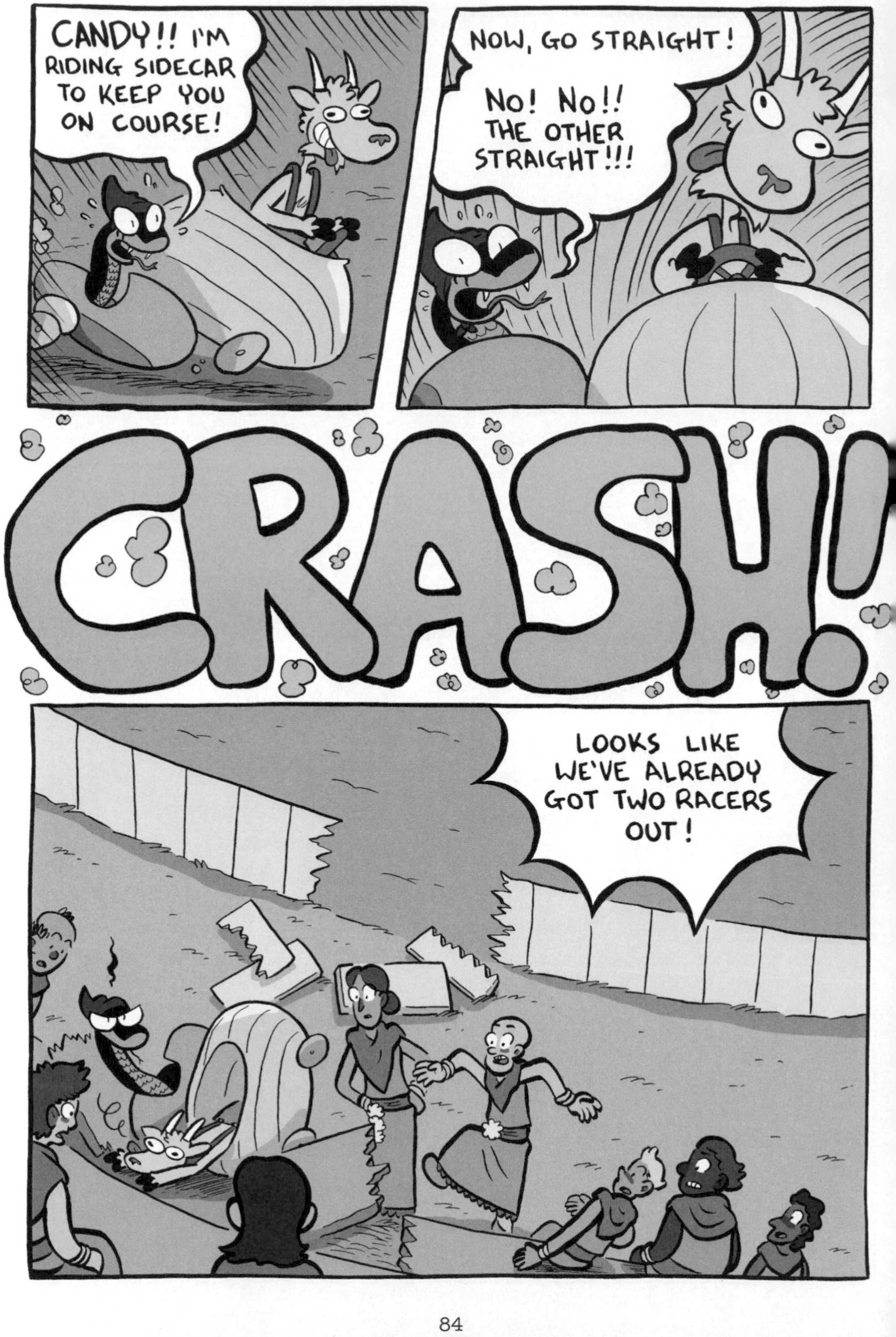
CANDY!! I'M RIDING SIDECAR TO KEEP YOU ON COURSE!
NOW, GO STRAIGHT!
NO! NO!! THE OTHER STRAIGHT!!!
CRASH!!
LOOKS LIKE WE'VE ALREADY GOT TWO RACERS OUT!

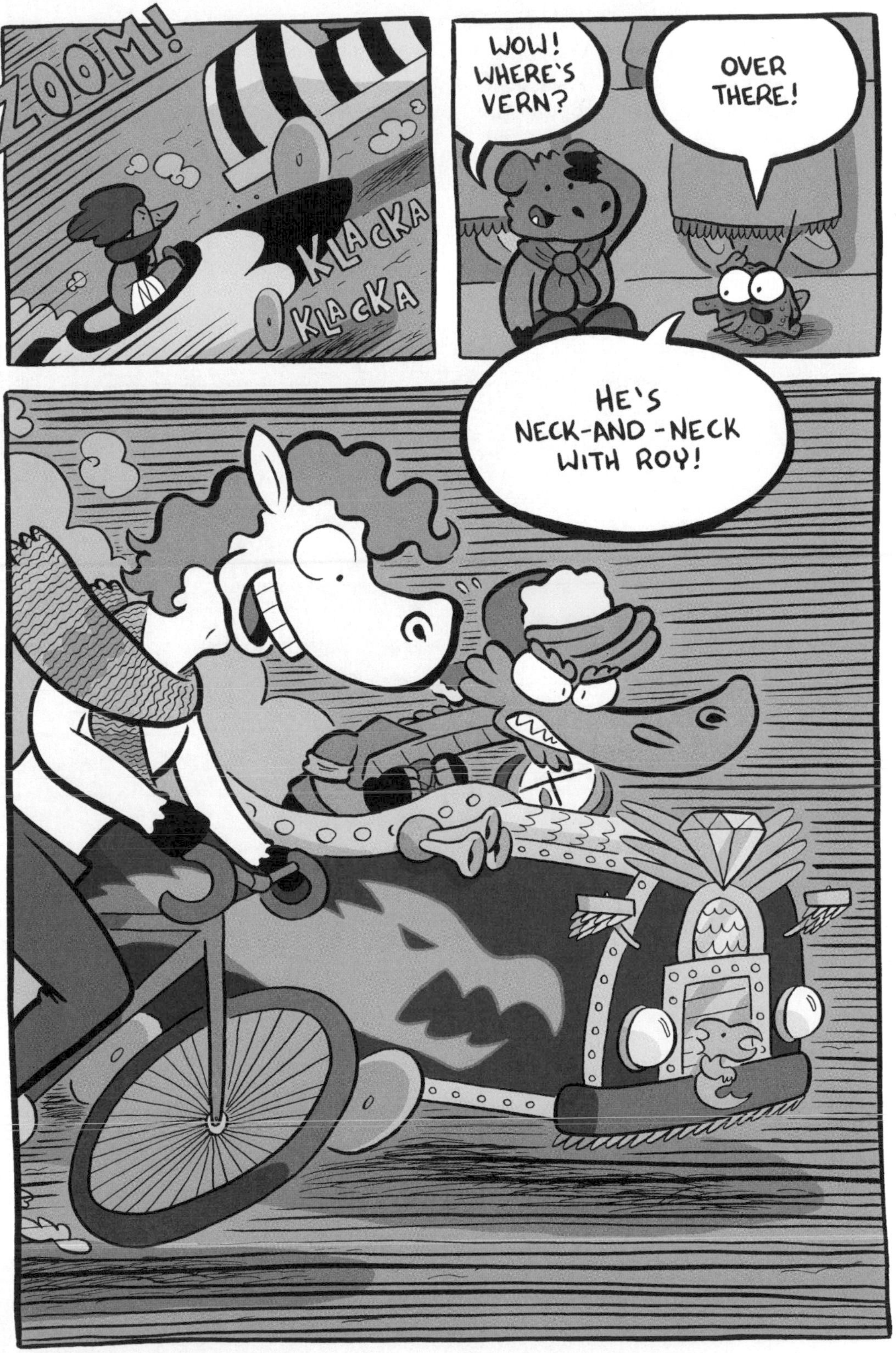
ZOOM!
KLACKA
KLACKA
WOW! WHERE'S VERN?
OVER THERE!
HE'S NECK-AND-NECK WITH ROY!

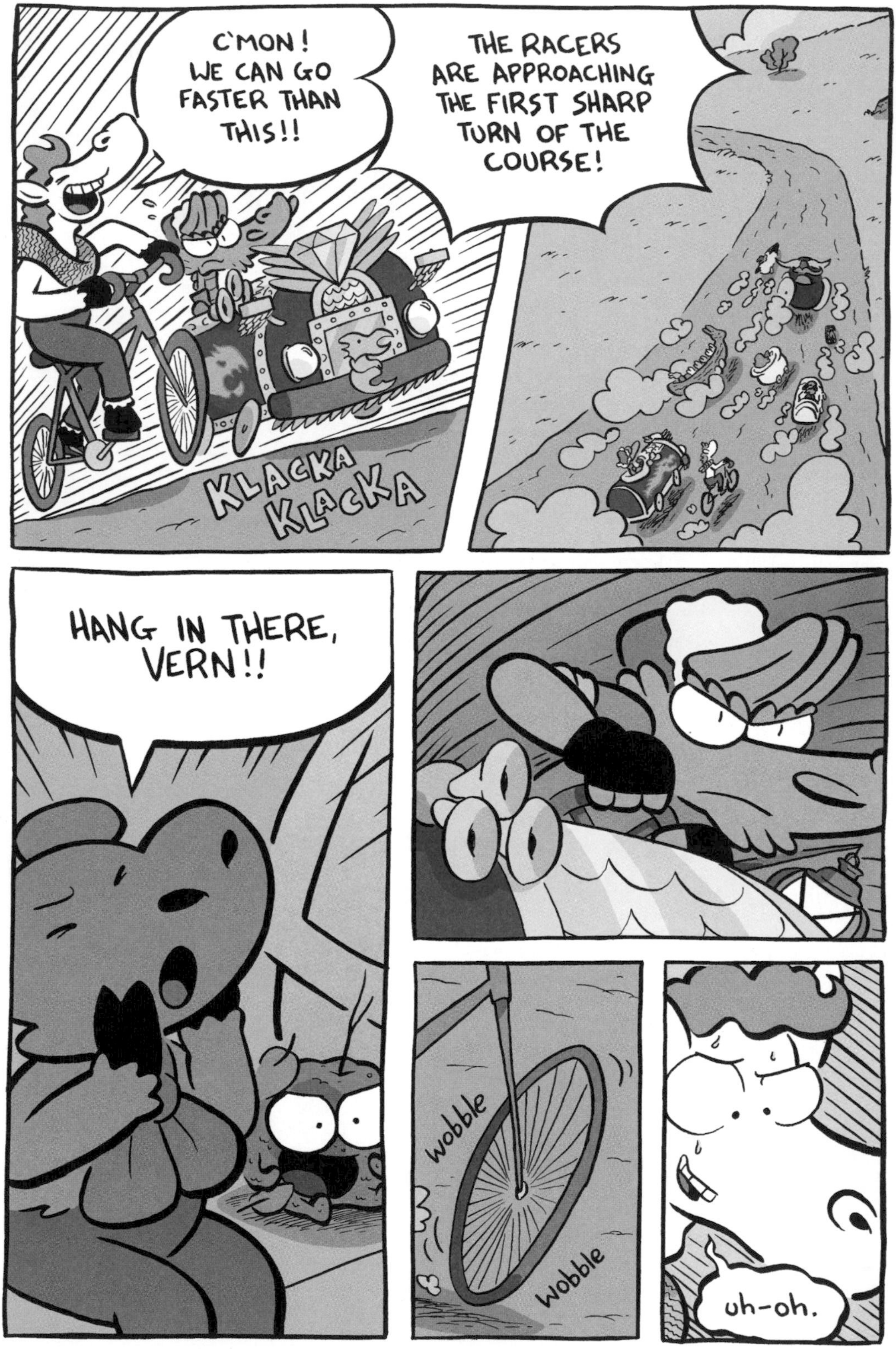
C'MON! WE CAN GO FASTER THAN THIS!!
KLACKA KLACKA
THE RACERS ARE APPROACHING THE FIRST SHARP TURN OF THE COURSE!
HANG IN THERE, VERN!!
wobble
wobble
uh-oh.

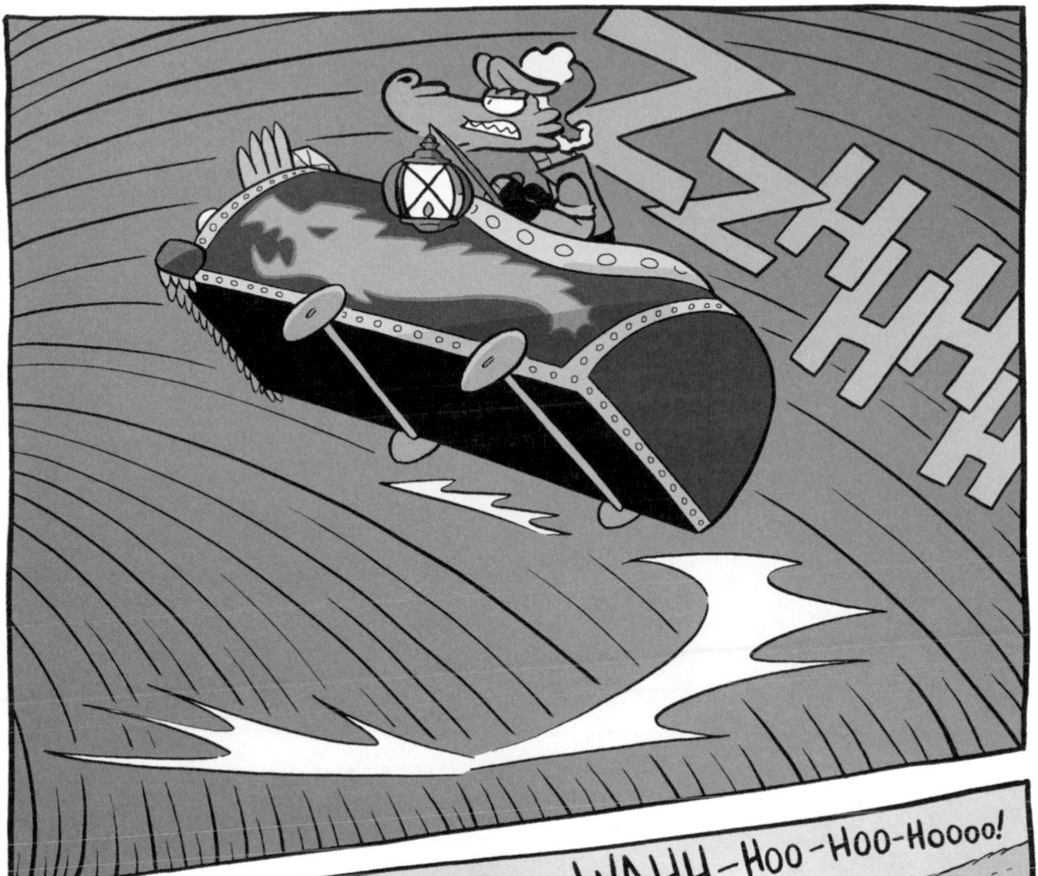
ZHHHH

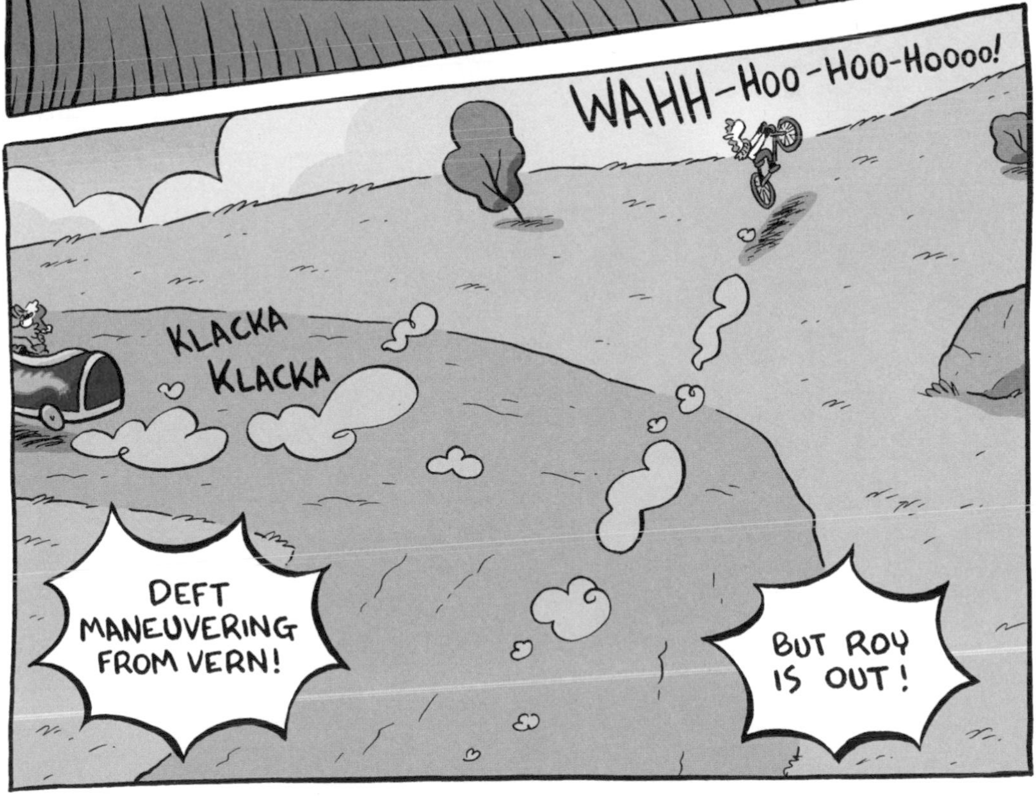
WAHH-Hoo-Hoo-Hoooo!
KLACKA KLACKA
DEFT MANEUVERING FROM VERN!
BUT ROY IS OUT!

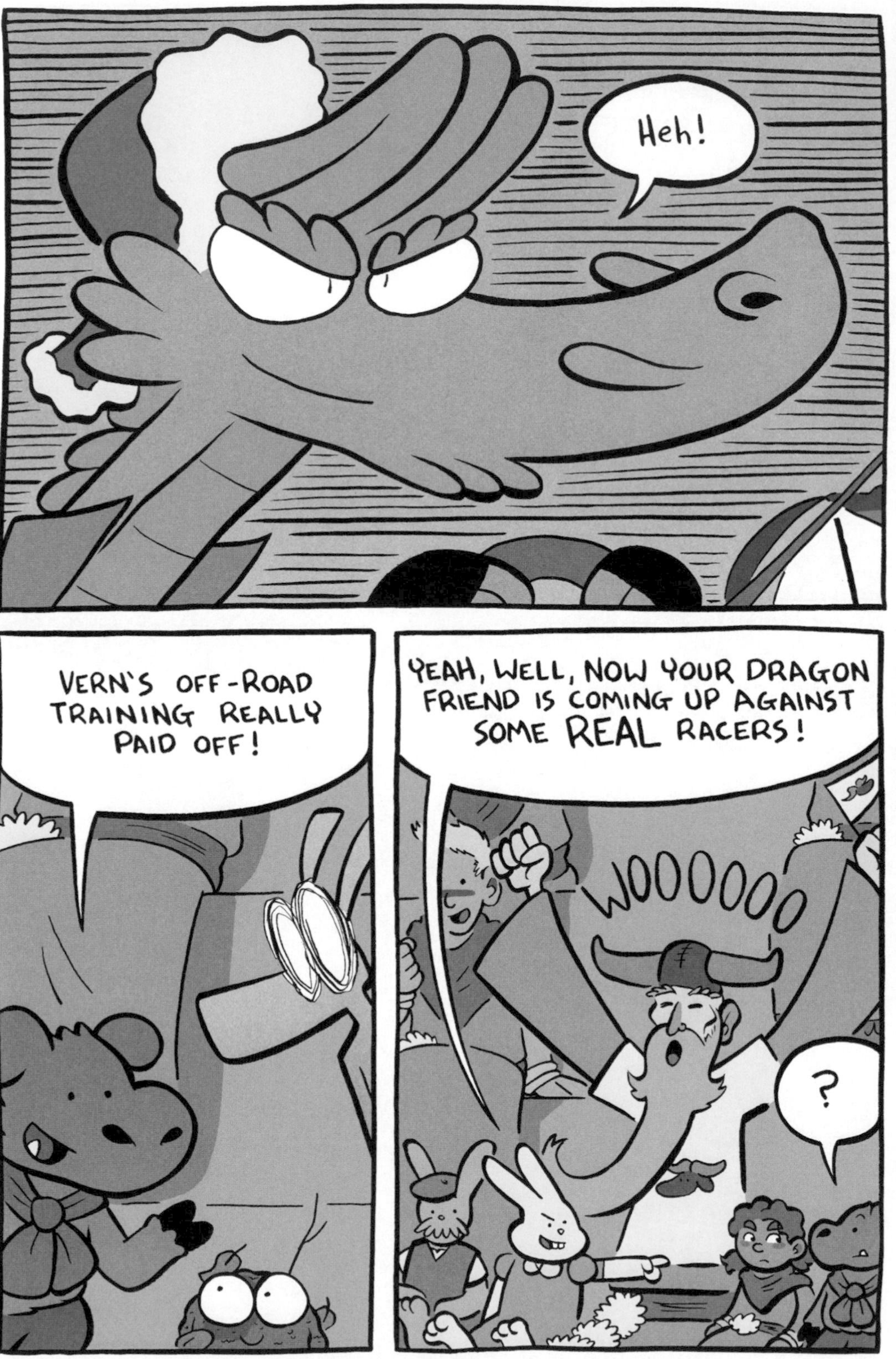
Heh!
VERN'S OFF-ROAD TRAINING REALLY PAID OFF!
YEAH, WELL, NOW YOUR DRAGON FRIEND IS COMING UP AGAINST SOME REAL RACERS!
WOOOOOOO
?

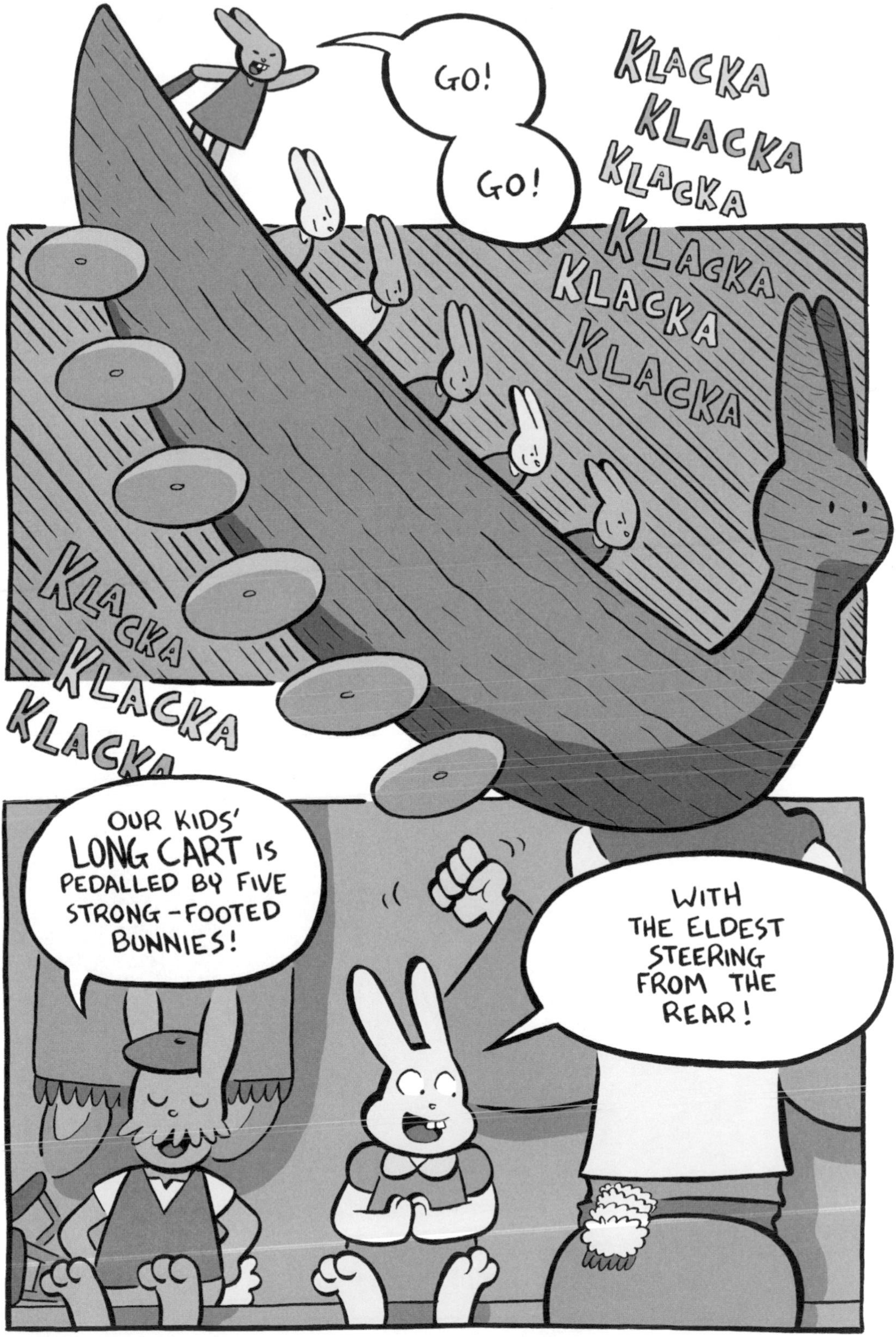
GO!
GO!
KLACKA KLACKA KLACKA KLACKA KLACKA KLACKA
KLACKA KLACKA KLACKA
OUR KIDS' LONG CART IS PEDALLED BY FIVE STRONG-FOOTED BUNNIES!
WITH THE ELDEST STEERING FROM THE REAR!

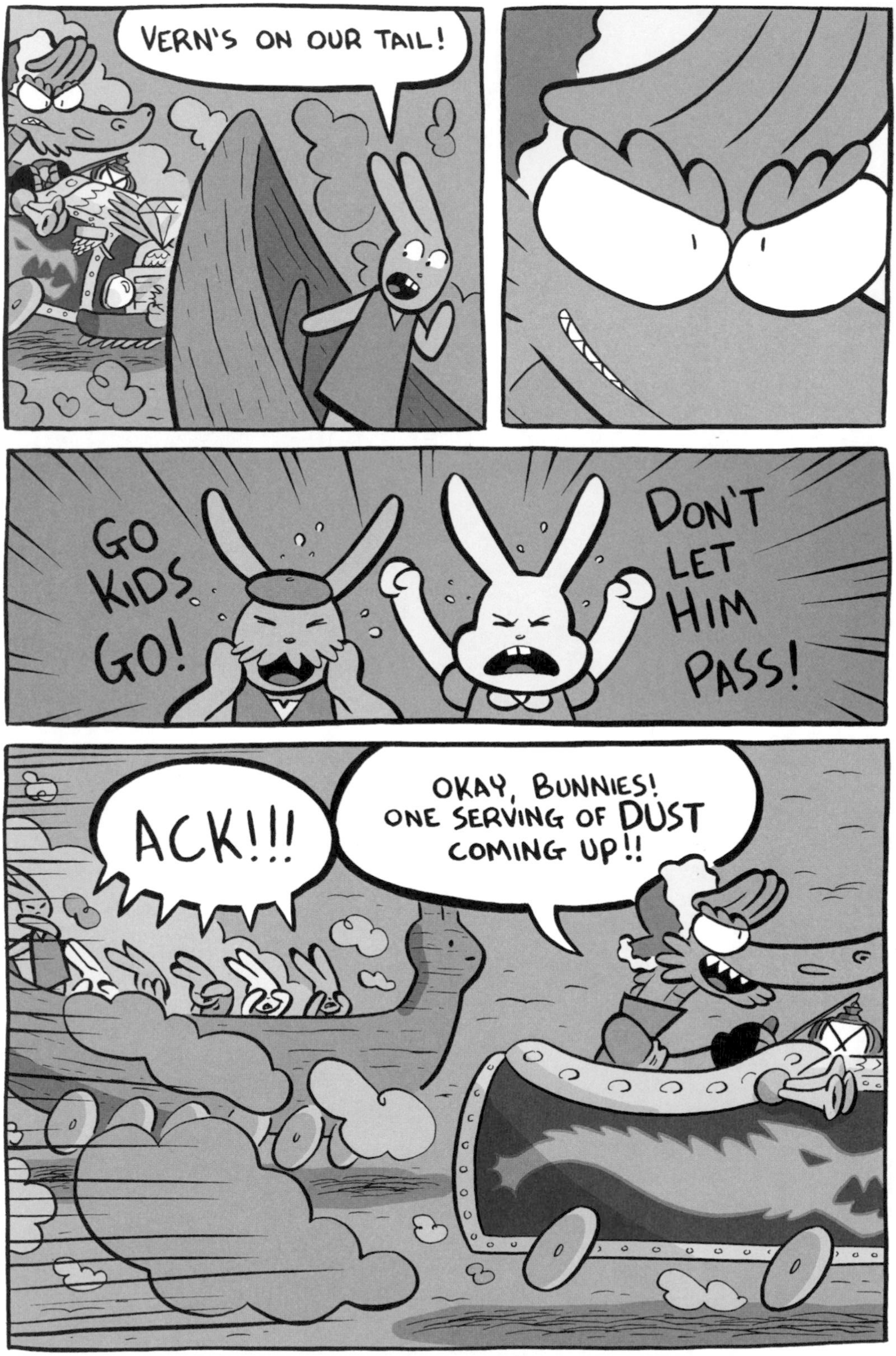
VERN'S ON OUR TAIL!
GO KIDS GO!
DON'T LET HIM PASS!
ACK!!!
OKAY, BUNNIES! ONE SERVING OF DUST COMING UP!!

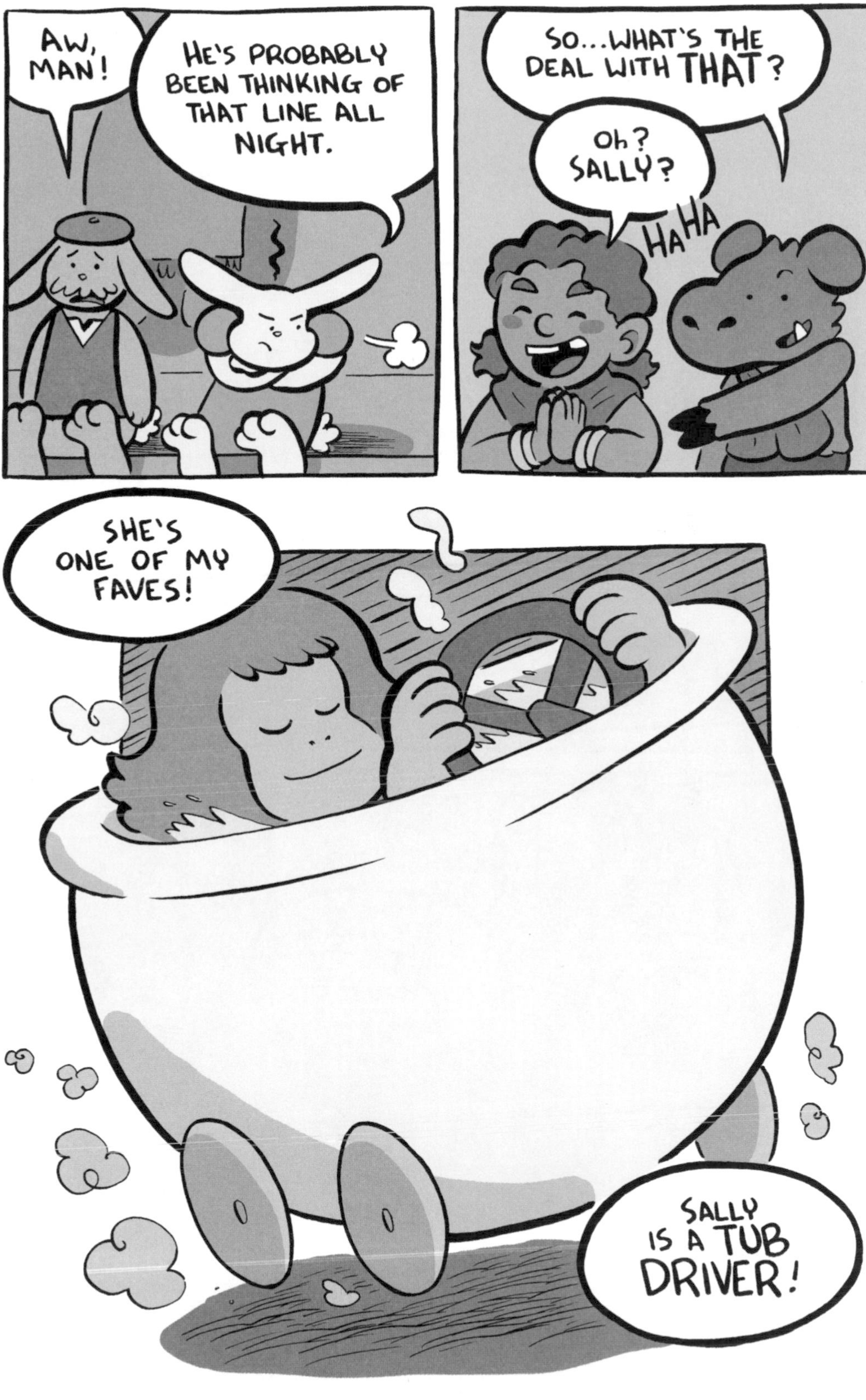
AW, MAN!
HE'S PROBABLY BEEN THINKING OF THAT LINE ALL NIGHT.
SO...WHAT'S THE DEAL WITH THAT?
Oh? SALLY?
HAHA
SHE'S ONE OF MY FAVES!
SALLY IS A TUB DRIVER!

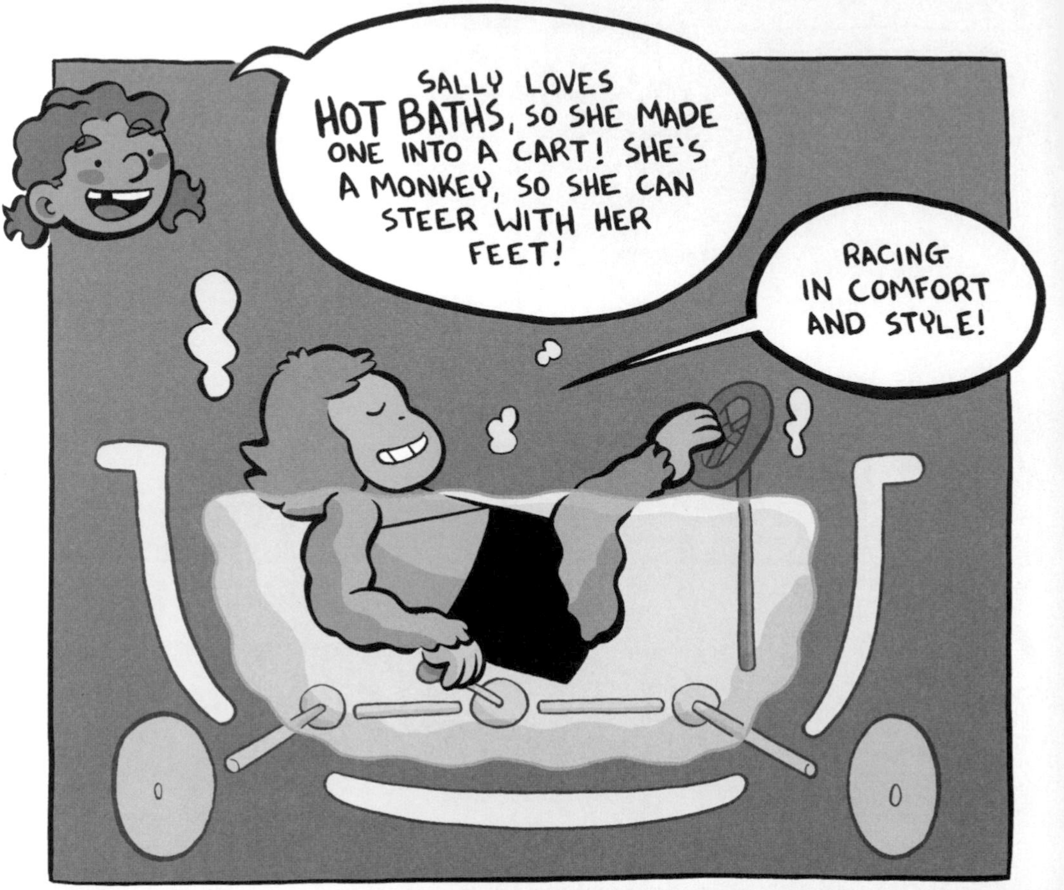
SALLY LOVES HOT BATHS, SO SHE MADE ONE INTO A CART! SHE'S A MONKEY, SO SHE CAN STEER WITH HER FEET!
RACING IN COMFORT AND STYLE!

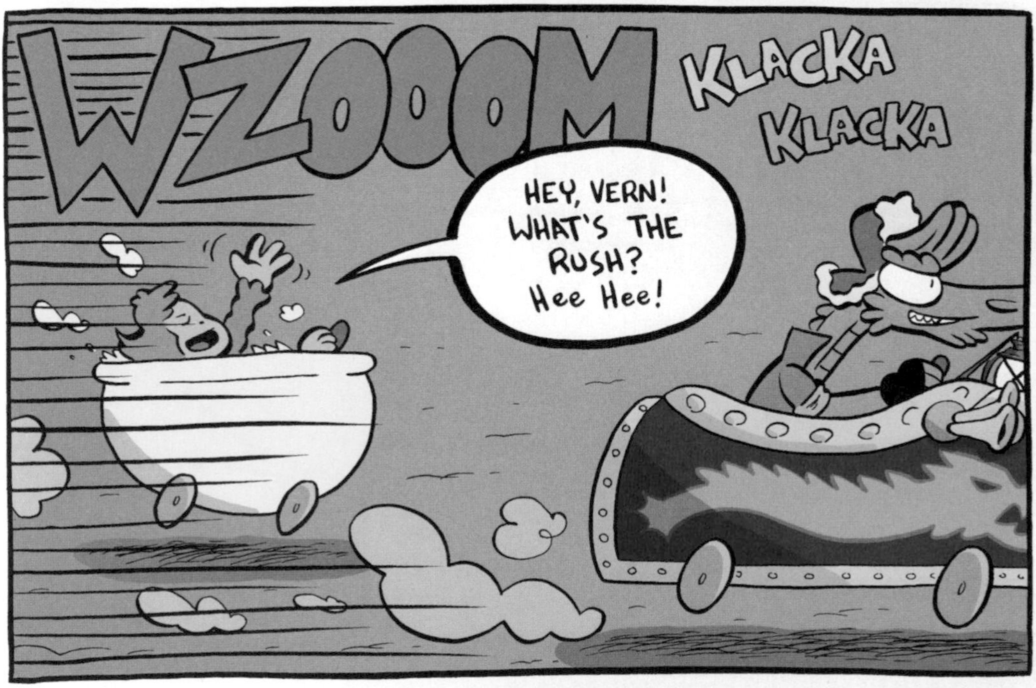
WZOOOM
KLACKA KLACKA
HEY, VERN! WHAT'S THE RUSH? Hee Hee!

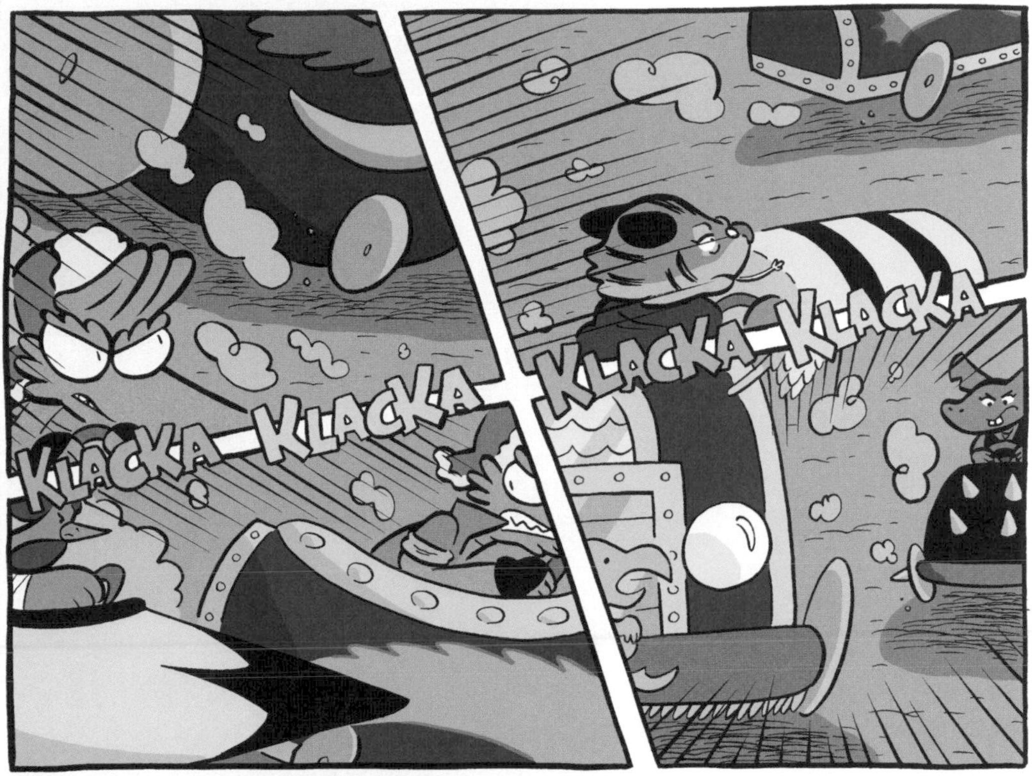
KLACKA KLACKA KLACKA KLACKA

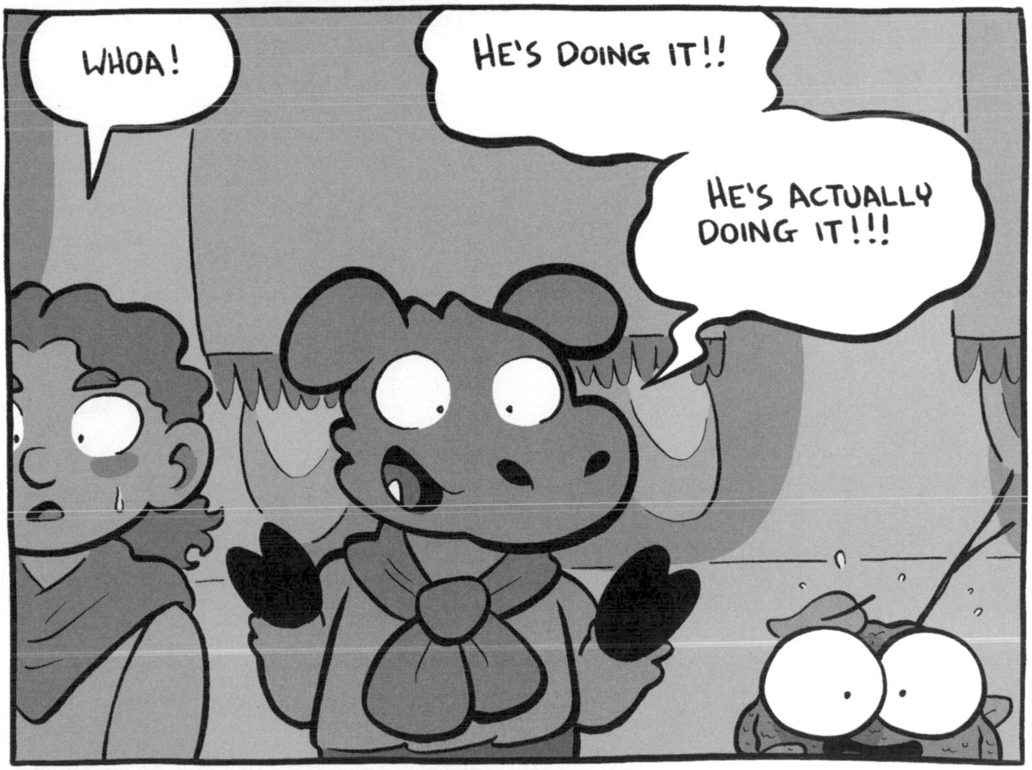
WHOA!
HE'S DOING IT!!
HE'S ACTUALLY DOING IT!!!

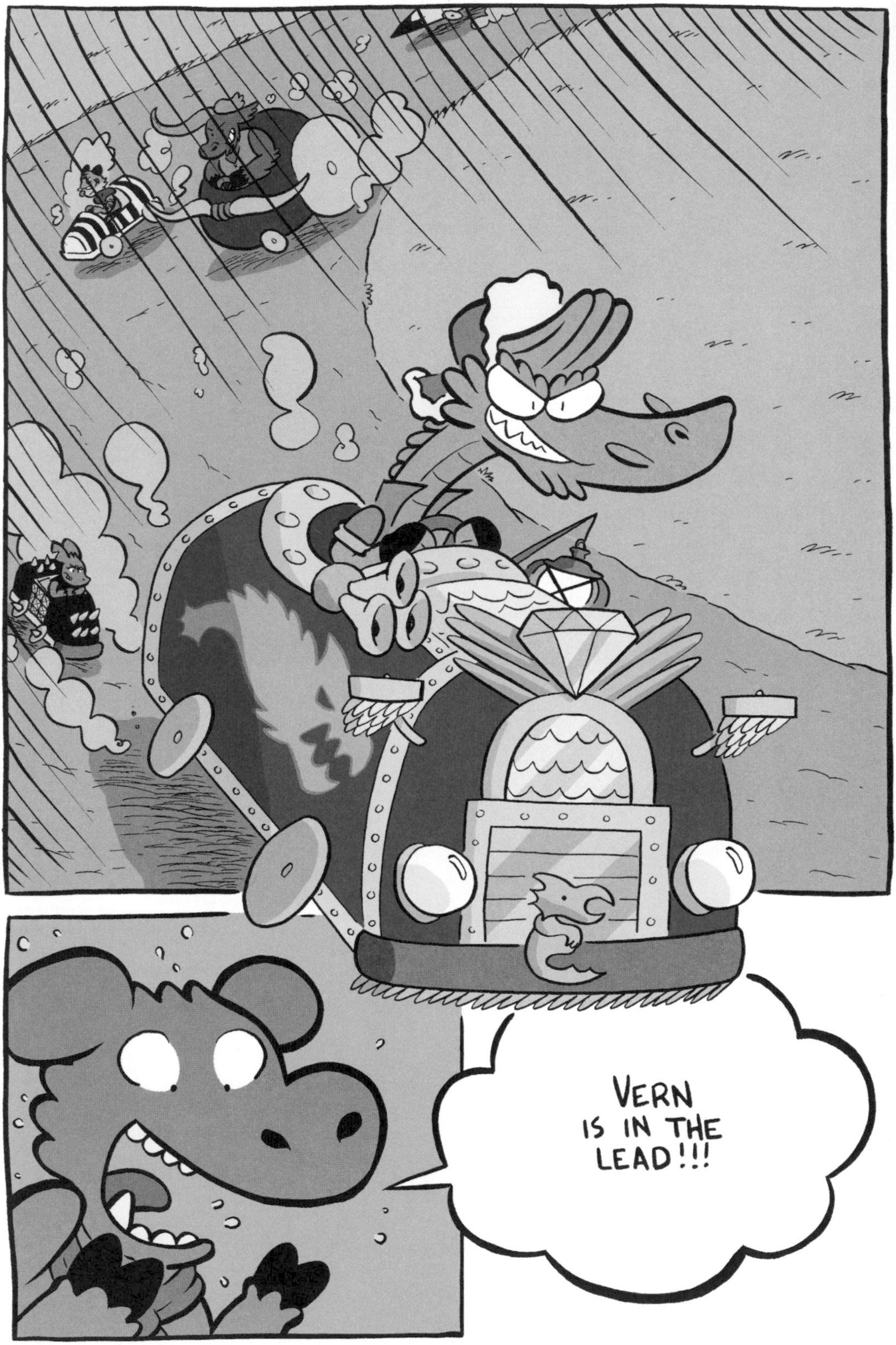
VERN IS IN THE LEAD!!!

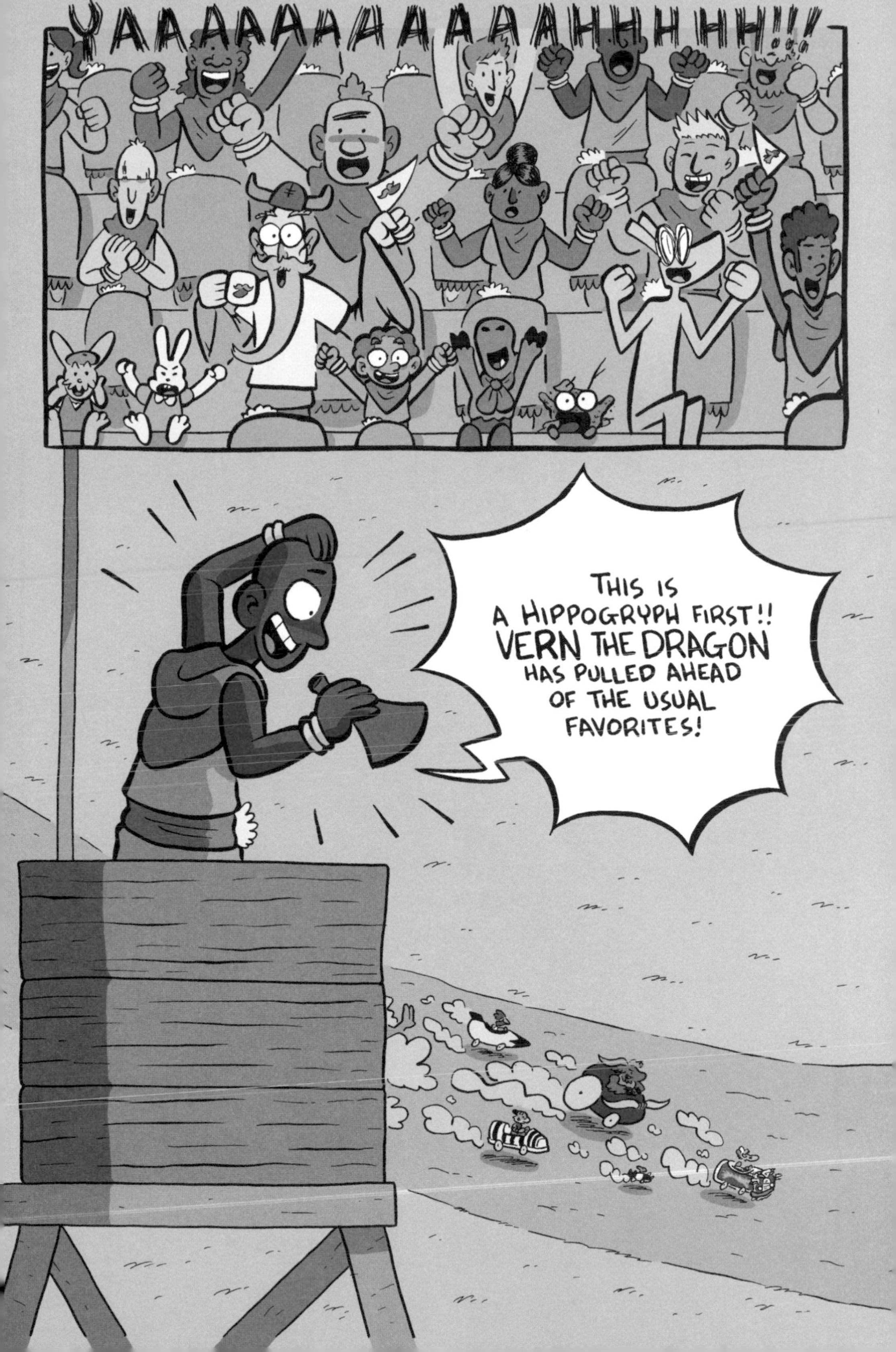
YAAAAAAAAAAAAHHHHHH!!!
THIS IS A HIPPOGRYPH FIRST!! VERN THE DRAGON HAS PULLED AHEAD OF THE USUAL FAVORITES!

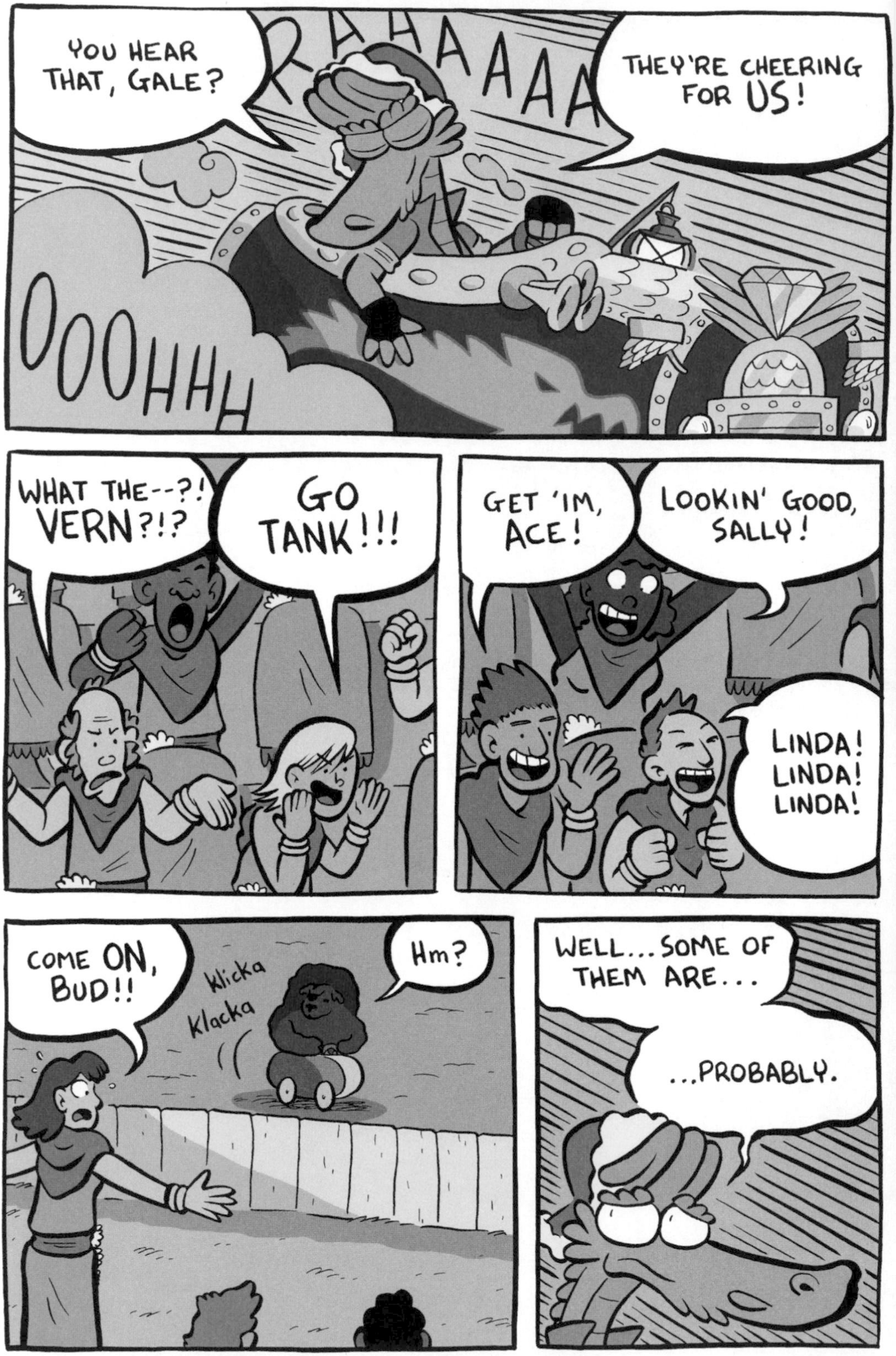
YOU HEAR THAT, GALE?
RAAAAAAA
THEY'RE CHEERING FOR US!
OOOHHHH
WHAT THE--?! VERN?!?
GO TANK!!!
GET 'IM, ACE!
LOOKIN' GOOD, SALLY!
LINDA! LINDA! LINDA!
COME ON, BUD!!
klicka
klacka
Hm?
WELL... SOME OF THEM ARE...
...PROBABLY.

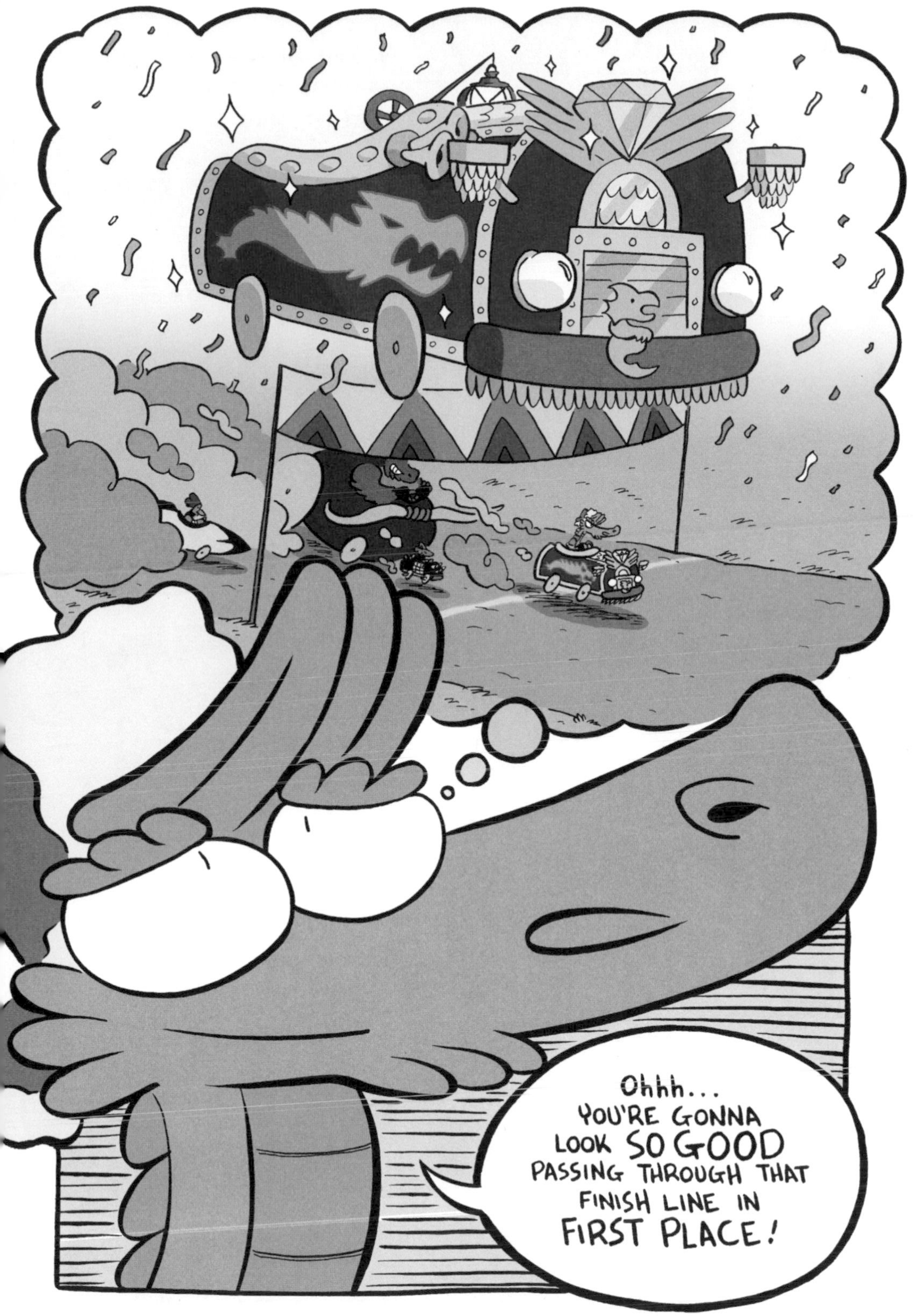
Ohhh... YOU'RE GONNA LOOK SO GOOD PASSING THROUGH THAT FINISH LINE IN FIRST PLACE!

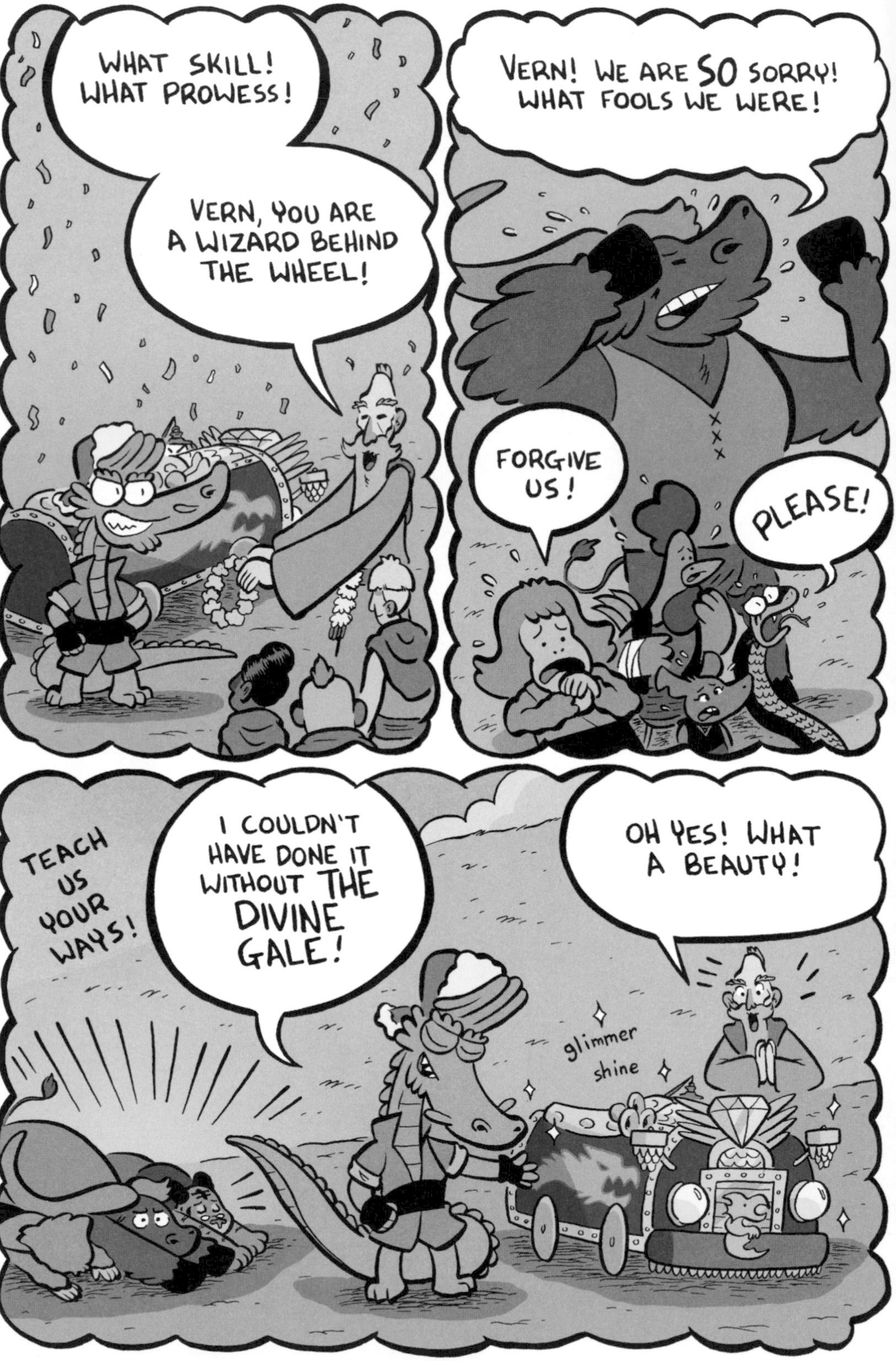
WHAT SKILL! WHAT PROWESS!
VERN, YOU ARE A WIZARD BEHIND THE WHEEL!
VERN! WE ARE SO SORRY! WHAT FOOLS WE WERE!
FORGIVE US!
PLEASE!
TEACH US YOUR WAYS!
I COULDN'T HAVE DONE IT WITHOUT THE DIVINE GALE!
OH YES! WHAT A BEAUTY!
glimmer
shine

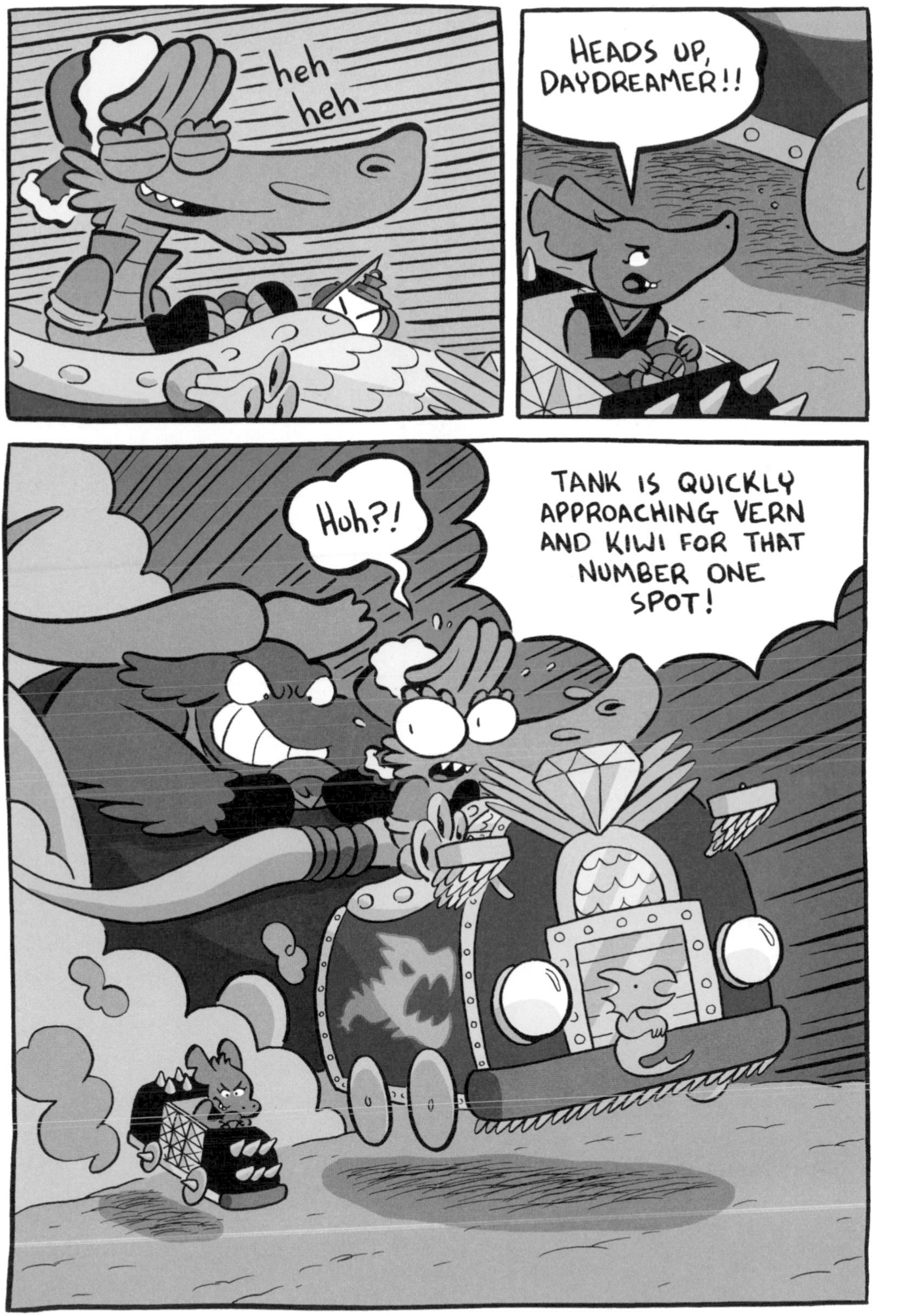
heh
heh
HEADS UP, DAYDREAMER!!
Huh?!
TANK IS QUICKLY APPROACHING VERN AND KIWI FOR THAT NUMBER ONE SPOT!

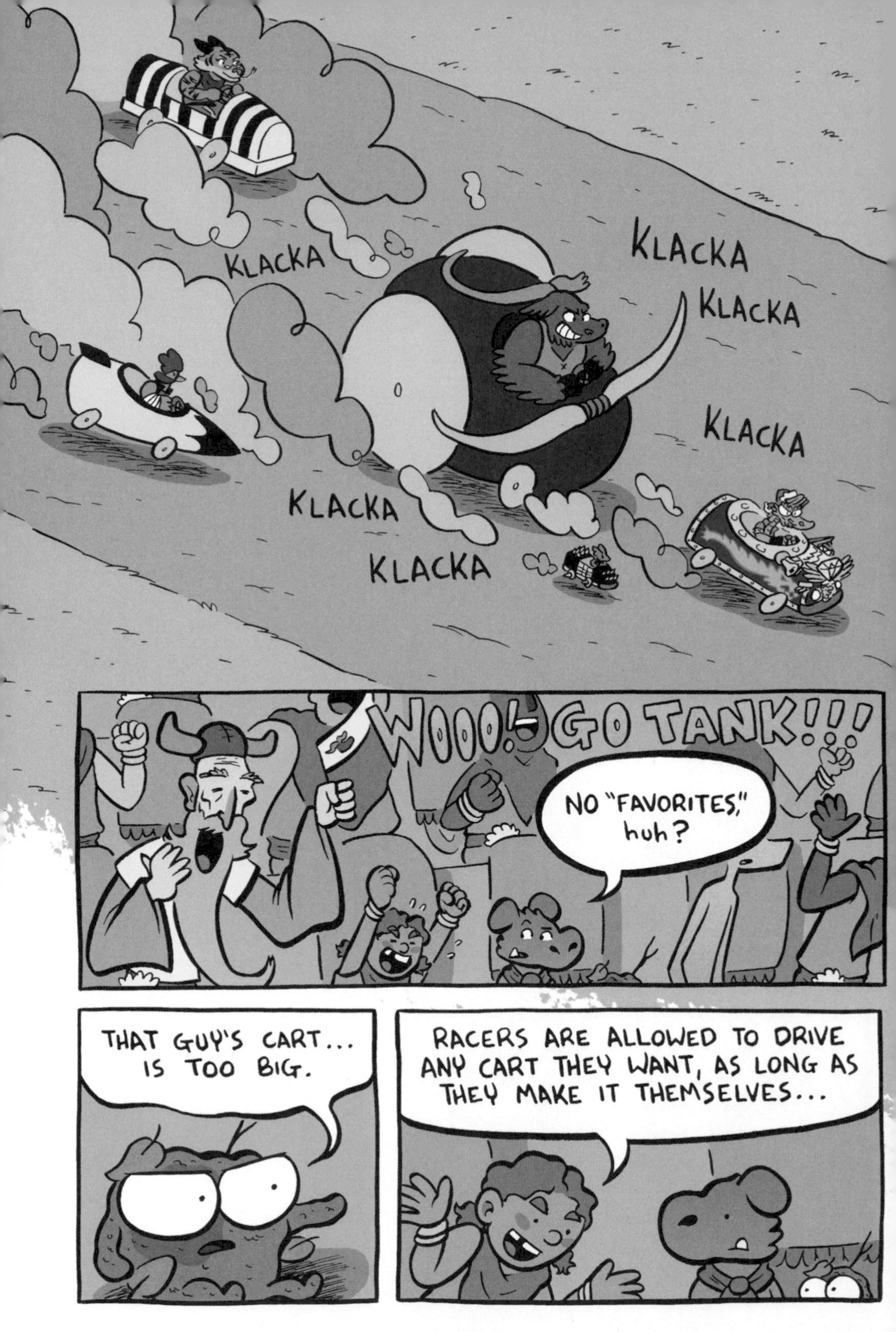

KLACKA
KLACKA
KLACKA
KLACKA
KLACKA
KLACKA
WOOO! GO TANK!!!
NO "FAVORITES," huh?
THAT GUY'S CART... IS TOO BIG.
RACERS ARE ALLOWED TO DRIVE ANY CART THEY WANT, AS LONG AS THEY MAKE IT THEMSELVES...

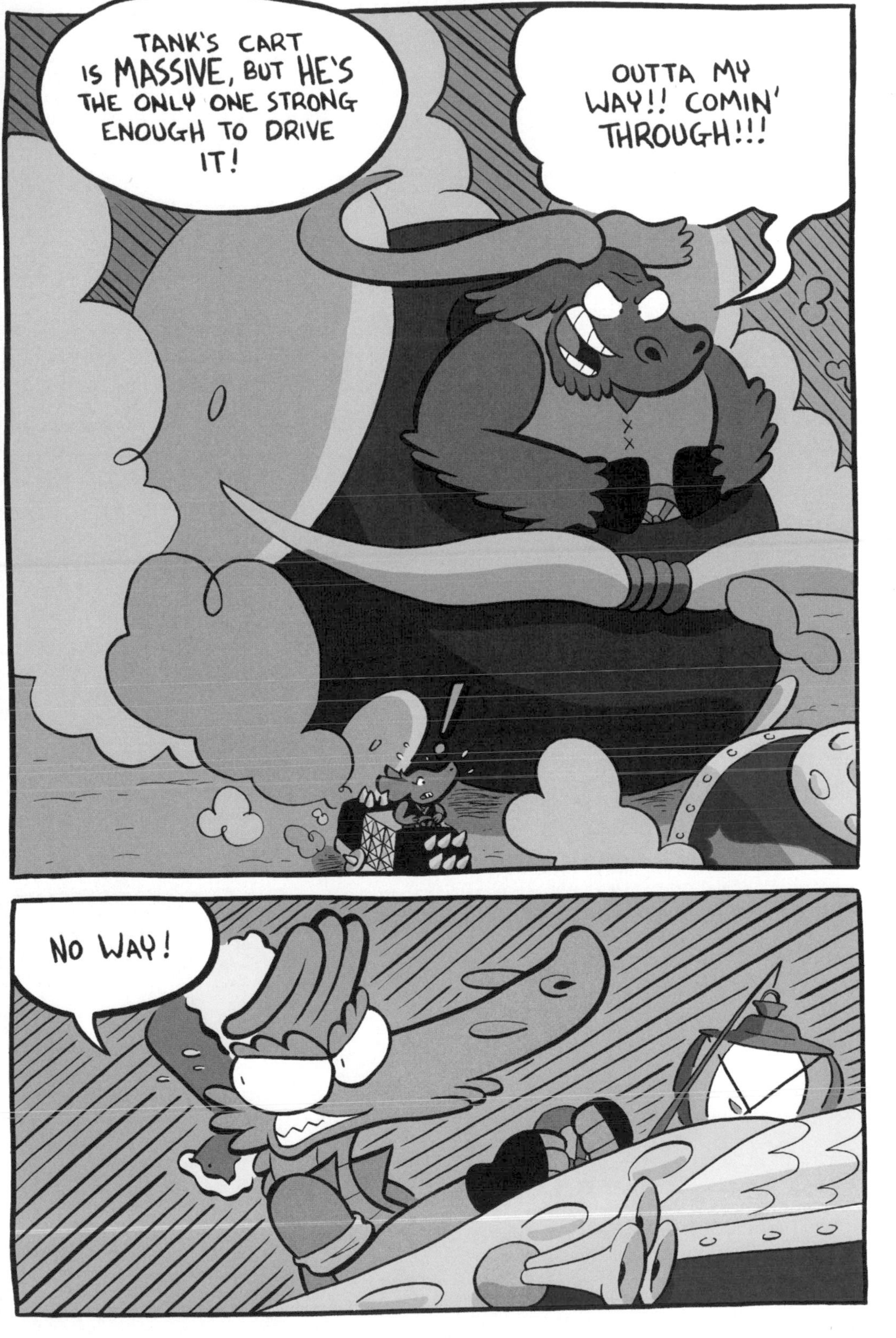
TANK'S CART IS MASSIVE, BUT HE'S THE ONLY ONE STRONG ENOUGH TO DRIVE IT!
OUTTA MY WAY!! COMIN' THROUGH!!!
!
NO WAY!

LISTEN, VERN!

IF YOU DON'T MOVE...

...I CAN'T GUARANTEE THE SAFETY OF YOUR LI'L WORK OF ART!

SIGH

SWERVE!

'ATTA BOY!

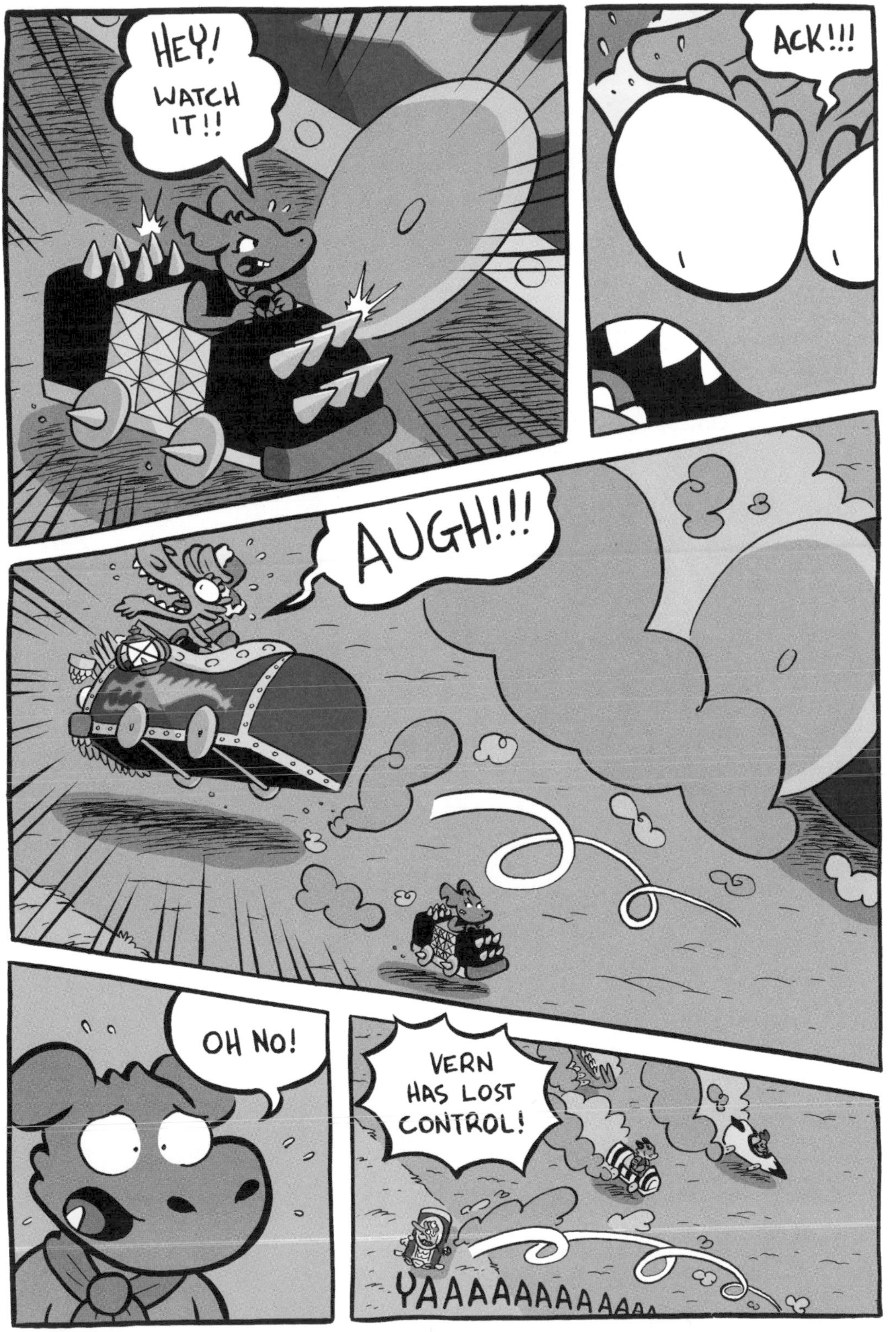
HEY! WATCH IT!!
ACK!!!
AUGH!!!
OH NO!
VERN HAS LOST CONTROL!
YAAAAAAAAAAA

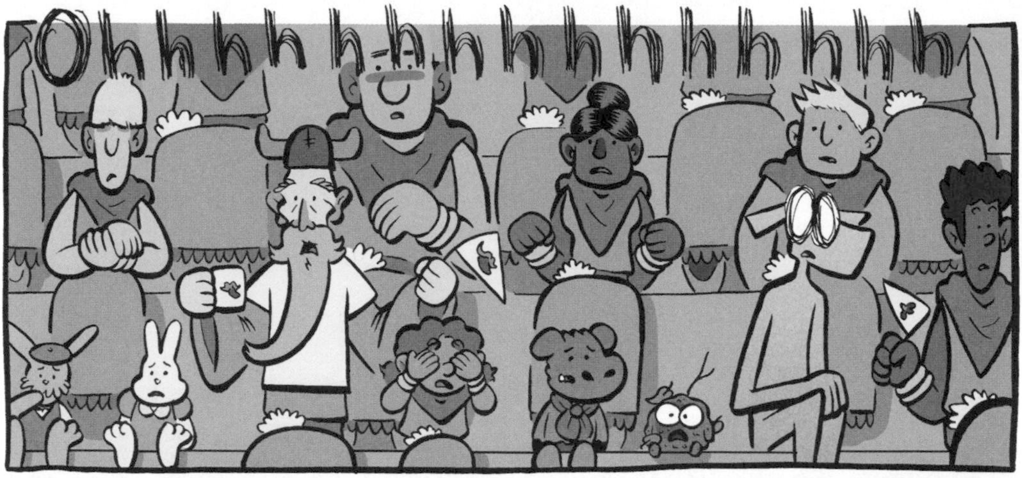
Ohhhhhhhhhhhhhhhh

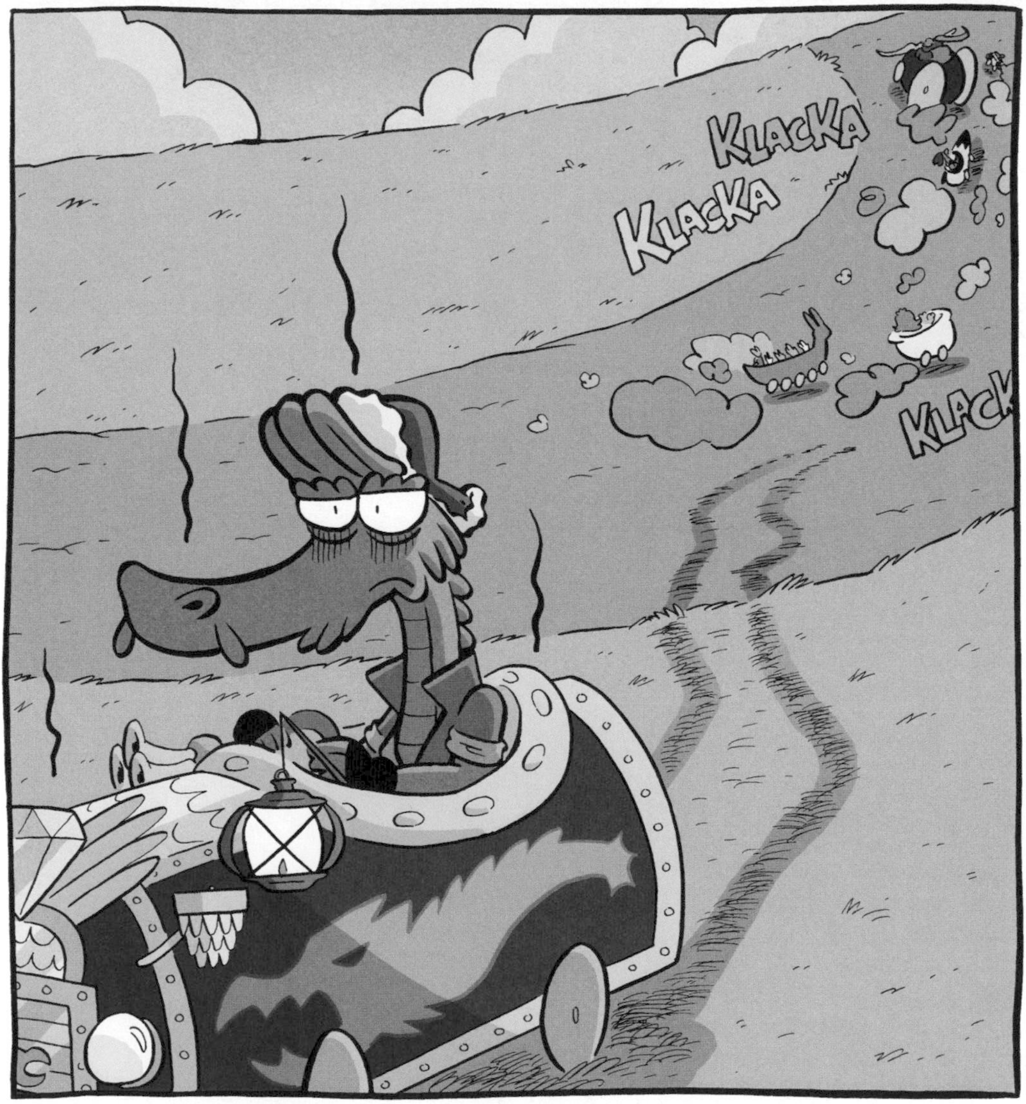
KLACKA
KLACKA
KLACK

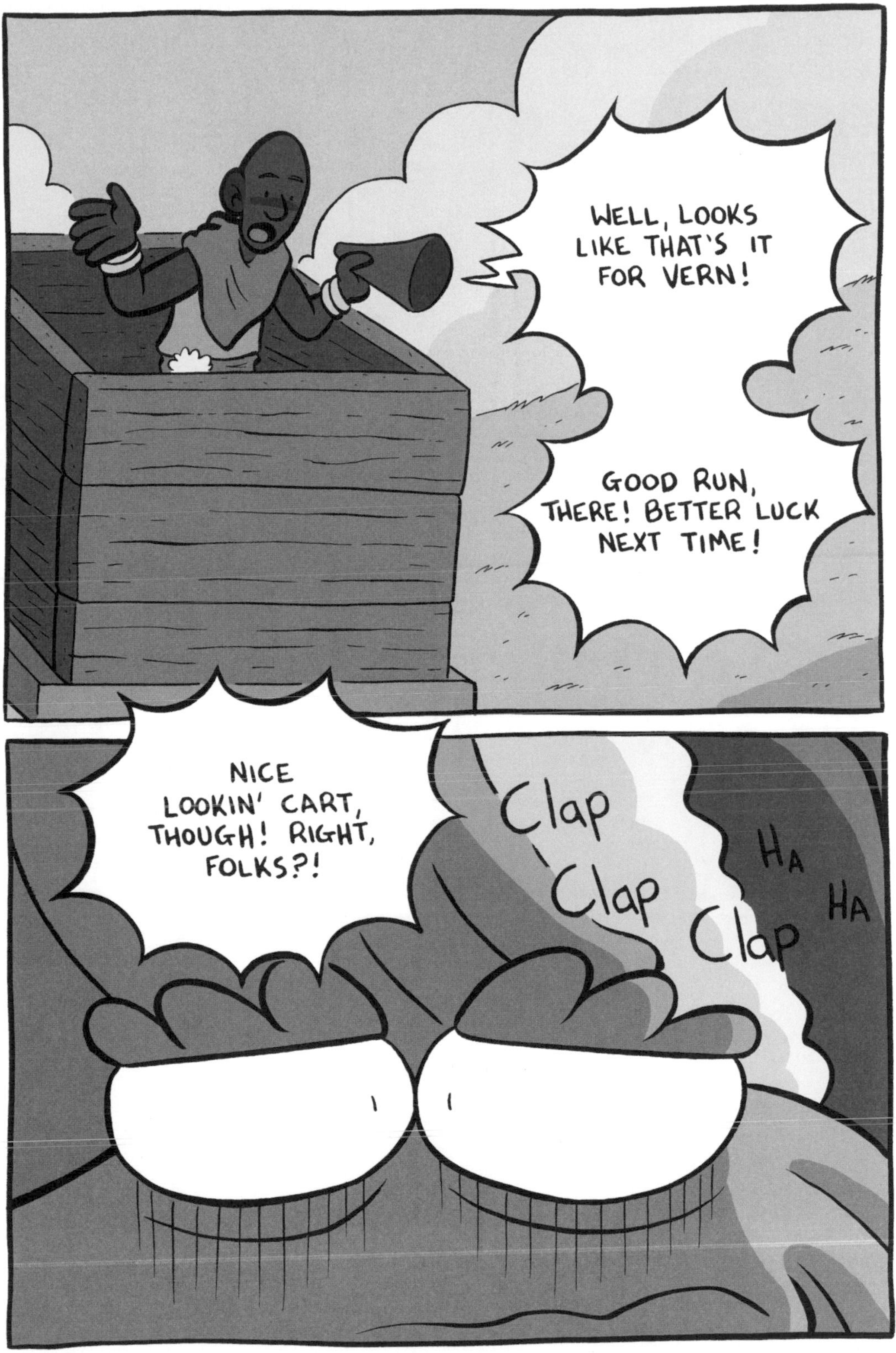
WELL, LOOKS LIKE THAT'S IT FOR VERN!
GOOD RUN, THERE! BETTER LUCK NEXT TIME!
NICE LOOKIN' CART, THOUGH! RIGHT, FOLKS?!
Clap
Clap
Clap
HA
HA

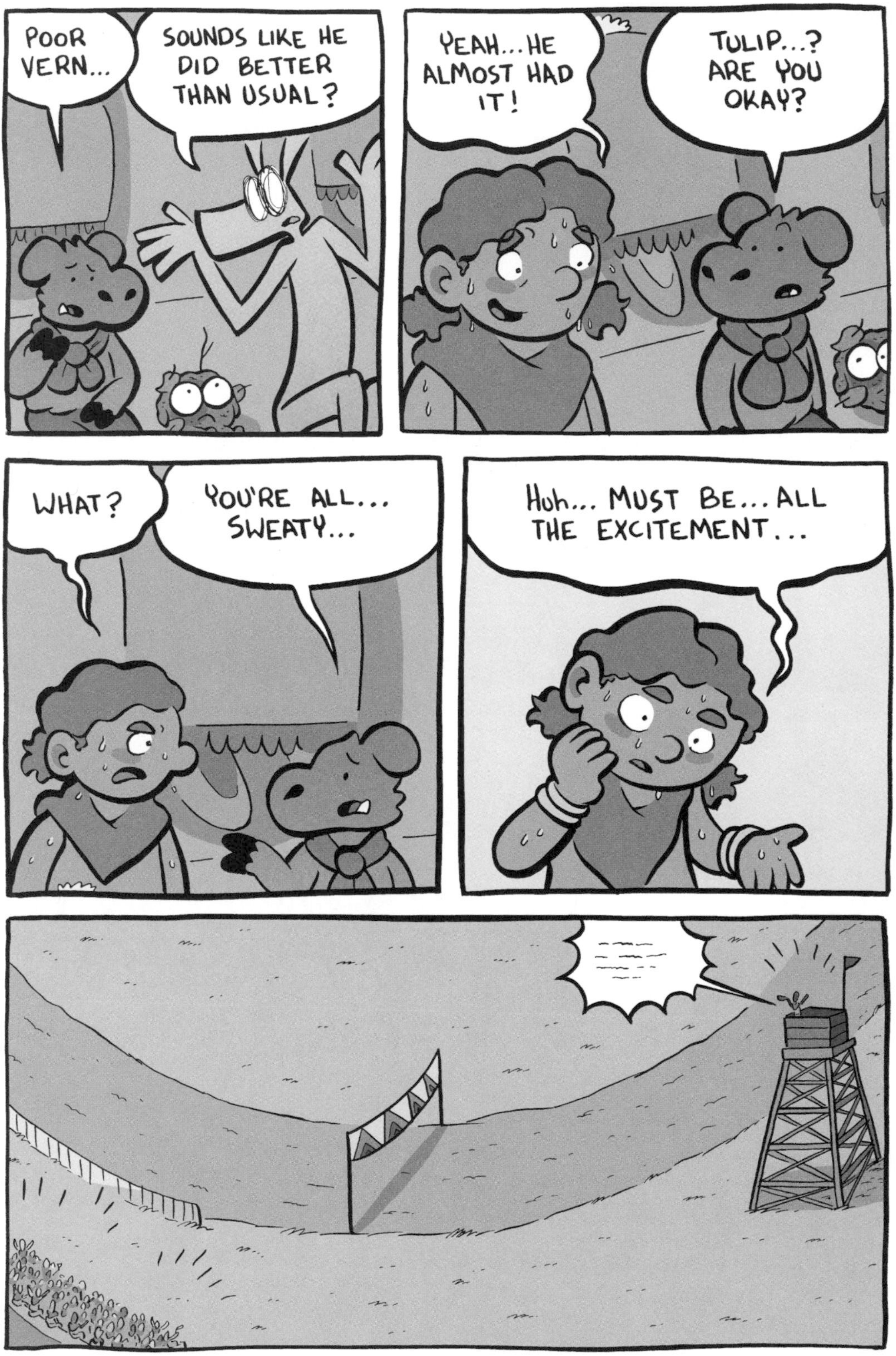
POOR VERN...
SOUNDS LIKE HE DID BETTER THAN USUAL?
YEAH... HE ALMOST HAD IT!
TULIP...? ARE YOU OKAY?
WHAT?
YOU'RE ALL... SWEATY...
Huh... MUST BE... ALL THE EXCITEMENT...

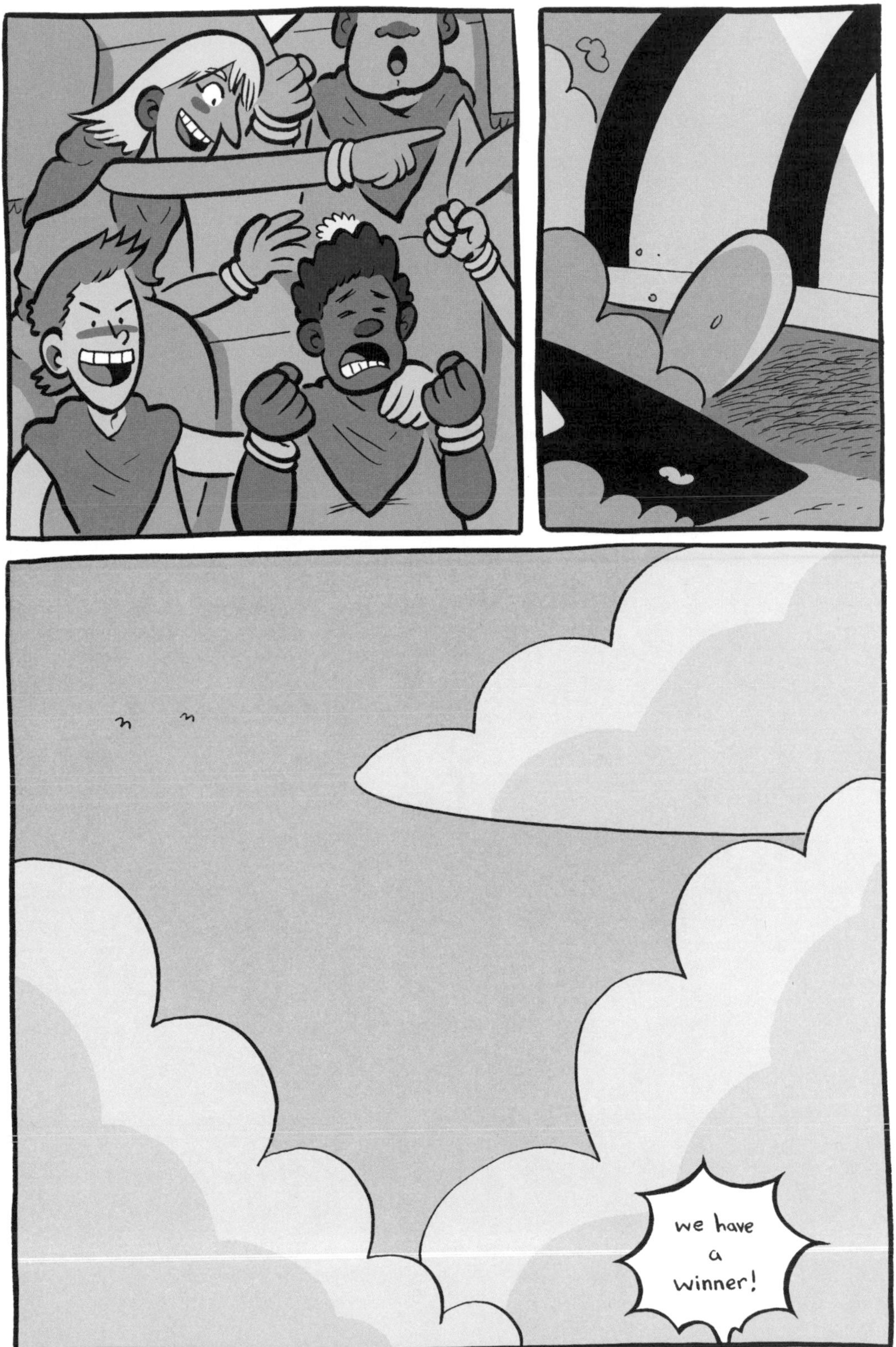
we have a winner!

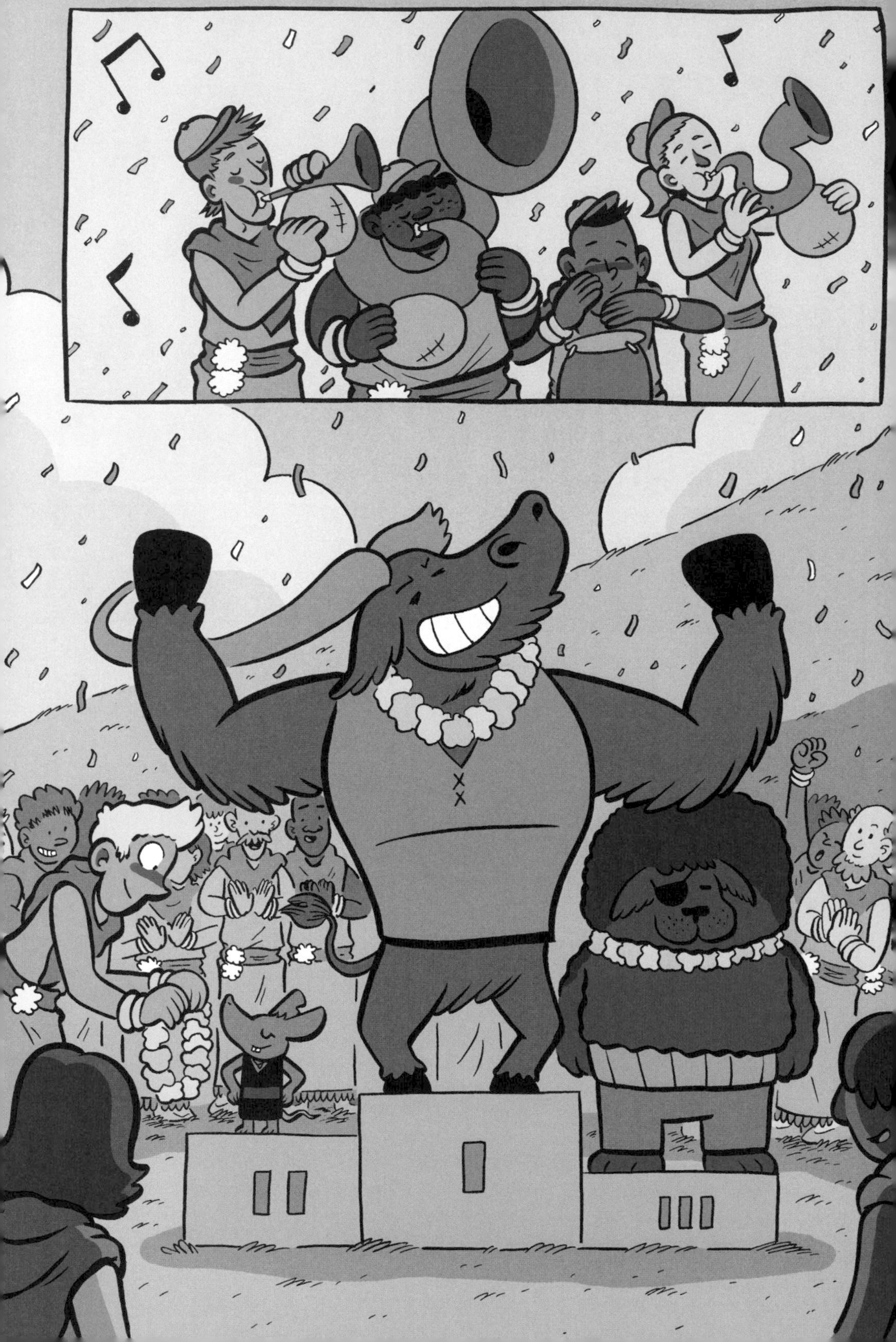

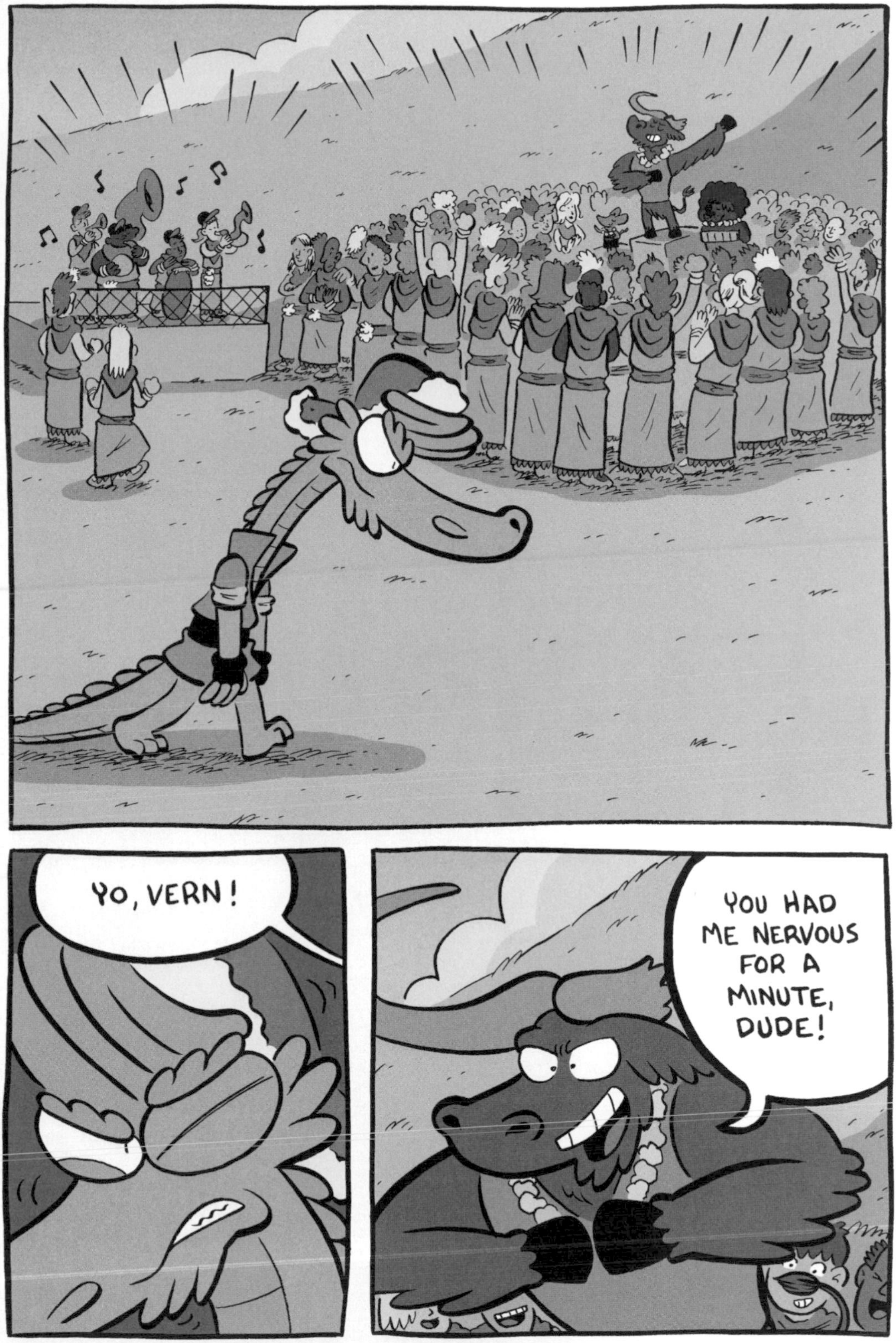
YO, VERN!
YOU HAD ME NERVOUS FOR A MINUTE, DUDE!

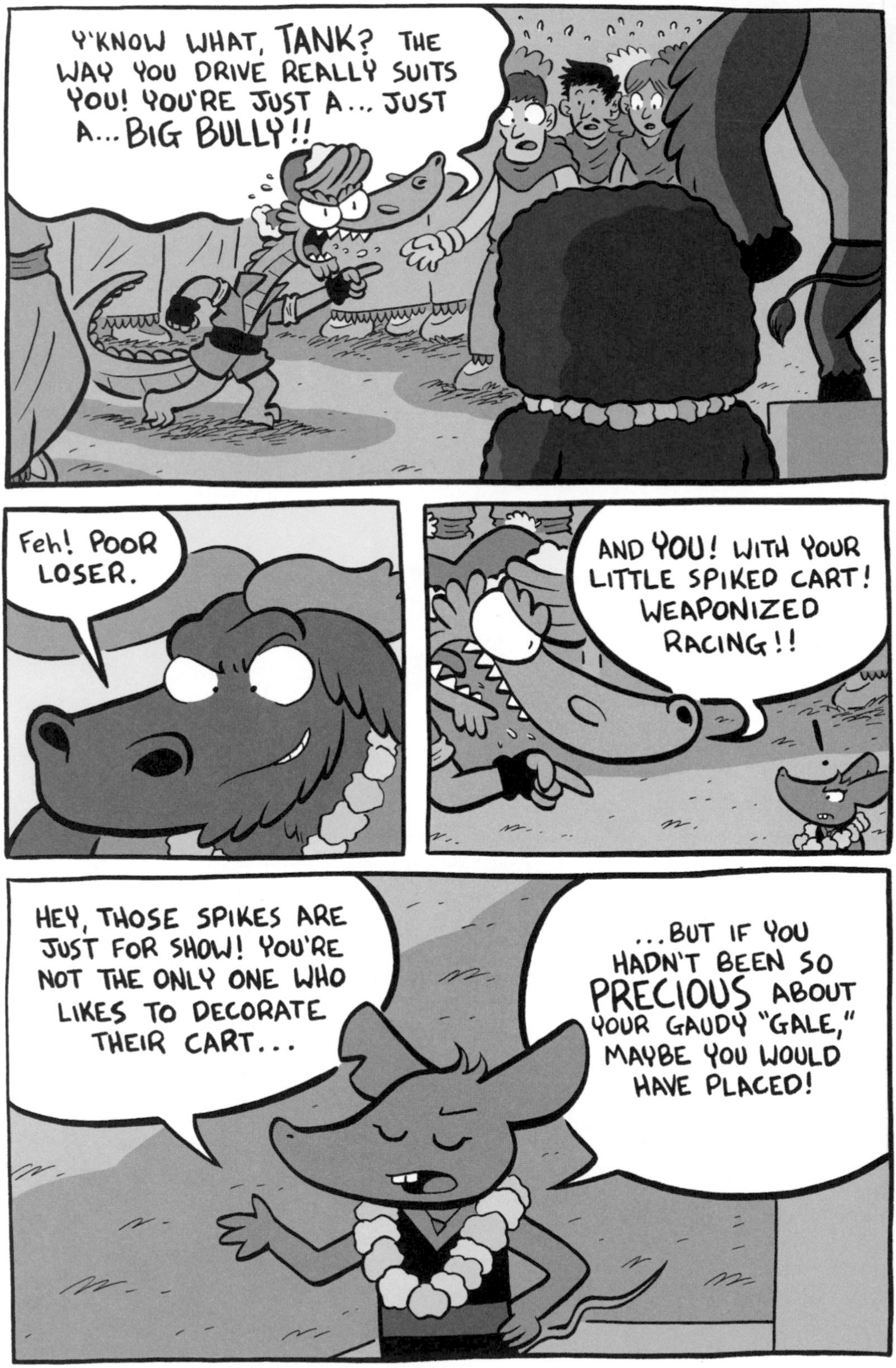

Y'KNOW WHAT, TANK? THE WAY YOU DRIVE REALLY SUITS YOU! YOU'RE JUST A... JUST A... BIG BULLY!!
Feh! POOR LOSER.
AND YOU! WITH YOUR LITTLE SPIKED CART! WEAPONIZED RACING!!
!
HEY, THOSE SPIKES ARE JUST FOR SHOW! YOU'RE NOT THE ONLY ONE WHO LIKES TO DECORATE THEIR CART...
...BUT IF YOU HADN'T BEEN SO PRECIOUS ABOUT YOUR GAUDY "GALE," MAYBE YOU WOULD HAVE PLACED!

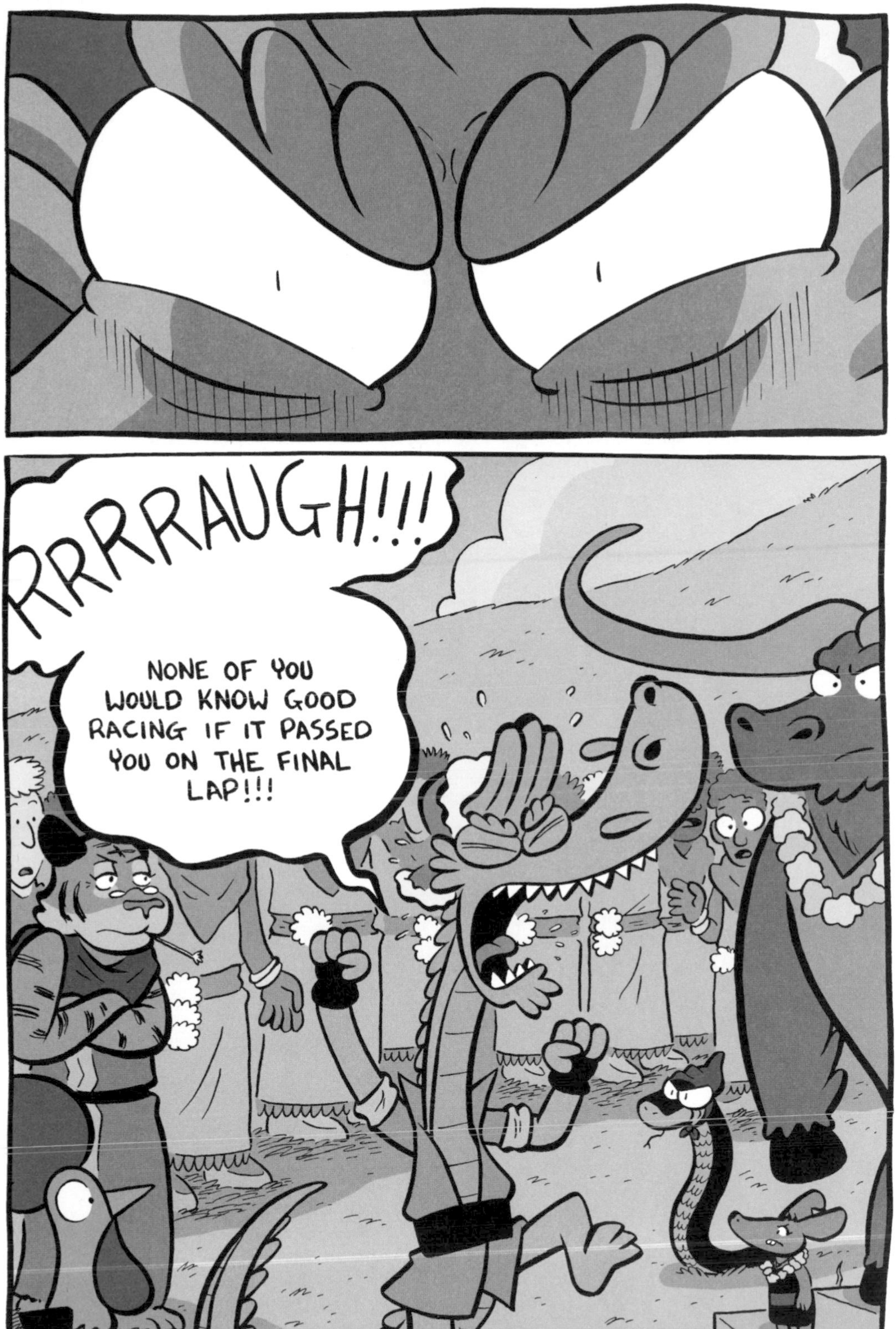
RRRRAUGH!!!
NONE OF YOU WOULD KNOW GOOD RACING IF IT PASSED YOU ON THE FINAL LAP!!!

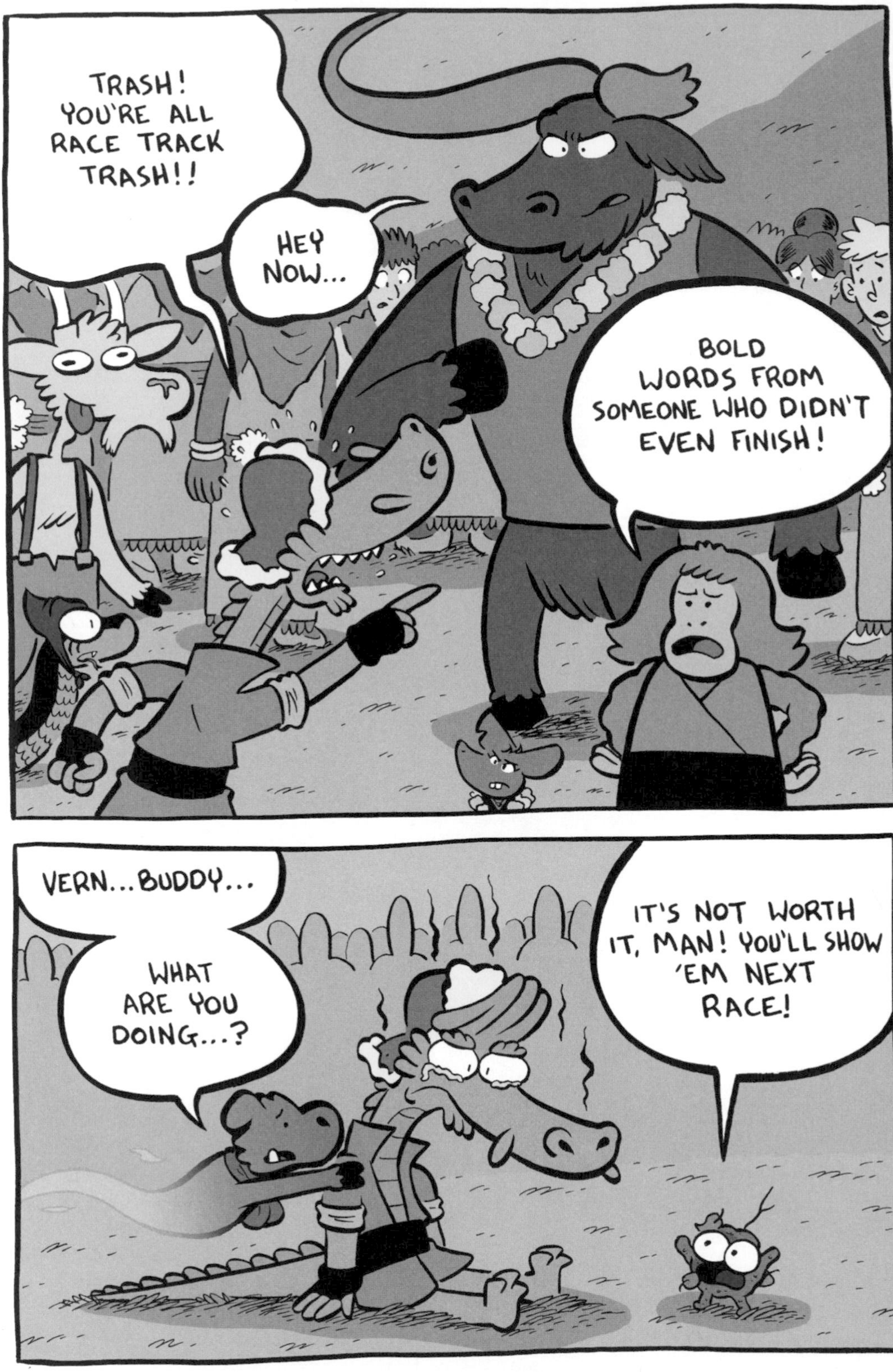
TRASH! YOU'RE ALL RACE TRACK TRASH!!
HEY NOW...
BOLD WORDS FROM SOMEONE WHO DIDN'T EVEN FINISH!
VERN...BUDDY...
WHAT ARE YOU DOING...?
IT'S NOT WORTH IT, MAN! YOU'LL SHOW 'EM NEXT RACE!

VERN, THIS OUTBURST IS NOT THE KIND OF SPORTSMANSHIP THAT ELDER GUST PRACTICED.

I...I'M SORRY, ELDER KNOTT. I JUST--

SIGH...I DON'T KNOW...

...MAYBE I'M NOT CUT OUT TO BE A GREAT RACER AFTER ALL...

GASP!

WHAT HAPPENED?

IS SHE ALRIGHT??

Huh?

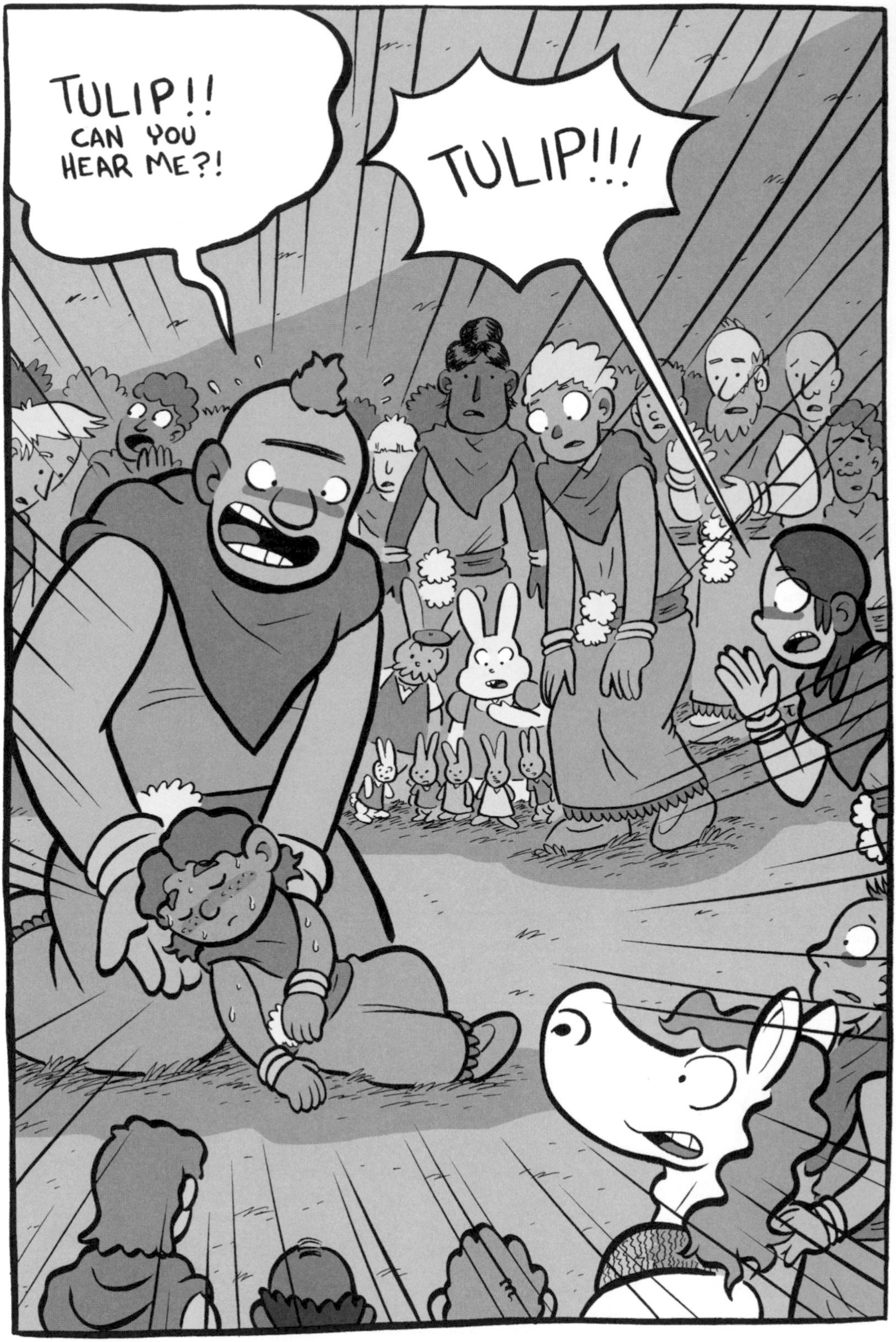
TULIP!! CAN YOU HEAR ME?!
TULIP!!!

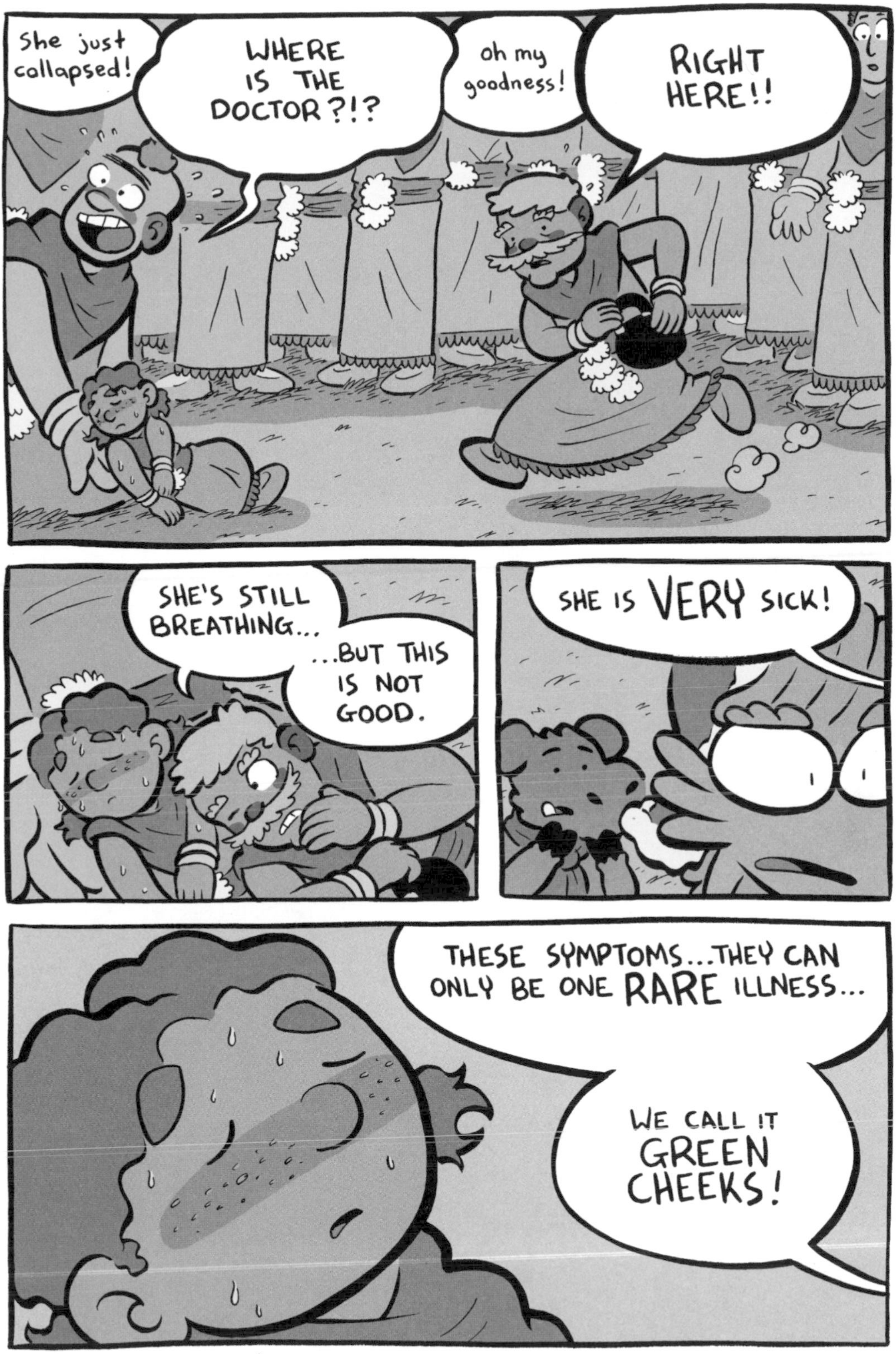
She just collapsed!
WHERE IS THE DOCTOR?!?
oh my goodness!
RIGHT HERE!!
SHE'S STILL BREATHING...
...BUT THIS IS NOT GOOD.
SHE IS VERY SICK!
THESE SYMPTOMS...THEY CAN ONLY BE ONE RARE ILLNESS...
WE CALL IT GREEN CHEEKS!

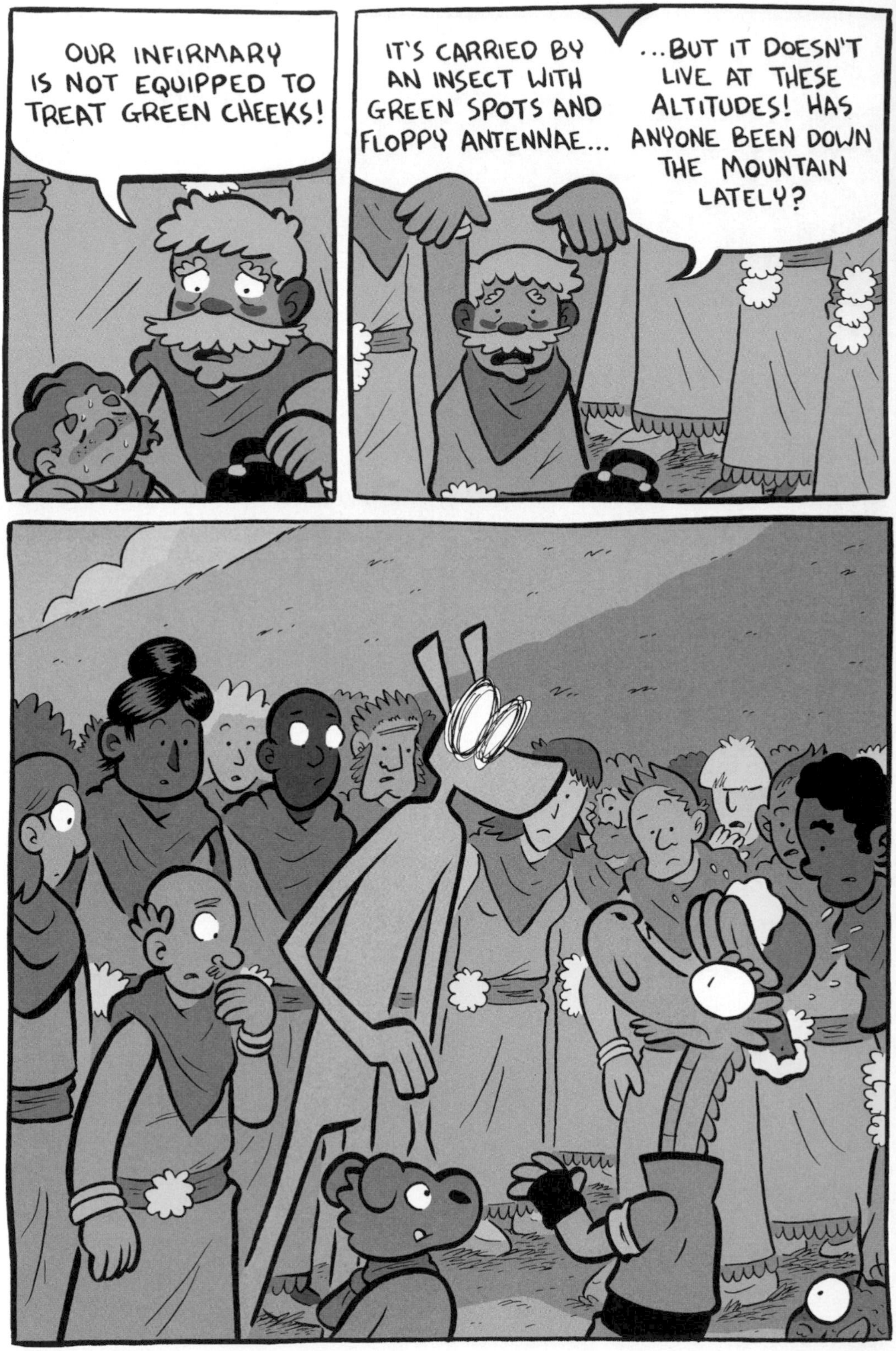
OUR INFIRMARY IS NOT EQUIPPED TO TREAT GREEN CHEEKS!
IT'S CARRIED BY AN INSECT WITH GREEN SPOTS AND FLOPPY ANTENNAE...
...BUT IT DOESN'T LIVE AT THESE ALTITUDES! HAS ANYONE BEEN DOWN THE MOUNTAIN LATELY?

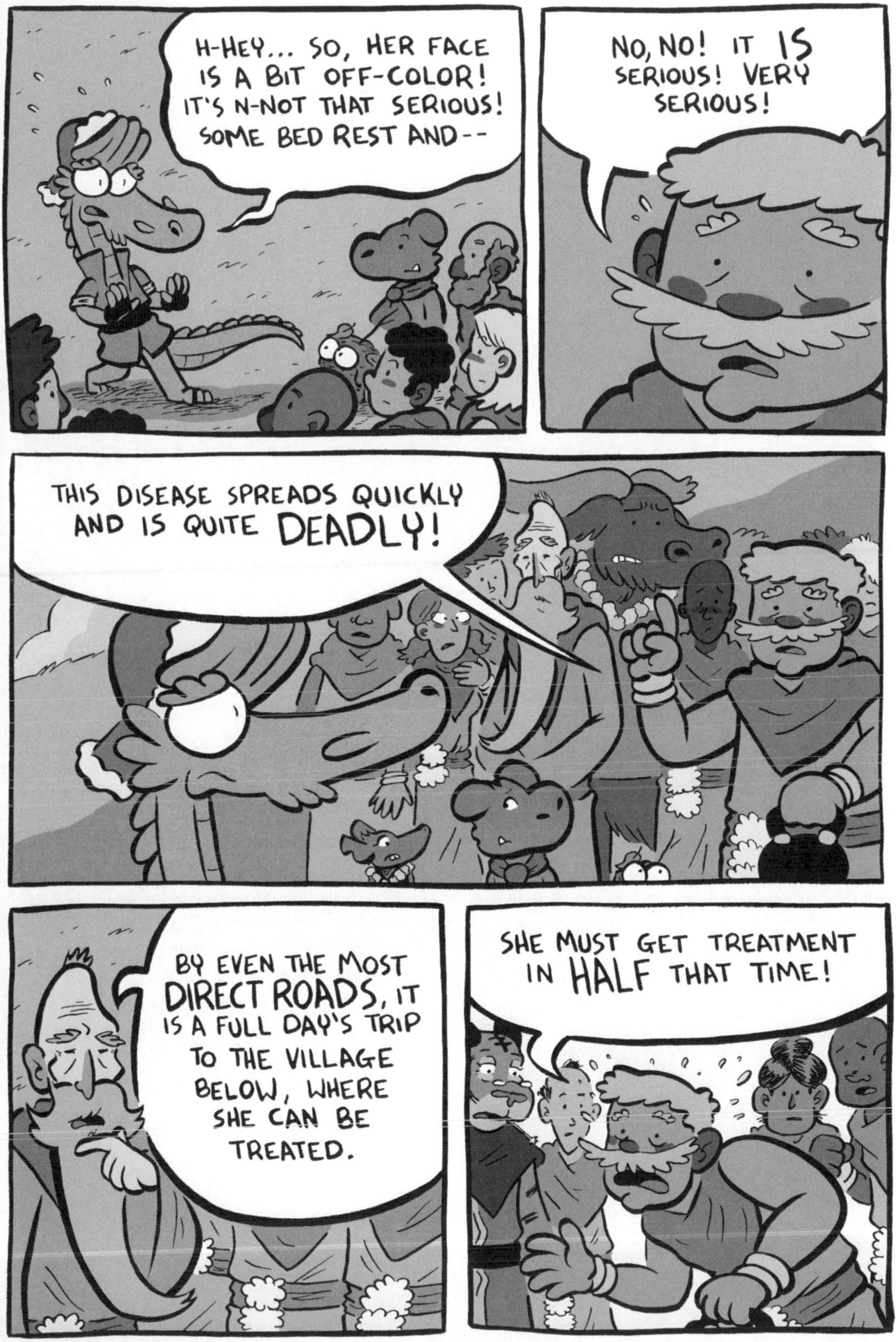
H-HEY... SO, HER FACE IS A BIT OFF-COLOR! IT'S N-NOT THAT SERIOUS! SOME BED REST AND--
NO, NO! IT IS SERIOUS! VERY SERIOUS!
THIS DISEASE SPREADS QUICKLY AND IS QUITE DEADLY!
BY EVEN THE MOST DIRECT ROADS, IT IS A FULL DAY'S TRIP TO THE VILLAGE BELOW, WHERE SHE CAN BE TREATED.
SHE MUST GET TREATMENT IN HALF THAT TIME!

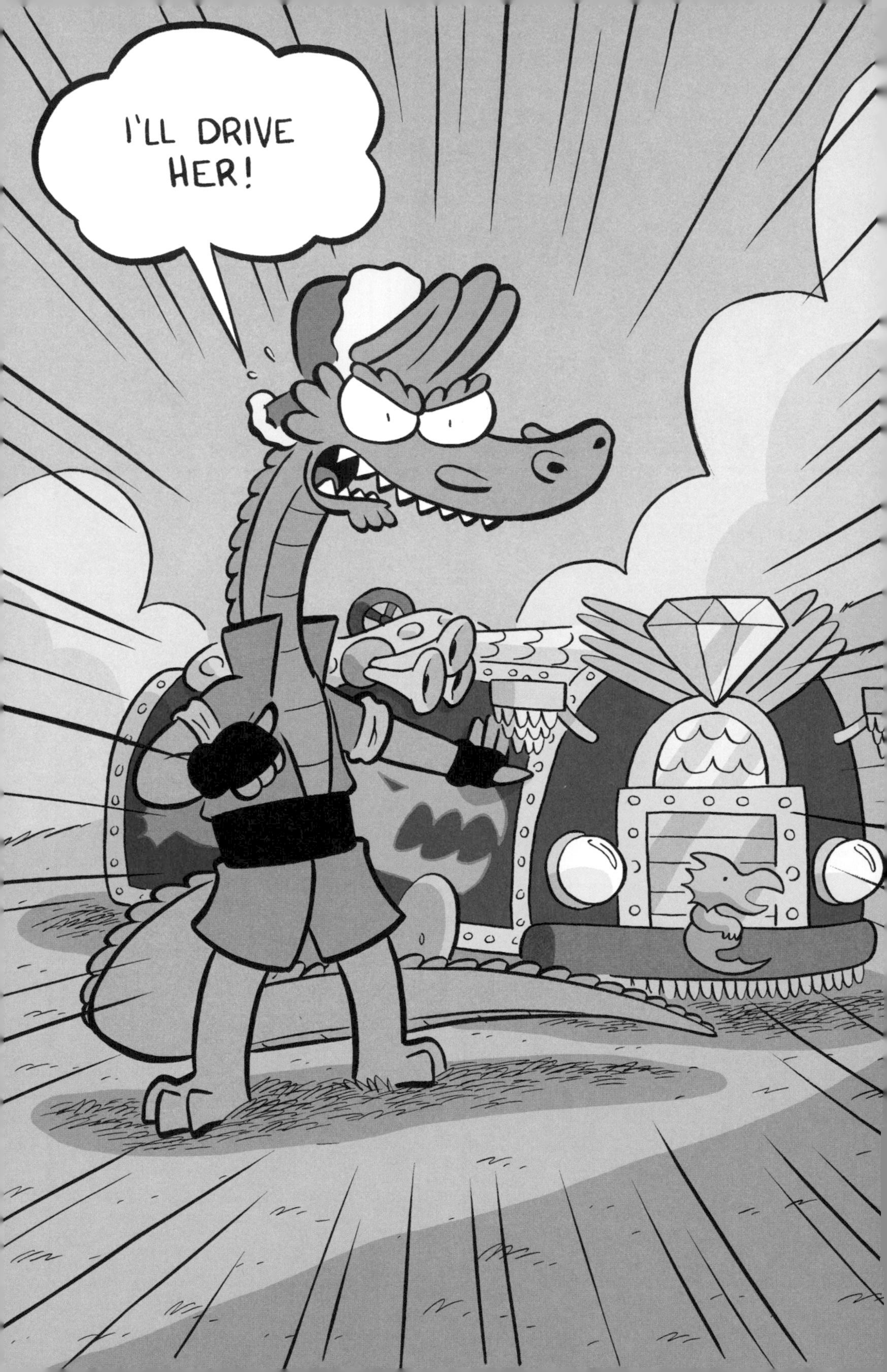
I'LL DRIVE HER!

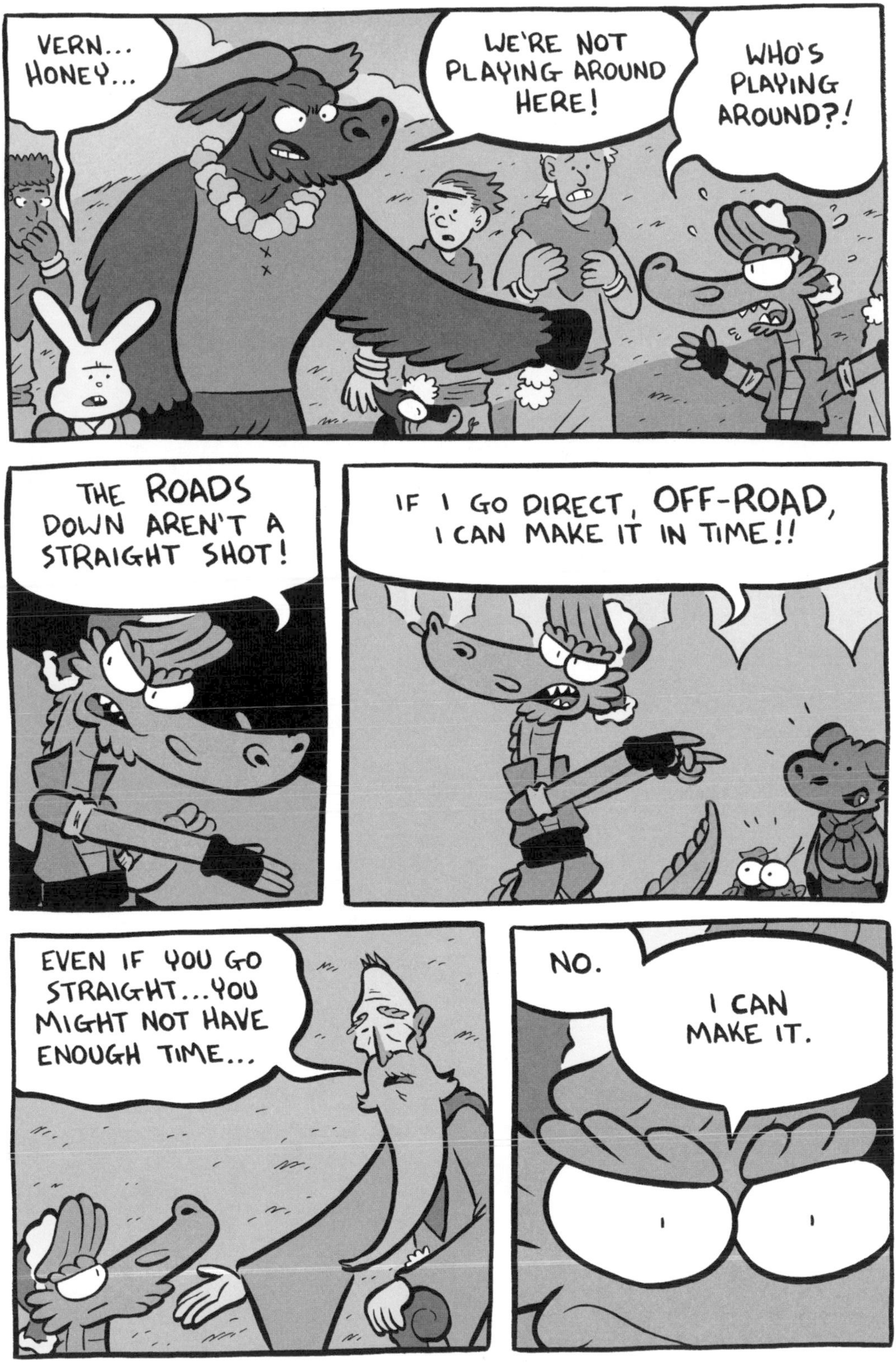
VERN... HONEY...
WE'RE NOT PLAYING AROUND HERE!
WHO'S PLAYING AROUND?!
THE ROADS DOWN AREN'T A STRAIGHT SHOT!
IF I GO DIRECT, OFF-ROAD, I CAN MAKE IT IN TIME!!
EVEN IF YOU GO STRAIGHT...YOU MIGHT NOT HAVE ENOUGH TIME...
NO.
I CAN MAKE IT.

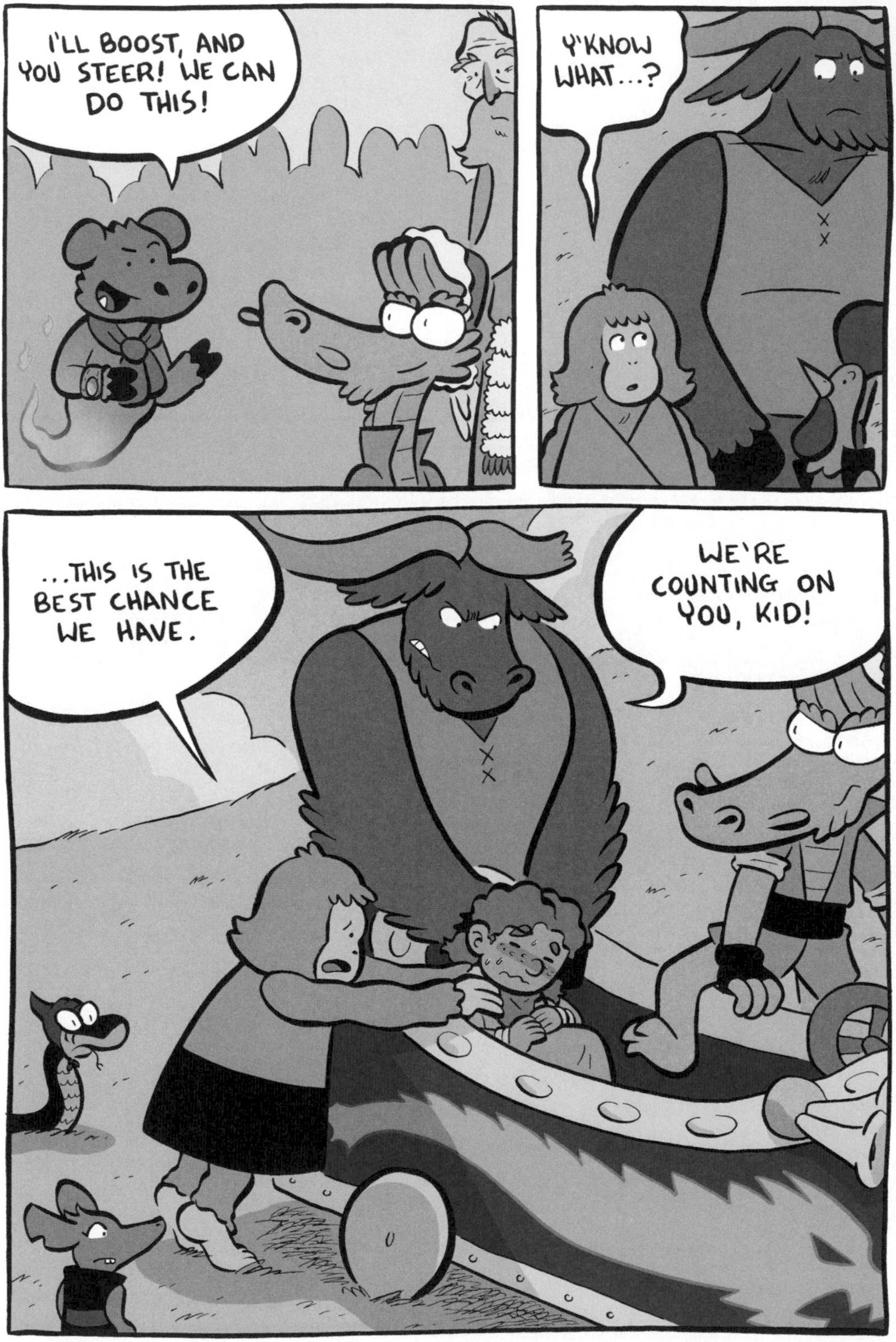
I'LL BOOST, AND YOU STEER! WE CAN DO THIS!
Y'KNOW WHAT...?
...THIS IS THE BEST CHANCE WE HAVE.
WE'RE COUNTING ON YOU, KID!

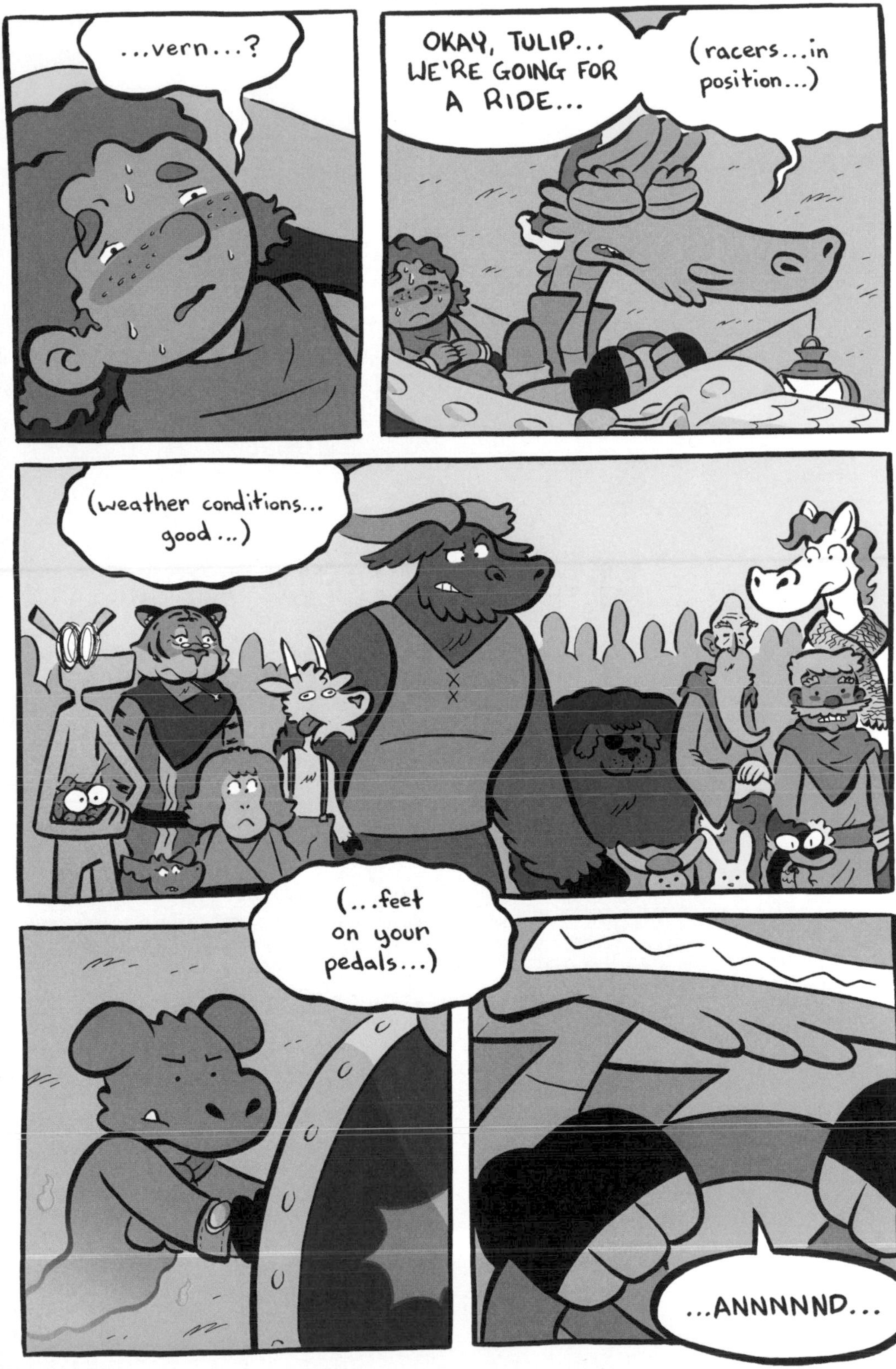
...vern...?
OKAY, TULIP... WE'RE GOING FOR A RIDE...
(racers...in position...)
(weather conditions... good...)
(...feet on your pedals...)
...ANNNNND...

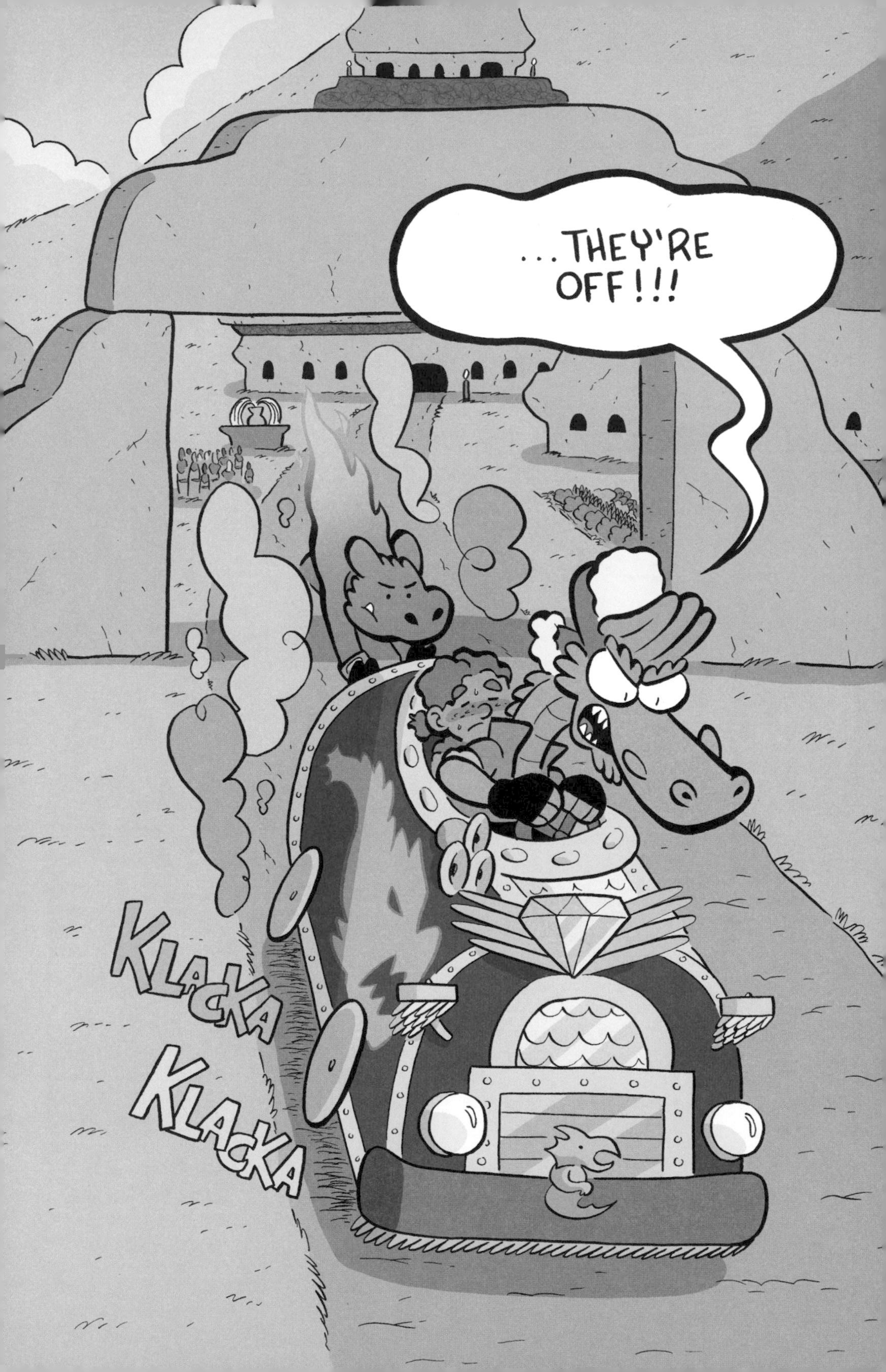
...THEY'RE OFF!!!
KLACKA
KLACKA

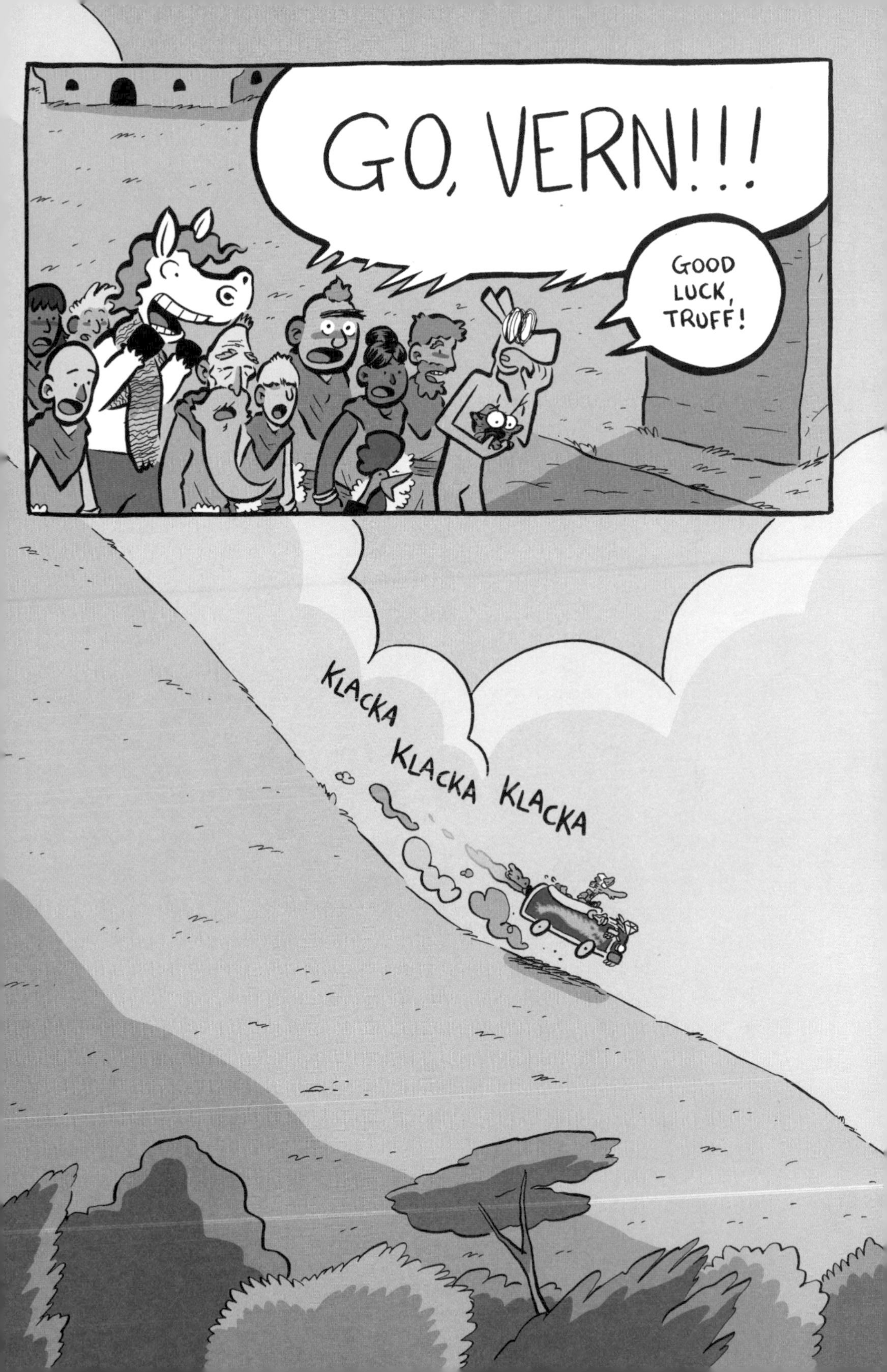
GO, VERN!!!
GOOD LUCK, TRUFF!
KLACKA
KLACKA KLACKA
KLACKA

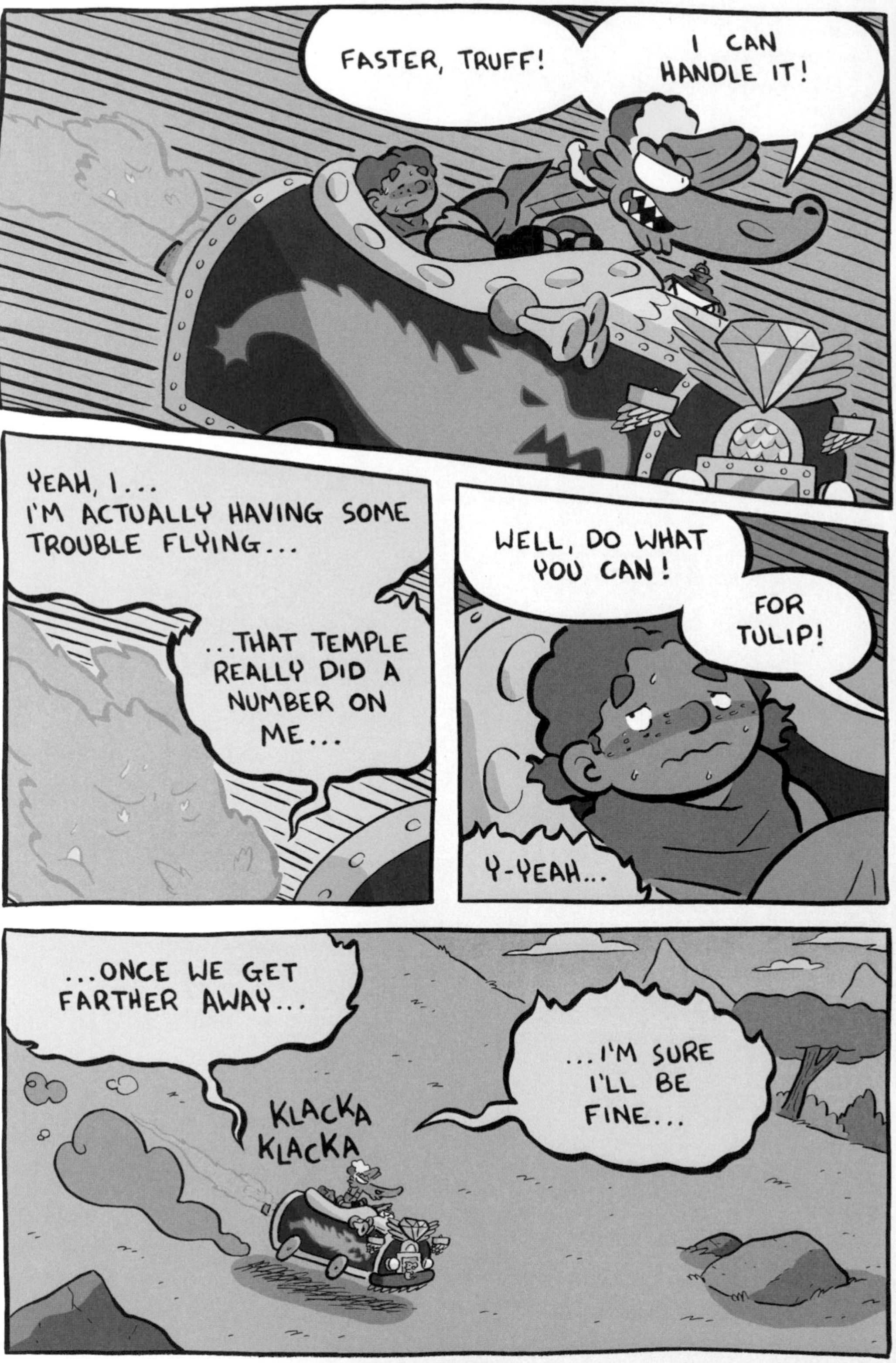
FASTER, TRUFF!
I CAN HANDLE IT!
YEAH, I... I'M ACTUALLY HAVING SOME TROUBLE FLYING...
...THAT TEMPLE REALLY DID A NUMBER ON ME...
WELL, DO WHAT YOU CAN!
FOR TULIP!
Y-YEAH...
...ONCE WE GET FARTHER AWAY...
KLACKA KLACKA
...I'M SURE I'LL BE FINE...

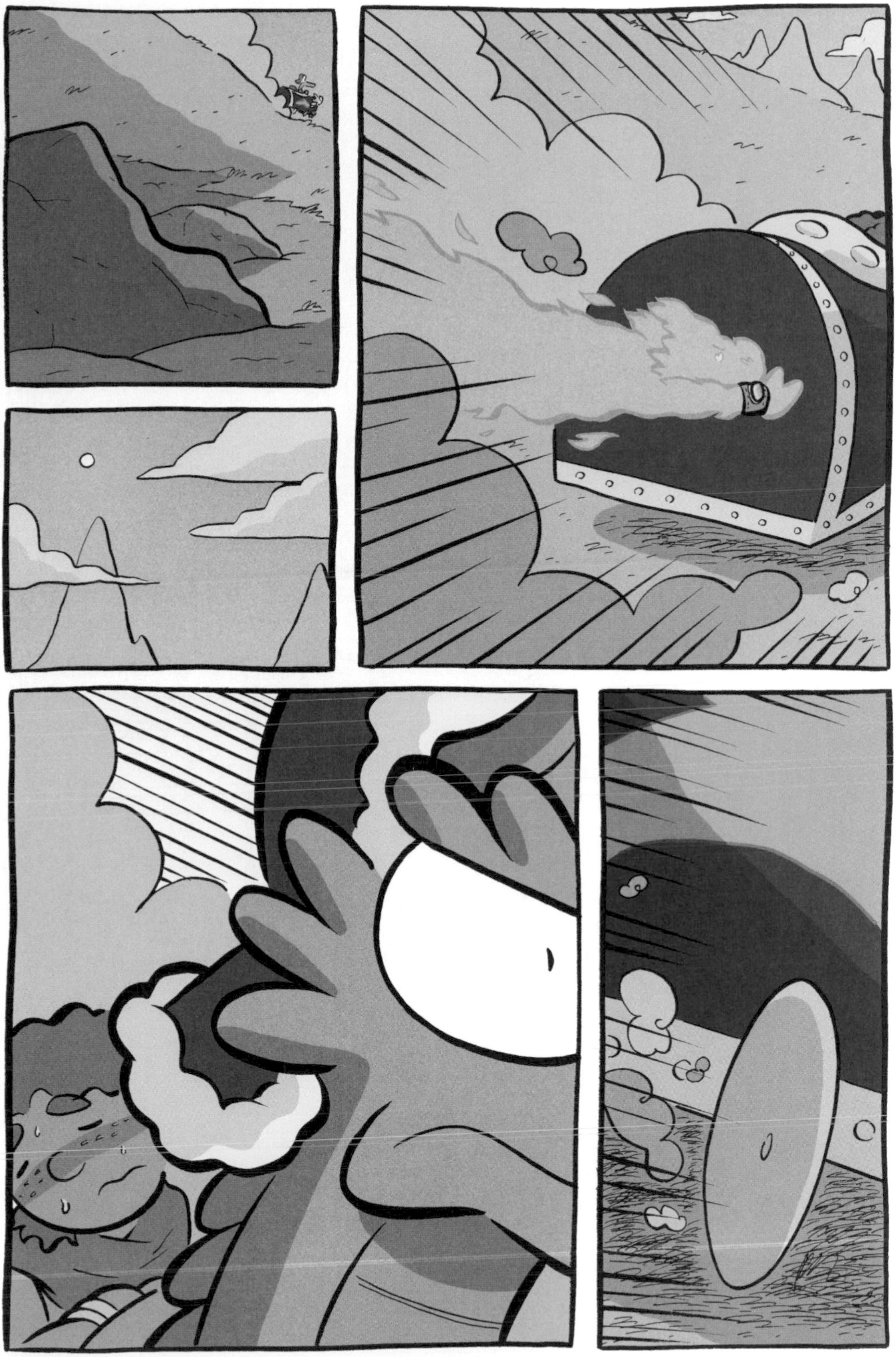

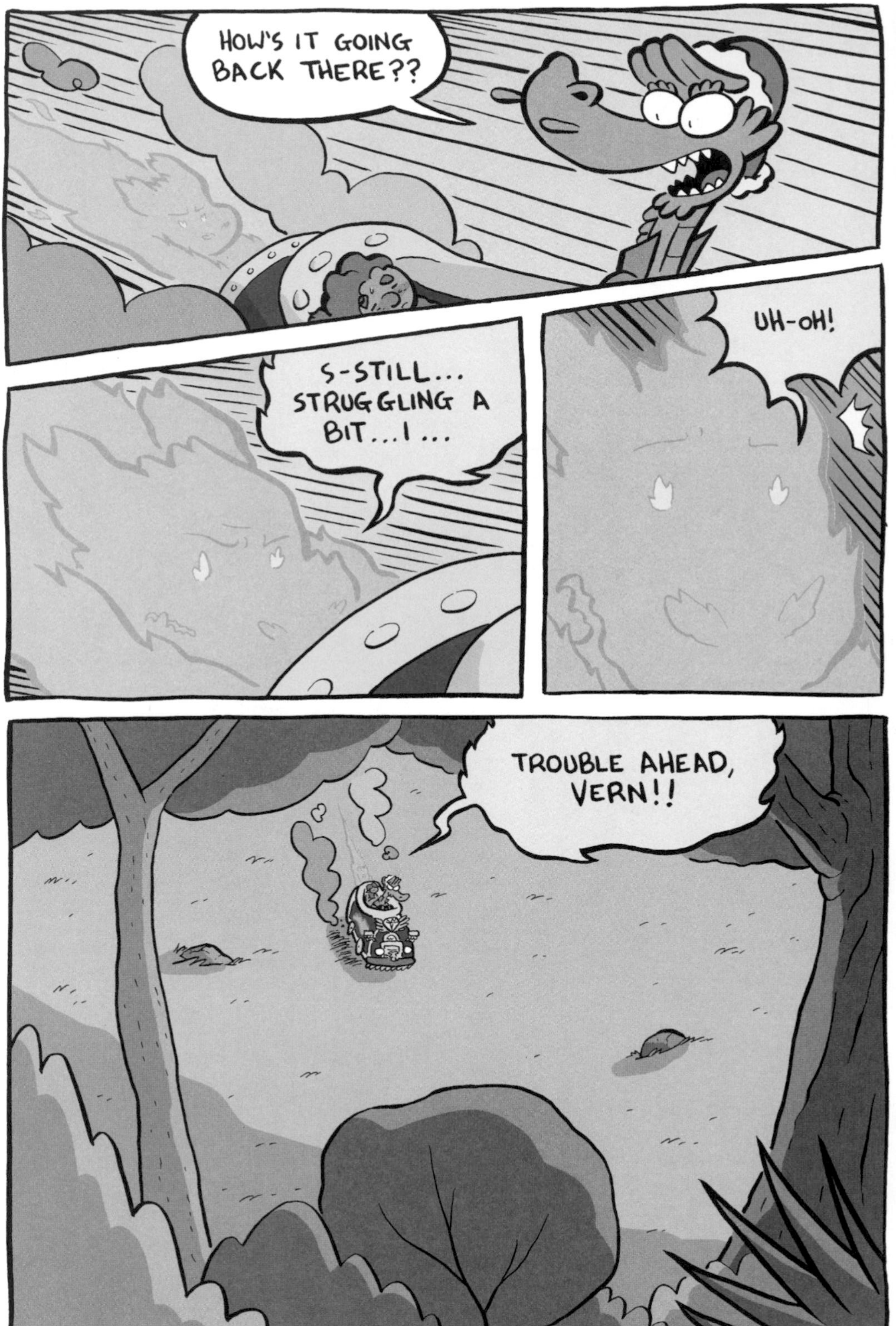
HOW'S IT GOING BACK THERE??
S-STILL... STRUGGLING A BIT...I...
UH-OH!
TROUBLE AHEAD, VERN!!

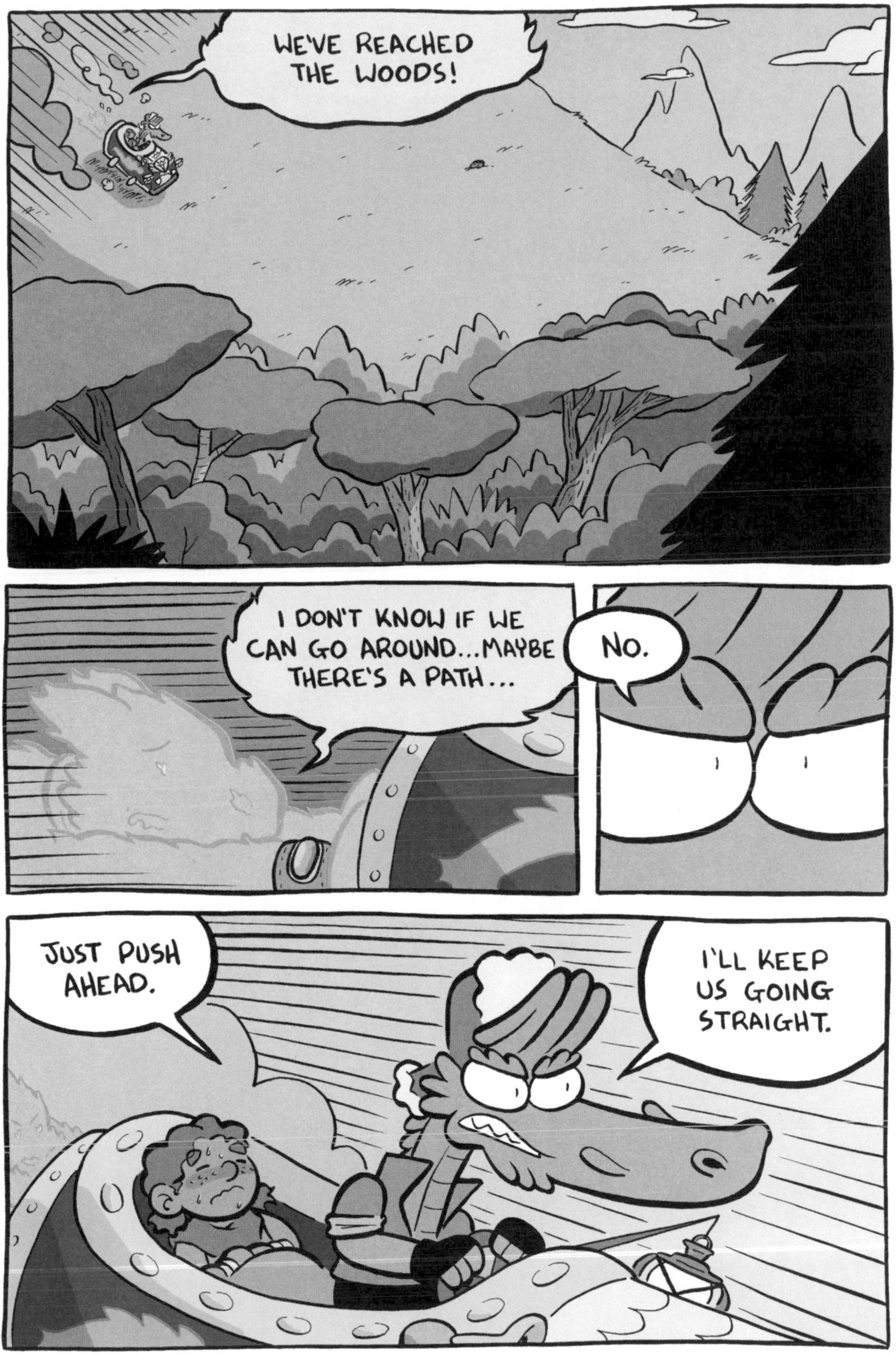
WE'VE REACHED THE WOODS!
I DON'T KNOW IF WE CAN GO AROUND...MAYBE THERE'S A PATH...
NO.
JUST PUSH AHEAD.
I'LL KEEP US GOING STRAIGHT.

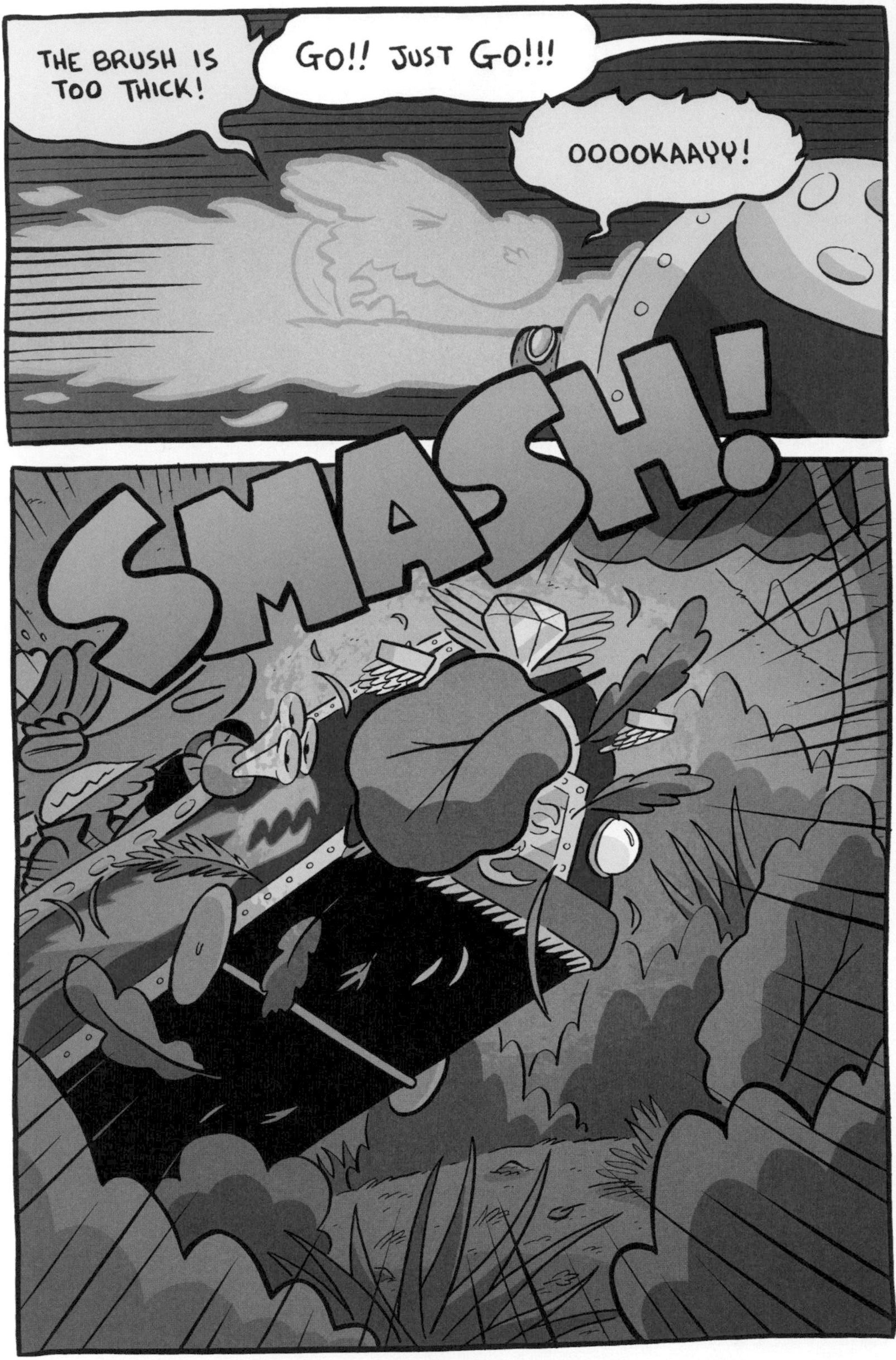
THE BRUSH IS TOO THICK!
GO!! JUST GO!!!
OOOOKAAYY!
SMASH!

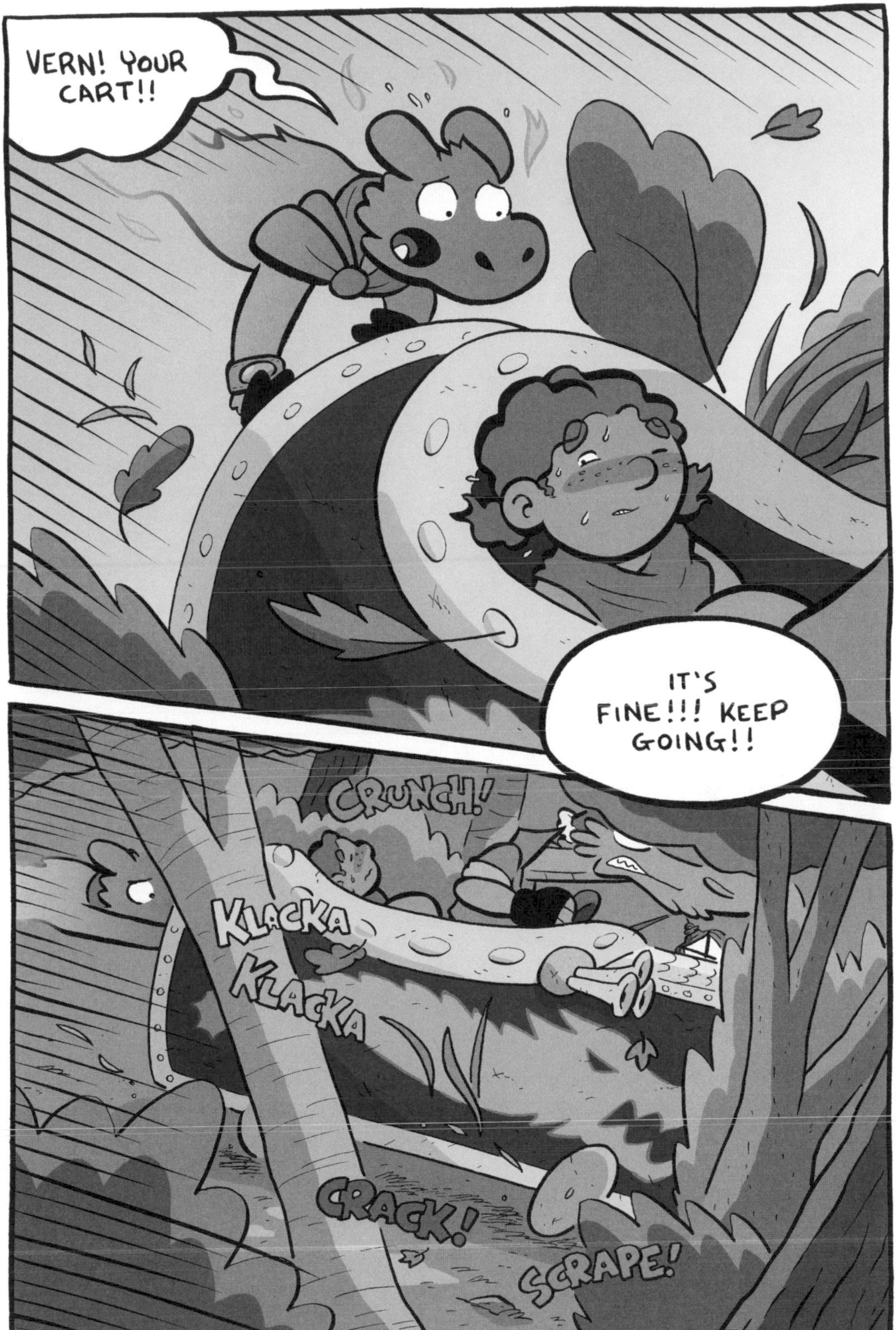
VERN! YOUR CART!!
IT'S FINE!!! KEEP GOING!!
CRUNCH!
KLACKA
KLACKA
CRACK!
SCRAPE!

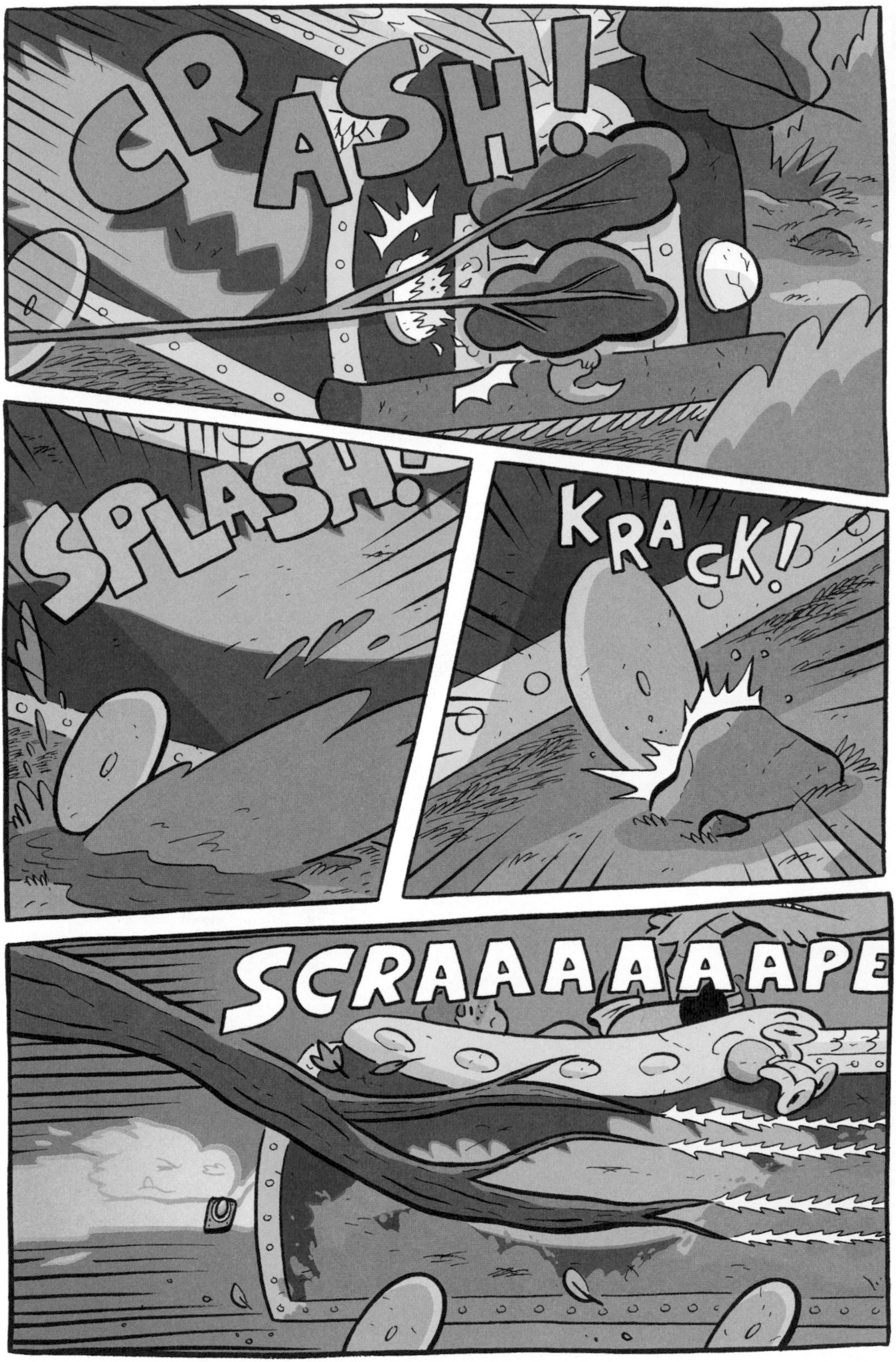
CRASH!
SPLASH!
KRACK!
SCRAAAAAAPE

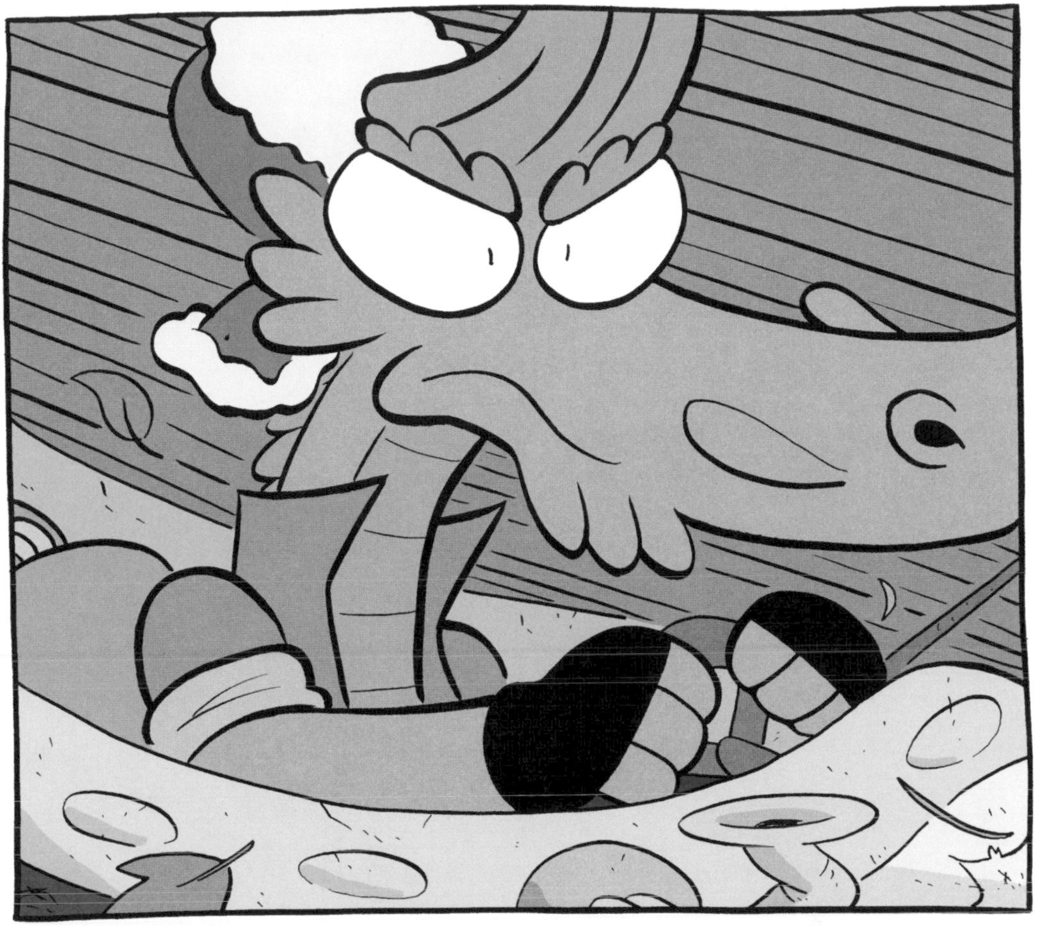

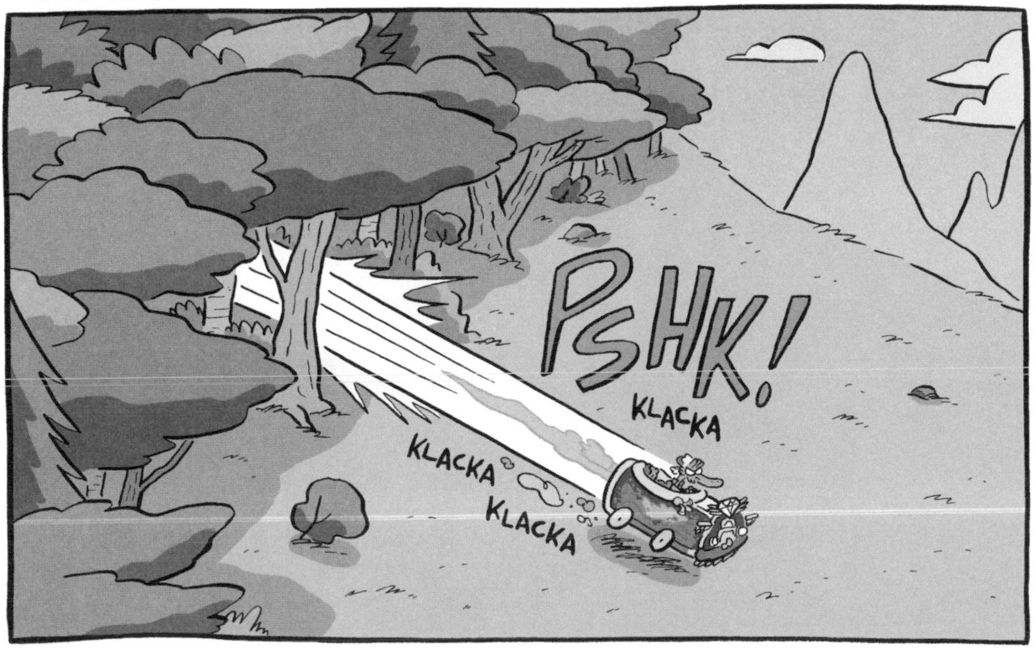
PSHK!
KLACKA
KLACKA
KLACKA

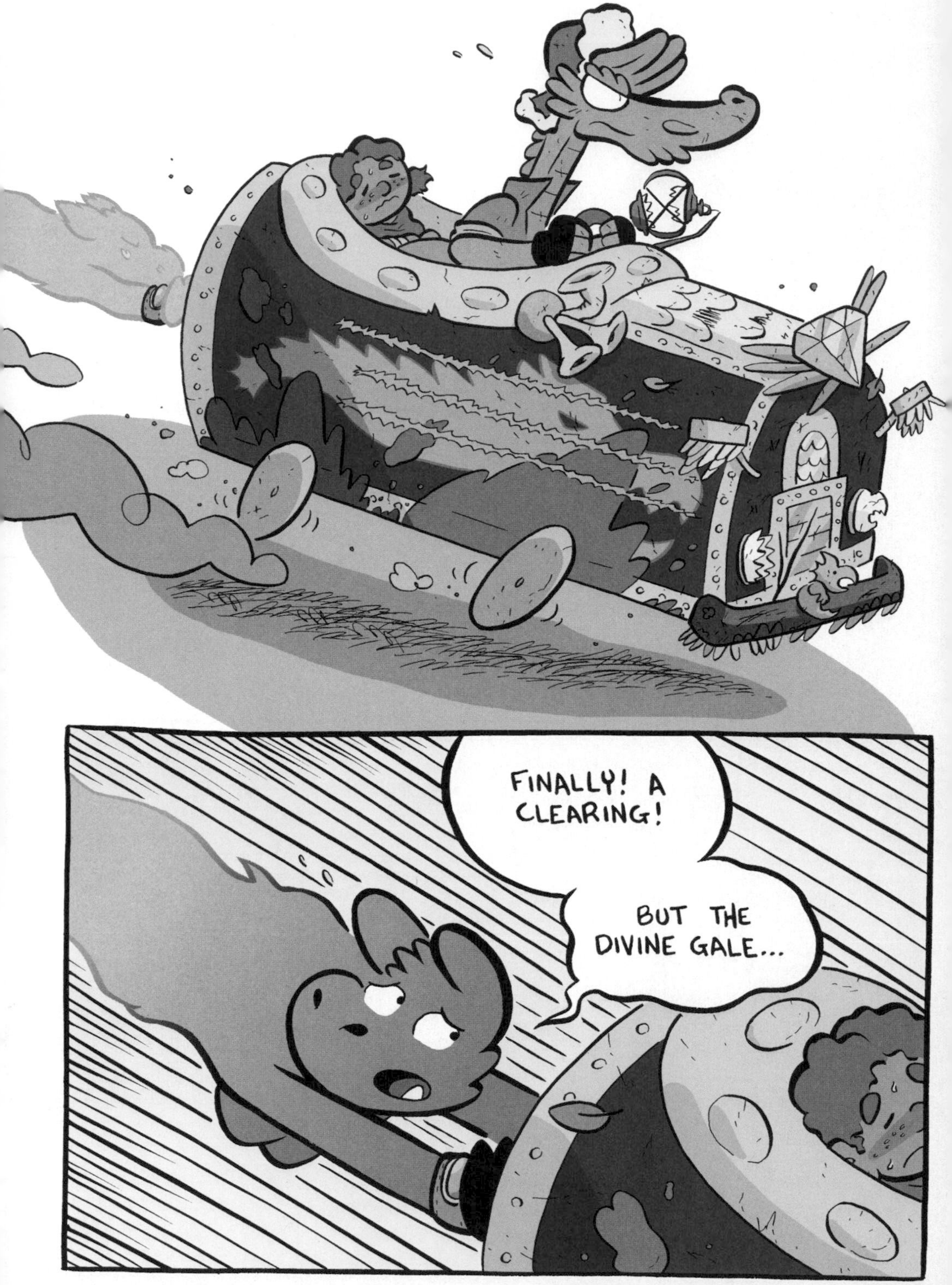
FINALLY! A CLEARING!
BUT THE DIVINE GALE...

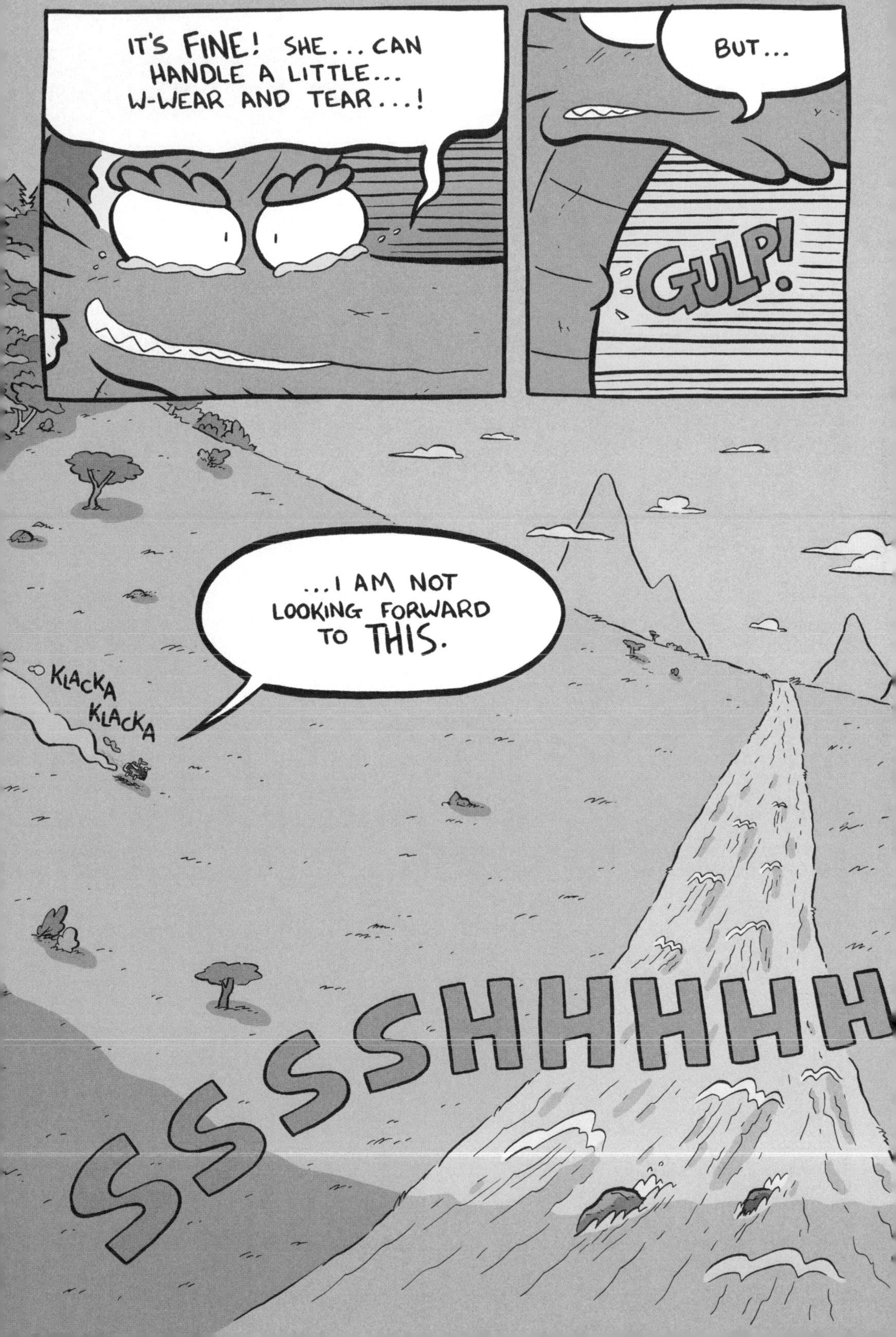
IT'S FINE! SHE... CAN HANDLE A LITTLE... W-WEAR AND TEAR...!
BUT...
GULP!
...I AM NOT LOOKING FORWARD TO THIS.
KLACKA KLACKA
SSSSHHHHH

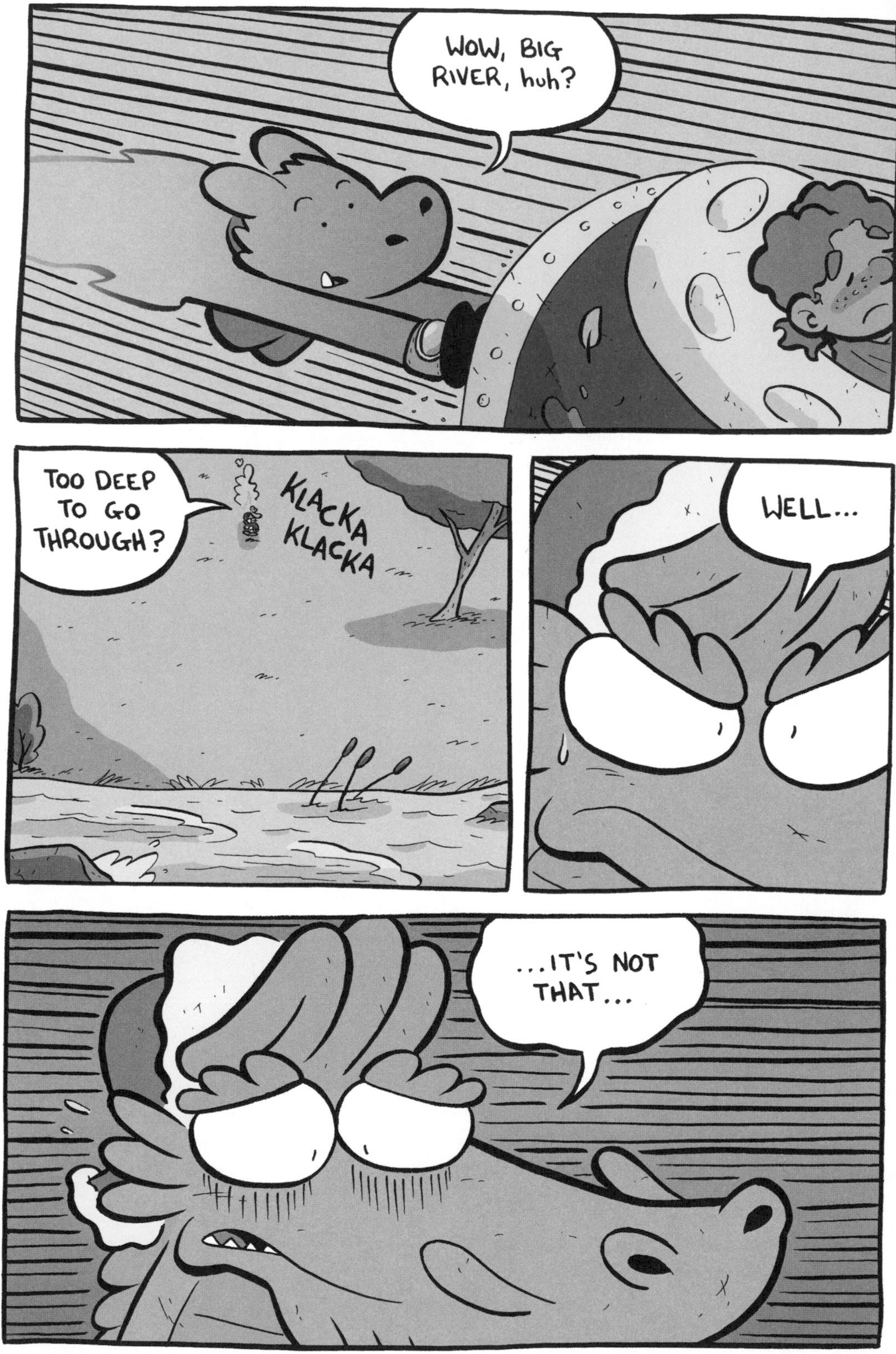
WOW, BIG RIVER, huh?
TOO DEEP TO GO THROUGH?
KLACKA KLACKA
WELL...
...IT'S NOT THAT...

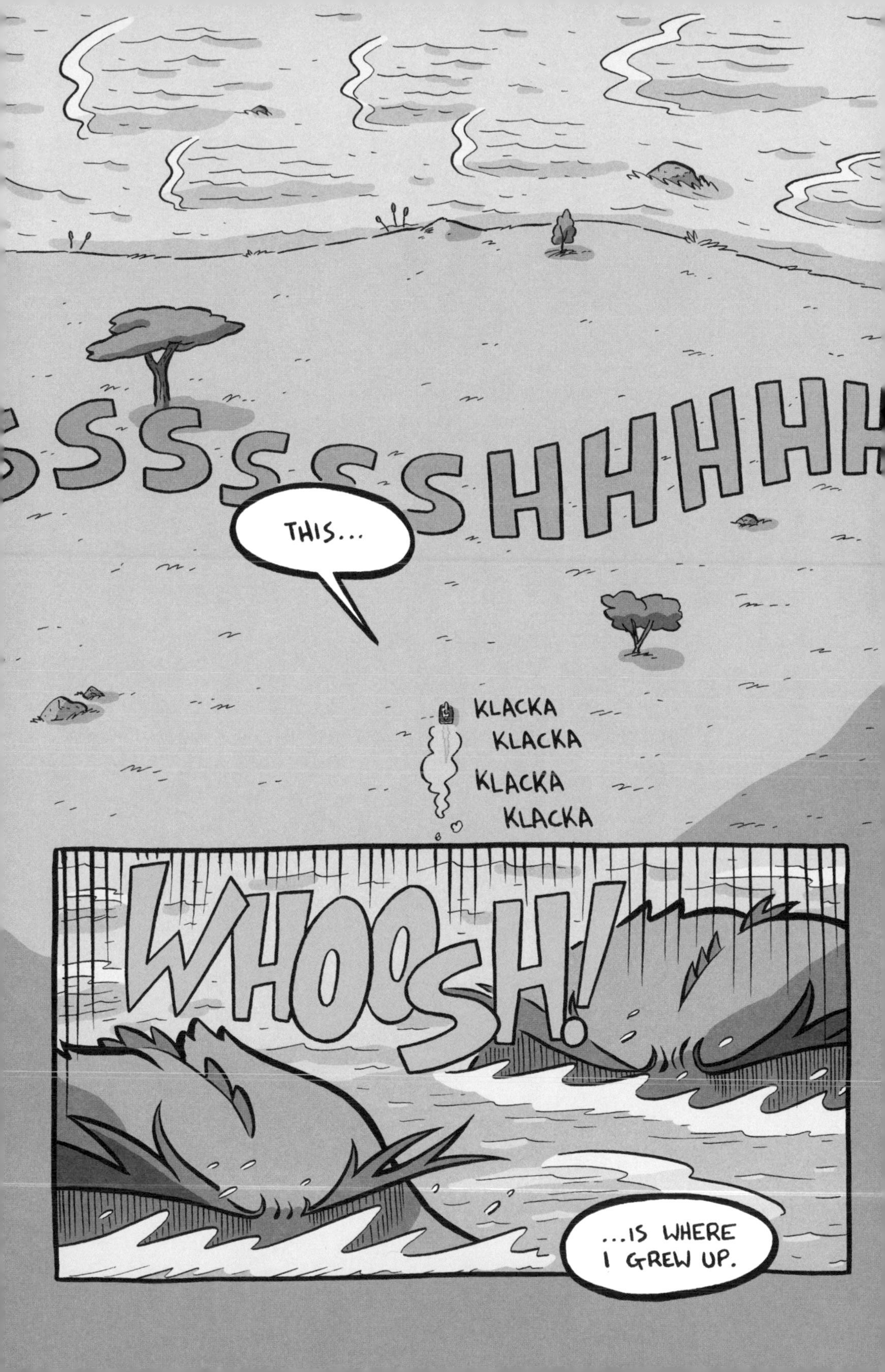
SSSSSSHHHHH
THIS...
KLACKA
KLACKA
KLACKA
KLACKA
WHOOSH!
...IS WHERE I GREW UP.

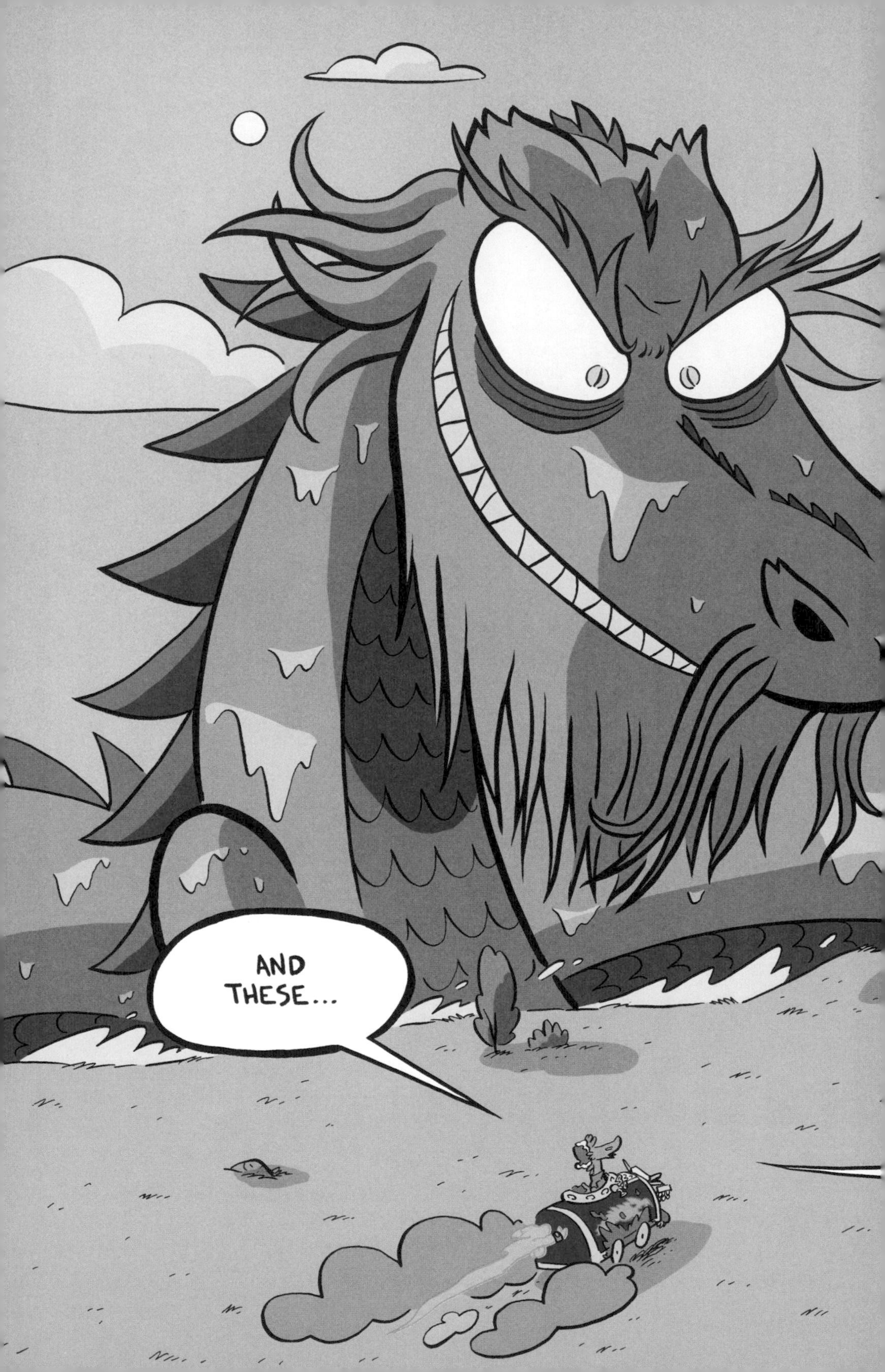
AND THESE...

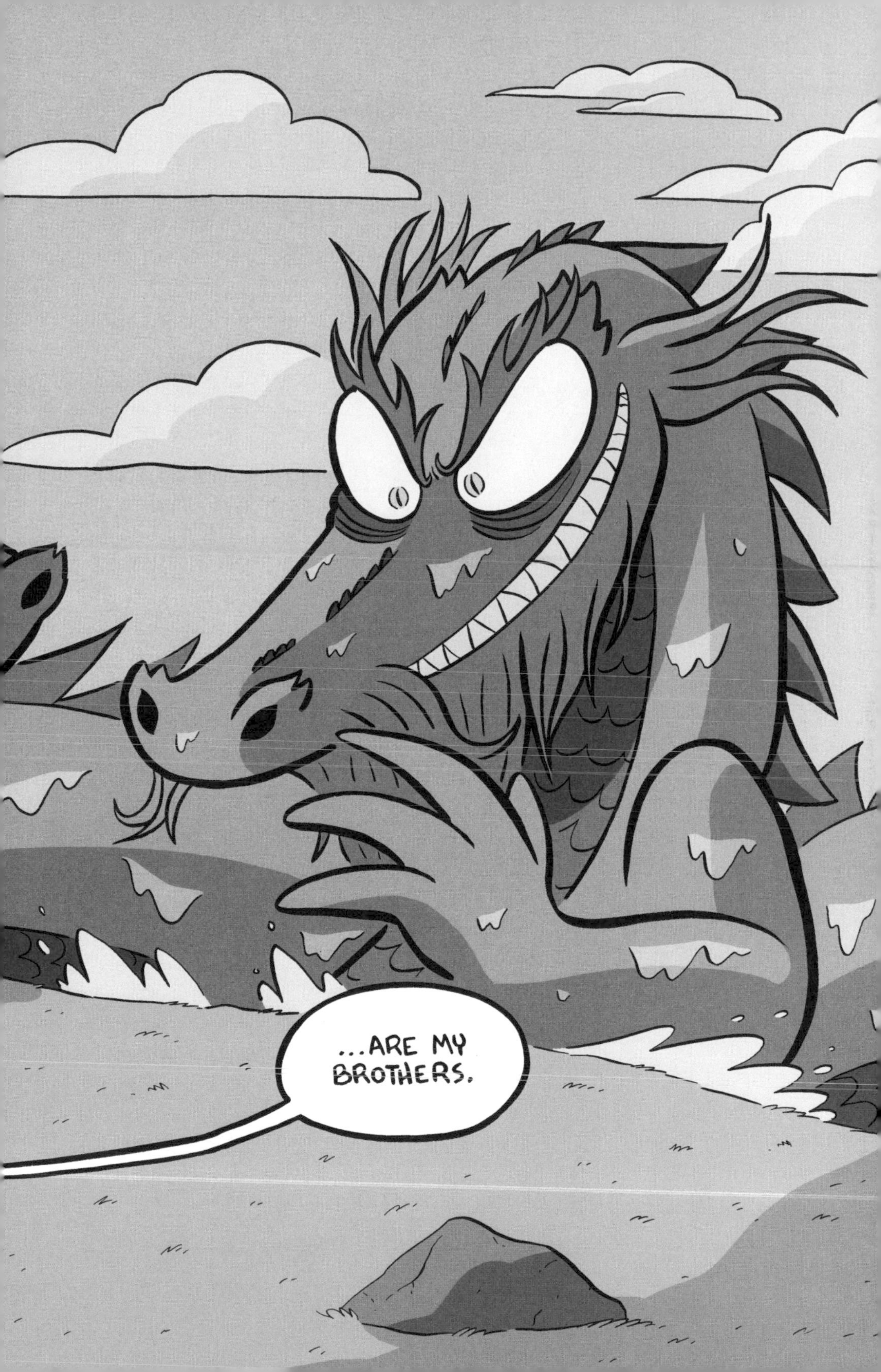
...ARE MY BROTHERS.

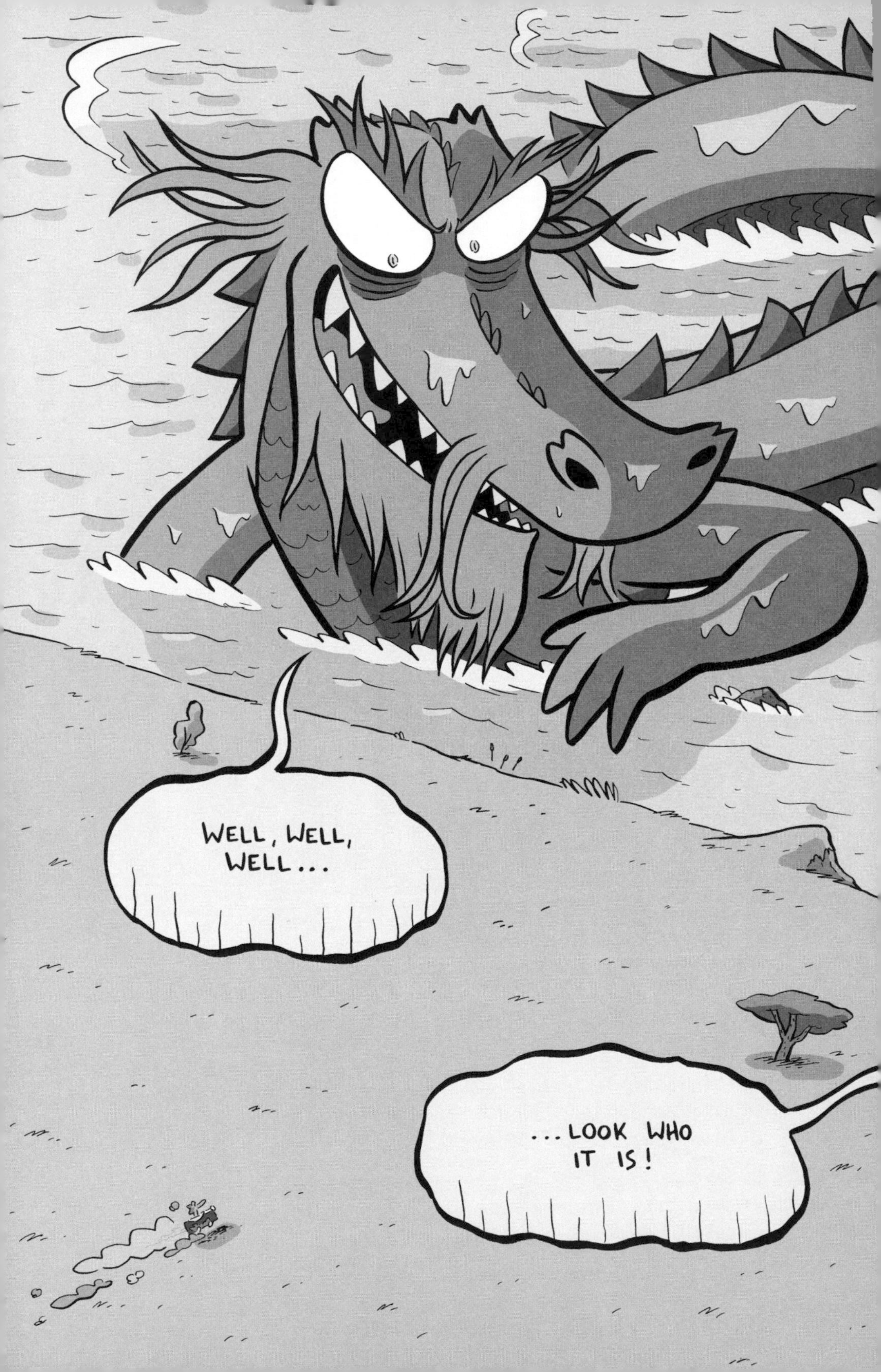
WELL, WELL, WELL...
...LOOK WHO IT IS!

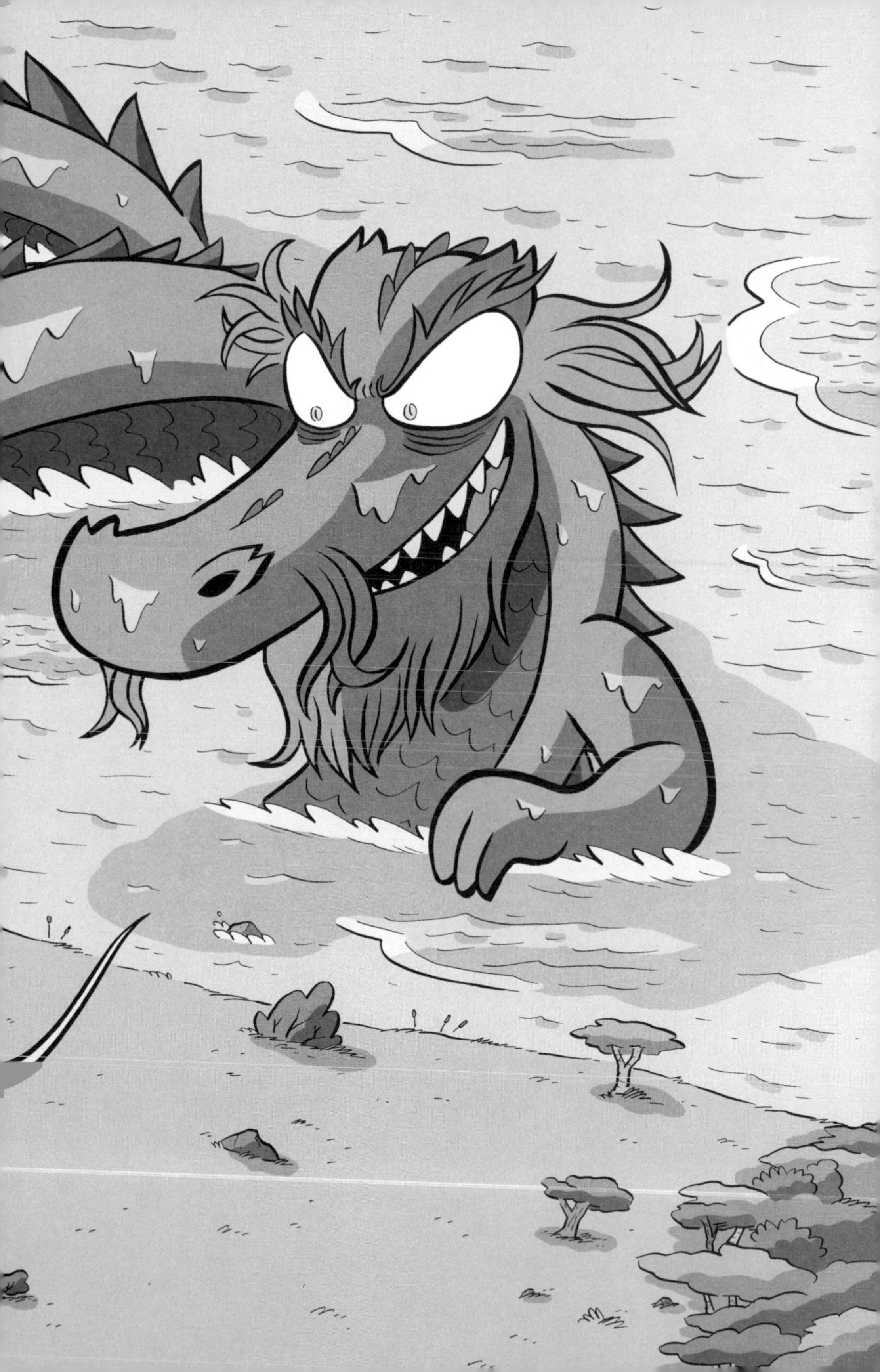

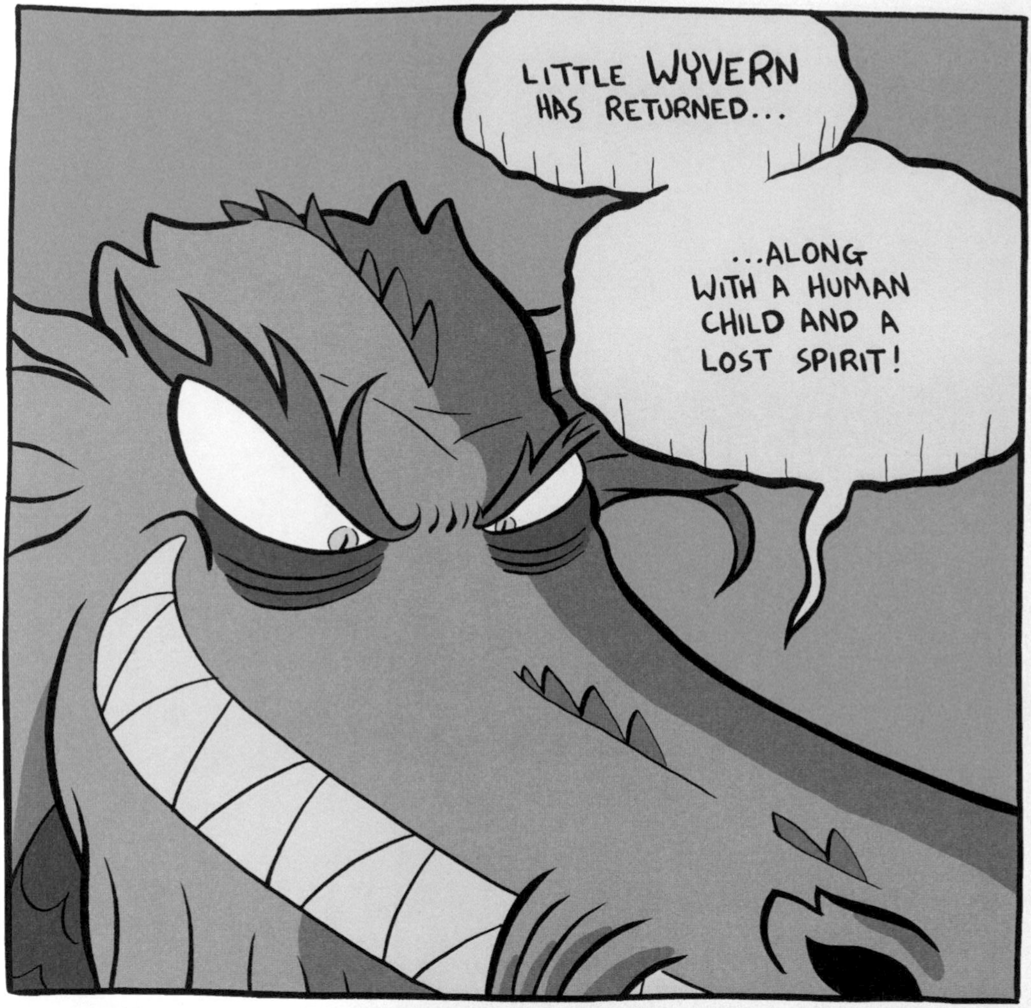
LITTLE WYVERN HAS RETURNED...
...ALONG WITH A HUMAN CHILD AND A LOST SPIRIT!

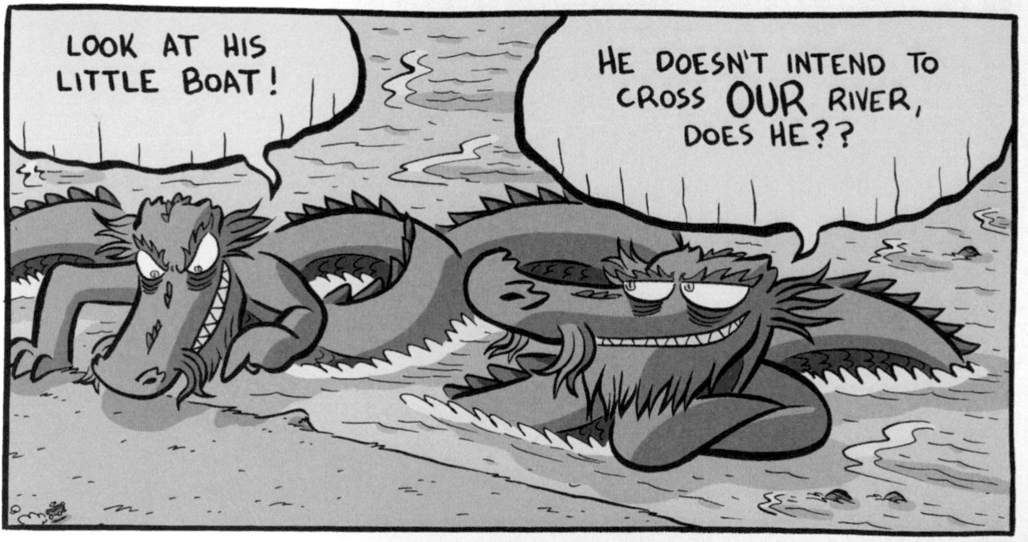
LOOK AT HIS LITTLE BOAT!
HE DOESN'T INTEND TO CROSS OUR RIVER, DOES HE??

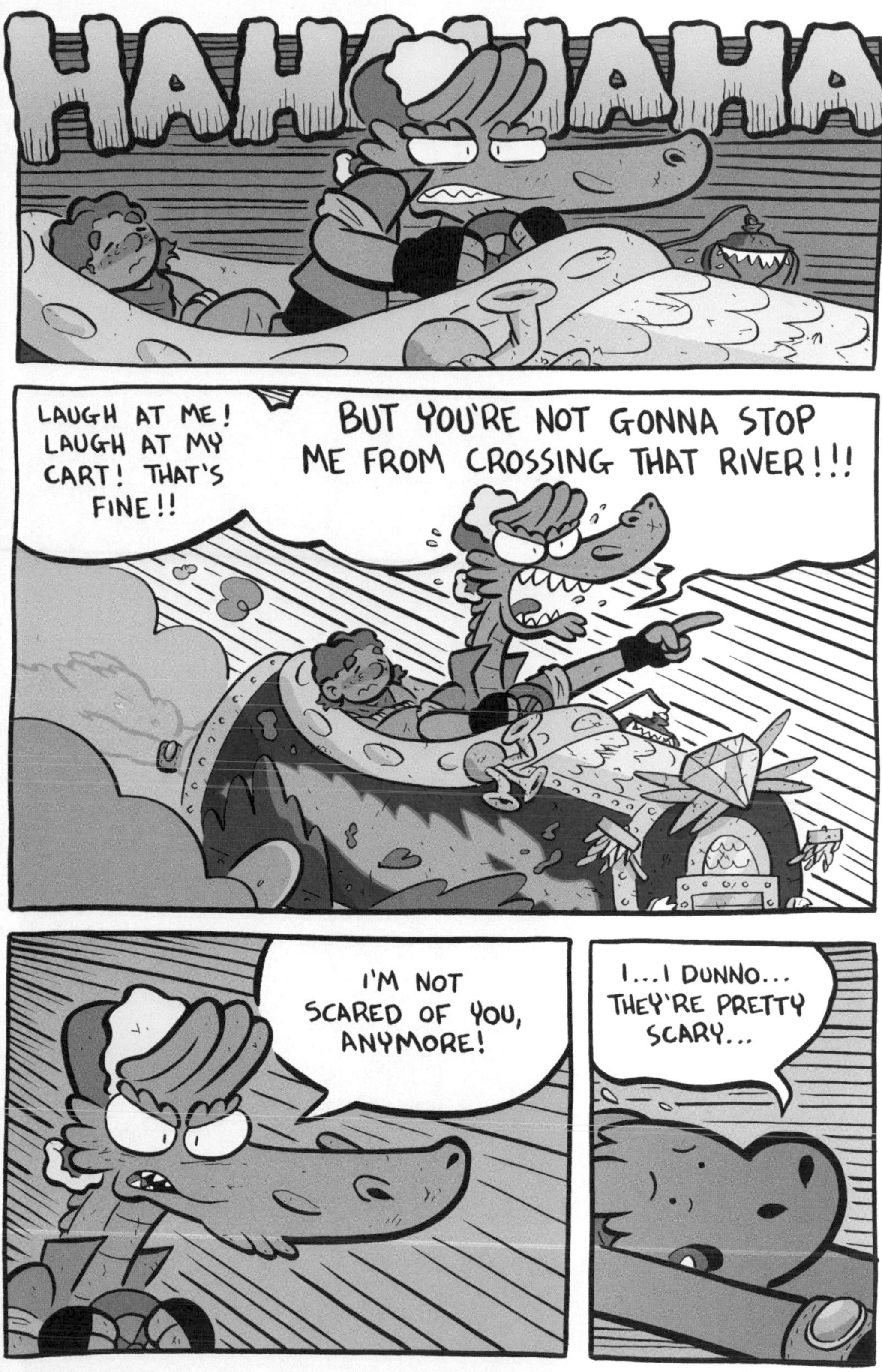
HAHAHAHAHA
LAUGH AT ME! LAUGH AT MY CART! THAT'S FINE!!
BUT YOU'RE NOT GONNA STOP ME FROM CROSSING THAT RIVER!!!
I'M NOT SCARED OF YOU, ANYMORE!
I...I DUNNO... THEY'RE PRETTY SCARY...

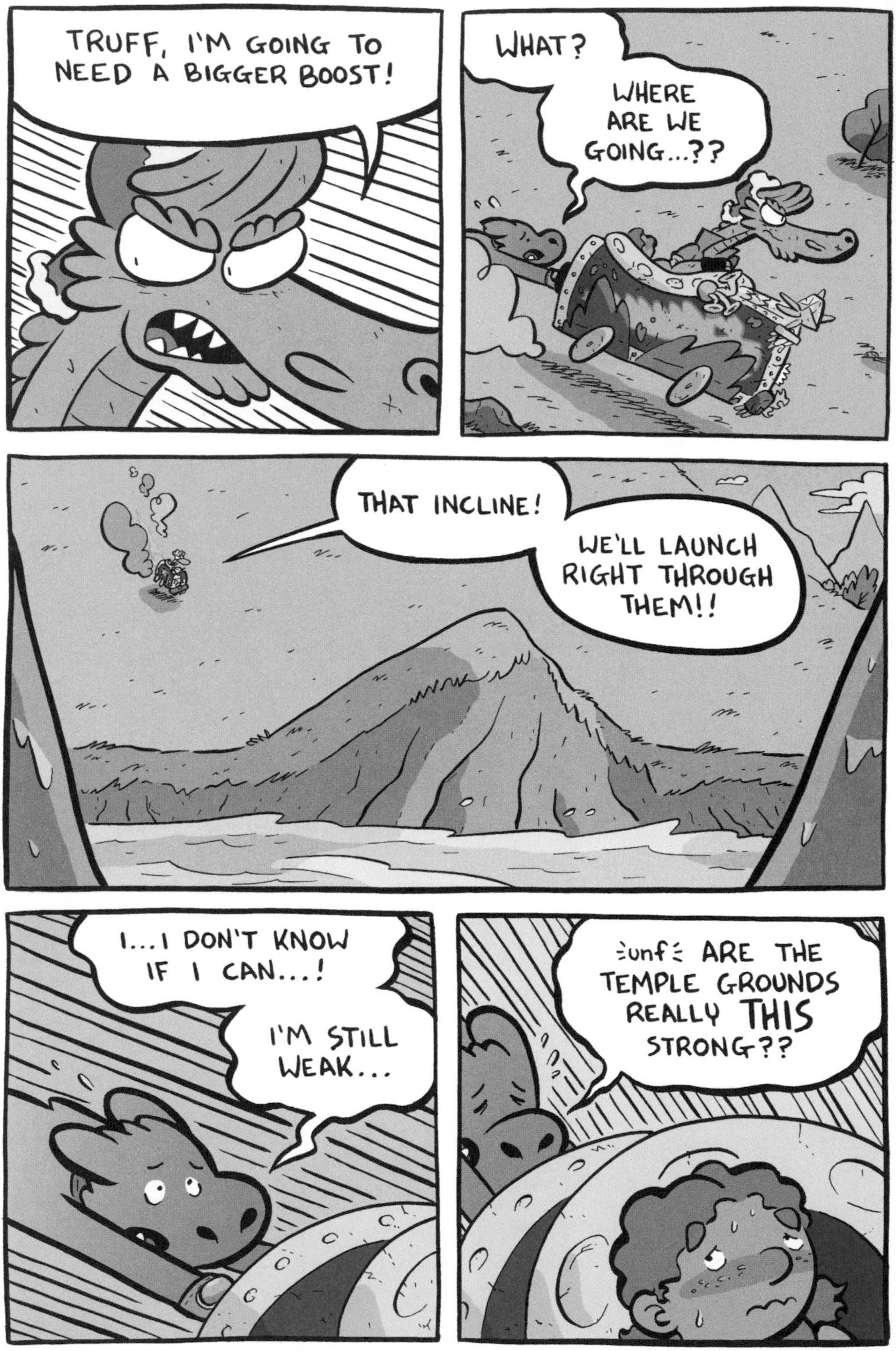
TRUFF, I'M GOING TO NEED A BIGGER BOOST!
WHAT?
WHERE ARE WE GOING...??
THAT INCLINE!
WE'LL LAUNCH RIGHT THROUGH THEM!!
I...I DON'T KNOW IF I CAN...!
I'M STILL WEAK...
unf ARE THE TEMPLE GROUNDS REALLY THIS STRONG??

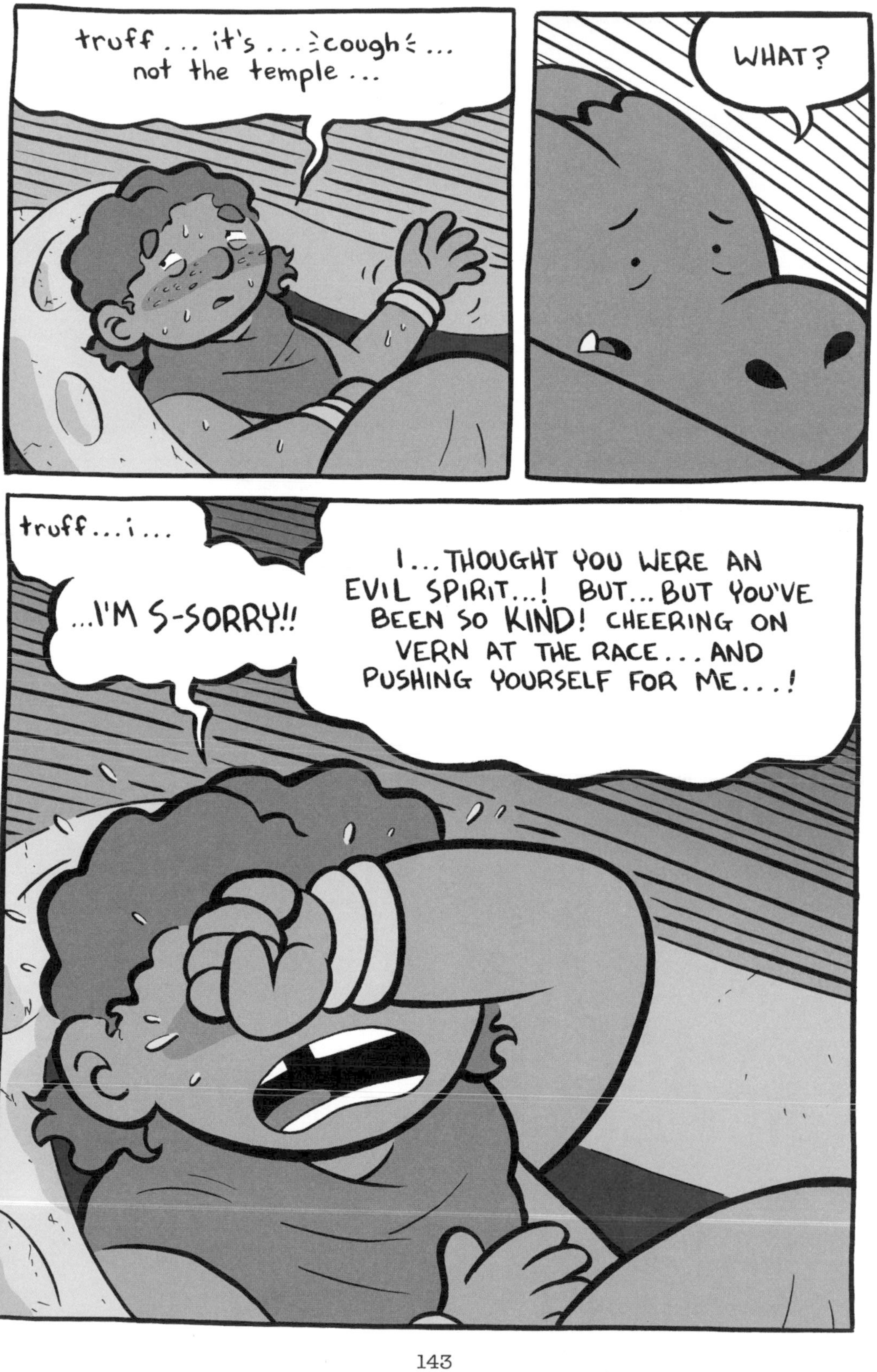
truff ... it's ... ≷cough≶ ... not the temple ...
WHAT?
truff ... i ...
... I'M S-SORRY!!
I ... THOUGHT YOU WERE AN EVIL SPIRIT ...! BUT ... BUT YOU'VE BEEN SO KIND! CHEERING ON VERN AT THE RACE ... AND PUSHING YOURSELF FOR ME ...!

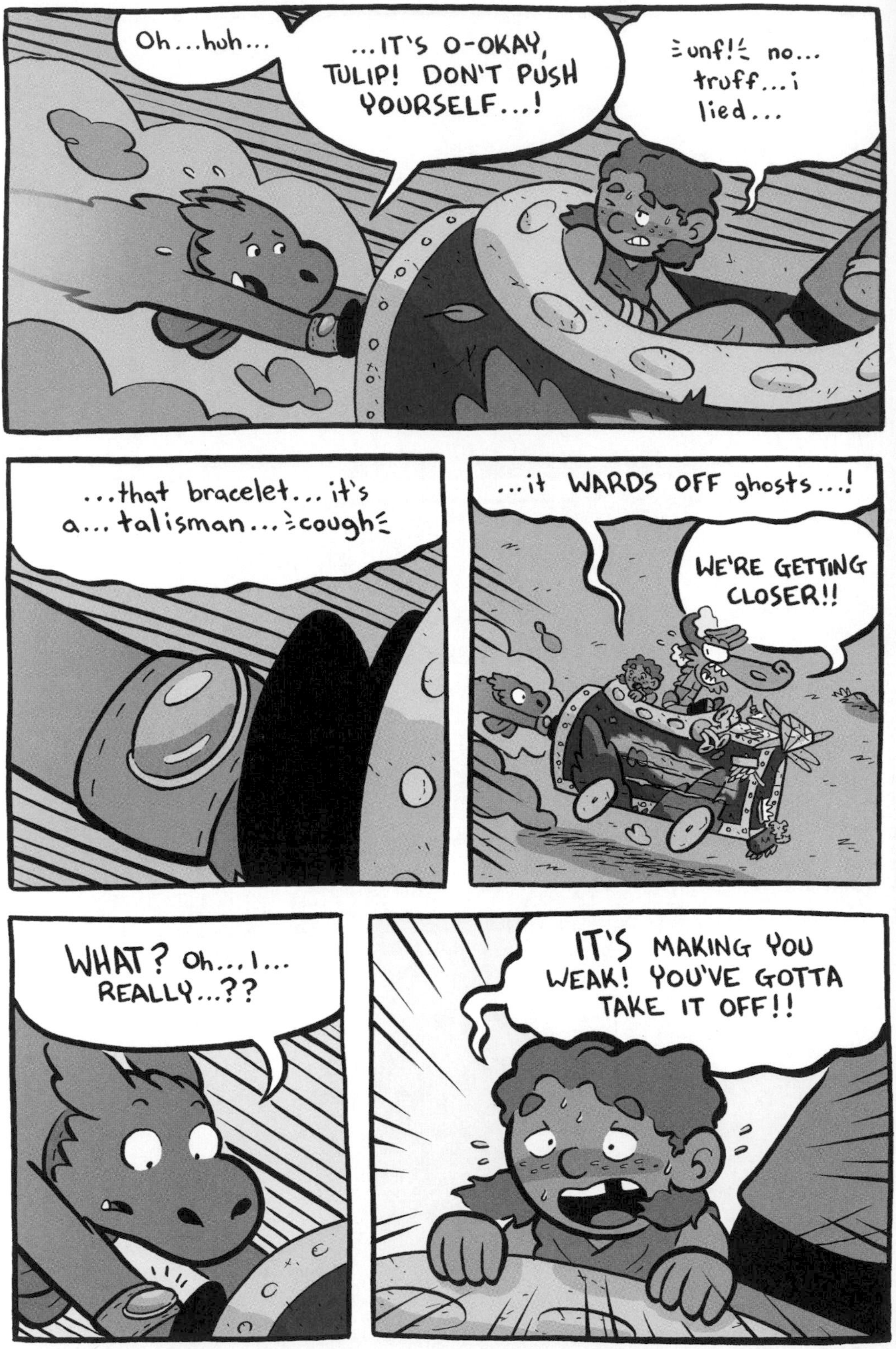
Oh...huh...
...IT'S O-OKAY, TULIP! DON'T PUSH YOURSELF...!
unf! no... truff...i lied...
...that bracelet... it's a... talisman... cough
...it WARDS OFF ghosts...!
WE'RE GETTING CLOSER!!
WHAT? Oh...I... REALLY...??
IT'S MAKING YOU WEAK! YOU'VE GOTTA TAKE IT OFF!!

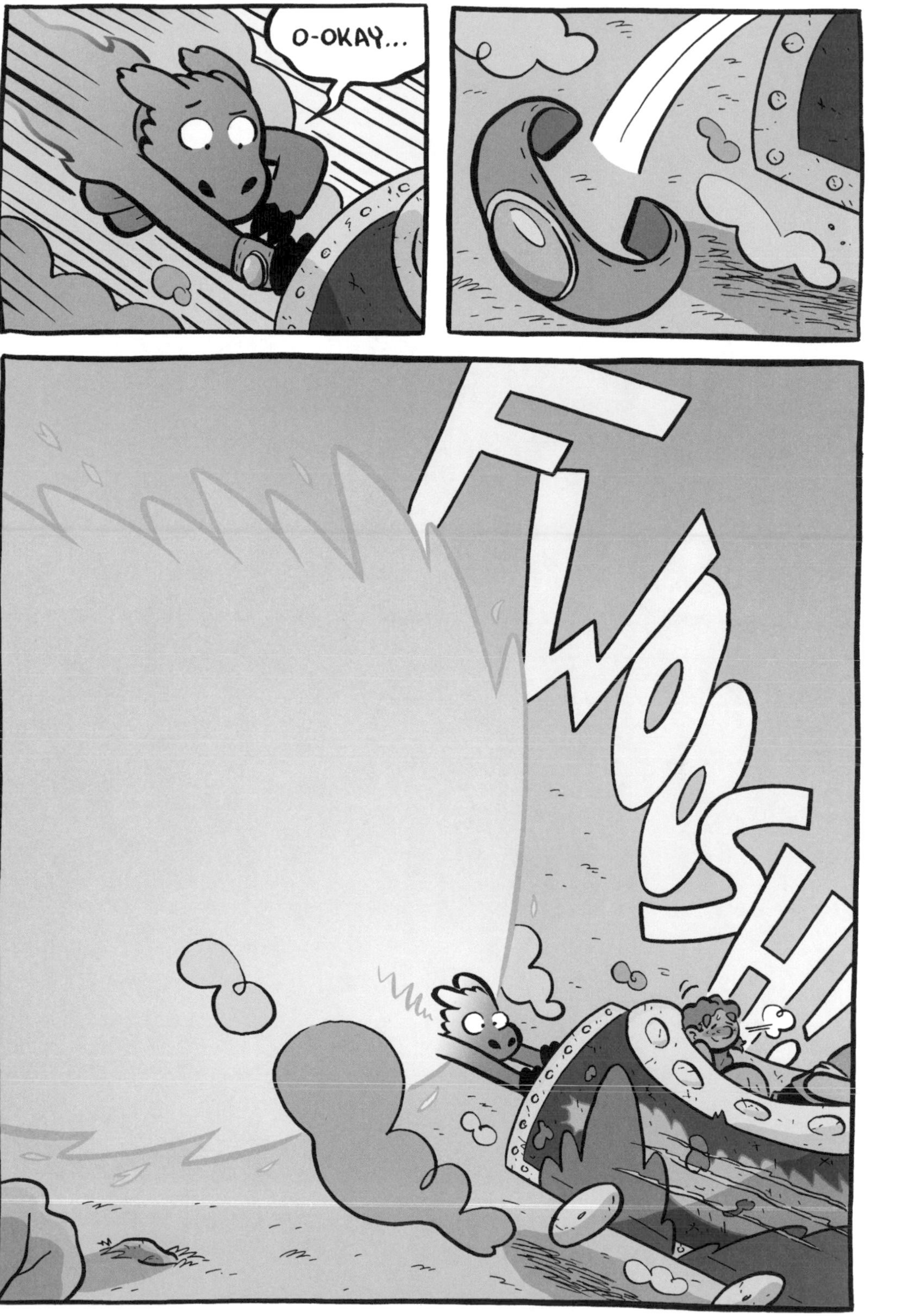
O-OKAY...
FWOOSH!!

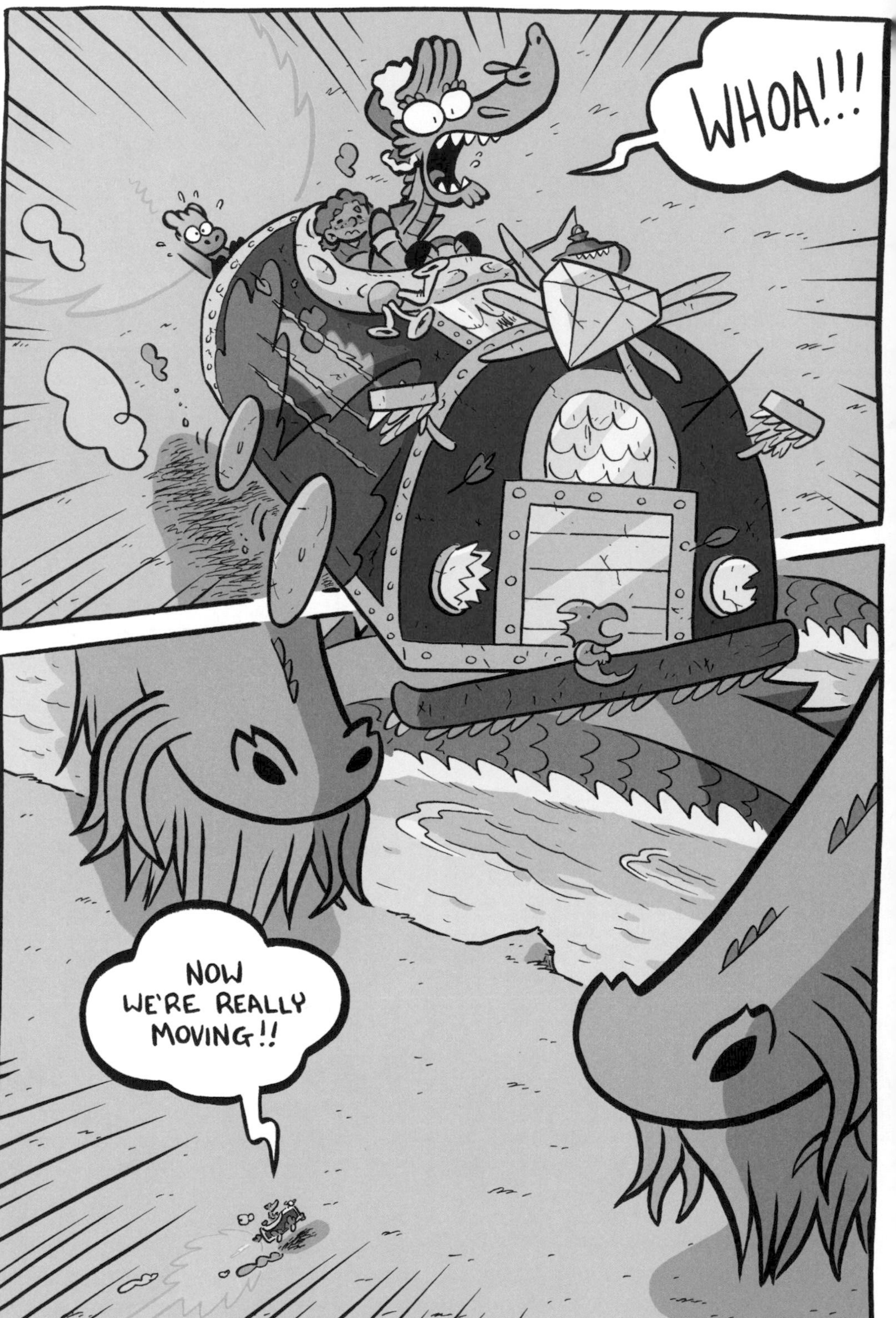
WHOA!!!
NOW WE'RE REALLY MOVING!!

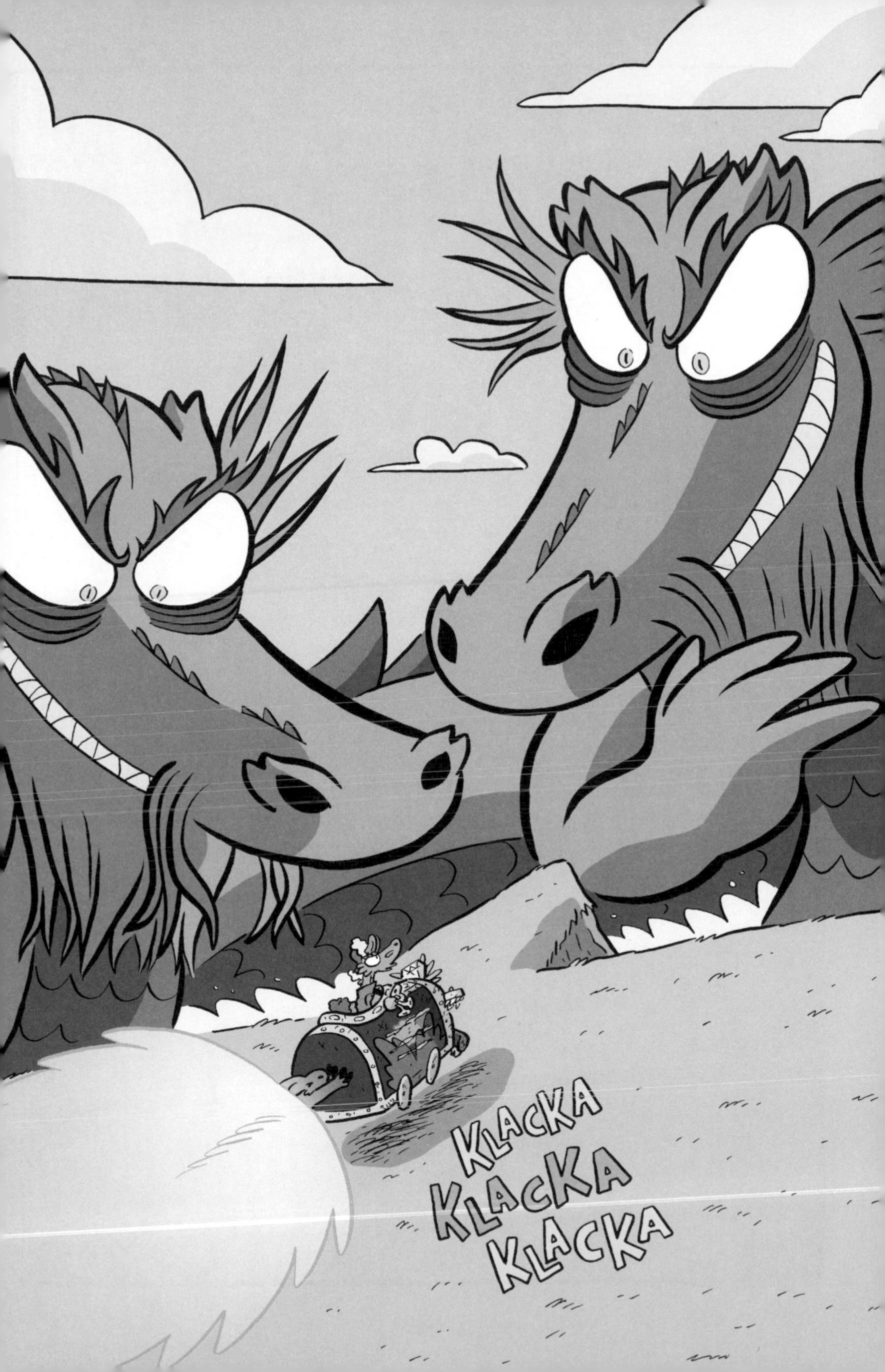
KLACKA
KLACKA
KLACKA

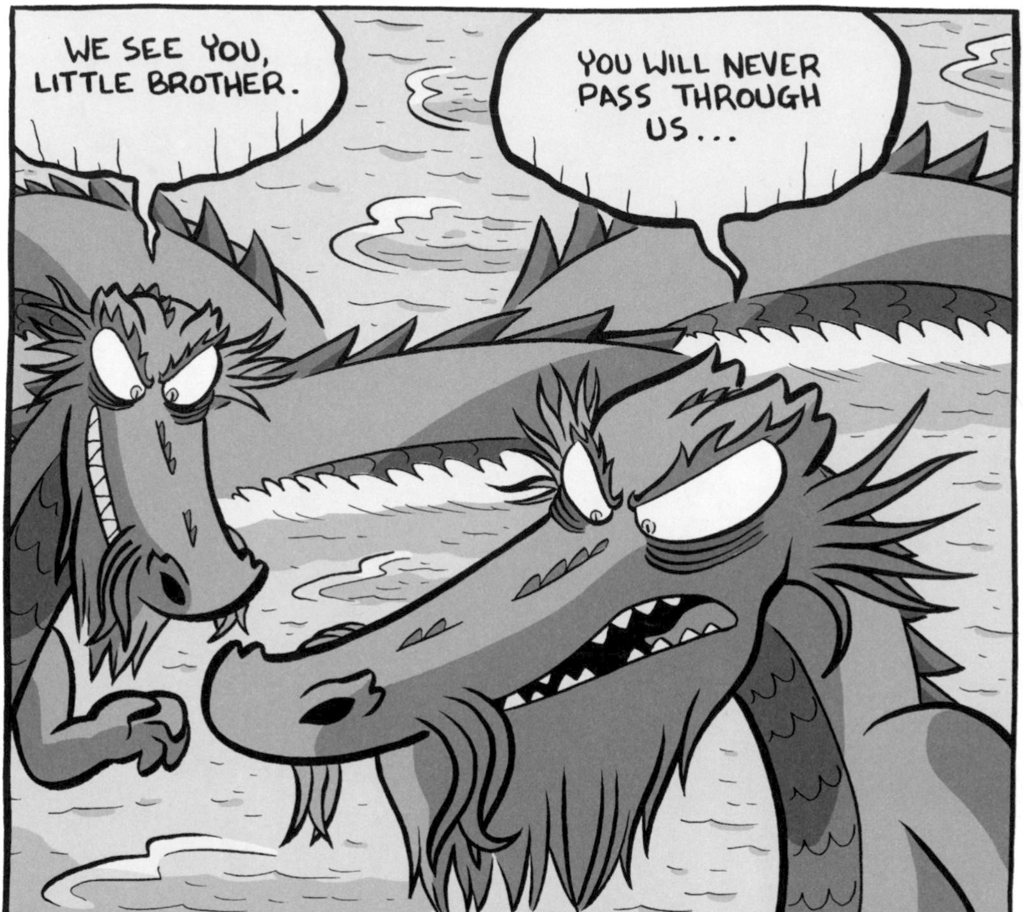
WE SEE YOU, LITTLE BROTHER.
YOU WILL NEVER PASS THROUGH US...

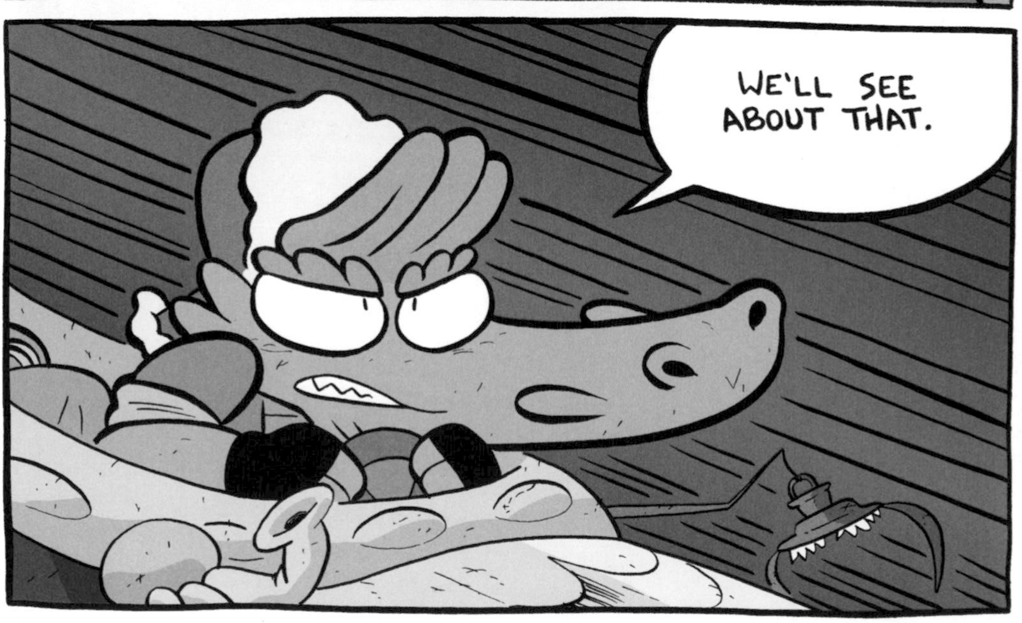
WE'LL SEE ABOUT THAT.

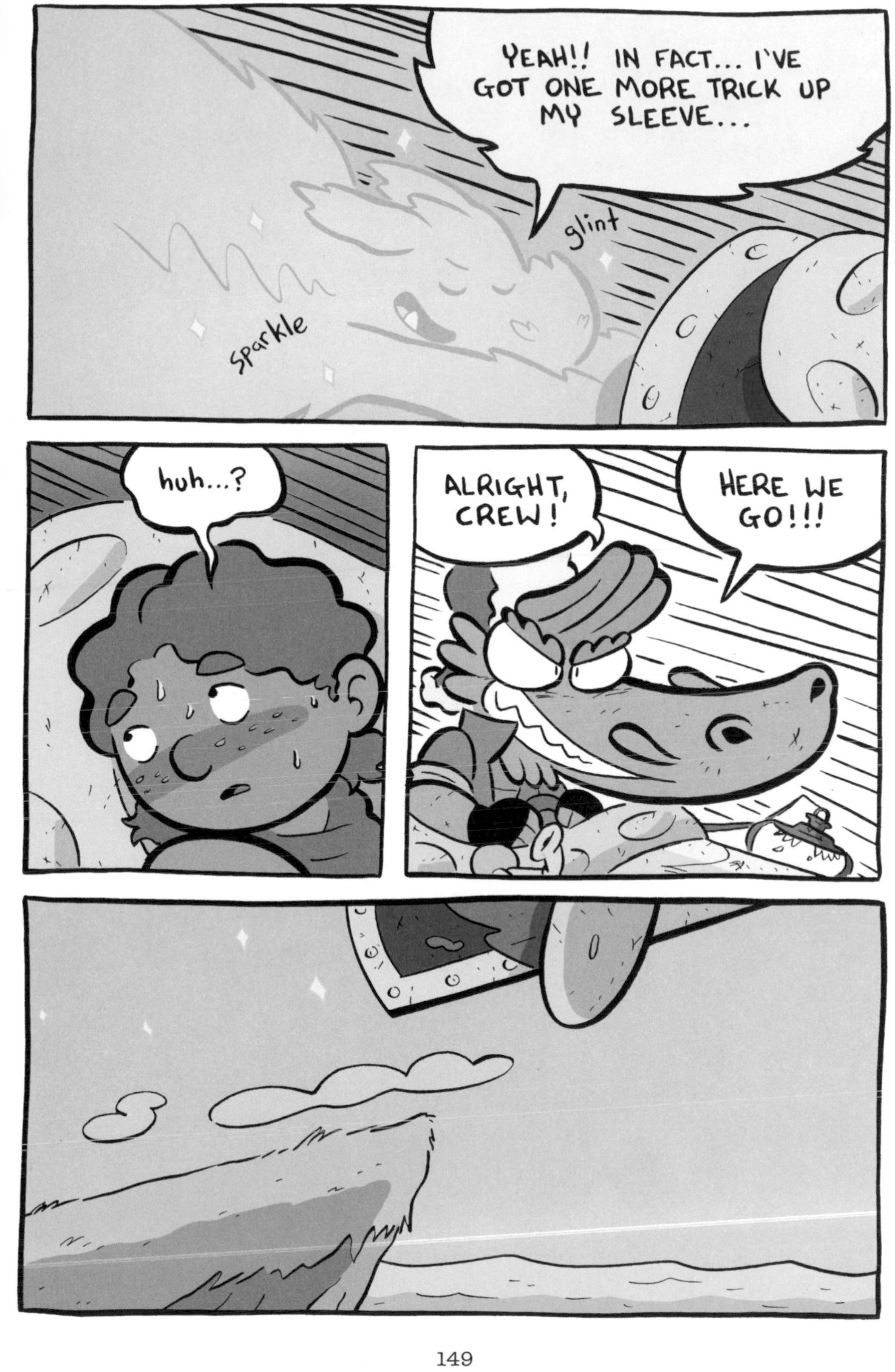
YEAH!! IN FACT... I'VE GOT ONE MORE TRICK UP MY SLEEVE...
glint
sparkle
huh...?
ALRIGHT, CREW!
HERE WE GO!!!

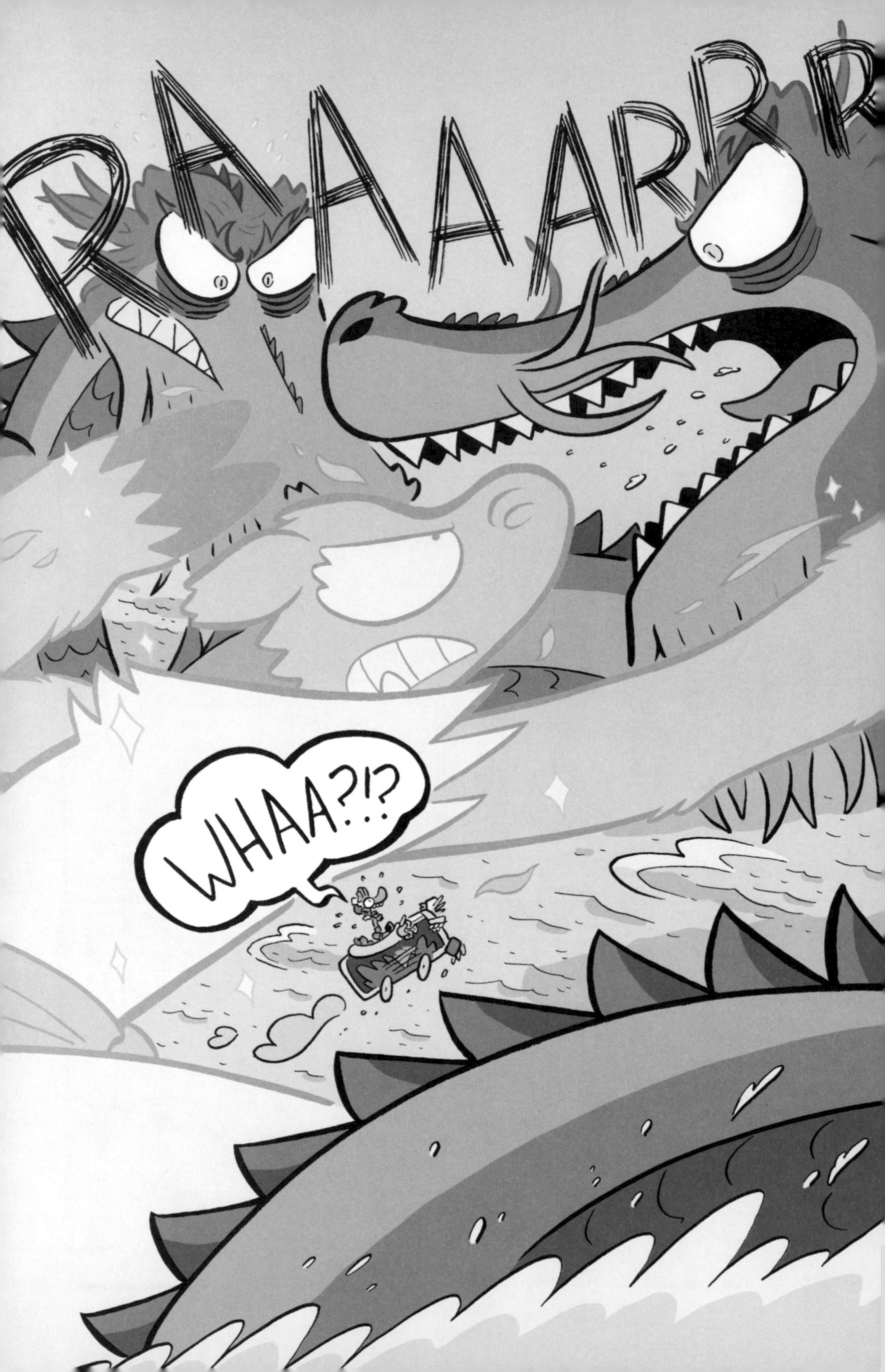
RAAAARRRR
WHAA?!?

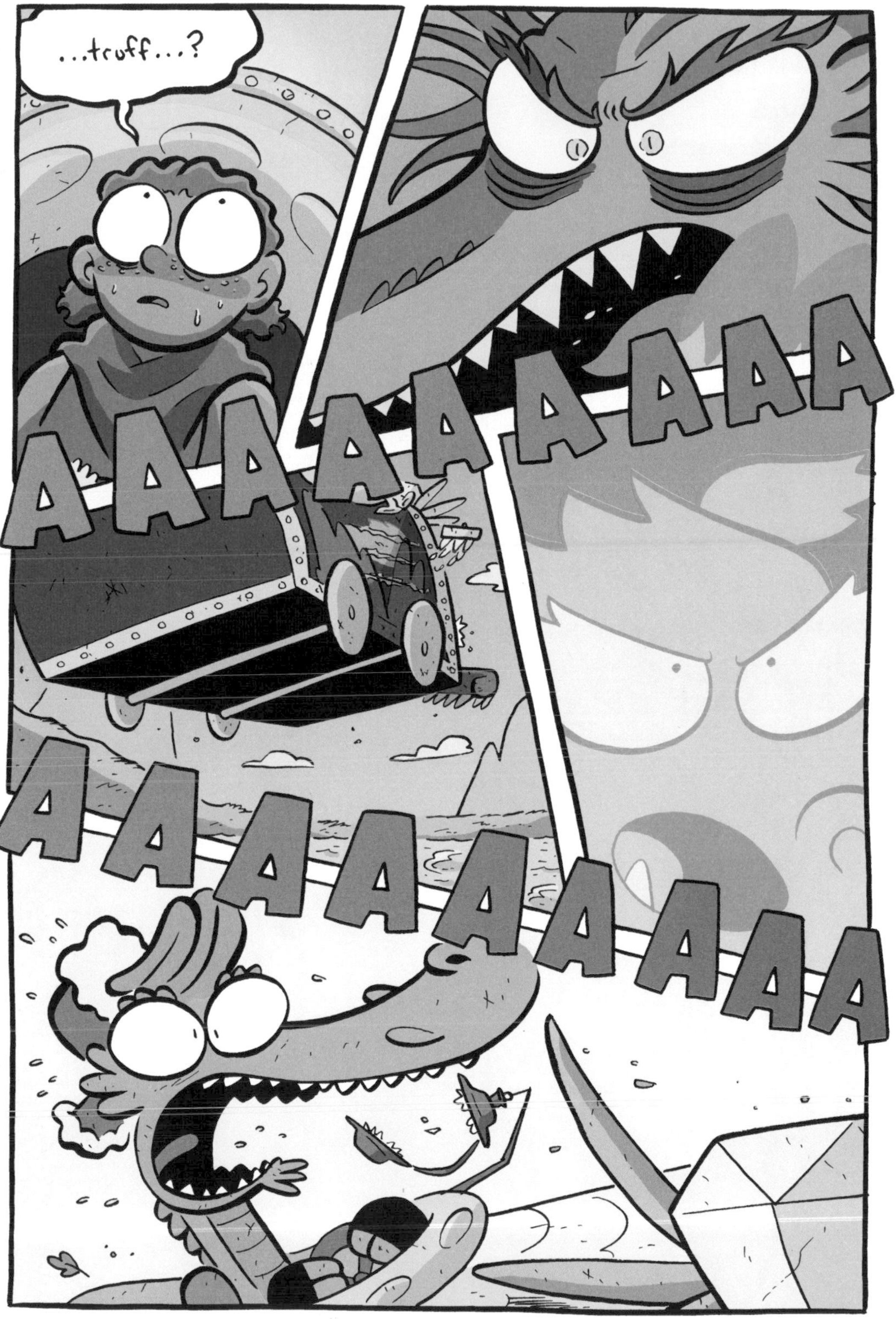
...truff...?
AAAAAAAAAA
AAAAAAAAAAAAA

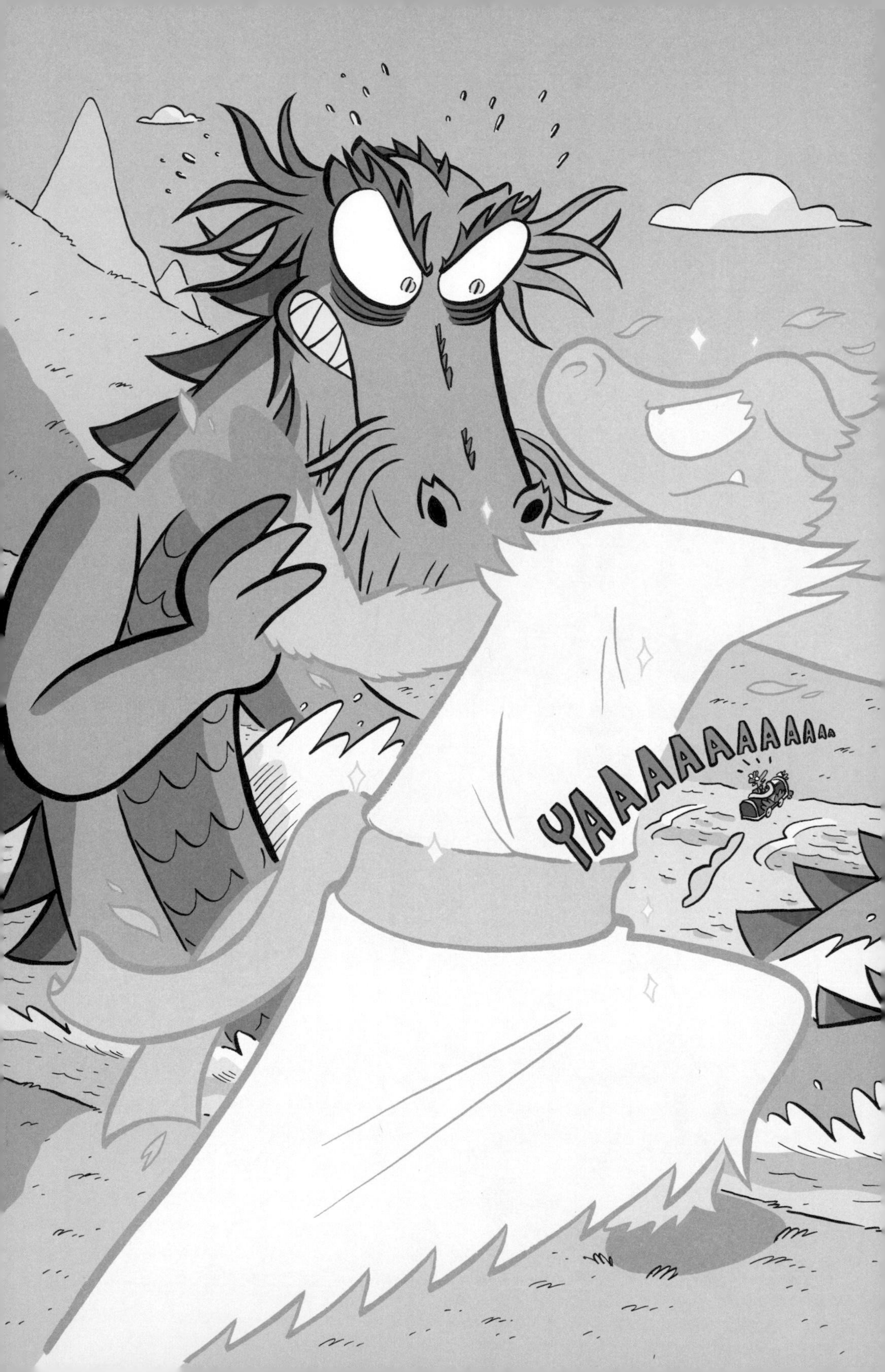
YAAAAAAAAAAaa

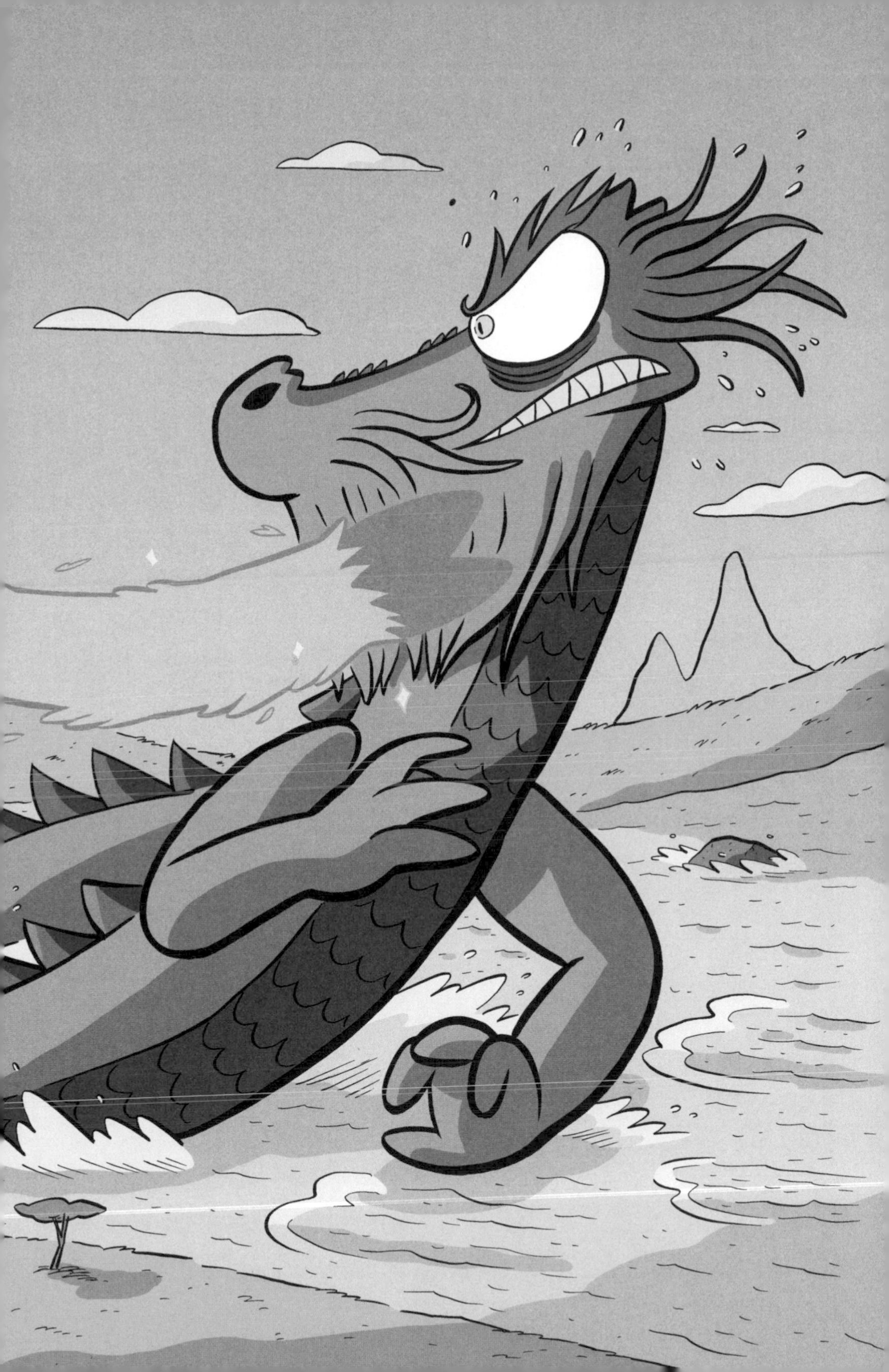

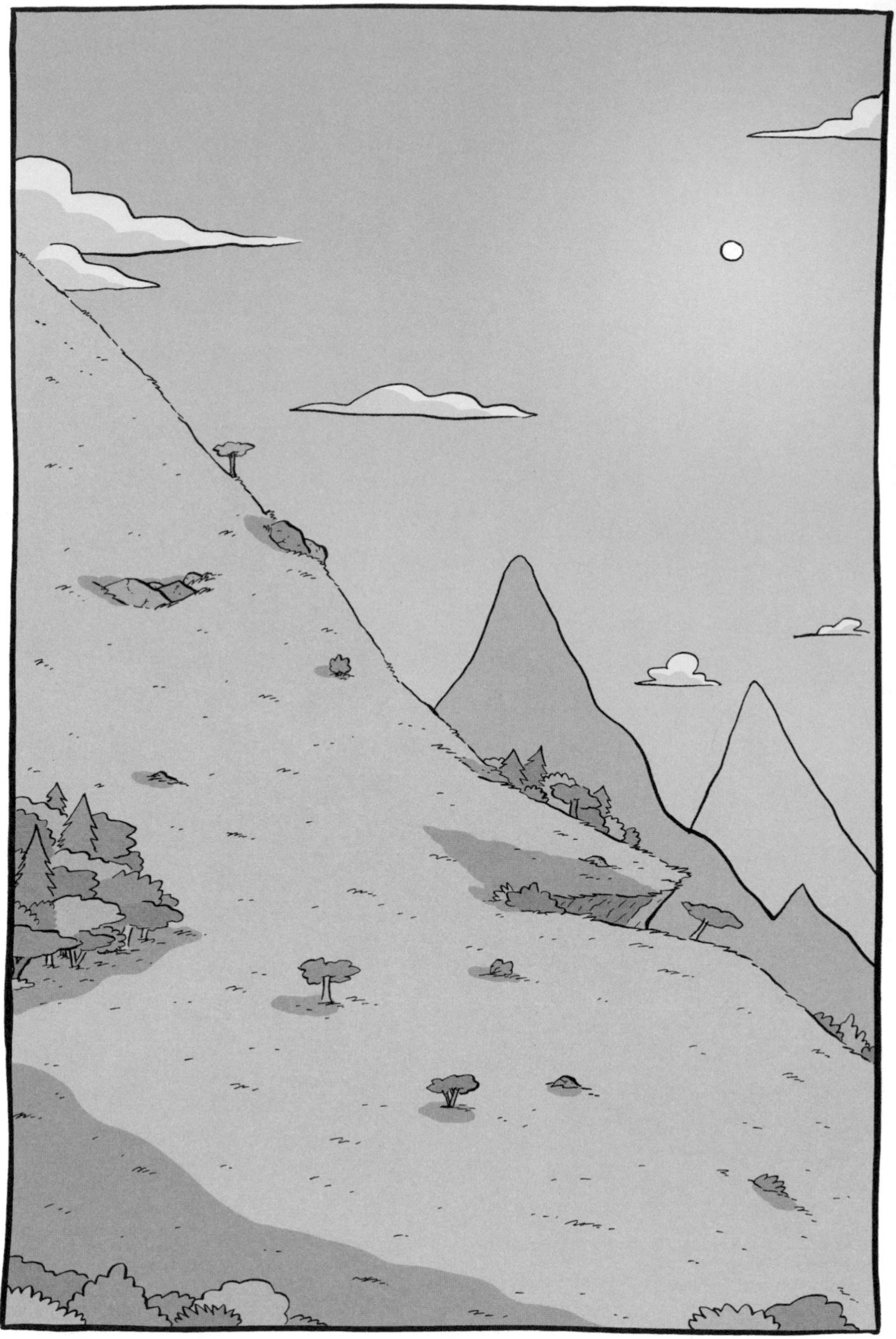

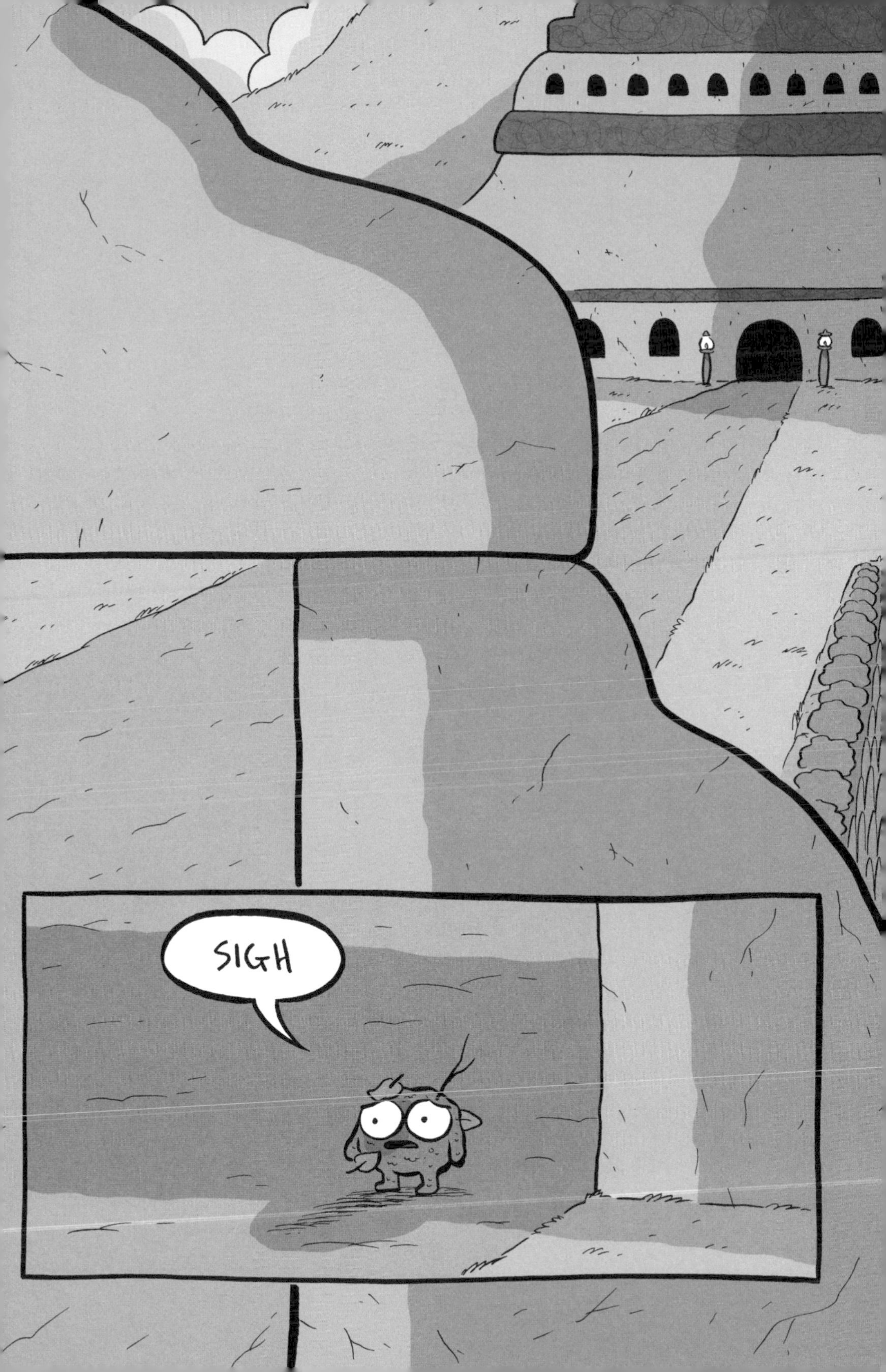
SIGH

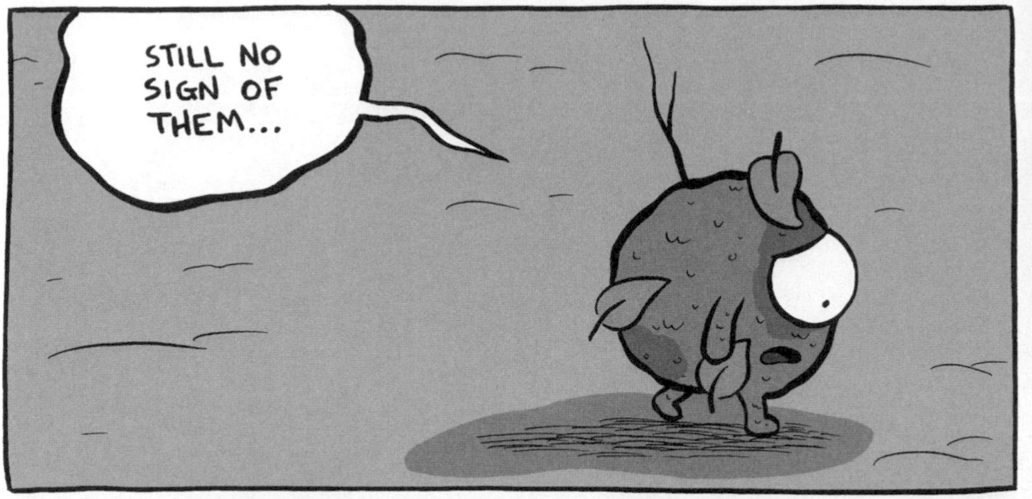
STILL NO SIGN OF THEM...

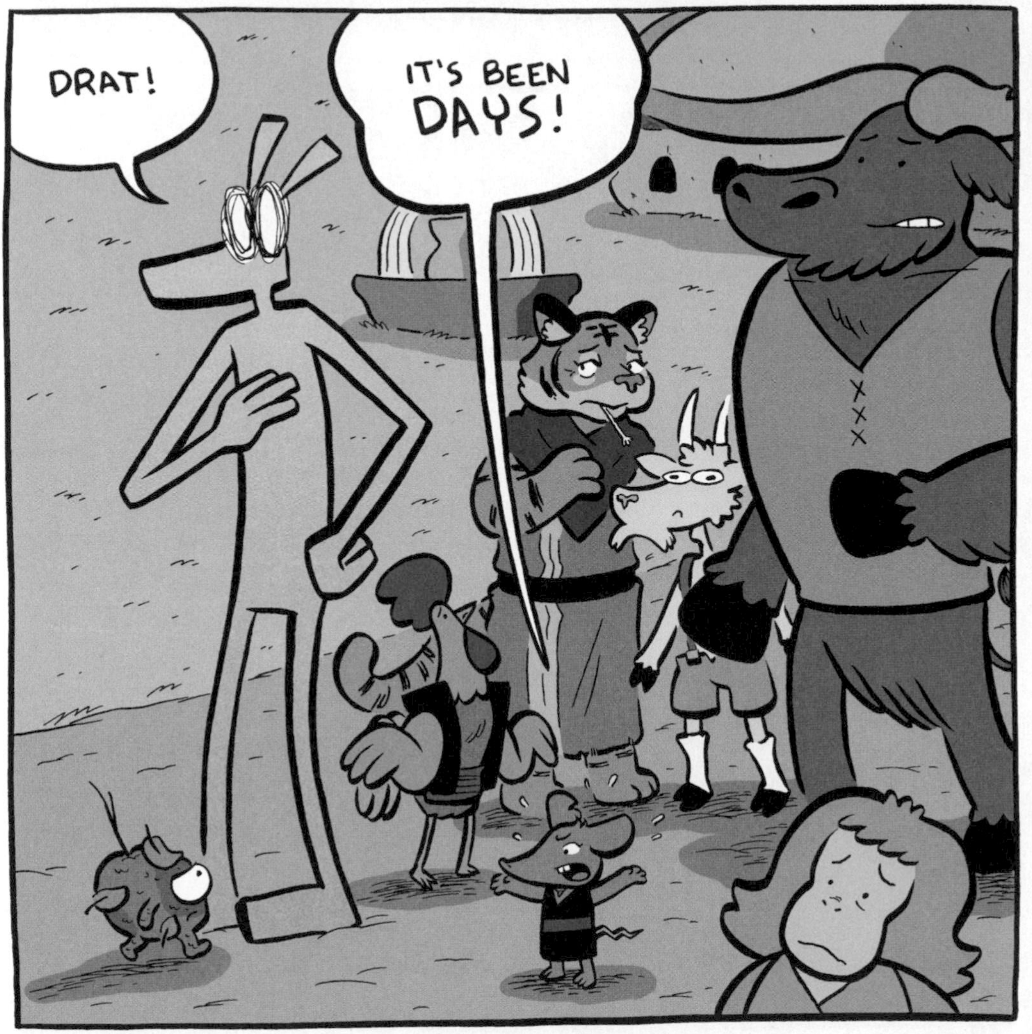
DRAT!
IT'S BEEN DAYS!

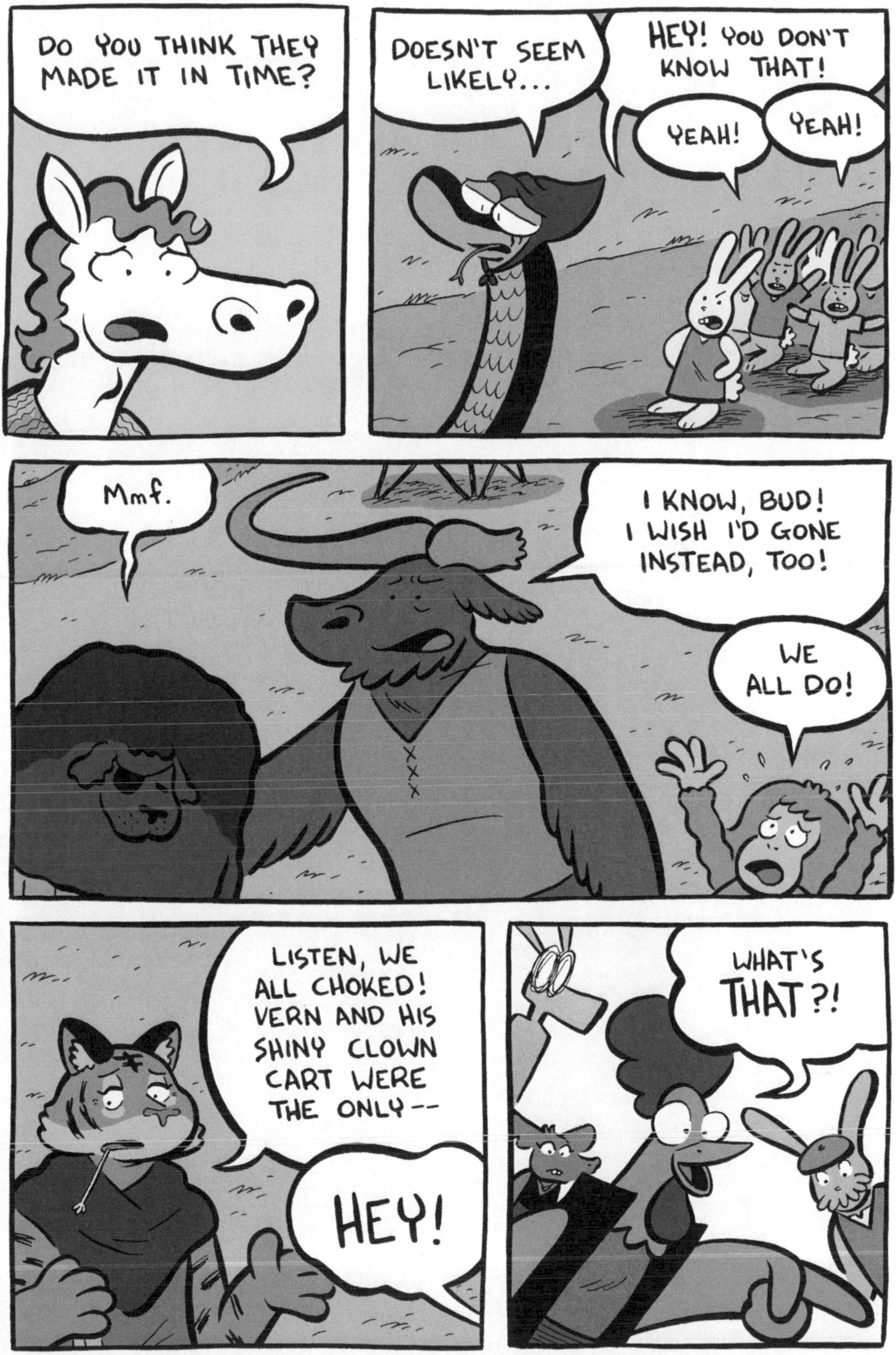
DO YOU THINK THEY MADE IT IN TIME?
DOESN'T SEEM LIKELY...
HEY! YOU DON'T KNOW THAT!
YEAH!
YEAH!
Mmf.
I KNOW, BUD! I WISH I'D GONE INSTEAD, TOO!
WE ALL DO!
LISTEN, WE ALL CHOKED! VERN AND HIS SHINY CLOWN CART WERE THE ONLY--
HEY!
WHAT'S THAT?!

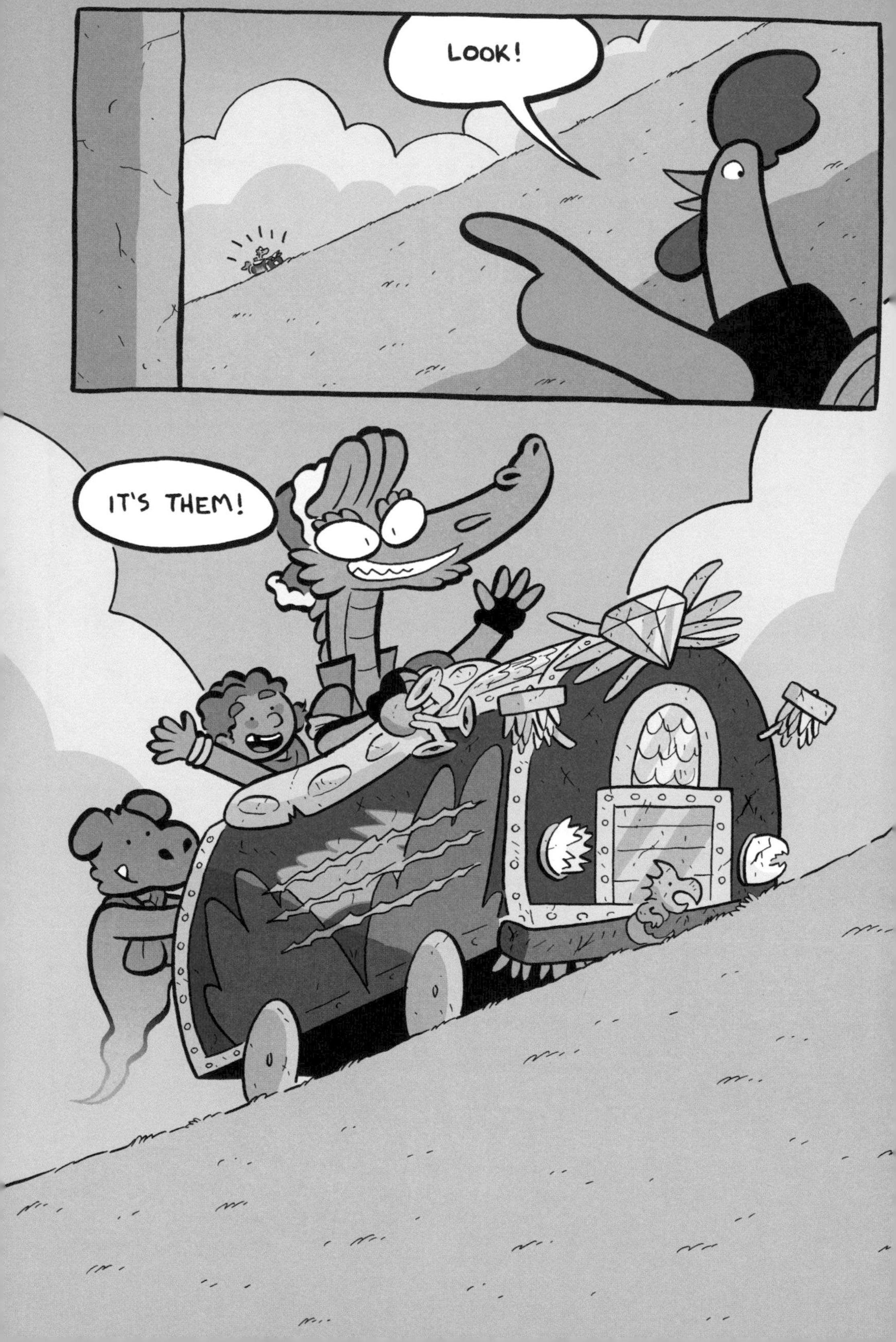
LOOK!
IT'S THEM!

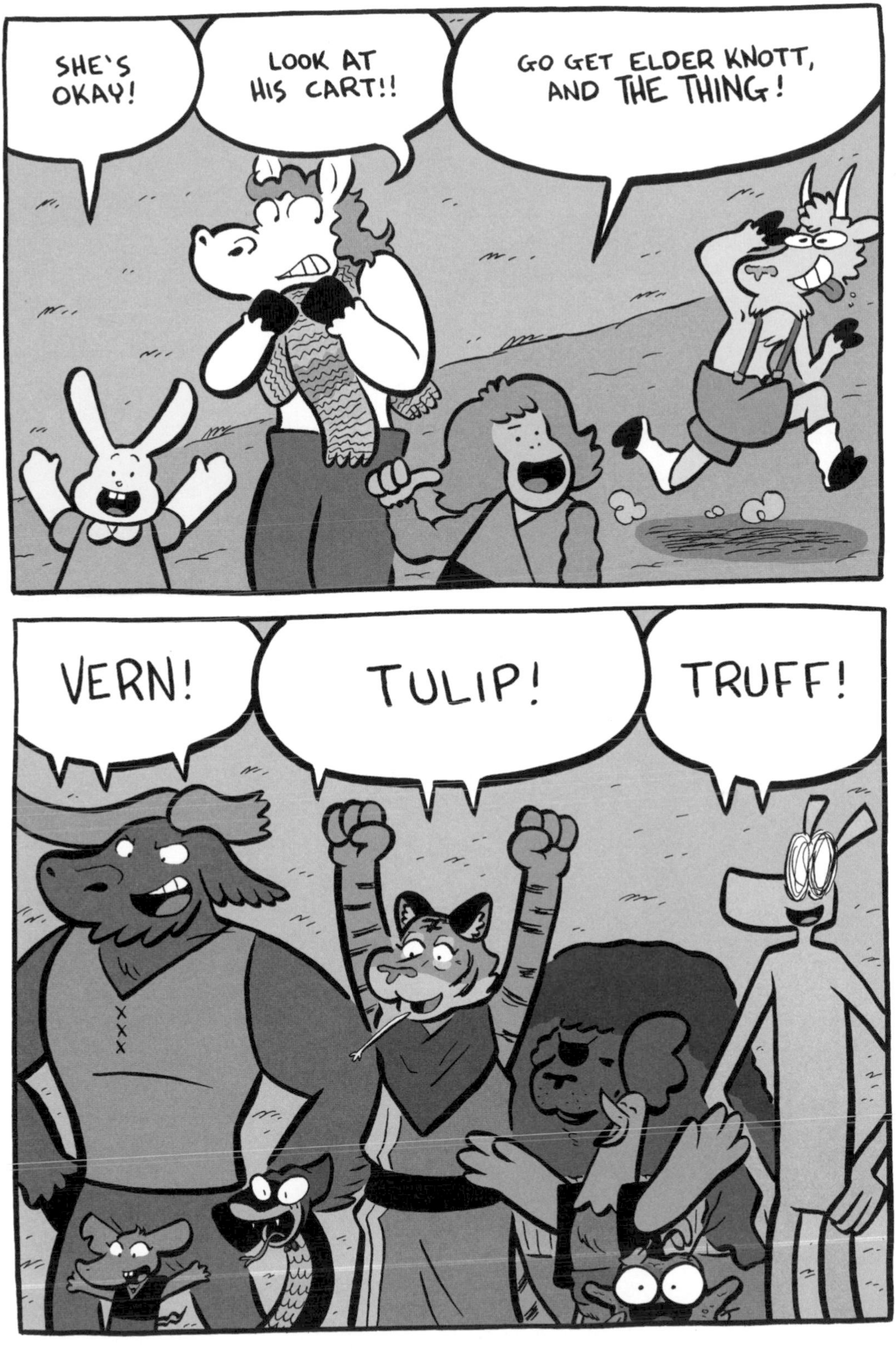
SHE'S OKAY!
LOOK AT HIS CART!!
GO GET ELDER KNOTT, AND THE THING!
VERN!
TULIP!
TRUFF!

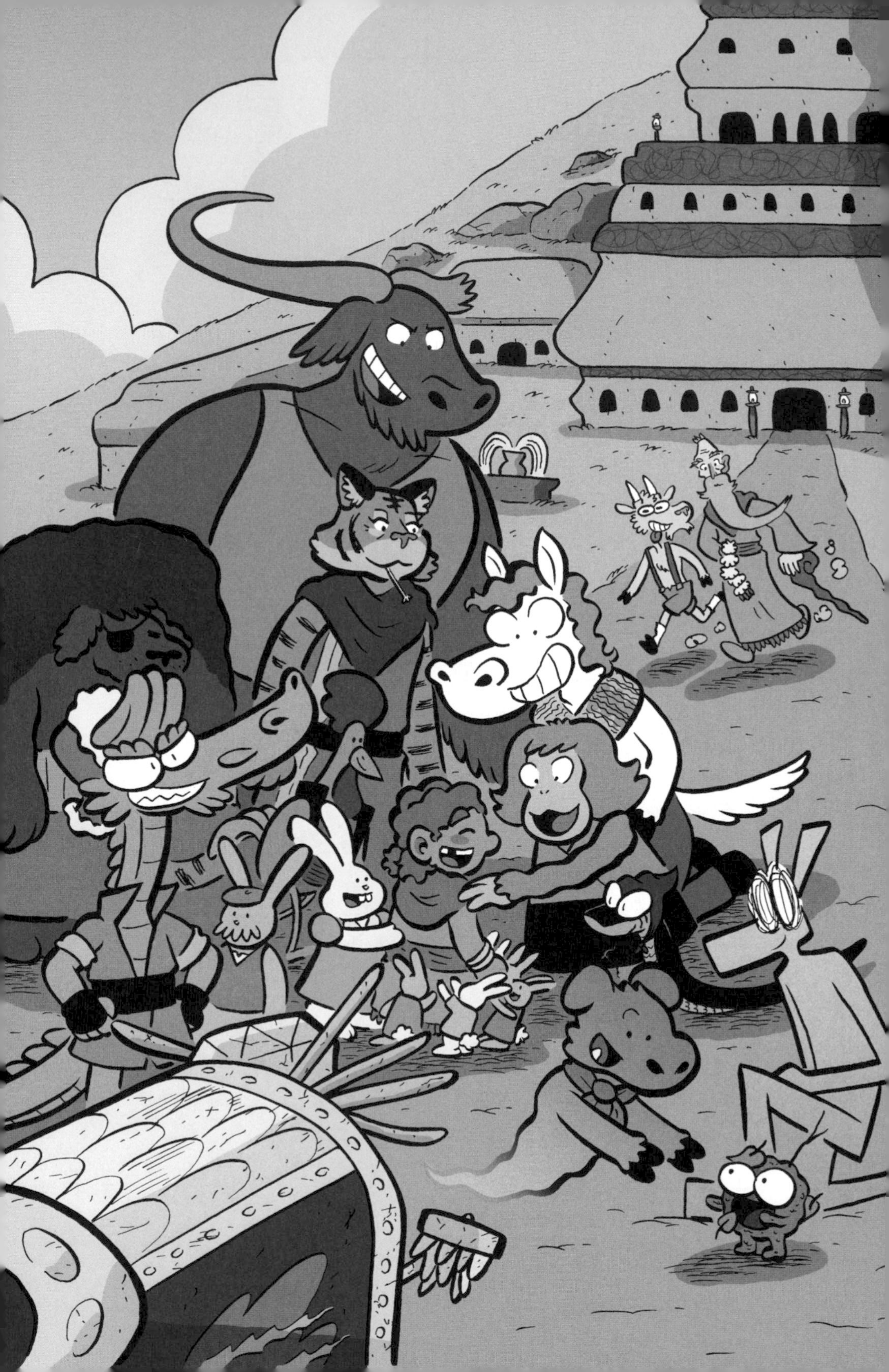

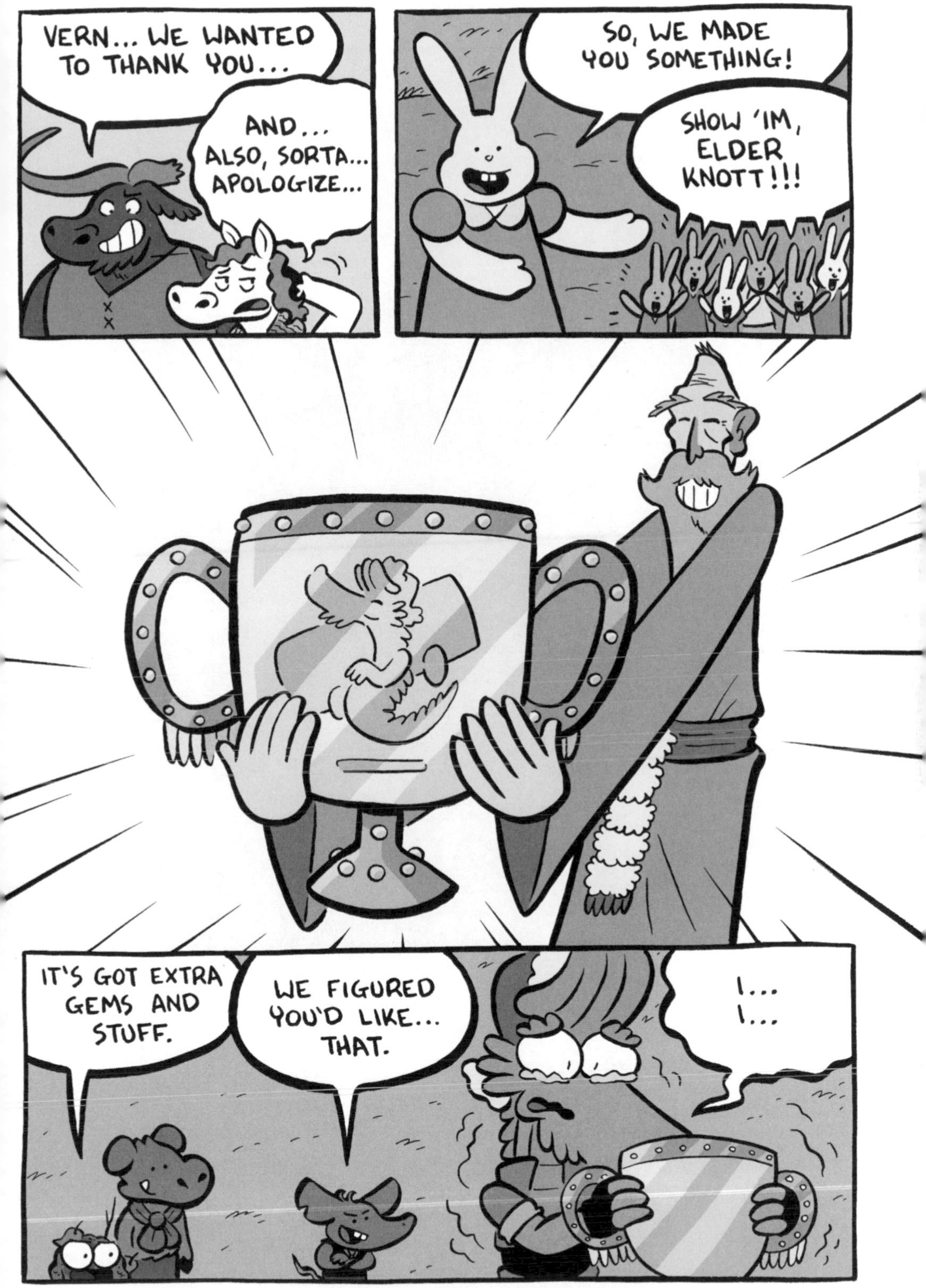
VERN... WE WANTED TO THANK YOU...
AND... ALSO, SORTA... APOLOGIZE...
SO, WE MADE YOU SOMETHING!
SHOW 'IM, ELDER KNOTT!!!
IT'S GOT EXTRA GEMS AND STUFF.
WE FIGURED YOU'D LIKE... THAT.
I... I...

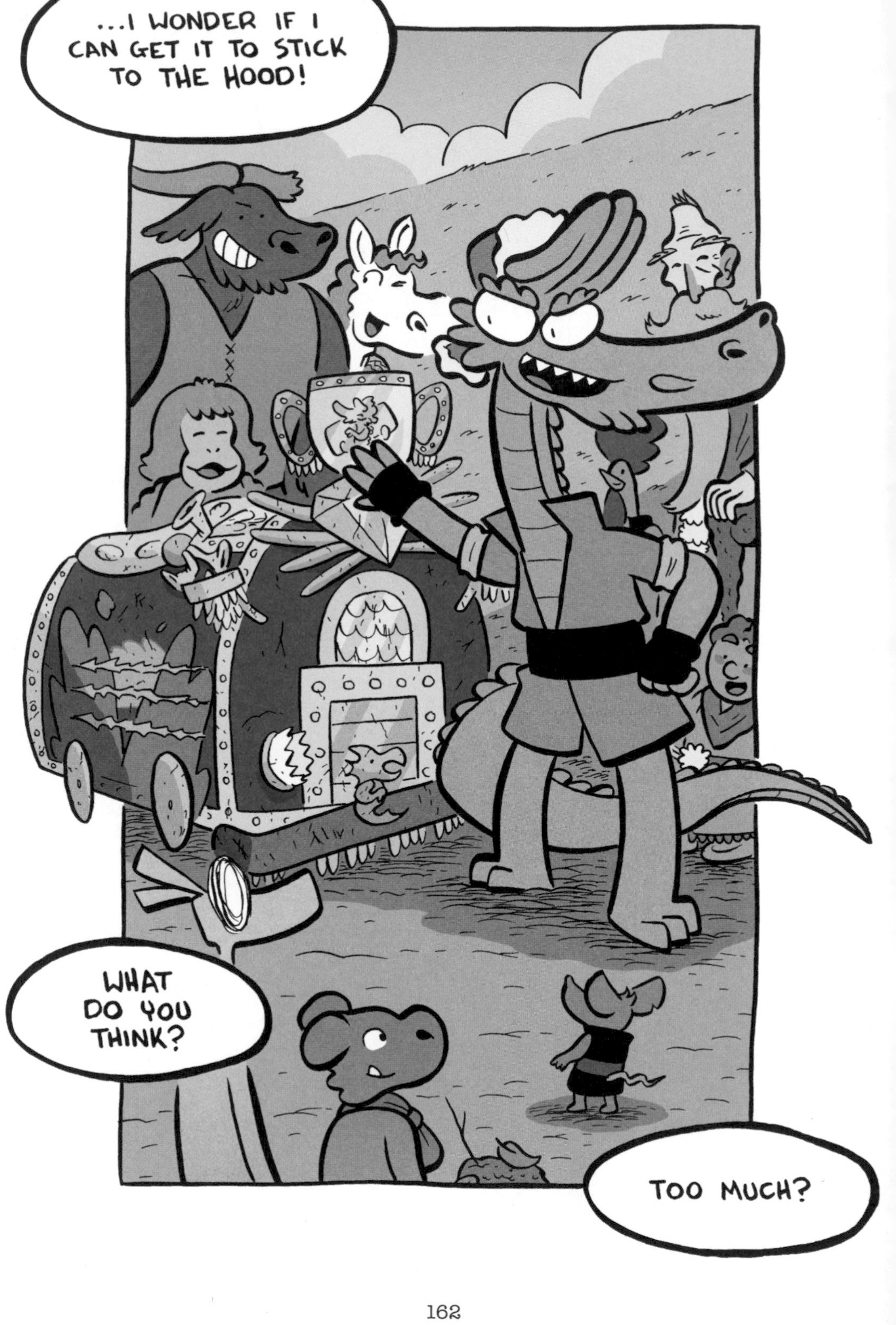
...I WONDER IF I CAN GET IT TO STICK TO THE HOOD!
WHAT DO YOU THINK?
TOO MUCH?

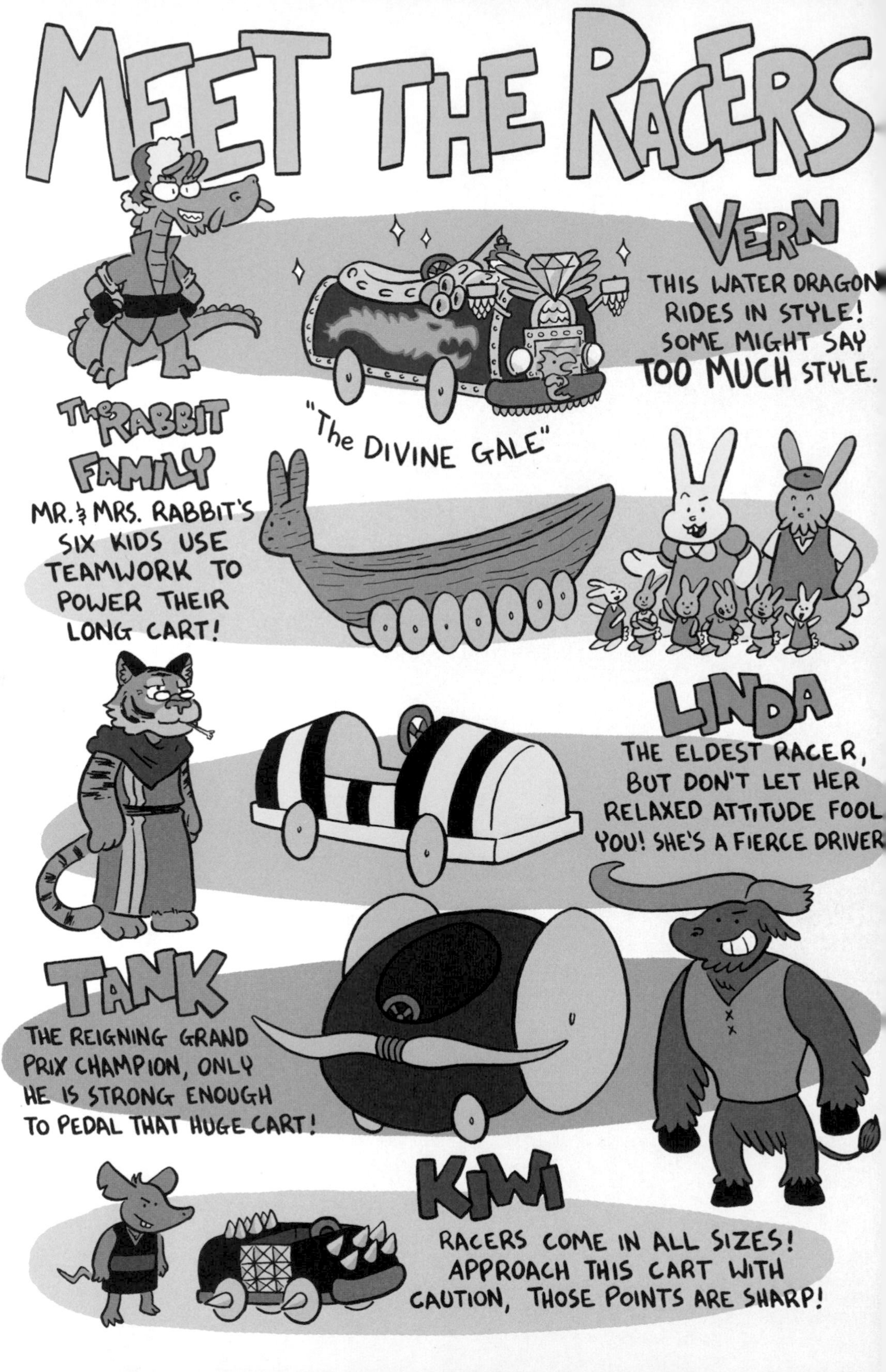
MEET THE RACERS
VERN
THIS WATER DRAGON RIDES IN STYLE! SOME MIGHT SAY TOO MUCH STYLE.
"The DIVINE GALE"
The RABBIT FAMILY
MR. & MRS. RABBIT'S SIX KIDS USE TEAMWORK TO POWER THEIR LONG CART!
LINDA
THE ELDEST RACER, BUT DON'T LET HER RELAXED ATTITUDE FOOL YOU! SHE'S A FIERCE DRIVER
TANK
THE REIGNING GRAND PRIX CHAMPION, ONLY HE IS STRONG ENOUGH TO PEDAL THAT HUGE CART!
KIWI
RACERS COME IN ALL SIZES! APPROACH THIS CART WITH CAUTION, THOSE POINTS ARE SHARP!

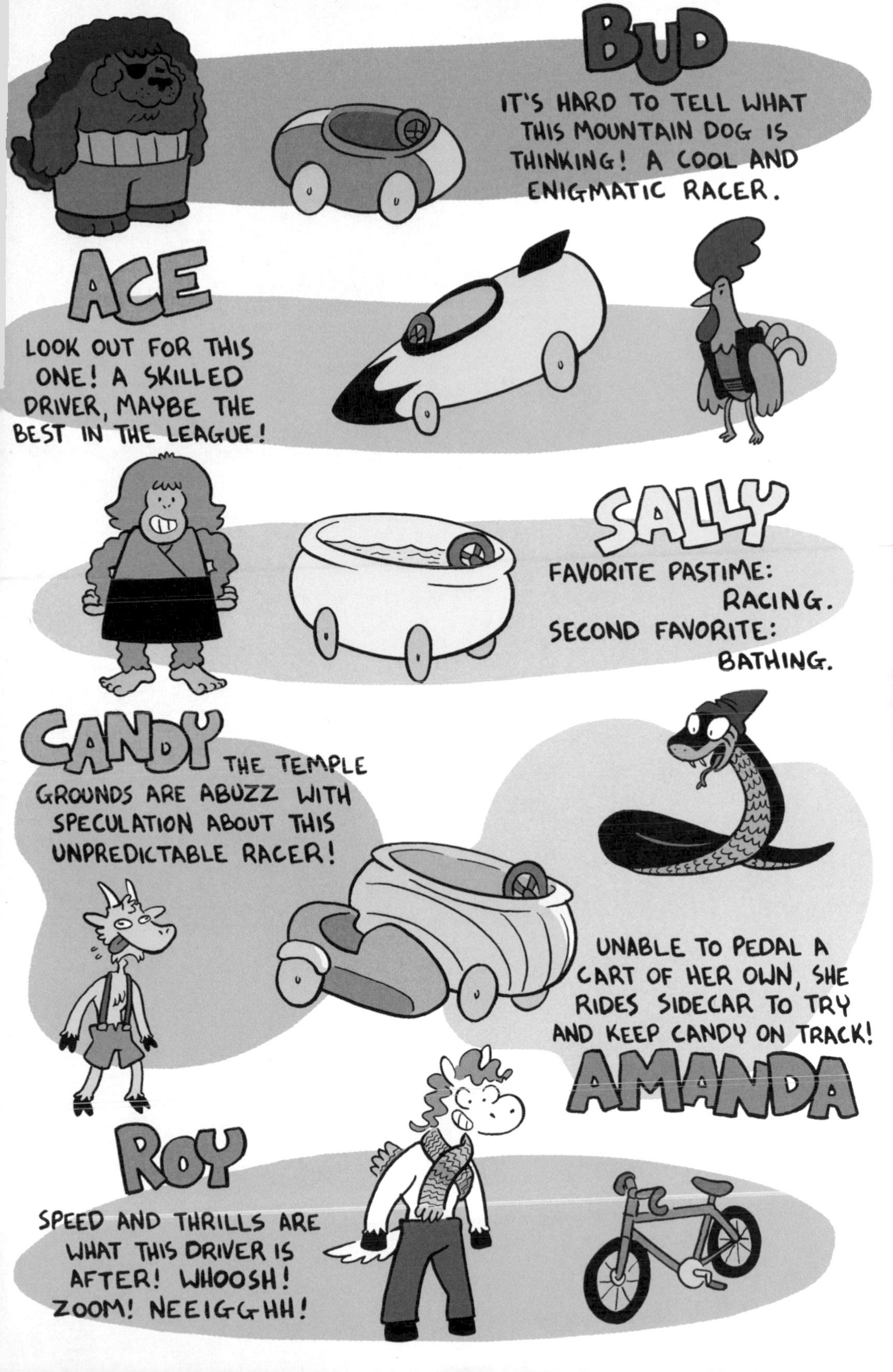
BUD
IT'S HARD TO TELL WHAT THIS MOUNTAIN DOG IS THINKING! A COOL AND ENIGMATIC RACER.
ACE
LOOK OUT FOR THIS ONE! A SKILLED DRIVER, MAYBE THE BEST IN THE LEAGUE!
SALLY
FAVORITE PASTIME: RACING. SECOND FAVORITE: BATHING.
CANDY
THE TEMPLE GROUNDS ARE ABUZZ WITH SPECULATION ABOUT THIS UNPREDICTABLE RACER!
UNABLE TO PEDAL A CART OF HER OWN, SHE RIDES SIDECAR TO TRY AND KEEP CANDY ON TRACK!
AMANDA
ROY
SPEED AND THRILLS ARE WHAT THIS DRIVER IS AFTER! WHOOSH! ZOOM! NEEIGGHH!

PROCESS SKETCHES!

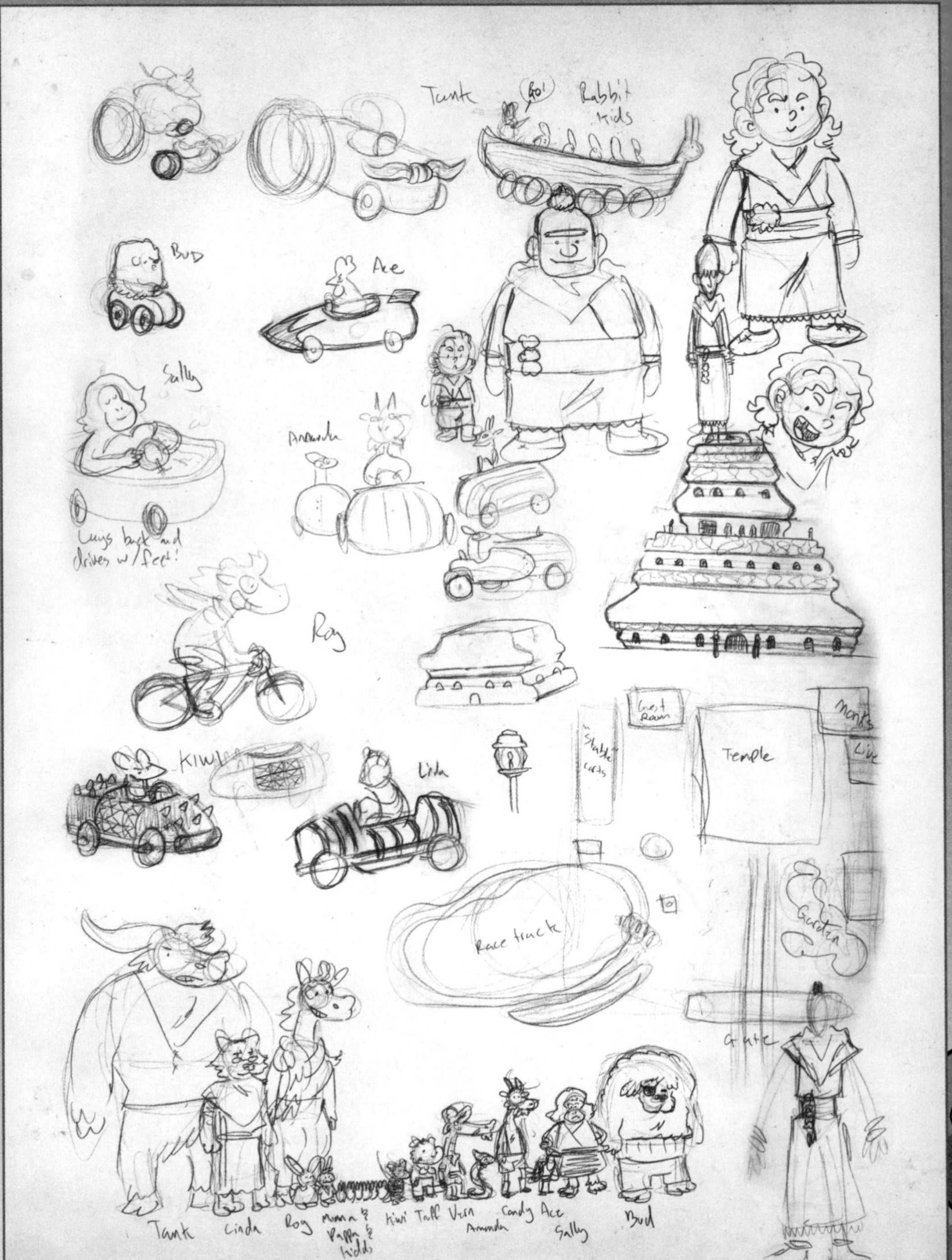
Tank
Go!
Rabbit kids
Bud
Ace
Sally
Amanda
Lungs back and drives w/ feet!
Roy
KIWI
Lida
Guest Room
"Stable" carts
Temple
Race track
Garden
Gate
Tank
Linda
Roy
Momma & Pappa & kids
Kiwi
Truff
Vern
Amanda
Candy
Ace
Sally
Bud

Joey Weiser is the Eisner Award–nominated author of *Ghost Hog* and *the Mermin* graphic novel series from Oni Press. His comics work ranges from writing and drawing for SpongeBob comics to coloring the *Jedi Academy: A New Class* series. His first graphic novel, *The Ride Home*, was published in 2007 by AdHouse Books. He is a graduate of the Savannah College of Art & Design and currently lives in Athens, Georgia.

MORE books from Joey Weiser!

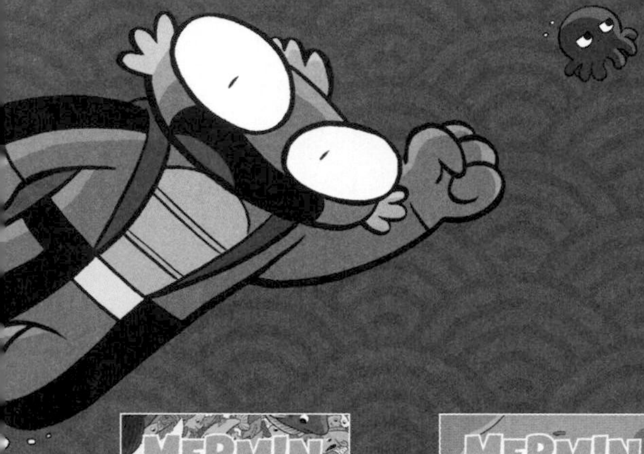

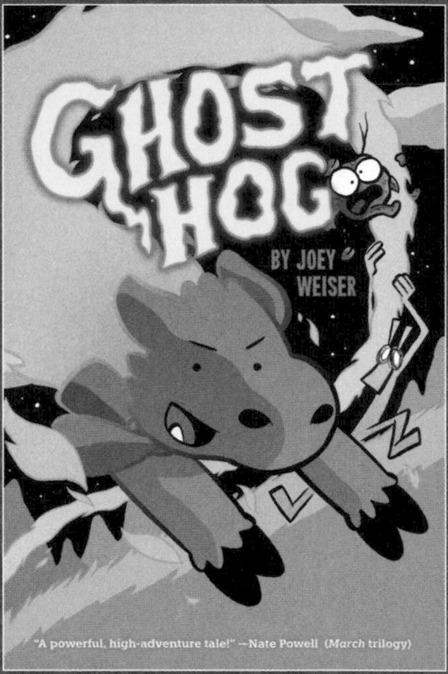
GHOST HOG
BY JOEY WEISER
"A powerful, high-adventure tale!" --Nate Powell (*March* trilogy)

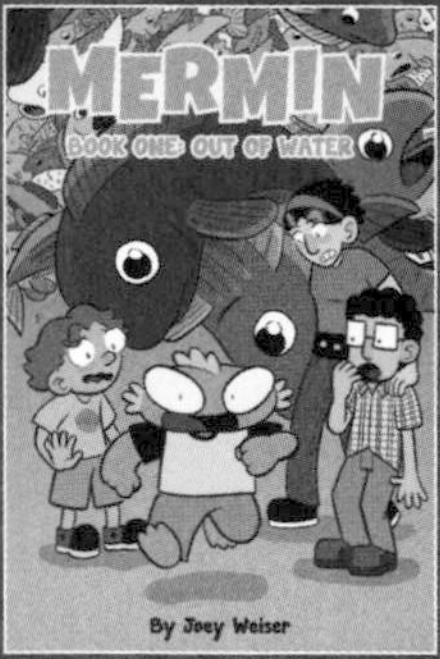
MERMIN
BOOK ONE: OUT OF WATER
By Joey Weiser

MERMIN BOOK ONE:
OUT OF WATER

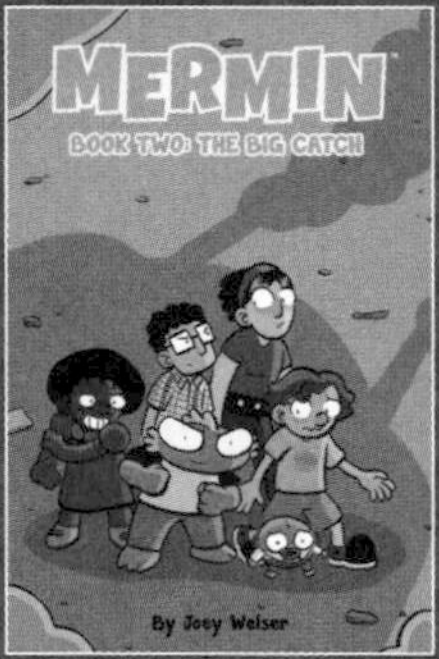
MERMIN
BOOK TWO: THE BIG CATCH
By Joey Weiser

MERMIN BOOK TWO:
THE BIG CATCH

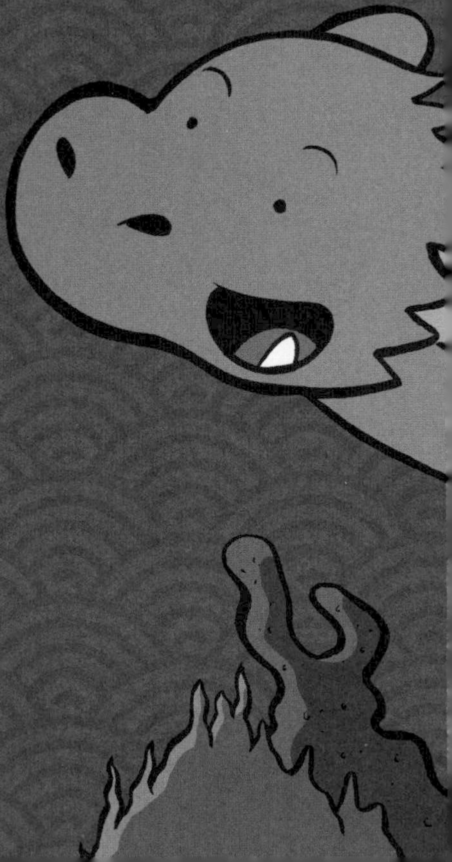

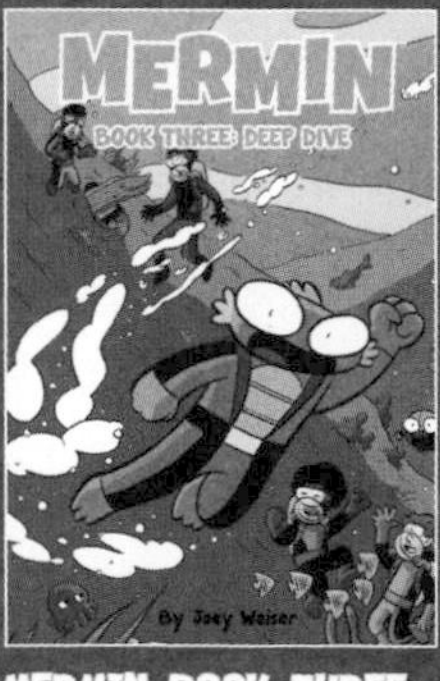
MERMIN
BOOK THREE: DEEP DIVE
By Joey Weiser

MERMIN BOOK THREE:
DEEP DIVE

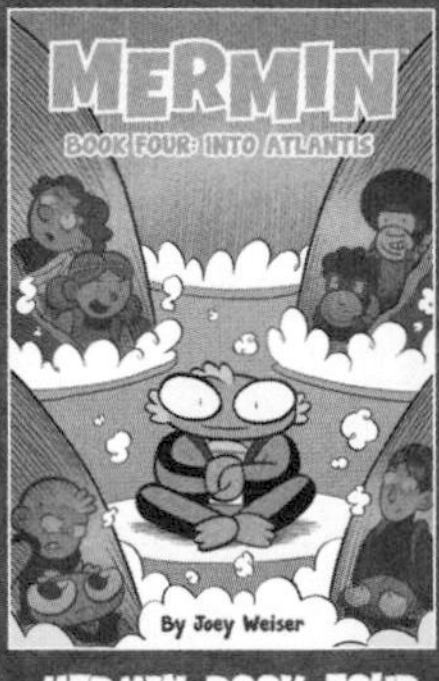
MERMIN
BOOK FOUR: INTO ATLANTIS
By Joey Weiser

MERMIN BOOK FOUR:
INTO ATLANTIS